THE REVEALING

Also by L. A. Marzulli

Nephilim
The Unholy Deception

THE NEPHILIM SERIES 3

THE REVEALING

THE TIME IS NOW

L. A. MARZULLI

GRAND RAPIDS, MICHIGAN 49530 USA

ZONDERVAN™

The Revealing
Copyright © 2004 by Lynn Marzulli

Requests for information should be addressed to:
Zondervan, *Grand Rapids, Michigan 49530*

Library of Congress Cataloging-in-Publication Data

Marzulli, L. A. (Lynn A.), 1950–
　　The revealing / L. A. Marzulli.
　　　　p. cm.
　　ISBN 0-310-24086-7 (softcover)
　　　1. Human–alien encounters—Fiction.　2. Middle East—Fiction.
　3. Antichrist—Fiction.　I. Title.
　PS3563.A778R488　2004
　813'.54—dc22

2004013485

Interior design by Laura Klynstra

Printed in the United States of America

---

04 05 06 07 08 09 10 /❖ DC/ 10 9 8 7 6 5 4 3 2 1

As we hurtle forward to the past, we just might find ourselves in the days of Noah once again. It's nice to know Lynn Marzulli is paying attention under the guise of fiction. One can only hope he has more listeners than Noah did.

Michael S. Heiser, Ph.D.
Author of *The Facade*

I've been in full-time ministry for twenty-five years and have never seen such rapid deployment of Bible prophecy. The push for peace in Israel, the call for a one-world order, a revived Roman Empire, buying and selling through alphanumeric systems injected beneath the skin, widespread earthquake activity. Then, just when I thought it couldn't get any better, Lynn Marzulli takes us to the imminent possibility of fearful sights, great signs, and lying wonders in the heavens.

Thomas Horn
Author of *Return to the Stones of Fire*

To
Dr. I. D. E. Thomas

* o *

Author's Note

This is the third and last book in the Nephilim series. I have spent over a decade examining the UFO phenomena. While the Nephilim series is fiction, I believe that UFOs are a real part of the end-time Luciferian agenda. More specifically, that that agenda is one of deception. The deception is multi-faceted in its scope and manifests itself in diverse ways. Let us be aware . . .

L. A. Marzulli
Spring 2004

Acknowledgments

I would like to thank the following people who helped make this book possible:

My father, Lynn Q. Marzulli ... you too, Mom!

Pastors Dave and Sylvia Owen and the Malibu Vineyard Christian Fellowship.

Thanks once again to Dave Lambert and Lori Vanden-Bosch, two of the greatest editors living and breathing on the planet today!

Bill Myers, Mike Heiser, Tom Horn, Gary Schultz, Dave Flynn, Jim Tetlow, Chris Pinto, Steve and Iliana Schoelkopf, Antoinette Dick, Tom and Cherie Doherty, Dale and Carol Kornreich, D. David Morin, Mark Duncan, and Linda. A special thanks to Chris Heeber, who proofread the manuscript and gave me some great feedback.

Thanks to Gary Zethraeus for his input on the kingdom of fear versus the kingdom of faith.

To Karen Ball, Sue Brower, Joyce Ondersma, Cindy Wilcox, and the rest of the great folks at Zondervan for their help.

To the artist who brought the cover idea to life ... Great job!

Most of all to my wife, Peggy, and my two daughters, Corrie and Sarah.

THE REVEALING

Prelude:
Nazi Germany, the Last Days of the Third Reich

Wolfgang Von Schverdt hurried up the last few steps of the Fuehrerbunke, the vast underground complex that Adolph Hitler had constructed for his protection, and had made his home for the last 105 days of his life. Pushing open a heavy steel door, he saw an overcast May sky, his first glimpse of daylight in over a week. Then he gasped in astonishment at the twisted steel, broken concrete, and rubble that surrounded him . . . all that was left of the Reichschancellery. The Allied bombing had been unrelenting, pounding Berlin day and night without letting up, until much of the city had been reduced to ashes. An ubiquitous layer of dust and smoke, combined with the smell of rotting corpses and seared flesh, created a living hell.

Von Schverdt breathed the foul air deeply, enjoying it, tasting it with the tip of his tongue. He loved the smell of war, relished it, was born for it. *If only that madman, Hitler, had not proven to be such a weak vessel, things might have been different. If only someone else with more vitality had been chosen* . . . He let his thoughts slip away as his adjutant, who carried two overstuffed satchels of papers, caught up with him. Von Schverdt picked his way through the rubble to where the garden had once been. There he came upon a small group of Nazi SS who were dousing two bodies with gasoline.

A captain who noticed Von Schverdt snapped to attention. "Heil, Hitler!" he shouted as another soldier threw a match on the gasoline which exploded in a rush of flames.

"Look around you, you idiot! The war is over," Von Schverdt said, and glared at the man.

The captain, unsure how to react, remained at attention.

Von Schverdt walked closer to the shallow pit and looked at the bodies of Adolph Hitler and Eva Braun, his mistress. He gathered a mouthful of saliva and spat toward the flaming bodies, then pivoted on the heels of his boots and walked away.

He turned up the sleeve of his black leather greatcoat and glanced at his watch. It was almost five. He had less than an hour to meet the Americans and surrender.

A burst of machine gun fire sounded very close, and he reacted with a start.

The Russians will be here soon. That realization made him hurry toward a car that was waiting nearby.

Shortly after Hitler had committed suicide by shooting himself, General Wolfgang Von Schverdt had made a series of telephone calls to the Americans from his private room in the Fuehrer's bunker. He had offered them information, and as he had expected, they had responded eagerly.

Others in the bunker had begun to flee, knowing that capture by the Russians would mean imprisonment or death. Those remaining in the bunker had all agreed that it would be better to surrender to the Americans than to fall into the hands of the Red Army.

Von Schverdt stepped next to the waiting car. He glanced at the driver. *Little more than a boy,* he thought.

"Heil, Hitler," the youth blurted.

Von Schverdt smiled with feigned affection. "Heil, Hitler," he responded, and returned the salute.

His adjutant, Heinz, struggled with two bulging satchels, put them down a moment to rest, and then, getting a fresh grip, continued toward the car. Von Schverdt leaned against the car and watched as the man approached.

"Put them in the back," Von Schverdt ordered as he stepped away from the car.

"*Ja vol,*" Heinz puffed, as he set the briefcases down and opened the rear door of the car. He lifted one of them, set it on the floor of the backseat, and then turned to retrieve the other.

Von Schverdt watched Heinz's every move, as he slowly undid the leather strap on his holster and brought the P.38 to his side, fitting the silencer to it.

It's a pity, he thought, *Heinz has been loyal. Still...*

Von Schverdt waited until the man had finished his task and faced him, awaiting new orders.

Von Schverdt raised the handgun and Heinz took a step backward, a mixture of terror and confusion filling his face. "No, Herr Von Schver—"

Von Schverdt fired once, and the bullet went neatly through the forehead of the man, the force of it driving him into the rear door of the car, where his lifeless body slumped to the ground.

Von Schverdt moved, catlike, to the driver's door, opened it, and caught the boy by the oversized sleeve of his uniform, and yanked him out of the car.

The boy fell in a heap at Von Schverdt's feet and began to claw at his boots, crying out for mercy. Von Schverdt fired once and the boy lay still. He unfastened the silencer, reholstered his sidearm, and as he did so, noticed that a few spots of blood had splattered on his boots. He went over and wiped them off on the dead boy's pant legs. That done, he slid into the driver's seat and sped off to his meeting place with the Americans.

The drive was treacherous. More than once he fired his gun to ward off those attempting to hijack his car. At one point a group of fleeing women and children clogged the road. Von Schverdt held his hand on the horn, but didn't slow the car. Women and children scrambled to get out of the way. One old woman tripped and fell on the road in front of the speeding car. Von Schverdt ran over her, not even glancing in the rearview mirror as the car sped on. *Desperate times require desperate measures,* he reminded himself.

There's nothing left . . . They've destroyed everything, he thought, as the car rolled by block after block of leveled, smoldering buildings. He had trouble getting his bearings, as many of the street signs were missing, and most of the familiar landmarks that would have aided him had vanished.

He stopped the car and looked around, trying to get a sense of where he was.

Nothing here . . . But wait. He noticed the base of a statue by the side of the road, all that was left of a beautiful bronze sculpture he had once admired.

He turned the car, stepped hard on the gas pedal, and the car lurched forward.

Only a few more miles and then, the Americans. The thought made him anxious. *How much of his work had been destroyed, or discovered?* He gripped the steering wheel tighter.

A short time later he saw a roadblock with an American flag flying alongside it and a dozen armed American GIs brandishing rifles. To the left a machine gun nest was lined by rows of sandbags.

Von Schverdt slowed the car and stopped twenty yards away from the roadblock. He opened the door of the car and stepped out, being careful to raise his hands over his head as he did so.

One of the Americans shouted to him in very bad German, *"Ubergeben sie sich mit ihren hande hoch!"* (Surrender with your hands up.)

Von Schverdt raised his hands higher and stood motionless.

More shouting, this time from behind the roadblock. Four GIs approached.

Another one called out, *"Bewegen siesich weg von den auto."* (Move away from the car.)

Von Schverdt chuckled. *Idiots,* he thought. *How could they have beaten us?*

His mind raced back to a better time, years ago in Nuremberg, when Hitler was cresting to the peak of his power just before the war. Thousands of flashlights, each held by Hitler

Youth, illuminated enormous swastika flags encircling the arena, which billowed in the cool breeze of a German spring night. Endless rows of helmeted soldiers melted in the distance. Von Schverdt, along with other Nazi party leaders, was seated on a platform above the gathered throng, and, just in front of him, the Fuehrer himself was in the midst of an impassioned speech: coercing, whispering, then his voice exploding in a thunderous crescendo. But not by his own power. The force that filled and swelled the dictator was not human. Von Schverdt knew only too well what it was that came and filled the little corporal with such tremendous force and power that even he, who had helped the possession to occur in the first place, was awed by the magnitude of its power, and the visceral vitality of it.

And this is all that is left of our thousand years of rule? Our thousand-year reich? What happened? he mused as he watched the Americans, the victors, draw closer.

The Americans stopped twenty feet away, their guns pointed at him. Von Schverdt heard them ask each other the German words for "kneel down."

Stupid, he thought, as he slowly dropped to his knees.

The American soldiers surrounded him. Two of the men took his arms and, pinning them behind his back, yanked him to a standing position. They checked his sidearm holster and found it empty.

"Hey, will you look at this," called one of the Americans. He pulled Von Schverdt's coat away from his shoulders.

"Looks like we got ourselves a general." A sergeant ambled forward, gumming the butt of a cigarette.

The others crowded around, peering at his uniform.

"I am *SS-Obergruppenfuehrer,* Wolfgang Von Schverdt," Von Schverdt said, in almost perfect English, but with a heavy accent.

The Americans looked at each other in astonishment.

"I have very important information there, in the back of the car, for your superiors. They are expecting me." And he gestured toward the rear of the car.

"Take a look, Charlie," the sergeant ordered.

Charlie, a stocky youth with unshaven stubble on his face, hurried over to the car and opened the rear door.

"Two satchels ... lots of papers, Sarge. Hey, he's got a handgun lying on the front seat."

"Bring 'em along," Sarge replied.

The soldier slung his rifle onto his shoulder and hoisted the satchels out of the car, then retrieved the Luger.

They escorted Von Schverdt toward the roadblock. Von Schverdt's eyes darted about, searching for the official that had promised he would meet him. When they reached the roadblock, one of the soldiers raised the wooden crossbar and Von Schverdt passed under it. He heard the sound of a jeep growing closer from behind him.

"Hey, looks like we got more company," one of the American soldiers, manning the machine gun, yelled out.

"Looks like the Russians," someone else replied.

Von Schverdt saw an officer emerge from the shell of a burned-out building, with the remains of shaving cream still on his chin.

Shaving at this time of day ... Where is the discipline of this army? Von Schverdt wondered.

"Who's this?" the officer asked, throwing a glance at Von Schverdt as he buckled his sidearm to his waist.

"Looks like a general, sir. He just pulled up outta nowhere and surrendered to us," the sergeant replied.

Von Schverdt turned his head and looked at the incoming jeep with a bright red Russian star painted on the hood and flags flying from each of the front fenders. The jeep came to a stop inches from the wooden crossbar. A tall, thin man in civilian clothes climbed out.

One of the American MPs called out, "What can we do you for?"

The civilian crossed his arms in front of him. "I am Vladimir Patchenko, Russian Secret Service."

The American officer took a step forward. "Captain Decker, Ninth Army."

Patchenko nodded. "We saw his car speeding through the streets and followed him here." He glanced at Von Schverdt. "We want him for interrogation."

Captain Decker shifted his weight and remained unfazed. "This man's surrendered to us, and I have orders from my higher-ups regarding the surrender of Nazi officers."

Von Schverdt eyed the Russian. *How far will he go with the American?* he wondered. *If somehow this Russian asserts himself over the American captain, then my work, all of it, is lost. And I am, most likely, a dead man.*

Patchenko took a few steps closer to Von Schverdt. "I'm sure we can work something out, Captain, yes?"

Decker shook his head, fumbled in his pocket, and produced a pack of Luckys. It was fresh and unopened. He tapped it in the palm of his left hand several times, then pried off the wrapper. "Smoke?" He held out the pack to Patchenko.

A smile broke over Patchenko's face. "This is a luxury, Captain," he replied, taking one. "May I have another, for later?"

"Be my guest. In fact, why not take the whole pack?" Decker held the pack out in front of the man. Patchenko hesitated a moment, then took the cigarettes and slipped them into his jacket pocket.

Decker slid his hand into the other pocket of his pants and came up with a lighter. He flicked the scratched cover open, thumbed a flame, then lit Patchenko's cigarette. "Bought this the day we shipped out from the States."

Patchenko nodded and inhaled deeply, then let a stream of smoke escape from his mouth. "Captain, I'm grateful for this and—"

Decker cut the man off. "No gratitude necessary, Mr. Patchenko. Just let's leave things as they are with my prisoner. Okay?"

Von Schverdt feigned indifference and looked away from the men as he held his breath.

Patchenko took another drag and then began to nod his head in agreement.

"So we have a deal then?" Decker cocked his head to one side, smiling as he extended his hand.

"Deal," Patchenko replied. They shook hands, and he headed back to his jeep.

"Visit us again," Decker called out.

Patchenko's driver fired the engine and a moment later the jeep sped away.

Von Schverdt let his breath out, relieved at the outcome.

"You speak any English?" Decker asked.

"Fluently, Captain," Von Schverdt replied, then added, "I was instructed by a Colonel Dougherty to surrender here. He assured me that he would be present."

Decker raised his eyebrow. "Sarge, the radio. Call HQ and see if there's a Colonel Dougherty that knows about this."

Von Schverdt saw the man disappear into the same burned-out shell from which the captain had emerged.

"What's your rank?" Decker asked.

"I am an *SS-Obergruppenfuehrer*. A general."

Decker nodded and looked at the two satchels of papers. "And those?"

"Colonel Dougherty expressed a keen interest in them," Von Schverdt replied.

"What was your command?"

"I'm afraid I cannot discuss any of this," Von Schverdt answered. "Only with Colonel Dougherty."

Their conversation was interrupted as the sergeant returned. "It's legit, Cap. HQ says Colonel Dougherty left an hour or so ago. He's OSS."

"OSS," Decker repeated. "Intel boys."

"Must have gotten lost, huh, Cap?" Sarge offered.

Such incompetence, Von Schverdt thought.

"Bring an ammo crate for the general to sit on. Have two men guard him until the colonel arrives," Decker ordered. "Sarge, do a search of the bags and make sure they're clean."

"Got it, Cap."

"Captain, please, I assure you that the satchels contain confidential papers, and will . . ."

Decker cut the general off and repeated his order, "Search the bags, Sarge."

A soldier appeared with an ammo crate and set it next to Von Schverdt, who chose instead to remain standing with both of his hands clasped together behind his back. *What if this man understands what he is looking at? What if he sees the drawings, the photos?*

The sergeant opened one of the satchels. "Nothing but papers in this one, Cap."

"Look in the other," Decker ordered.

Von Schverdt saw the sergeant open the other satchel.

"More of the same Cap . . . except this one has a lot of photos. Want to look at them?" he said, pulling some of them out.

A voice rang out behind Von Schverdt. "We got company."

Decker turned and faced him. "Let's hope it's Colonel Dougherty."

Von Schverdt nodded. His eyes darted toward two jeeps speeding toward him and then back to the sergeant who had taken a few of the photos out.

"Hey, Cap," the sarge called.

Von Schverdt heard the fear in the man's voice.

"Maybe you should take a look at these . . ."

"Stow it," he heard Decker reply.

The jeeps pulled up and Von Schverdt saw the distinct armband on the soldiers in the lead jeep, signifying them to be Military Police. Von Schverdt reckoned that the other man seated in the passenger seat of the second jeep was probably Colonel Dougherty.

The MPs got out of the jeep and stood at attention while a stout man with a shock of premature white hair climbed out.

Decker gave a snappy salute. "Atten-hut!" Decker barked, and his men snapped to attention.

"As you were," Dougherty replied. The men relaxed.

Von Schverdt made brief eye contact with Dougherty.

"We took a wrong turn about a mile out from HQ. Got us all fouled up. We've got to do something about the road signs," Dougherty grumbled.

"Yes, sir," Decker replied.

"This him?" Dougherty asked.

"Yes, sir."

Von Schverdt snapped to attention, clicked his boot heels together, and saluted. "General Wolfgang Von Schverdt of the SS."

Dougherty returned the salute, his eyes were on the two satchels.

Von Schverdt extended a gloved hand gesturing toward the bags.

"Like I said, Colonel, much of the information is here, but of course there is more . . ."

Dougherty went over to the satchels and pulled out a file that contained several pictures. Von Schverdt studied the man, scrutinizing every muscle on his face. Watching for a twitch of an eye, stiffening of a lip, a crease in the brow, or anything that Von Schverdt might use for his advantage. After a moment Dougherty closed the file and remained motionless for almost a full minute, his eyes downcast.

The man is shaken, Von Schverdt thought. *Good.*

"Colonel?" Captain Decker called out.

Colonel Dougherty gathered himself together. "Sorry, Captain. Have one of your men load these into my jeep." He turned to his escort of MPs. "Corporal, take charge of the prisoner."

The man saluted and drew his sidearm as he and the other MP descended upon Von Schverdt, who noticed that the corporal had produced a set of handcuffs.

"Really, Colonel, are these necessary?"

"I'm afraid so, General," Dougherty replied.

Von Schverdt extended his hands in front of him and the MPs cuffed him. He was then escorted to one of the jeeps, where he was placed in the passenger seat. The MP with the handgun sat behind him. Colonel Dougherty and Captain Decker saluted each other, then the jeeps turned around and sped off down the road.

* ○ *

The debriefing lasted for more than four hours. Von Schverdt had been taken to a large tent at the American Army headquarters. There, seated with Colonel Dougherty and two other men, he spoke and answered questions. Photographs and papers from Von Schverdt's satchel littered the table.

"General," Colonel Dougherty addressed him, "have you any idea of the condition of the . . . craft? With all of the bombing, is there going to be anything left of them?"

Von Schverdt tapped his forefinger against the death's head skull ring on his other hand. "I have no way of knowing that, Herr Colonel. I constructed the underground hangar to withstand such bombing, but who knows, *ja?* May I suggest that we go to see it ourselves?"

Von Schverdt saw Dougherty eye the other men. "How far is it from here?"

"Perhaps two hours, providing of course that the roads are passable."

Dougherty reached for a map that had been brought in during the debriefing. "Show us," he said, and passed it to Von Schverdt.

Von Schverdt studied it for a moment. "Here. Near Peenemunde. I had the hangar constructed to look like a dairy barn. We even had cows in the pasture." He chuckled.

"So, in the morning you can take us there?" Dougherty asked.

Von Schverdt nodded. "Yes, in the morning."

The debriefing ended and Dougherty, along with several MPs, escorted Von Schverdt to a makeshift cell which had been prepared for him.

Von Schverdt surveyed the accommodations. A barbed-wire fence encircled a tent placed on a deck made of wooden pallets. The tent's flaps and sides had been rolled up, showing an army cot and one chair. "I trust you'll be comfortable, General," Dougherty said. "One of the MPs will bring you something to eat. It won't be much, though."

"Thank you, Colonel. I'm grateful for anything you might provide."

An MP opened a gate and Von Schverdt stepped into the enclosure.

"In the morning," Colonel Dougherty said.

"Yes, I look forward to it," Von Schverdt replied as the MP closed the gate, latched it, and then positioned himself beside it.

Von Schverdt made his way to the cot and tested it with the palm of his hand before sitting on it. He took off his greatcoat and folded it over the metal chair, then stretched himself on the cot. *What if there is nothing left? What if the hangar didn't hold up?* he wondered. *I still have the capsule of cyanide in the heel of my boot, but the Americans are eager for more. If the craft is undamaged, then all will be well.* Von Schverdt constructed every conceivable scenario he could think of concerning what he might find when morning came. He carefully scrutinized each one down to the last detail, and then, when he felt he had exhausted all of the possible outcomes, he drifted off into an uneasy sleep.

The next morning Von Schverdt awakened at his customary time of 5:30. Dougherty arrived a short time later, and after a hasty breakfast of runny eggs and burnt toast, Von Schverdt was escorted to an Army staff car and sandwiched in the rear next to Colonel Dougherty and one of the men who had been present at the meeting the night before. The third sat in the front passenger seat.

Von Schverdt had not been formerly introduced to the two men. No names had been exchanged, and he knew nothing about them other than that they were part of an American organization called the Office of Strategic Services, or OSS. One of the OSS guy's ears stuck out, so he called him Dumbo, after the character in the Disney movie. Hitler had been fond of Disney movies, and Von Schverdt had watched several of them with *Der Fuehrer* at his mountain retreat, Wolf's Lair. The other man was fair-skinned with hardly a trace of facial hair, so he called the man Snow White. He enjoyed his private defamation of the two men, and it bolstered his spirits, making him feel superior.

The staff car was escorted in the front and rear by Military Police jeeps as it moved out of the Army headquarter's compound and headed southwest toward Peenemunde.

Von Schverdt looked out the window at the ravaged countryside as he answered yet another of the endless questions posed to him by the men from the OSS.

"You mentioned that the craft you had was operational?" Dumbo asked from the front seat.

"Yes, it was operational."

Dumbo and Snow White exchanged glances.

"Are you aware that our Air Force pilots reported this kind of aircraft as they were flying sorties over Berlin? They nicknamed them 'Foo fighters.'"

"No, I wasn't aware of that." *How much should I tell them . . . should I give them something now? A little tidbit, something to whet their appetites?* Von Schverdt toyed with several bits of information.

"But the craft at your facility were never used in a combat-type scenario?" Dumbo asked.

"Correct." Von Schverdt shifted in his seat so that he faced Colonel Dougherty. "*They've* been here for thousands of years, Colonel," Von Schverdt said, and he saw that his statement made the men very uncomfortable.

"How can you be so sure?" Dougherty asked.

"Because I communicated with one of them." Von Schverdt waited a moment, letting the full realization of what he had said begin to sink in.

"You communicated . . . how?" Snow White asked.

Von Schverdt pointed a gloved forefinger to his temple. "Telepathically. They are more evolved than we are. They are the old ones that make up much of the world's—what is your English word?—mythos."

"I'm not sure I follow you on that," Dougherty said.

"They can project thoughts into your mind. They can show you what has happened on this planet for thousands of years. Their involvement concerning man's ascent from apes, for one thing."

Silence followed.

Good, Von Schverdt thought, *I have planted a seed. And it will grow when they see what lies ahead,* ja?

They took several detours due to large craters in the road from Allied bombs. Bridges were either burned out or missing. Several hours later the cars stopped at the driveway of what appeared to be a deserted dairy farm on the outskirts of Peenemunde. The farm was located in a small, verdant valley several miles from Peenemunde, where the V1 and V2 rockets had been produced. Fenced fields that a short time ago contained dairy cows were now pockmarked with craters from bombs. The farmhouse had been ransacked: windows broken, the front door halfway off its hinges, furniture strewn about on the uncut lawn.

"Now we are here, *ja?*" Von Schverdt said, and he leaned forward with worried expectation.

The staff car made its way up the driveway, which was wide enough to accommodate two vehicles. Von Schverdt saw the familiar pens, usually filled with livestock, with gates open and vacant.

What has happened here? he wondered as he stared out the window.

As the car got to the disguised dairy barn, Von Schverdt's heart sank as he saw that the rear half of the building was gone, and a fire had gutted a good portion of it.

The men got out of the car and Von Schverdt began to run to the barn.

"General!" he heard Dougherty call out, but he kept running.

Von Schverdt reached the center of what had been the secret hangar for the flying disks, its floor a thick slab of steel-reinforced concrete. Just as he stopped, two MPs came up next to him with weapons drawn, followed a moment later by an angry Colonel Dougherty.

"Next time I'll tell them to shoot," Dougherty threatened.

"I'm sorry, Herr Colonel. It's just that I poured so much of myself into this. But here ..." He went to the center of the barn and with his gloved hands began to clear away the dirt and burnt timbers from the floor.

"Colonel, have your men help me."

"Do as he says," Dougherty commanded.

Two MPs came alongside Von Schverdt. "Like this," he instructed, as he stood up to move another timber. He dropped back to his knees and swept away the ash and dirt, exposing the floor, which had a blackened metal band running flush to the concrete.

"We clear this," he instructed the MPs. "It is our doorway to what the colonel needs to see."

"How does it open, General?" Snow White asked.

"First, we clear the debris ... then you will see," Von Schverdt answered.

"Sir," one of the MPs spoke up. "I've never seen metal like this ... some kind of alloy or something. It's not even burned by the fire."

Dougherty eyed Von Schverdt, wanting an explanation.

"Yes, it's an alloy ... similar to what the craft is made from," Von Schverdt explained.

Two hours went by with all of the men including Colonel Dougherty helping to clear the floor of the hangar.

Von Schverdt had taken off his shirt. His muscular torso was sweaty and soot-stained as the last of the debris was moved, revealing a forty-by-thirty-foot rectangular metal seam in the floor.

"Now we can open it," Von Schverdt exclaimed, as he made his way to the rear of the hangar, accompanied by one of the MPs. "Here." And he pointed toward a panel that was housed in a protective metal enclosure. He pulled a key from under the panel that had been hidden there and handed it to the MP. "Open it."

He watched as the MP fitted the key into the lock, and a moment later the door of the panel slid open to reveal a control box. "I'm going to open the doors, Colonel," Von Schverdt stated, as he began to reach for the controls.

"Not so fast, General," Dougherty called, as he approached with Snow White and Dumbo.

Von Schverdt stood up and waited until the men were next to him.

"Where's the power source?" Dougherty asked.

"I had everything buried underground. This facility has its own generators and is powered by synthetic fuel."

"Go ahead, General." Dougherty nodded at the controls.

Von Schverdt reached into the box and flipped a switch, waited a few seconds, and then fitted the palm of his hand over a red knob, giving it three turns to the right before pushing it in.

The relative quiet of the hangar was interrupted as the men heard a loud crack. Then, with a rush of air, the large concrete panel in the floor began to open. Von Schverdt led them over to the edge, where the group of men watched as the rectangle dropped a foot beneath them before it disappeared. "Here . . . the stairs." Von Schverdt reached down and pulled up the last section of handrail, then fastened it to the side of the opening.

Colonel Dougherty gasped, "I don't believe it."

Von Schverdt chuckled. "You are looking at one of the crafts that was given to us." And he pointed to a metallic-looking silver disk that rested on the floor forty feet below.

Von Schverdt saw the mixture of fear and uncertainty as Colonel Dougherty asked, "By them?" and pointed to the sky.

"Yes, but not there." Von Schverdt gestured upward with his index finger. "They are beneath us, Colonel, deep within the bowels of the earth. They have an extensive tunnel system that creates a grid underneath the planet. Like I said earlier, they have been here for thousands of years."

Von Schverdt saw, to his satisfaction, that Snow White and Dumbo looked shaken, as did the MPs. "I have something I think you will find of interest, Colonel," Von Schverdt said, "but you must go to my private office." He smiled.

Dougherty looked to Dumbo and Snow White, and both gave a nod of approval. "Good, then if you will follow me." Von Schverdt began to descend the stairs, followed by Colonel Dougherty and the rest of the men. They reached the bottom and Von Schverdt waited for the group to assemble before he continued. He flipped a switch, and the lights came on. Air ducts and water pipes ran along the ceiling. A cluster of thick electrical cables ran along the floor.

Von Schverdt watched with satisfaction as Colonel Dougherty and his men walked around the saucer, touching it, examining it.

"Where's the power source, the engine?" Dumbo asked.

Von Schverdt shook his head. "I can assure you that it's unlike anything you have ever imagined . . . but again, if you will allow me to show you my private office, much of what you ask is there."

Colonel Dougherty looked tense, as if he expected some sort of trap.

"Colonel, what are you expecting? I'm unarmed, and as you can see, the base has been abandoned, *ja?*"

"Draw your weapons, men," Dougherty ordered, and the MPs drew their .45 automatics.

"I can assure you, Colonel, that this is not necessary, but I understand. You don't trust me," he said matter-of-factly.

Dougherty tightened his lips and looked to the other men for agreement.

Dumbo cleared his throat. "It might be a trap."

Snow White nodded. "I agree, sir, the guns are cheap insurance."

"The MPs' weapons stay at ready," Dougherty said.

"Suit yourself, Colonel," Von Schverdt said, and led them down a corridor past several prototypes that were in various stages of construction. He showed them what remained of blueprints and schematics that were strewn about the floor, evidence of a hasty departure. Except for the distant whine of a generator, the place was eerily still.

"We have done some back-engineering, as you can see," Von Schverdt offered.

"When were you last here?" Dougherty asked.

Von Schverdt shrugged. "Two weeks ago, Colonel." He stopped and pointed toward an opened door fifty feet away. "My office, just there," he said.

"Colonel, there's something in the doorway," one of the MPs said, indicating the office that Von Schverdt had directed their attention to.

"What's going on, General?" Dougherty asked.

"Look and see for yourself, Colonel," Von Schverdt said. He motioned toward the doorway with his hand and a small figure came into view.

"It looks like a child," one of the MPs said.

"I assure you it's not a child," Von Schverdt replied, as a small gray being, with an enlarged head and large black almond-shaped eyes, stepped into the light. It had a thin torso and spindly arms and pale, gray skin. In fact, the MP's description was accurate, for it did look like a helpless child.

Von Schverdt heard a collective gasp from the men behind him as they got their first look at an alien life-form.

He stopped and turned back. The MPs had dropped their guns and were holding their heads. He saw the terror in their eyes.

"Make it stop," one of them yelled. "Make it stop!"

Von Schverdt tilted his head to one side and observed the men, who had dropped to their knees. One of the MPs had

THE REVEALING / 33

begun to convulse, white foam gathering around the corners of his mouth, while the other started to bang his head against the floor.

"General, what is going on?" Colonel Dougherty shouted.

Von Schverdt raised his hands to the small figure. The MPs collapsed to the floor, both men gasping for breath.

"I could have had *him* kill you all," Von Schverdt said, as the alien came up next to Von Schverdt. "Now, Colonel, I want you to listen very carefully." His face hardened and took on an air of superiority. "These are my demands."

1

---

* ◻ *

Mr. Wyan was very clever, and so was Azazel, for they were one and the same. A Jekyl-and-Hyde supergenius manifesting itself in the three-dimensional space-time continuum called earth.

Mr. Wyan moved about in the world of men undetected except, perhaps, for his unusual height and ugly scar that ran across his forehead over his left eye. But he was truly part of another dimension. For he was also Azazel, a fallen angel, a reptilian shape-shifter. He, along with others of his kind, had been cast down from heaven. It had been long ago in another age when he had come to earth the first time. He and the other fallen angels had taken many wives from the race of men and reproduced. Their offspring became known as the Nephilim, and they had spread out over the face of the earth.

When the deluge came, Azazel had sought refuge in the Abyss. He was enraged at the slaughter of his children as they drowned in the Flood and became disembodied spirits, or, as men would call them later, *demons*. His legions were thwarted by the barrier that the Enemy had set over the earth. The barrier had been put in place to prevent him, and the minions of the One they served, from manifesting themselves on the earth. It had been millennia since they had been allowed to roam there.

But that barrier was finally broken.

It was near midnight in the city of Jerusalem. A crescent moon peeked out through the clouds for a moment and then disappeared. The streets were deserted and Wyan moved quickly, his black trench coat trailing behind like a cape as he walked in the shadows of the closed shops and vendors. He had come to the Old City in search of the ancient scroll.

He thought about the last time he had seen it, as it was handed to a man he had come to know as MacKenzie. Incredibly MacKenzie, along with the help of others, had ruined one of his plans. There were three men in particular that he vowed to destroy. Oh, how he hated them.

He concentrated on the face of the first man, Art MacKenzie, and mulled over what he had come to know about him. *Hadn't he been a drunk, tended to by one of the Master's underlings? Divorced from his wife and family, and wallowing in self-pity and bitterness over the death of his son? But then the Enemy had taken an interest in this worthless sod, and the man had become free, and in such a short time had become a real nemesis. And to think I almost succeeded in killing him.* The thought sent a ripple of pleasure through him.

Now MacKenzie was under the tutelage of the second man he despised, a man he had come to know as Johanen. But not an ordinary man . . . For some reason the Enemy had given this one power over death itself. Over the centuries, other fallen angels had spoken of him as the "Immortal One," saying that he had been assigned special emissaries to guard over him, and that he had done miracles in the sight of men and interfered with many of their Master's wishes.

The third man in this loosely knit confederacy was an archeologist and old Messianic Jew, Elisha BenHassen. He had uncovered under the Temple Mount in Jerusalem one of the last remaining pieces of evidence of the Nephilim. A skeleton over ten feet in length, it was direct evidence of the union between beings like himself and the daughters of men.

Humankind, in general, had come to deny the existence of the spirit world. Good and evil, God and devil, had become things of superstition. But there were those who still knew where the battle lines were drawn. Men like MacKenzie, Johanen, and BenHassen. He thought how wonderful it would be to take these three men's heads in his hands and slowly choke the life out of them.

He was nearing the place where the scroll he sought was being kept—the Tower of David Museum. Earlier in the day he had shape-shifted into one of the guards. When the scroll had arrived he followed it to the laboratory where it would be photographed, cleaned, and finally translated. The scroll had been under close scrutiny and no opportunity had presented itself to steal it. So Azazel had left to wait for another chance. Now he stood near the entrance of the museum, which was well-lit. Azazel stopped across the street and then transformed himself into a mist and floated across the street and under the door of the ancient tower. He moved down the empty halls, a foglike specter, staying close to the baseboard along the floor. At one point he passed a guard who had no idea of the creature that moved silently just a few feet away from where he stood.

He found the room and slid under the door. Once inside, he resumed the form of Mr. Wyan. Glancing around, he saw what he was looking for. The scroll had been unrolled and was placed under a sheet of glass. He moved the glass aside, letting his hand run over the surface of the scroll, and looked at the strange writing. *What is this?* He didn't recognize the strange shapes. *No matter, Von Schverdt will have his people look into it and with their computers decipher it.* He rolled it up and tucked it into the inside of his trench coat as he walked to the door.

He unlocked the bolts and moved out into the hall. Listening, he heard a multitude of sounds: the boilers in the basement, a rat scurrying in the wall on the floor level below, the ticking of clocks in every room and lab in the building, the whine of computers, a passing car outside. He focused on the sound that he sought: the breathing of the security guard on the lower floor. He located two other guards, one on the floor above him and another in the building's commissary. Then he walked down the hall, staying near the wall. He saw the camera at the end of the hall and paused a moment. He reached toward it with one hand and an inky cloud enveloped the camera.

Coming to the staircase, he bounded up the three flights to the door that opened onto the roof. It had an alarm attached to it. Azazel reached his hand out again, and the wires that ran from the alarm melted and fused together. Opening the door, he stepped out onto the roof. Then he spread out his arms and shape-shifted into his true form—a reptilian creature with dark wings folded across its back. He unfolded his wings, then leaped from the building and flew into the night air, clutching the scroll in his clawed hand.

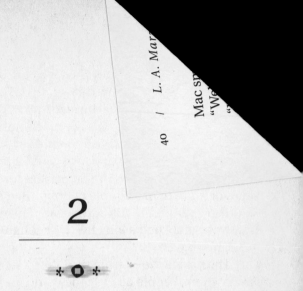

2

A rt MacKenzie brushed a dark lock of hair from his fore-head and then ran his fingers through his scalp. He had awakened early, just at daybreak, and wondered for a minute where he was, then realized he was at Elisha BenHassen's house just outside Jerusalem. He got out of bed and, after slipping into his jeans and a T-shirt, went in search of a cup of coffee. The house was still, and he assumed Elisha had not yet risen. He found the coffee and started a fresh pot brewing. Minutes later, hot coffee in hand, he made his way to Elisha's library.

Mac glanced at the rows of books that lay in all directions. Most had slips of paper marking particular passages. Others were opened and lay atop other books in the shelf. Three computers, their screen savers showing an endless universe, sat atop of what was once a dining room table. A large map of the Middle East was suspended on the far wall. A fax machine had spewed dozens of pages that were scattered over the floor, due to a broken tray that lay next to the machine.

"Good morning, MacKenzie," Elisha said. The old man came into the room holding a mug of coffee. He was in his bathrobe, and his disheveled hair and trifocal glasses made him look a little like Einstein.

miled. "Good morning, Elisha."

ll, MacKenzie, how did you sleep?"

Very well, thank you," he lied.

Elisha went over to the fax machine and gathered the paper from the floor. "I wish I could say the same. Restless night."

"I lied," Mac confessed. "Same goes for me. I don't think I slept for more than a couple of hours. Bad dreams."

Elisha nodded. "You have really been through it from what you said. I had a long talk with Johanen before he left."

"Oh, what about?"

"The next move . . . from the Enemy. He believes that time is very short. People all over the world are talking about the mysterious sign in the heavens."

"Yeah, the man on the street is scared. And who wouldn't be? When was the last time anything like that happened?"

Elisha thought for a moment. "Fatima, Portugal, in 1917. Seventy thousand people saw something. It was called the 'Miracle of the Sun.' I've been researching this, and I believe it was a precursor of things to come. A harbinger from the Enemy, one of the signs that Scripture tells us to be aware of in the last days."

Mac took a sip of coffee. "What happened?"

"A long story, Mac, but the short of it is, that seventy thousand people saw the sun spin and fall to the ground. Of course it was a local occurrence; the sun didn't spin or fall from the sky anywhere else in the world, only in Fatima."

"You called it a harbinger?"

"Yes, I believe that in the Last Days counterfeit miracles will be shown to those on earth."

"And the sign that we saw—the supposed reemergence of the Bethlehem star—is just such a sign."

"The Internet is buzzing with chat about it. TV, radio, everyone has an opinion on it. Even the pope commented on it. Of course, we know who is behind it and how it is going to be used to deceive the nations."

Mac and Elisha were discussing a false sign that had appeared over the country of Yemen a few days earlier, a supposed reoccurrence of the star of Bethlehem. Mac and Johanen had seen it firsthand and knew that it was part of an elaborate scheme designed to deceive.

"I think it already has, to some degree," Mac said.

"People are believing the lie from the Enemy because they have abandoned the truth of God's Word."

Mac nodded. "Yeah, it amazes me. It's actually written down for everybody to see for themselves, but most people still don't get it. 'There but for the grace of God go I,' if it hadn't have been for Johanen and you."

"Yes, the Scriptures tell us that only the wise will understand."

Mac asked, "What's on the agenda today?"

"We're going back to Mossad headquarters to meet with Uri." Elisha's grandson Uri worked with Elisha researching the UFO phenomena. "We need to discuss the sign in more detail and also the scroll which was stolen. And there are other developments that have my ear to the ground."

"Such as?"

"Troop movements in neighboring countries. It was one of the reasons I had little sleep. It seems that Iran is engaging in military maneuvers. Nothing unusual about that, except that they were joined by Egypt. Now that Iran is armed with nuclear capability it becomes unsettling."

"Any word on the scroll?" Mac asked, referring to the ancient scroll that had been handed off to him by a mysterious robed figure in Yemen, then, somehow, stolen from the Tower of David Museum two nights ago. Johanen had believed that the scroll contained vital information that might help them in their ongoing conflict with the Cadre.

Elisha turned away from MacKenzie. "Nothing yet. But Johanen believes that the Cadre has something to do with it."

"How could they have broken into the museum and stolen it?" Mac asked.

Mac watched Elisha adjust several books on the shelf in front of him. "Truly a mystery," Elisha began. "There were no signs of a break-in. One of the security cameras suddenly clouded over, but the people who examined it believe it was most likely a transmission malfunction. And the guards reported nothing out of the ordinary—yet the scroll is gone."

Elisha wearily sank into a chair. "We need to keep a watchful eye, MacKenzie. Johanen believes, as I do, that the time is very near for them to begin the Great Deception. In some ways it has already begun with the appearance of the sign. The time of the end appears to be upon us."

"So what's next, Doctor?"

Elisha shook his head. "We'll have to wait and see."

3

"Come on, Nora, hurry it up," a lanky black man coaxed, his bloodshot eyes darting over his shoulder and up the garbage-infested alleyway.

"You want to do it?" Nora challenged back, letting her hands fall to her sides.

"No way, man. I know nothing 'bout this and that's a fact."

"Say you're sorry then." She balled her fists and stuffed them into the pockets of a dirty pair of men's trousers several sizes too big for her.

The man took a step back and looked up the alley. He ran his hand nervously over his forehead and licked his lips. "Man, I'm gonna just walk outta here and we not gonna get nothin'. You'll see." He took a step back.

Nora's laughter echoed through the alleyway.

"Somebody gonna hear you with that crazy laugh o' yours and then they gonna find us here."

"We done nothin' wrong . . . yet," she said, looking at him with a grimy angelic face and a shoulder-length mane of unkempt, dark brown hair.

"I'm gonna leave you, Nora, 'less you go on an' do it."

"Say you're sorry," she demanded.

The black man scowled back at her. "No way, man, I ain't sorry for jack."

44 / L. A. Marzulli

"Then you can find somebody else to get you in."

The man kicked a Styrofoam cup that still held some coffee, which splattered back on his pants as he sent it flying against the alley wall. "Now look what you made me do."

Nora laughed again.

"That laugh o' yours gets more creepier by the day," the black man said. "You been takin' your pills?"

Nora ignored the question. "Say you're sorry, Jerry," she demanded.

Jerry licked his lips again. He was coming down from amphetamines and he needed to get more. His body was beginning to ache and his hands trembled uncontrollably for a second or two as he angrily eyed the woman, who, in his mind, had made such an unreasonable demand on him. After all, he hadn't said anything to offend her. He had just told her to hurry it up. His left arm shuddered, forcing a decision. "All right . . . I'm sorry."

Nora showed him a tired smile, with a few missing teeth. She pulled her hands from her pockets and once again set to work on a padlock that held a thick chain that was wrapped around the back door of a convenience store. Jerry took a few steps so that he was right behind her. He watched her delicate ivory fingers work the lock pick. A moment later Nora pulled down on the lock and it opened.

"You amazing, you know that," Jerry said, genuinely astounded at Nora's ability. "I'll do my part now, be ready to get out here, soon as you see me." He pulled an old pillowcase from the inside of his sweatshirt, then slowly unwound the chain and slipped into the store.

Jerry let his eyes adjust to the dimly lit room. Cocking his head, he listened to the muted conversation and the blare of a radio that came from the front of the store. Then he made his way to one of the shelves that held canned foods, some of which were still in half-opened boxes. He picked up one and carefully slipped it into his sack. Then he grabbed the next one and carefully set it against the first can, at the bottom lest he should make any unwanted noise. *It's my lucky day*, he thought, as he filled his sack up and glanced back at Nora. *Crazy chick*. He wondered where she had learned to pick locks like a pro. The bag nearly full, he grabbed for another can, and as he did his hand trembled uncontrollably. The can slipped from his grasp and fell to the floor. Jerry froze and waited, eyeing the door that led directly to the front counter. He saw it begin to open. He picked up another can as he made for the back door.

"Hey, you!" a fat old Korean man shouted at him.

Jerry threw the can and it slammed into the man's shoulder. As the man yelled in pain and fell to the floor, Jerry darted through the doorway and into the alley. Nora was running next to him, laughing like a crazed woman.

"Crazy chick," Jerry muttered under his breath as he made for the back of the alley. He saw Nora go over the chain-link fence, catlike.

Jerry got to the fence. Glancing behind him, he saw that the angry Korean grocer had made it to the doorway and had a gun. "You stop. I shoot!"

On the run, Jerry tied the top of the pillowcase and threw it over the fence into Nora's waiting arms. He scrambled up the fence, and as he reached the top, he heard the gun go off.

The bullet whizzed over his head. Jerry was now really scared. *He's gonna kill me over a few cans of food*, he thought, as he dropped to the ground. He grabbed the sack from Nora and the pair began to run down another alleyway.

They ducked into a doorway and were hidden from sight.

"You think he's gonna follow us?" Nora asked, her breath coming in little pants.

"He too fat 'n' old for this . . . no way, man," Jerry said, and he grinned at Nora. He peered around the blackened brick. "He's at the fence, wavin' his gun around."

"You hear that?" Nora said, and she grabbed Jerry's sweat-shirt.

"They ain't gonna find us," Jerry blustered, as he nodded toward the police sirens that echoed through the labyrinth of buildings near New York's Central Park. "Besides, nobody gonna mess with a couple of mole people." He grinned.

He motioned for her to stay close and, crouching low, they made their way along the wall of the alley.

"Up here." Jerry pointed to part of a rusted fire escape that had been gerry-rigged over the alley's rear wall. The pair climbed over the wall and fell into the rear of a burned-out shell of an apartment building, which, in spite of the fence, had been a catch-all for the community's garbage and unwanted items.

"Look at all this," Jerry said as he picked up a torn mattress.

"We can use it back at the condo," Nora said.

"Yeah, I'll come back for it, after we eat . . ." Jerry pushed Nora down.

"Hey, what are you doing?" Nora said.

"They knows we here. Look, they in front of us," Jerry pointed to a squad car with its lights flashing in front of the lot.

"They're not getting me," Nora whispered, and she moved closer to Jerry.

"Nothin' gonna happen . . . they ain't comin' here through all this. Too many rats." Jerry pointed to one that scurried a few feet past them.

A bullhorn cracked to life. "We know you two are in there. Come out with your hands up."

"Yeah, like I'm just gonna give up my food to you, man," Jerry taunted in a whisper.

"I don't like this, Jerry. They know we're here," Nora said.

"I knows somethin' that they don't," Jerry said, as he tapped his head with his index finger knowingly.

"Like what?" Nora asked.

"You 'pologize to me for making me say sorry to you back there," Jerry insisted and folded his arms across his chest.

Nora looked defiant.

"Come on, man, no chick gonna hit me with that stuff 'cept my ol' lady, an' you ain't her."

"Come out now . . . this is the police . . . you're both under arrest," the cop ordered.

"Yeah, like I'm gonna come out with my hands up and everything," Jerry mocked.

"All right, I'm sorry I made you do it," Nora said, clearly growing more nervous with the police presence.

"Good . . . Now stay low an' follow me," Jerry ordered as he crept forward on his hands and knees, holding the sack in front of him. He made his way past a huge pile of broken concrete and bricks and then toward a large pile of scrap wood and building materials. "It's comin' up now."

"I don't see anything," Nora whined as she crawled behind him. "They ain't gonna get me and I ain't goin' back to that place."

"Don't worry, nobody's gonna get ya."

"So where is it?" Nora asked again.

"Tim told me about it, an' he never lied 'bout nothin' to nobody." Jerry allowed himself to chuckle.

"This is the police . . ."

Jerry laughed. "Hey, man, these guys really think we're comin' out an everythin'?"

"How much farther?" Nora asked.

"It's up here. See that pile of trash that was throwed into that kinda basement there?"

"Yeah."

"There's a tunnel in there, connects to the sewer."

Jerry led them into the basement, which was surrounded by the remains of brick walls that rose several stories above them. "It's supposed to be here." He hurried over to the rusted hood of an automobile leaning against the wall. Pushing it aside he chuckled again. "It's here . . . just like Tim said it would be."

Nora slid past him into the tunnel. Jerry followed but put back the hood to conceal the entrance. The two of them sat for a moment, allowing their eyes to adjust to the darkness, before scrambling down the tunnel.

"Where's it end?" Nora asked.

"Tim say it goes into a main sewer."

They crawled for a few minutes more in what now was complete darkness. Their scuffing shoes and panting breath echoed down the pipe.

"Hey, it's here," Nora whispered.

"Just like Tim said it would be," Jerry added.

The pipe intersected into a main sewer, allowing them to stand upright and walk through ankle-deep sewer water.

"When you want to pop up?" Nora asked.

"We go a little more ways just to make sure," Jerry responded.

"What did you get?" Nora asked.

"Lots of canned stuff. Yams, beans, oriental vegetables, I don't know—it's all stuffed in the bag here." Jerry moved his shoulders upward which made a few of the cans jostle in the bag.

"What about this one?" Nora asked, pointing to a shaft of light that poured through a manhole cover.

Jerry shook his head sagelike. "Let's do the next one just to be safe."

They continued walking and came to another manhole cover.

"I'll go up first," Jerry said, handing Nora the bag. He climbed the rusted ladder and pressed upward on the manhole cover. "It's down tight," he muttered as he heaved against it with his shoulder. Finally the cover loosened and he held one corner of it. Light poured in and, for a moment, stunned him. He blinked his eyes and then squinted outside and looked around.

"Well?" Nora asked impatiently.

Jerry didn't answer. He moved the other side of the lid upward and looked around some more. Finally he pushed the whole thing over the side and it was gone.

"Hand the bag," he ordered.

Nora handed him the bag and Jerry took it and threw it out of the manhole then followed after it.

Nora scrambled up the ladder after him. The two stood in a small side street. Jerry elbowed her to look at a few startled pedestrians who gawked at their sudden appearance from the underworld.

Jerry set the lid back over the manhole and grinned. "Looks like we're gonna be eatin' like kings back at the Condos."

"Like kings and queens," Nora added.

The two set off and several blocks later crept through a hole in a chain-link fence that led to a littered vacant lot that bordered the underground subway tracks. They slid down the angled concrete embankment, dropping almost thirty feet to the single set of train tracks below.

"We did it, Nora," Jerry laughed, as they walked leisurely along the tracks.

"Yeah. Hey, train coming," Nora warned, and a few moments later the headlight of a train could be seen in the recess of the tunnel that opened up before them.

They moved to the mouth of the tunnel and waited. Jerry grabbed the bag as the train streaked past. He looked up just as the last car was going by and caught a glimpse of a man reading a newspaper, oblivious to him and Nora just a few feet away.

"No place like home," Jerry said, as he and Nora moved back into the tunnel, following the tracks that disappeared under the streets of New York City.

4

Brian Fitzpatrick took another breath of air in two distinct gulps timed with the stride of his legs, as he ran up a hill that he had jokingly named Heartbreak Hill, in New York City's Central Park. Then, as if his legs were pistons that were tied to the rhythm of his breath, he let out the air in one long stream that took up two more strides. He snatched another breath of air and leaned forward into the hill, feeling the burn in the back of his thighs as he passed the halfway mark. Sweat poured down his forehead and he yanked his sweatband, pulling it down toward his eyes.

He passed another jogger, a woman, who was taking the hill in short, almost babylike steps. He shouted, "You can do it," as he passed close to her. Two minutes later he crested the hill and let his body relax into an easier pace, as this part of his run was flat. He looked forward to mornings when he didn't have to work, when at the crack of dawn he would jump out of bed, don his sweats, and head to the park. He relished the time alone, away from the constant demands of the Doomsday Clock Project Think Tank.

"The Tank," as it was nicknamed, consisted of a staff of people who monitored world events twenty-four hours a day and fed the information into a state-of-the-art computer.

Since the Industrial Revolution, progress and technology had increased exponentially to the point that no one person could get a decent overview of all that was happening. Life had become a complex interlocking web of commerce, industry, and art.

A negative by-product to this technology was that humans had succeeded in gaining the potential to annihilate every living soul on planet earth . . . many times over. Fitzpatrick had been employed at the Tank for his knowledge of eschatological prophecies from different cultures spanning thousands of years. He had read and studied everything from Hopi Indian legends to Hebrew apocalyptic scrolls.

Because by personal preference he lived in New York City even though the Tank was based near Washington, D.C., it wasn't unusual for him to spend as many as three consecutive days at the Tank, catching a short nap in the staff lounge every now and then to ward off fatigue. In fact, he had just finished a three-day shift.

His mind started to run off on a linguistic problem involving translation from an ancient Canaanite text. But he firmly stopped it, shoving it back to the compartment that it belonged in as he looked at the brilliant hues of a maple tree that was backlit by the rising sun.

He quickened his pace, nearing the end of his run. For the last fifty yards he sprinted for all he was worth, imagining himself at a track meet at his former high school. At the finish line he slowed, walking in a large circle on the grass holding his hands above his head. A sudden nip of cold fall air made him turn up his collar on his jacket. He dropped to the ground and stretched his legs, taking care to massage the backs of his calves. *Not bad for someone over forty,* he mused.

As he headed out of the park he spotted a homeless person sleeping on a park bench. He detoured a little out of his way and looked at the sleeping figure of a man. A shopping cart with a New York Mets' flag attached was parked near the bench. He smelled the alcohol and saw the empty bottle tossed a few feet away from the bench. Remembering that he had a five-dollar bill in his jacket earmarked for a Starbucks' latte, he retrieved the cash and stuck it in the threadbare sleeve of the man's coat.

Then he made his way to Columbus Circle, where he noticed a black limo parked on the corner ahead of him. At first he didn't give it a thought, but as he drew nearer, the blacked-out window disappeared and he recognized the face of Anthony Titwell, his driver.

He tightened his lips and straightened his back as he drew closer to the vehicle.

"How did you find me?" he asked as he stood a few feet from the limo.

Titwell grinned. "You got your watch on, don't you?"

Fitzpatrick looked down at his watch and remembered that it had a global positioning device that enabled its wearer to be found with pinpoint accuracy.

"Emergency, then?" Fitzpatrick asked.

Titwell got out of the car and opened the rear door. "That's why I'm here."

Fitzpatrick knew that Titwell wouldn't know what the call was about. He was just doing his job in finding him.

"Thanks, Titwell," Fitzpatrick replied, as he slid into the back of the limo. "Do I have time to shower and change?"

Titwell put the limo in gear and pulled away from the curb. "Nope."

"The airport then?"

"Yep. Your jet's on the runway waiting for you."

Fitzpatrick settled back in the seat and wondered what was so important that his weekend would be interrupted. He took the satellite phone off its cradle and made sure the voice scrambler was on before he punched in a series of numbers.

"Good morning, Fitzpatrick." A voice with a heavy German accent came over the receiver.

"Good morning, sir," Fitzpatrick answered.

"We've got something that needs your attention immediately."

"I'm on my way," Fitzpatrick replied. "What is it?"

"Let's not go into that right now. Suffice it to say that it's very ancient and at the moment indecipherable."

"Any idea of what language it is?"

"That's why you're headed to the Tank." A pause, then: "Call me when you have any information on it."

"I'll do that, sir."

Fitzpatrick turned the phone off and put the receiver back in the cradle. He didn't trust the man he worked for. He didn't like the way everyone at the Tank was treated as an inferior underling. He took umbrage at the way the man flaunted his wealth and position, and how he went out of his way to make the point that his ancestors were German royalty and had been in the service of the Kaiser. A little over a year ago, the man had wooed him away from a modest university teaching position, offering a six-figure income that Fitzpatrick had found irresistible. Fitzpatrick planned to work for a few years, bank the money, and then retire to Rome, where he could scour the vast archival Vatican libraries.

Fitzpatrick had found the Tank to be an enigma. There were soldiers like Titwell, and military MPs, but they weren't tied into any particular branch of the service he could identify. Fitzpatrick had come to realize that he didn't know whom he actually worked for—the United States government, the private sector, a rogue element, or even the Chinese, for that matter. All he knew for certain was that the man he reported to, nicknamed the Hag by everyone in the Tank, was in charge.

Another unsettling fact was the realization that he didn't know what became of his work. Or for that matter, what interest his employer would find in tracking certain prophecies from diverse civilizations, and looking for some universal constant in them. It sobered him to realize that the information that came his way was very classified and was very up-to-the-minute intel.

An hour later his unmarked jet touched down on a special runway near Washington, D.C. Fitzpatrick was hurried to a waiting car and motored to a building just outside the Washington Beltway. Titwell stopped at the gate to the underground parking garage and punched in the code. The gate opened and the car went down into the parking area. Several turns later it reached a wall—at least, what appeared to be a wall. Fitzpatrick looked out his window as the car gave a little jolt, and then the section of the floor that the car rested on began to go down into the earth. After several minutes it came to rest.

An MP opened the door and Fitzpatrick got out and waited, holding his right hand in front of him. The MPs grabbed his hand and slipped it into a machine that covered his hand glovelike, to his wrist. Fitzpatrick felt an almost imperceptible sting, as a needle pricked his skin and withdrew a tiny amount of blood.

Without a word the MP took the sample to a machine that was imbedded into a large stainless steel door. He watched the monitor as the blood sample's DNA was matched.

"You're free to go, Mr. Fitzpatrick," he called, as he keyed a small locked box that had held the release for the door.

Fitzpatrick waited as the stainless steel doors slid noiselessly open. Walking alone down a dimly lit corridor, he nodded at several coworkers he passed. He opened the door to his department, a large room filled with desks and computers. Bookshelves covered three walls, and the fourth wall held a digital map of the world.

Fitzpatrick unbuttoned his sweat jacket and glanced around the room. Two men and two women were busy at the terminals. The Tank, as always, was in session.

"Morning, Fitz," Zach mumbled, as he typed on his keyboard. He was the group's statistician, specializing in third-world population growth and the relationships between emerging industry in those countries and the impact on the environment, surrounding nations, and the global economy.

"Coffee?" Mary asked, holding out a steaming cup and smiling.

Fitzpatrick took the cup and sipped. Mary was a tall, blond-haired woman who was approaching forty and had never married. She was still attractive when she wanted to be, and this morning she had taken the time to put on makeup and wear a skirt and sweater that flattered her trim figure. A graduate of Yale Medical School who had served a decade with the Center for Disease Control, she specialized in the research of rare diseases.

"What do we have?" Fitzpatrick asked, as he took another sip of his coffee.

"Look at this," Vinnie answered, using his mouse to highlight an area on his computer monitor that corresponded to the digital map on the wall. The image changed on the digital screen against the far wall.

Vinnie's specialty was supertechnology. While still in college, he had designed a faster computer chip that was bought by a leading company.

"What is it?" Fitzpatrick asked, noting that the images appeared to have been shot with a night-vision camera.

"Infrared satellite image of an incident that happened in Yemen forty-eight hours ago. I think you'll find it very interesting," Vinnie stated.

"You've all seen it then?" Fitzpatrick asked.

"Several times," Joyce offered. "We have some very extraordinary footage here."

Joyce, a middle-aged hippy, was an expert in the paranormal. For Joyce to think it extraordinary meant that it was more than the typical UFO footage, or mutilated cattle carcasses, or apparitions of the Virgin Mary.

Fitzpatrick settled in his chair as the footage rolled. A fiery object entered the camera's field.

"Meteor?" Fitzpatrick asked.

"My first guess, but meteors don't stop and start again," Mary offered.

Fitzpatrick watched as the object slowed down and then took off again. "Close-up?" he asked.

"Yeah . . . here it comes." Vinnie typed in a command on his keyboard.

Fitzpatrick stared with genuine wonder. "Incredible," he whispered. "It looks like a craft of some kind, but where was it made and by whom?"

"The press is hailing it as the reemergence of the Bethlehem star," Joyce added, "but it's unlike anything I've ever seen."

"People all over the world have heard about it," Zach said. "An *Al Jazeera* film crew caught it on tape. They've been showing it nonstop."

"And our media picked it up from them?" Fitzpatrick asked.

Zach nodded. "Yeah, Fox News and CNN are running with it."

"Any idea as to what it is?" Mary asked.

Fitzpatrick shook his head.

"Anything in the ancient prophecies about it?" Mary asked.

Fitzpatrick shook his head. "Nothing that comes to mind."

"It seems to have been centralized over the country of Yemen."

Fitzpatrick nodded. "Mideast update? Anything affected?"

"Syria moved some troops around to their border with Lebanon. The Iranians are doing military exercises in the Persian Gulf. Other than that, status quo," Zach stated.

There was a knock on the door and a military attaché entered carrying a sealed packet. "Mr. Fitzpatrick," he said, as he placed the packet in Fitzpatrick's hands.

Fitzpatrick signed the release form and the man left the office.

All eyes were on him as he opened the packet and unfolded the copy of an ancient scroll. "This is why the Hag interrupted my weekend," Fitzpatrick said, as he got his first look at the strange writing.

"You recognize it?" Joyce asked.

"No, I don't ... very interesting though ... It's not Chaldean ...," Fitzpatrick mumbled as he made his way to his desk, so absorbed in the new find that he forgot his colleagues.

5

***

A rt MacKenzie and Elisha BenHassen arrived in front of Mossad headquarters, having been informed that a top-secret communiqué awaited Mr. MacKenzie. They were going to see Elisha's grandson Uri and the Major, an old friend of Elisha's who had helped found the Israeli Mossad, the Israeli version of the CIA.

Mac saw several armed guards in front of the building. The street was fairly crowded, and people bustled about their business in the early morning hour.

"Tight security," he said, motioning to the armed guards as they headed toward the entrance.

"We cannot let our guard down for a moment, MacKenzie," Elisha said, pushing his trifocals up on the bridge of his nose.

Mac glanced up the street at a handful of people waiting for a bus fifty yards away.

"Shalom," Elisha said to one of the guards as he produced his credentials.

A woman yelled from the bus stop up the street. Suddenly one of the guards shoved Elisha down onto the pavement. Both guards then bolted toward the commotion.

"Get down, MacKenzie!" Elisha shouted.

Mac had one knee on the pavement when he heard another scream. He stood up to get a better look. He saw people diving into shops, while others ducked behind any shelter they could find, leaving a young woman with a veil struggling with an older woman who was tearing at her clothes and yelling. Mac saw the crowded bus come to a stop beside them.

What are they fighting over? he wondered.

"MacKenzie, get down!" Elisha yelled, and Mac felt the man's hand tug at his pant leg.

Then he heard a piercing cry of "*Allah Akbar,*" from the veiled woman, followed by a blinding flash and a violent explosion. Mac was thrown off his feet as the shock wave from the blast threw him to the pavement.

There was a moment of eerie silence and a thick cloud of dark smoke enveloped him. Then the shrieks of the wounded erupted. Mac wiped his eyes and then to his horror, noticed the severed lower part of an arm next to him. It looked surreal to him, as if it were part of a mannequin or a doll, and not the warm flesh and blood that, moments ago, had been part of a human being. He stared at the wedding band on the blackened finger.

Fighting the urge to vomit he turned the other way as another wave of black smoke washed over him.

"MacKenzie?"

"I'm okay," he called to Elisha, then slowly got to his knees and tried to get his bearings. He looked down at his clothes and saw that his pants had been torn and his shirt ripped.

"Over here, MacKenzie," Elisha called out through the smoke.

A siren blared in the distance.

Mac stumbled toward Elisha. Then his ears began to ring. He worked his jaw up and down trying to clear his ears, but he couldn't shake the ringing. Dizzy, his eyes burned from the black smoke, he staggered like a drunken man.

The wind switched directions, revealing the spot where the suicide bomber had destroyed herself. He saw the littered remains of dead and wounded people scattered over the street and sidewalk. Shop windows had been shattered and the bus that had pulled up to the stop was on fire, its side ripped open like it was no more than a soda can.

An ambulance streaked by followed by several police cars, but Mac could barely hear the sirens. He put his fingers in his ears, trying to clear them.

Elisha hurried over, waving to him and talking. Mac shook his head and pointed to his ears, then yelled, "I can't hear you!"

Elisha reached him and helped him get to the interior of Mossad headquarters. Mac collapsed on a bench, and his body began to shake. He looked at Elisha and saw him mouth the words, "suicide bomber."

Mac nodded and felt the room spin around him for a moment. Elisha reached out and steadied him. "Will you be all right?" he mouthed.

Mac nodded, made a gesture for something to drink. Elisha hurried away down the hall.

Mac let his head fall back so that it rested on the wall behind the bench. A flurry of men and women hurried in all directions, bringing wounded people into the building and setting them near him.

Elisha returned with a paper cup full of water. Mac sipped the water, grateful that the acrid taste in his mouth was washed away. He swallowed and felt his ears unplug, but the ringing continued.

"My ears are ringing," he mumbled to Elisha.

"It will go away in a while," Elisha offered. "But your hearing is fine?"

"I think so," Mac said, putting a finger inside his ear and moving it around. "I saw her . . . she looked right at me just before she blew herself up," Mac said. "She was young . . . in her twenties . . . and pretty. What a waste of life."

Elisha nodded. "Are you able to get to the Major's office?" Elisha asked. "It's just down the hall."

Mac nodded and Elisha helped him to his feet.

"Elisha, MacKenzie, are you all right?"

Mac saw the Major running down the hall toward them.

"He was stunned by the blast," Elisha said as the Major reached them.

"You see," the Major said, "this is what we live with. They don't want peace. They want every Jew dead."

"Easy, old friend," Elisha counseled. "Not every Arab hates us. There are many who want peace, and some even recognize that we have a right to the land."

The Major shook his head, then turned to Mac. "Are you sure you're all right? Should I call for a doctor just to make sure?"

Mac shook his head. "I'm okay, Major, thank you." He worked his jaw again to see if it would stop the ringing. "How soon can we see the communiqué?"

"As soon as we get to my office." The Major led them through a reception area to his private office and motioned for Elisha and MacKenzie to take a seat. "Here it is, MacKenzie," the Major said, as he handed him a sealed envelope.

Mac opened it and blinked his eyes a few times before beginning to read. "He wants me to come to Rome." He handed the letter to Elisha.

"Frankly, I wish he had summoned me instead," Elisha said.

"Do you think it has something to do with the scroll? Does Johanen know it was stolen?" Mac asked.

"I sent a communiqué to him, via the Major, shortly after we received the news," Elisha said.

"You told me that you believed the same people we shut down in Yemen were responsible for the theft," the Major stated.

Elisha shrugged. "The evidence points to them. After all, we disrupted their broadcast and thwarted their plans to reveal the extraterrestrial presence . . . at least temporarily."

"You know what is really strange?" Mac asked. "Maggie was supposed to fly in, and at the last minute she canceled because my daughter, Sarah, had come down with appendicitis."

"God is looking after you, MacKenzie," Elisha stated.

Mac nodded, wondering what awaited him in Rome with Johanen.

6

Johanen paused at the iron gate that led to the small court-yard and rose garden that had once been tended by the late Cardinal Fiorre. He ran his hand over the brass handle and prayed, asking for strength and wisdom. He had gone without sleep for the last twenty-four hours, flying from Israel to Naples and then to his castle in the Alps. There he was informed of the jailhouse suicide of Stephan, once one of his most trusted aides, who had betrayed him and his organization known as Spiral of Life. He was greatly troubled further by the news that Cardinal Fiorre, a longtime trusted friend and Vatican informant, had apparently died of a massive stroke. Fiorre had left him some papers, but no trace of the papers could be found at the castle. Johanen believed that Stephan had destroyed them. So now he had come in haste to Rome, to see if Father Thomas knew anything about their content.

He unlatched the gate and entered the courtyard. A small fountain gurgled in the far corner and the scent of roses and freshly turned earth filled the air. He stopped, gathered a cream-colored rose in his fingers, and inhaled its fragrance. He then made his way to the heavy wooden door, grabbed the head of a hideous-looking gargoyle, and let the knocker fall with a muffled thud.

A young priest with a boyish face and a shock of red hair opened the door. "Johanen?" he asked, a smile spreading across his face.

Johanen extended his hand. "Yes, good to meet you, Father Thomas. I came as soon as I got your word."

"Cardinal Fiorre spoke often of you. Come in, won't you?"

After Johanen entered the house the priest closed the door behind him, then gestured to a seat at a dining room table stacked with papers and books.

"I will miss him," Johanen said as they seated themselves.

Thomas nodded, then leaned forward in his chair. "He was like a grandfather to me. But something very pressing is happening." Thomas lowered his voice. "I have wanted to tell someone . . . but . . . there has been an incident concerning His Holiness."

Johanen frowned and waited for the man to continue.

"It's being kept quiet. His Holiness has had a stroke. I have even heard that he is not expected to live past tonight."

"When did this happen?"

"Only a few hours ago . . . I only know because I was working late at the Vatican, in Cardinal Fiorre's private chambers. His Holiness was saying Mass in his private chapel when it happened. They rushed him secretly to a hospital."

"It won't be long before the media gets wind of it," Johanen replied.

"Cardinal Fiorre's funeral was scheduled for tomorrow, but now . . . who knows?"

"If the pope dies, then, I agree, most things will be put on hold until his successor is elected."

"Are you aware that His Eminence requested an autopsy to be performed in the event of his death?" Father Thomas said, changing the subject.

"No, I wasn't aware of that. Has it been carried out?"

"Yes. The results confirmed that he died of a massive stroke. But there's something that you should know."

Johanen waited.

"I saw the body, and his face was contorted . . . He looked like a man who had seen the Evil One himself."

"What did the coroner say about that?"

"That facial contortions often accompany severe strokes. But there's something else. When I arrived, I found this." Thomas held up a silver cross. "I found it lying next to the wall there." He pointed behind Johanen. "And what's more, there is a mark, a deep indentation in the plaster where the cross hit. Look." The man got out of his chair and went over to the wall. He placed the cross next to the indentation.

"It's like it was thrown with great force, yes?" Thomas stated.

Johanen got up from his seat and went over to get a closer look. He let his finger trace the indentation. "I agree, this certainly is very strange."

"Another thing that is very odd. His Eminence was working on something that had been directly commissioned by His Holiness."

"Cardinal Fiorre spoke to me of the manuscript he completed," Johanen said.

"I've searched everywhere and the manuscript is gone," Thomas said.

"I received a message that he was going to send me a copy of it."

"Yes, I was aware of that," Thomas said. "You said you never received it?"

"I believe it was destroyed."

"He left some very specific instructions in the event of his death. I was entrusted with an envelope. I was told in the event of his death to mail it immediately."

"Where was it addressed?"

"To an address in New York. It was addressed to a Brian Fitzpatrick."

"Did the cardinal ever mention him to you?"

"Here." Thomas took a photograph from the sideboard behind him. "It's a picture that was taken almost ten years ago."

Johanen looked at the photo. "Is this Fitzpatrick with the cardinal?"

"Yes."

"Then he was ordained?" Johanen said with surprise as he looked at the collar around the man's neck, marking him as a priest.

"He was a Dominican," Thomas answered.

"Was?"

"He left his holy orders. There was something in his past that haunted him. I believe Cardinal Fiorre knew, but His Eminence never confided in me."

"It appears that they worked closely together," Johanen said.

"His Eminence confided that they were *very* close . . . but the man fell away."

Johanen fitted the cross into the indentation that it had left in the plaster. "Someone other than Cardinal Fiorre is responsible for this."

Johanen saw Thomas look at him questioningly.

"I cannot imagine Cardinal Fiorre throwing the object that he venerated for any reason."

"So you suspect . . . someone else was responsible?" Thomas asked.

"Yes, I do."

"But who?"

Johanen handed the cross back to Thomas. "Those who want to make sure that Cardinal Fiorre's work never reached His Holiness."

7

Nora sat around a small campfire in front of Jerry's card-board house, four stories below the streets of New York City. Around her, a half a dozen people of diverse ethnicity and age warmed themselves. Nora eyed the two track rabbits that were slowly cooking on a spit over the fire. They were in fact two rats that were a little smaller than rabbits, and were considered a staple by those who dwelled in the subterranean world known as the Condos.

The Condos was a natural cavern, separated from the underground subway tracks by a large outcropping of rocks that dimmed the frequent roar of passing subway trains. Over one hundred homeless men and women lived here, in a loosely knit commune. Someone had diverted an electrical wire and rigged it to light lamps that illuminated the interiors of a smattering of cardboard huts, making them look like mis-shapen Japanese lanterns. Water came from several pipes that leaked overhead and was collected in cans and buckets.

Nora kept her eye on Jerry, as he was busy opening several cans that they had stolen from the grocery store. He had already traded several cans for some speed, and the drug had put him in good spirits again.

"You shoulda seen her." Jerry nodded toward Nora. "Like a real pro." He lifted his can opener and used it as a prop for

Nora's lock picks. "She just opened that lock like it was nothing." He snapped his finger.

"Tell them how you almost got shot," Nora reminded him.

"Ain't safe up there no more," Laverne, a middle-aged woman and a junkie, groaned.

"That's right . . . It's not safe anymore," added an old white man with a battered face.

"I don't know how you manage to do it," said a man who looked like he could have been a banker. "It's been over a year since I went out."

Some of the others nodded their agreement.

"Aw, it's nothing," Jerry said, as he pried the lid back. Grabbing it with a pair of fire-blackened pliers, he placed the can on the fire. "They don't scare me. Besides, most people don't want to mess with us mole people." This nickname came from the subway workers and police, and the tunnel dwellers used it as well.

The can settled down on the coals and the group watched as the flames licked its sides, burning off the label.

Five minutes later Nora said, "Don't overcook it, Jerry."

Jerry ignored her and, taking a fork, poked the track rabbit to see if it was done. "It's soup," Jerry called, announcing that the "rabbit" was finished.

The mole people produced cups and plates seemingly from nowhere.

Jerry pulled out the metal spit that had skewered the rats over the fire. He motioned to Nora and she held out her plate, which had a faded picture of Barney on it. Jerry dropped two very thin slices of the meat, along with several hot yams from the tin, onto it.

Nora took the food and then hurried away from the fire to Jerry's cardboard house.

"Nora? You okay?" Jerry called out.

The banker whispered as he held out his plate, "Her lights are going off again."

"She ain't takin' her pills, that's all," Jerry replied, scooping yams out onto the banker's plate.

"What you gonna do with her?" the old man with the battered face asked, as he spooned a mouthful of rabbit into an almost toothless mouth.

Jerry shrugged and took the first bite of his dinner. He was Nora's protector. As long as Nora took the pills she did okay. Where the pills came from remained a mystery that he still wasn't able to figure out. All he knew was that she always had a supply. He had read the label, hoping that they were drugs he could maybe use. The label had a long name that he couldn't pronounce, so he left the pills alone.

He had first noticed her picking the locked door of a bakery. He had watched with admiration as, moments later, the door opened, and Nora had entered, returning quickly with an armful of donuts. He had followed her, and when it was night and she had curled up on a bench in the park, it was he who had chased off a would-be rapist. He then took her underground and introduced her to the group at the Condos. At first she was a big hit because of her lock-picking skills. But soon the others noticed that Nora was "a real crazy."

Nora took to living in the tunnels, but she often sneaked away at night, leaving Jerry's cardboard house and going to deeper levels of the tunnels. Other times she would sit in the house and rock back and forth, staring into space, not eating or sleeping. Jerry would spoon-feed her chicken broth and nurse her as best he could. At first, these episodes would last a few days, but they were growing more frequent as time went on. Jerry had learned over the months that when Nora took her pills she was somewhat normal. But when several days elapsed without her taking them, her erratic behavior would return.

Jerry finished his meal and wiped his plate with an old towel.

"I better go an' check on her," he muttered, moving away from the fire toward his cardboard house. He saw that Nora hadn't lit the candle, and he took that as a bad sign. He rapped his knuckles on the flap of cardboard that served as a door and called out, "Nora? It's Jerry. You decent?"

He waited for a moment but there was no answer. So he went in.

"Nora, what are you doin'?" She had taken a razor blade and was sitting in the semidarkness pulling strands of her hair and cutting it close to her scalp.

"C'mon, girl, give me that thing." He grabbed the razor out of her hand. He found a pack of matches and, striking one, lit the candle.

"Why you do that, girl? Trying to make yourself a freak, or what?" He shook his head.

Nora didn't answer. She just stared out into space and played with a length of hair that she hadn't cut yet.

"Nora, what am I gonna do with you?" Jerry grabbed a blanket and put it around her shoulders. "Where are your pills, girl?"

She ignored him, so Jerry looked over at a little stack of bricks where Nora kept her stuff. He found the pills, popped the lid, and offered one of them to Nora. "Come on and take it, girl," he coaxed.

She finally took it out of his hand and put it in her mouth and swallowed.

"Let me see," Jerry said.

Nora opened her mouth and stuck out her tongue, showing him that she had swallowed the pill.

He watched her until the candle burned down almost an inch. Then he gently pushed her down into her bed of papers and pulled the blankets over her. He went to his bed and lay there wondering what he was going to do with this crazy woman, until the effects of the speed began to lessen and he went to sleep.

8

Art MacKenzie followed a line of people of diverse nationalities through the boarding tube to the terminal gate in the Rome International Airport. Although he was travel weary, he looked forward to seeing the man whom he considered his spiritual mentor and friend, Johanen.

MacKenzie searched the crowd. *What a zoo,* he thought, as he heard half a dozen languages being spoken within earshot. A turbaned Pakistani with a bushy beard and a cell phone glued to his ear hurried by. A Moslem mother, her *abaya* concealing her body except for an opening revealing her wary eyes, led her children through the throng of people. An American couple, perhaps on their honeymoon, were discussing the star of Bethlehem. "I saw it on CNN," the petite newlywed said. "It was freaky-looking."

Her husband shook his head. "Yeah, I know what you mean. I thought it looked like something out of the *X-Files,* appearing out of nowhere, and then vanishing."

"The news said it wasn't a comet, and besides, the . . ." The last part of her sentence was lost as the couple moved out of earshot.

Mac fought the urge to comment. After all, he had been there, in Yemen. He had seen the Bethlehem star and knew what it was . . . a false sign from the Enemy, sent to deceive the nations of earth into believing that extraterrestrials were somehow linked to the birth of Jesus. Even though Johanen and he had destroyed the bogus tomb of Jesus and interrupted the broadcast that was supposed to reveal to a select cadre of people the extraterrestrial presence, the sign had been picked up by the Arab news agency *Al Jazeera*. It then found its way to England, via satellite, and finally, to the American mainstream press, who had a field day with it. The pundits on CNN, Fox News, and the major networks all had commentary and theories on what it might have been. Mac realized that the deception had begun. His mind flashed back to Yemen, and he involuntarily shuddered.

Do I stay here and wait? Mac wondered, as he carried his small bag, made his way to a concrete column, and leaned against it.

He looked down the main corridor crowded with people, but what drew his attention was a group of Roman Catholic clergy. They were hurrying en masse toward him, and as they passed he heard them talking in grave tones. He overheard "His Holiness" several times and wondered what to make of it.

He felt a tap on his shoulder that startled him.

"Welcome to Rome, MacKenzie," the familiar voice of Johanen greeted him.

"Johanen," Mac gasped, and the realization of who he was standing in front of pressed in on him. *The beloved disciple, John the apostle, is here at Rome International Airport, and he greets me like an old school chum.*

Johanen reached out and, grabbing Mac's shoulder, said, "Good to see you, MacKenzie."

He then pointed to the cluster of clergy, who were distancing themselves from them. He leaned close and whispered, "The pope is on his deathbed. He's not expected to live through the night. The media doesn't know."

Mac whistled between his teeth.

"Something else, MacKenzie. Cardinal Fiorre, a very dear friend whom I have known for years, was found dead in his house a few days ago. At first it appeared to be a stroke, but his protégé, Father Thomas, and I believe he was murdered. The manuscript that Fiorre had labored on for years has been stolen. Father Thomas informed me that a copy was sent to me, but I never got it. I believe Stephan intercepted it and destroyed it, or allowed it to fall into the wrong hands. By the way, Stephan committed suicide . . . hung himself in his jail cell."

"Did you have a chance to talk to him before he . . . ?"

Johanen shook his head. "No, I did not." He looked troubled. "But getting back to Fiorre. Father Thomas informed me that there was a disk, along with photographs and papers, that he sent to someone in the States. New York City, to be precise. Apparently the recipient was at one time very close to Cardinal Fiorre."

"Do you think the disk is a copy of Fiorre's manuscript?"

"Yes, I do, and so does Father Thomas. You'll meet him shortly."

"How do the fallen angels figure in this . . . or don't they?"

Mac watched Johanen frown. "I am not certain, MacKenzie, but I have a feeling that somehow they were involved in Cardinal Fiorre's death. The project that the cardinal was working on involved the identity of the man whom Satan would possess—the Antichrist—and the group of men who would be essential in implementing his plans. He had names."

"Of those in the Cadre?" Mac asked.

"Yes, MacKenzie, and I think he had a good idea of their timetable. The information alone is what got him killed."

"If that's true, then this man in the States is in danger."

"I agree. That is why we are headed to New York when we finish our business here."

The two men walked the rest of the concourse, entered the main terminal, and found their way to the curb, where Johanen hailed a cab. He gave a running commentary of the various statues, fountains, architecture, and sights that flew by as the cab made its way toward Vatican City.

A short while later, Mac and Johanen climbed out of the cab. Johanen paid the fare.

"This way, MacKenzie." Johanen opened a decorative wrought iron gate that led to an enclosed rose garden. They made their way to the front door, where Johanen took the gargoyle knocker and struck it several times.

The door opened and Johanen made the introductions as Father Thomas led them into the house.

"Have you been able to learn more about this man in New York?" Johanen asked.

Father Thomas nodded. "Brian Fitzpatrick was ordained almost ten years. He is a man of great intellect. He speaks over a dozen languages and holds two doctorate degrees. He is a linguist and is able to read, verbatim, from many ancient manuscripts. He also has a photographic memory. Cardinal Fiorre and he had worked very closely until the day of his departure."

"And he just left, in the middle of the research?" Mac asked.

Father Thomas nodded, then the telephone rang and he excused himself to answer it.

"What would make a man leave his calling like that?" Mac asked Johanen.

"I am not certain, MacKenzie. I must admit it puzzles me."

Father Thomas hurried back into the room. Mac saw that all of the color had drained from his face.

"His Holiness has just died," the father blurted. His eyes filled with tears as he crossed himself, bowed his head, and began to pray.

9

━━━━━━━━━━

✳ ⬤ ✳

Nora dreamed she was alone in a big church and there were many candles. Then a strong wind blew the flames so that they started a fire that burned down the church. Then she found herself in a small room with padded walls and every time she touched them she received a shock of electricity.

She awakened with a start and sat upright, her mind a jumble of thoughts and ghostly images. The sounds of a snoring man next to her brought her back. *That's Jerry*, she told herself.

She wondered how she had gotten to bed the night before and couldn't remember anything after sitting around the fire eating the track rabbit. She rubbed her head, then noticed that a patch of her hair was shaved close to her scalp and wondered how it had happened. Creeping out of the cardboard house, she looked around. Most everyone was still sleeping except Laverne, who was hunched near the fire which she had kept going with the supply of papers and scraps of wood that Jerry and some of the others brought to her. Nora didn't like her because she seemed to be vying for Jerry's attention. She eyed the bottle of pills but decided not to take one.

She tiptoed out of the camp and made her way out of the Condos and into the subway tunnel. A train approached and she stayed close to the wall as it went by. Afterward, she walked down the length of track toward the mouth of the tunnel, being careful to avoid the third rail, which carried the high voltage electricity that powered the trains. Jerry had told her that he once saw a man electrocute himself on it. The man had been drunk, tripped, and landed with his exposed arm on the third rail. The bottle he had carried broke and the liquid wet his arm. There had been a shower of sparks, the smell of burning flesh, and then it was over. All of the mole people had run away. No one had even bothered to go for help.

Nora shuddered and kept walking, always aware of the third rail. She touched the shaved spot on her head again and thought about going back to get a hat to cover it, but decided against it.

Half an hour later she was at the entrance to the tunnel. It was morning, and the city was in the grip of rush hour as a procession of crammed commuter trains rushed by her like ghostly phantoms from another world. She waited for another train to go by, then walked out of the tunnel and scrambled up the embankment that she and Jerry had slid down the day before. She hopped over the fence and walked through the vacant lot. At the smell of bacon and eggs cooking, her stomach growled. She slipped up the alley and saw the stray dog that she had named Boy. The mangy-looking animal wagged its tail but kept its distance from her.

"Come on, Boy," she called, as she bent over trying to coax him to her. The dog, however, remained steadfast and wouldn't budge. "I've got stuff to do, Boy. See you when I come back, and I'll bring you somethin'," she said as she left the alley.

Nora hurried to the park where she followed a jogging trail. She kept her eyes low, avoiding the glances of joggers who moved to the other side of the path to stay clear of her as they ran by.

She reached the end of the trail and left the park, hurrying past two winos on a bench who were stirring from sleep. At 90th Street she put her hands in her pockets and walked quickly, staying close to the buildings. There was a clock tower at the intersection, and she glanced at the time.

Big hand on the seven, she thought, and she realized that she had better walk faster or she was going to miss her opportunity. She quickened her pace, rounded a corner, and walked for another half block. Across the street was an apartment building with a forest-green canopy outside the lobby. A security guard was stationed in front, while a doorman sat on a stool next to the door.

Nora waited for the traffic to clear and then walked across the street. She crept close to the building and stopped fifty feet away, then moved closer until she was behind the guard.

"Hello, Nora," the guard said in a cheerful voice, even though his back was turned from her.

"How did you know I was here?" Nora asked, as she scurried around to the front of the man.

The guard, who was a retired dockworker in his sixties, glanced at the convex mirrors that were placed overhead in the framework of the canopy, enabling him to see behind him. "It's magic, Nora," he said. "Want a piece of gum?"

Nora giggled and held out her hand.

The guard gave her a pack of Juicy Fruit, which she tore open quickly, putting two sticks in her mouth.

"You be careful upstairs, and use the service elevator," he said.

Nora nodded. "Bye, Mr. Jenkins," she called, as she hurried around the side of the building down the alley to the service entrance.

The door was locked like always, so she fished into her baggy pants and brought her lock picks out. She selected one and set it into the lock. Moments later she was inside the building. She needed another pick to access the elevator. She activated it, the doors opened, and she entered, pressing the button for the fourteenth floor. The elevator stopped at the tenth and a painter entered, pushing a cart filled with paint cans, brushes, and other equipment. Nora moved to the rear of the elevator. The doors closed and it started its ascent. On the eleventh floor it stopped, the doors opened, and he rolled his cart out.

When the doors opened on the fourteenth floor Nora bolted down the plush carpeted hall. She stopped at apartment 1403 and looked up and down the hall, noticing the video surveillance cameras on opposite ends of the hall. Using her lock picks she opened the door and entered the apartment. She closed the door, stood with her back against it, and listened to the ticking of an antique grandfather clock a few feet away. Her eyes wandered over the rich Oriental carpet that graced the polished hardwood floors. Antique chairs, an ottoman made of an elephant's foot, and several statues graced the room, giving it an eclectic richness. Nora sniffed the air, smelling the warm mustiness of old books.

She moved away from the door and ran her hand along the bookcase that lined one entire wall of the room. Then she made a beeline for the kitchen. Opening the refrigerator door, she stuck her head in and began to sample the variety of cold cuts and cheeses that were stuffed into the drawers.

She tossed onto the floor several packs of hot dogs, some cheese, and two loaves of bread (one of which she earmarked for Boy). Then she turned her attention to the pantry, where she grabbed numerous cans of soup, vegetables, and beans. Leaving the kitchen, she walked back down the hall and opened a linen closet, where she grabbed a pillowcase.

Reentering the kitchen, she gathered the food from the floor into the pillowcase, and was about to leave when she noticed a bowl of fruit on the table. She went over to it and took several apples. She sat down, placed them on the table in front of her, and then arranged them in a pattern, that of a cross. She got up, looked at her handiwork, then throwing the plunder over her shoulder, retraced her steps. As she was about to leave the apartment she heard a noise on the other side of the door. The mail slot opened, and a flood of letters, magazines, and bills fell to the floor.

Nora waited a moment. She put her ear to the door and heard the mailman walking away. She then turned her attention to the mail on the floor. She sat down, crossed her legs underneath her, gathered the mail, and set it on her lap.

She started with a magazine, *Biblical Archeology Review*, and, not finding anything of much interest, tossed it aside. She opened the telephone bill. Seeing nothing but numbers on the paper, she crumpled it into a ball and threw it over her head behind her. One letter in a manila envelope caught her eye because of the row of colorful stamps.

She brought it close to her and looked at the stamps, slowly sounding out the word, "It . . . a . . . ly." She scratched at the corner of one of the stamps, hoping to peel it off so she could show Jerry back at the Condos. The stamp wouldn't budge. As she turned the envelope, she felt something hard inside and began to wonder what it was.

She pressed her dirty fingers against it and traced the outline of it. She looked around to make sure no one was watching and then she tore the envelope open and, bringing it close to her face, peered into it. She was disappointed. She reached in, took out the black square thing of plastic, and stared at it. Then she looked again at the pretty stamps and wondered to herself why there was nothing fun inside. She turned the envelope upside down, and a folded letter fell to the floor, which she ignored. She then put the plastic thing back into the envelope and, folding it in half, stuffed it into the pocket that she kept her lock picks in. Then she got to her feet, picked up the bag with the food, and opened the door.

Nobody, and that's good, she thought, as she peered down both ways of the corridor. She crept out, closed the door behind her, and ran to the service elevator. When it arrived she hurried into it and pressed the "L" button over and over again until the doors finally closed. The elevator lurched as it began its descent, and a few moments later it opened. Nora got out, and at the entrance to the service alley she waited until Mr. Jenkins, the security guard, had his back turned. Then she darted from the alley, unaware that Jenkins saw her in the video monitor, and was chuckling to himself at that very moment.

10

The Major hunched over his desk in his private office, deep underground in Tel Aviv. He rubbed at the corners of his mouth with his fingers and spoke into the phone that was cradled between his head and shoulder. "Are you sure our rockets killed everyone in the car?"

"Yes, sir, I am. We have confirmed it."

"Do the Iranians know what has happened?"

"They have news indirectly. But he shouldn't have been in the car in the first place."

"Yes . . . yes . . . that is true, but it doesn't change the fact that he *was* in the car and that he is now dead."

Another phone rang.

"Hold on for a moment; it's the red line." The Major put down the receiver and picked up the red phone.

"Major, this is the prime minister. I have very disturbing news. Have you heard? INF forces have killed an Iranian cleric."

"I know, I am on the phone with our intel," the Major replied.

"Yes, but do you know who this cleric is?" the prime minister asked. "He was the number-two man in line next to their prime minister. He just recently came into prominence."

"What was he doing here illegally?"

"We don't know."

"The strike was supposed to be on Hamas leadership in retaliation for the suicide bombing outside Mossad head-quarters a few days ago. You know about our policy to elimi-nate their leadership. The cleric was in the wrong place at the wrong time. What are the Iranians saying?" the Major asked.

"Their ambassador is livid, and there is talk of unre-strained retaliation. I want you to drop everything until we're out of the danger zone."

"Yes, sir," the Major replied, and the red phone line went dead. The Major picked up the other phone. "The prime min-ister said that the Iranians know about what happened."

"This might be the excuse they have been looking for to strike us."

The Major thought a moment then said, "Double the patrols on the borders and put the reserves on standby." He hung up the phone then opened the top drawer of his desk. He pulled out a bottle of No-Doze and popped several of the pills into his mouth. *It is going to be a long night . . . a very long night.*

11

Fitzpatrick sat at the conference table with the copy of the scroll he had received from the Hag in front of him.

"Well?" Mary pressed, as she leaned closer to the table to get a better look at the scroll.

Fitzpatrick wanted to ignore her, but glanced in her direction and gave the briefest of smiles. "I've never seen anything like it. Here's the strange part. The symbols don't link with any of the ancient Semitic languages, like Sumerian or Chaldean. It's like they're from an entirely new rootstock, a new language."

"Can you decipher it?" Joyce asked.

Fitzpatrick shrugged. "With enough computer time anything's possible." He turned to Vinnie. "How fast can you load this in?"

Vinnie toyed with the stubble on his pockmarked face, took a bite of a donut, and mumbled, "Maybe an hour or two."

"Good," Fitzpatrick said. "Let's get going on it, then."

"Where did the Hag get this?" Mary asked.

Fitzpatrick shrugged. "I don't know, but he thinks that it's important enough to get me down here after a three-day stint."

"No mercy," Mary kidded.

"None," Fitzpatrick agreed.

Zach, the group's statistician, tapped his ever-present mechanical pencil against a worn clipboard. "I've finished the calcs you asked for, Fitz."

"Anything of interest?"

"What calcs?" Mary inquired.

"The probability that prophecies from different cultures, written in different centuries from diverse religious and ethnic cultures, would somehow dovetail together into what appears to be an 'end-of-the-world-as-we-know-it' scenario."

Mary nodded slowly. "Can you repeat that?"

Fitzpatrick chuckled. "That's quite a mouthful, Zach. So what do you have?"

"The Native American Hopi Indians believe that it happens during what they call the Ninth Sign. Apparently the other eight have already happened, so we're in the time frame for it to happen now. Anyway, the Ninth Sign talks of a dwelling place in the heavens that falls with a great crash. I'm thinking the Space Station here." He paused a moment, thumbing through the notes on his clipboard, then began again. "The Mayans give 2012 as the date, and pinpoint it to coincide with the winter solstice. In the year 1514 Pope Leo IX said it would be another five hundred years, so that makes it 2015—close to the Mayans' date."

"That's only a decade away, and I'm not even married yet," Mary remarked, glancing at Fitzpatrick.

Zach ignored her. "Father Malachy, a priest living in the twelfth century, predicted all of the popes in succession until the end of the world."

"Yes, after this current pope, I believe we have one left to go," Fitzpatrick replied.

Zach tapped his clipboard. "Exactly. And that puts Malachy's prediction very close to the others I just mentioned. The point is, we have no collusion between these people, and yet their predictions converge very close in the time line. They all predict that something is going to happen, and don't set your watch by it, but it looks like it may happen soon. By the way, we may be looking at the last in the line of Father Malachy's popes. Vinnie picked up something earlier about the pope having a stroke."

Fitzpatrick raised his eyebrows. "Really, did he check into it further?"

Zach shook his head. "That's a big 'I don't know.' I was up to my cerebral cortex with this," and he tapped his clipboard.

"Back to what you were saying," Fitzpatrick began again. "What are the calcs of any of this happening anytime soon . . . as far as you can make them out?"

"It's off the charts. Try a number with about sixty zeroes after it. It could happen at any moment."

"That's sobering," Joyce said, under her breath.

"The end of the world is on our doorstep and I haven't started my Christmas shopping," Mary joked. The rest of the group remained silent, stunned by the sudden possible reality of what had only seemed like a vague, entertaining theory.

"Maybe these seers, prophets, could somehow see through time," Fitzpatrick suggested. "They all tapped into the same event, but because of their diverse backgrounds they viewed the same event in different ways, filtered by their own worldview."

Zach shrugged. "Who knows. Anyway . . . I'll give you the data after I load it all into the Beast and run the calcs on it. But it's my gut feeling that we'll soon move the clock to midnight."

The Beast was a supercomputer that had been especially constructed for the Tank. It was linked to all the major news services so that as the day's events unfolded, information would be sorted, analyzed, and then factored into the mix. The *mix* was the end result of all the data—specifically, how the events of the world would mix together to reach a climax, or, in other words, a likely end-of-the-world scenario. When Fitzpatrick had begun work at the Tank, the doomsday clock had been set at twenty minutes before midnight. With the ongoing tension in the Middle East, the instability of the former Soviet Union, civil unrest in many African nations, the

Iraqi war, North Korean nuclear capability, the ongoing Israeli/Palestinian conflict, and random acts of violence by terrorists, the doomsday clock had moved so it was just ten minutes before midnight.

"Yeah, it should be interesting to see how it affects the mix," Fitzpatrick replied.

"The Hag will be very interested in this," Mary added.

"Speaking of which, Mary told me that the Hag invited you to the gala," Zach said, as he walked backward away from Fitzpatrick. "The Hag" was the name that think-tank members used to refer to their boss. This negative nom-de-plume was bestowed on the man due to several factors, the least of which was his horrific-smelling breath and liver spots that blotched the man's face, which he tried to hide with thick makeup.

Fitzpatrick nodded. "A first, I assure you."

"I heard they get really wild," Zach remarked, and he turned and walked away, not waiting for an answer.

Fitzpatrick wondered about the Hag, the man who was hosting the gala. *Why would he invite me? What does he want?* he thought.

He walked toward his desk and slid the Japanese Shoji screen in place for a modicum of privacy. Taking a seat at his computer, he logged on using a very elaborate password. His computer, like the others in the Tank, worked on multilevels of security. One password allowed him access to the mainframe of the computer, but no farther. Another allowed him to navigate the Web, another allowed searches of government files. There were layers and layers of top-secret files, a world within a world.

Fitzpatrick typed in a command, and then authorization codes allowing him access to secret government files from 1940 to the present. He typed in the date 1945 and began to look at very old black-and-white photographs of some of the Nazi hierarchy. Next to the pictures he found entries like *Deceased 1978. Found guilty at the Nuremberg trials and sentenced to death. Believed to have escaped to South America. Last seen in Argentina circa 1965.* He was looking for his boss—Wolfgang Von Schverdt, the Hag.

Fitzpatrick had been somewhat reluctant at first to investigate his employer. But over the months he had a growing feeling that something wasn't right. He couldn't articulate what it was, but the feeling made him uneasy.

A decade earlier, he might have used religious terms to define that feeling, but he had abandoned his Christian worldview as being too dogmatic and narrow. He now embraced a potpourri of spirituality, believing all religions were, in fact, based on a synthesis of universal truth. His ability to study and read ancient documents had opened his eyes to what he had termed "The Universal Truth of Man." Gone was his former dogmatic thinking that a Savior, Jesus of Nazareth, was the only way to salvation. He had come to realize that through the ages humankind had been given information. His research had led him step-by-step to the unmistakable conclusion that there was a force that seemed to meddle in the affairs of men. This force had manifested itself in the likes of Buddha, Muhammed, and Krishna. Other manifestations were obscure, living in remote areas of the globe with only a small band of devotees. Yet, incredibly, they all seemed to say the very same thing: that God was within each of us. All humankind needed to do was to somehow make the link that we were all, in fact, divine. Even the words of Jesus echoed the very same thing, didn't they? That "the Kingdom of God was within you" and "you will do greater works than I"? Supporting documents had come to light in the twentieth century, such as the obscure manuscript *The Gospel of Thomas.* Once suppressed by the church, it was now being read by the common man, causing the dogma and doctrines of all religions to be questioned. He felt that he was charting a cosmic dialectic, where the conflict of religious diversity was about to be resolved in a synthesis—that synthesis being a new one-world religion.

He had put the pieces together and published an article through the university where he had been employed at the time. From that one article he had been contacted by the Hag himself, and landed the head position in the Tank. But after a year he wondered what ends his talents were serving, which had given him the impetus to start his own investigation on his enigmatic employer . . . the Hag.

Fitzpatrick had been able to place the Hag in Germany during World War II, but as of yet he had been unable to find any direct link with the Nazi party. He scrolled down through another list of Nazis. He examined their faces, reading the comments posted, and then, when he was certain that there was no resemblance, or that the person he was looking at didn't quite fit the bill, he would note the entry, delete it from his database, and move on to the next.

There had been several hits where the Hag might have been the man pictured. Fitzpatrick had the face aged, using the latest computer-imaging process, but so far his hunt had turned up nothing. However, several days ago he had stumbled onto something that had caught his attention. He had been looking at German scientists, who, after the war, became involved in the United States space program. He realized that although one set of records showed that the men had been involved in the death camps, a later one seemed to have any such indication of heinous acts removed from the files. He had cross-checked his information several times, and noticed that on the top of the page two words had been typed: *paper clip.* At first he had wondered what it could mean, but after a brief search he discovered that the files of Nazis that had been differentiated with the code word *paper clip* had been integrated into the American scientific community. So now Fitzpatrick narrowed his search to the paper-clip Nazis only, assuming that the Hag had been a Nazi, which Fitzpatrick was inclined to think he was.

The telephone rang and Fitzpatrick picked it up. "Fitzpatrick here," he replied, as he cradled the phone with his chin against his shoulder. His attention was still on the screen and he had scrolled down to the next name on the list.

"Hi, Fitz, it's Mary."

Fitzpatrick took his hands off the keyboard. "What's the scuttlebutt?"

"Are you going to go to the Hag's party or are you calling in sick at the last minute?" she asked. There was no mistaking the flirtatious overtones in her voice.

"Do I have a choice here?" Fitzpatrick asked as his eyes flashed back to the screen.

"I thought maybe we could go together," Mary suggested.

Having been a Dominican priest, he had missed the basic rudiments of dating, so he was taken aback by the woman's forwardness.

"Well, uh . . ."

Mary interrupted, "The Hag is sending a car for me. I could pick you up."

Vinnie popped his head over the Shoji screen. "Fitz . . . the pope's dead. It's official."

"Mary, the pope just died. Meet me at the conference table," and he hung up, glad to be off the hook.

"It's official," Vinnie started again as Fitzpatrick got out from behind his desk. "I mean, it's official to us, but the media hasn't gotten the intel yet."

"When is it supposed to break?"

Vinnie looked at his watch. "Less than half an hour."

Fitzpatrick thought a moment. "Give me a minute and I'll meet you all at the table."

"Got it," Vinnie chimed, and his head disappeared.

Fitzpatrick took one last look at the Nazis on the screen of his computer, earmarking the file so that later he could return to the same spot and renew his search. Following the links out of the database, he secured his terminal. A moment later his screen saver—an ancient Syriac manuscript—appeared, and Fitzpatrick left his desk.

12

Nora tried to throw the pillow sack over the chain-link fence that fenced in the vacant lot at the end of the alley, but it was too heavy for her and bounced off the fence back at her. She tried again but met with the same results. Then she remembered seeing a few discarded tires a little ways back down the path. She looked around, making sure no one else was near, and left the sack by the fence, then hurried down the path to where the tires were. Selecting one, she picked it up. It was filled with water and some of it splashed out and got her pants wet. She dropped it and picked up one end, allowing the rest of the water to drain.

She heard a dog bark and saw Boy at the end of the alleyway, wagging his tail.

"All right, Boy, I got somethin' for ya, all right," Nora said, and she went over to the sack and brought out the package of bread, opened it, and took out a slice. She held it out in front of her. "Come and get it, Boy," she coaxed. The dog lay down, wagged his tail, and moved a foot or two towards her. "Come on, Boy, you can do it," she said again. Boy barked at her and kept his tail wagging and moved another foot. Finally, Nora gave up and threw the bread at him. The dog fielded it in his mouth and was back down the alley and out of sight in an instant.

She went back to the tire and picked it up again, rolling it down the path to the fence where she propped it up against it, using it as a makeshift stepladder. She grabbed her sack and got up on the tire. It gave her the added height she needed to get the sack over the top of the chain link. She then scrambled over the top, snatched the sack up, and headed for the Condos.

At the entrance of the subway tunnel she stopped and listened as she let her eyes adjust to the dark. The sound of a train in the distance echoed eerily, and she could feel the slight trembling of the earth as it approached. Making her way over to the side of the tunnel, she kept walking. A minute later the train passed. She looked at the commuters, in the brightly lit cars that flashed by, like a ghostly intrusion.

Turning into a connecting tunnel she saw someone coming toward her. She held the heavy pillowcase tightly, ready to use it to fend off anyone who would try to take it. A few steps later, Nora realized that it was a woman, and relaxed. As she got closer, she recognized Lizzie, a heavyset older woman who didn't live in the Condos but had set up house nearby on a utility platform above the tracks.

"Hey, Lizzie, that you?" Nora called.

Lizzie shuffled a few steps. Nora heard the woman clear her throat. "Who wants to know?" a gravelly voice answered.

"It's me, Nora."

"Hey, sweetie, how you doin'," Lizzie called back.

"You goin' out?" Nora asked.

"Yeah, I need some things. Can't remember the last time I ate."

Nora set her pillowcase down and opened it. "Want some of this stuff?" She took out several of the canned foods. Lizzie's face lit up.

"You gonna let me have 'em?"

"I got plenty. You go 'head and take 'em." And she slid the cans over to her on the concrete walkway.

Lizzie set down a weather-worn shopping bag from Nordstroms, stuffed with useless miscellaneous items. Nora looked at Lizzie's swollen dirty feet tucked into bedroom slippers. The heels were bloodied, and several toes showed through the fabric.

"How you feelin', Lizzie?"

Lizzie slowly bent over and examined one of the cans.

"Oh, yams, I love 'em," she said, and her smile revealed missing teeth and blackened gums. Lizzie picked the other can up and looked at the label.

"Green beans . . . ." She looked at Nora with a dreamy expression. "When I was a little girl, Pappy would make a garden in the summer and plant corn an' tomatoes an' squash an' green beans, just like this. I'd go out in the evening an' pick a handful an' just stand there at the edge of the garden, staring at the sun as it was going down behind the trees at the end of the field. I'd look right into it as I shelled them beans and chewed 'em. My momma would see me starin' at the sun and she'd yell from the porch, 'Lizzie, you gonna go blind if you keep doin' that.'" Lizzie stopped a moment and began to laugh, which evolved into a wheezing cough. She clutched her hand to her chest, spat on the tracks, then continued, "I'd yell back, 'It's all right, Momma, sun's not so bright, I'm goin' to be fine.'"

Nora waited for the woman to go on with the story, but she saw moisture gather in the corner of her eyes.

"You gonna cook those beans and eat 'em as soon as you get home and that's gonna make you feel better, Lizzie," Nora offered. "I'll walk you back."

Lizzie sighed and picked up her bag, and the two women started to walk down the tunnel.

"You shouldn't stay down here, Nora," Lizzie said, after they had walked a ways. "This place isn't for you. You can make a go of it up there if you want to."

Nora looked at the woman but remained silent.

"I'm all used up and broken down, and I ain't got no place to go, but you, you're still young enough to make it all happen for you. Just have to stay away from the pimps and drugs, that's all. Either one of 'em will wreck your life, and I should know because that's why I'm here."

"You did that stuff . . . with the pimps and all?"

Lizzie nodded. "I came here right out of high school. I was tired of the little town in West Virginia I grew up in. Didn't know beans about the big city. Wasn't too long before I ran out of money and got down and out. The next thing I knew, some man offered me money for . . ." She paused a moment. "You know, the first time was hard and I cried after. But after a while I got used to it. Then came the drugs. But, Nora, you gotta know that it takes your soul right out of your body. That's what all of it does. It makes you empty and ashamed and you need more of the drugs to keep you goin'. And then one day you wake up and the men don't want you no more because you're old. Pretty soon the money's gone and so has ten years of your life. I bounced aroun' for a while. Did a waitress job. Parked cars, worked in a grocery store. But I didn't stay too long at any of 'em, and one thing led to another. A person has to sleep somewhere . . . so here I am. But, Nora, you don't have to be like me. Better get out now while you can. You know Big Jim?"

Nora nodded, thinking of a huge black man that lived in the tunnel below the Condos.

"He ain't been out for years now. Says he don't ever want to again. He's given up on goin' back to the world of the light. He wants the darkness and that's the end of it for him. That's what happens when you stay down here too long, Nora."

"But you go out, Lizzie," Nora reminded the older woman.

"Only when I has to. And it happens less and less." She had another coughing fit and spat on the tracks again. "You gotta promise me, Nora, that you're gonna get out of here."

Nora was silent.

"Promise ol' Lizzie."

Nora still didn't answer and the two walked a while in silence. The sound of Lizzie's shuffling feet, amplified by the tunnel, sounded like a snow shovel scraping on a driveway.

"Let's have a smokie," Lizzie said, and without waiting for an answer she stopped and leaned against the tunnel wall. The woman fished into her Nordstroms bag and took out a smaller, greasy brown bag. She opened it and pulled out a package of tobacco and some rolling papers. Holding one of the papers in one hand, she sprinkled the tobacco so that it filled the paper evenly. Then she rolled it between the thumb and index fingers of both hands and finally sealed it with a lick of her tongue. She handed it to Nora, who took it, and she repeated the process. Then she reached into the greasy bag again and brought out some wooden matches. She struck one on the wall of the tunnel, lit her cigarette, and then lit Nora's.

The women started walking again.

Nora took a puff but didn't inhale. She didn't like the taste but didn't want to seem ungrateful to Lizzie. She knew that mole people used cigarettes as a barter system, and this was Lizzie's way of making the score somewhat even for the cans of food that Nora had given her.

The end of Lizzie's cigarette glowed as the woman inhaled deeply. "These things are gonna kill me. I just know it," she said. "But maybe that ain't such a bad thing."

Before Nora could answer, they heard a loud moaning coming from ahead of them.

"What's that?" Nora asked.

"Sounds like somebody's hurt," Lizzie answered.

"Might be a trick or something," Nora suggested.

They heard the moaning again, and then afterward a whimper.

"Sounds like he's scared." Lizzie said.

"Think you know who it is?" Nora asked, knowing that Lizzie knew just about everybody in the tunnels.

"Can't make it out just yet. Let's get closer and see."

The women walked toward where they thought the sound was coming from.

"Who's up there?" Lizzie called out, when they reached the place where they thought they had heard the sound. It was a shelf notched into the wall and was used as a connection place for the hundreds of wires and pipes that ran through the tunnel system.

"Someone's under a blanket there," Lizzie said, as they reached the spot. "Hey, you all right?" she called.

They waited a moment and then from under the blanket they heard another whimper followed by a thin raspy voice. "Lizzie?"

"I think it's Rastaman," Lizzie said to Nora. "Rastaman? That you?" Lizzie called out.

The blanket began to move and a head with hair matted into dark dreadlocks appeared. "Ya, Lizzie, it's me, Rastaman." He sat up and pulled the blanket over himself.

"What happened to you?" Lizzie asked, as she delved into her bag and produced a candle, which she set on the ledge. Nora pulled out her lighter and lit it, then blinked her eyes a few times to get used to the light. She looked up at Rastaman. He was a tall, thin-as-a-rail black man from Jamaica who was addicted to heroin. In recent months he had become sick, and Nora and the others had speculated that he might have gotten AIDS from using infected needles.

Rastaman rocked back and forth on his haunches. "Sometin' got to me, mon, down there. Burn my face half off." He nodded his head in the direction below him, indicating that whatever had happened had been in one of the lower tunnels.

"His face," Nora said. "It's all red."

Lizzie picked up the candle and held it out in front of her. "Yeah, criminey, he's burnt or something," Lizzie agreed.

"Some kin' of monster did dis to me." He groaned again.

"You better come with us to the Condos," Lizzie suggested. "The Mayor needs to know about this. It might not be safe for any of us until we know who did this."

Nora agreed. "Yeah, Rastaman, the Mayor will know what to do. He'll protect you."

"I never get a long wit' da Mayor . . . he run me out, when he tink I got da AIDS, mon."

"You better come anyway. The Mayor needs to know," Lizzie said.

"There's sometin' comin' up from da deep places in da earth."

Nora shivered, as her mind conjured up some unearthly phantom lurking in the dark.

"Come down from there, Rastaman. You come with Nora and me," Lizzie ordered.

Nora watched Rastaman pull the blanket around his face as if by doing so maybe they would go away and leave him alone.

"Come on," Lizzie coaxed, "you can't stay out here by yourself. That burn's got to be cared for."

"You right, Lizzie, but da Mayor, no like me much. Still, I got ta do sometin' 'bout this," and he pointed to his face.

Rastaman moved to the edge and lowered himself to the concrete walkway. He was taller than Nora by at least a foot, and his dreadlocks hung down to his elbows.

Nora blew out the candle and handed it to Lizzie, who tucked it safely away in her bag. Then the two women got on either side of Rastaman, and the three of them slowly began the walk to the Condos.

"You gonna be all right, Rastaman," Lizzie mumbled as she shuffled along.

"Yeah," Nora seconded, "you're gonna be all right."

13

Elisha BenHassen sat in the Major's office at Mossad head-quarters in Jerusalem.

"What about the DNA testing?" he asked.

Elisha noticed the dark circles under the man's eyes.

"It was confirmed. He was the Iranian cleric. We've offered our sincerest apologies."

"Yes, but this has stirred up a hornets' nest of hatred throughout the Arab world."

The Major rubbed the stubble on his chin. "We've closed the borders. On top of that, there was a nasty skirmish on the Lebanese border. We lost almost a dozen men. It seems that the Hezbollah were probing our defenses."

"Do you think they're going to launch a full-scale invasion like in 1965?" Elisha asked.

The Major shrugged. The phone rang and the Major picked it up.

Elisha waited. The Major sucked in his breath, and the color drained from his face as he slowly put down the receiver.

"What is it?"

"The prime minister has had a massive heart attack. He isn't expected to recover."

"Does the press know?"

"Not yet . . . but they can't keep this hushed for very long."

Elisha frowned and looked at his old friend. "The Arabs will perceive this as the will of Allah for killing the cleric."

"Yes, and they may also interpret it as a sign to attack. We should go to the war room."

Elisha got up from his chair. "I'll call Uri, and I'll meet you there."

The Major nodded.

Elisha left the room and headed down the hallway. He suddenly felt very old.

14

It was half past four in the morning when Brian Fitzpatrick's private car dropped him off in front of his building.

"Hello, sir," the doorman greeted him as he opened the door to the building. "Your apartment had a visitor today."

A weary Fitzpatrick nodded and made his way up the elevator and down the hall to his apartment. He opened the door and switched on the light. The first thing he noticed was the mess of opened letters strewn about at his feet.

I'm too tired to deal with this now, he thought as he made his way to the bedroom. On the way he noticed another mess in the kitchen, where cans of food and a few wilted vegetables lay on the floor. And on the hallway floor by the linen closet, towels were piled in a disheveled heap. *At least the bedroom is untouched.* He pressed a series of numbers on the digital security lock pad on the door to his bedroom, which unlike other locks, couldn't be picked. He wanted one room in the apartment where his personal items, letters, research material, and rare books would remain sacrosanct. An inner sanctum, safe from prying eyes and eager hands. He went in, closed and locked the door, and undressed and crawled into bed.

At 9:30 he was awakened by the digital beeping alarm on his watch. He climbed out of bed and headed to the shower.

After putting the linens and towels that littered the floor back in their appropriate places, he showered, then dressed in a clean set of running sweats, although he wasn't planning on a run until later in the day.

In the kitchen, as he waited for his coffee to brew, he began to straighten up the mess. He noticed the arrangement of fruit on the table in the shape of a cross. He stared at it a moment, then gathered the fruit and put it back in the basket. He went to the living room, turned on the TV, and flicked through a few channels. *Every lens is on the death of the pope,* he thought, as he ping-ponged between the Fox News channel and CNN. He stared at the images flicking on the screen. Shots of Vatican City, then Saint Peter's Basilica, then to a group of cardinals, then to a multitude gathered in Saint Peter's Square. Already the process had begun to choose the successor.

Fitzpatrick's mind whirled. Was this the time of the black pope, the one that the prophecy has indicated, signaling the end of time? But what if the prophecy was wrong? What if this was another of the countless predictions that had failed in the past?

He reflected on several doomsday scenarios that had come up short. Bishop Gregory of Tours had predicted in 594 that the end would come between 799 and 806. He was wrong. In the fourteenth century, St. Vincent Ferrer set Italy, Spain, France, and England to trembling with his predictions of the Antichrist and the Last Judgment. He too had been wrong.

He paused a moment and rubbed his forehead. He knew too much, and what he knew he found impossible to reconcile, to hold together, and to put in a semblance of order. *Does something exist that is outside the space-time continuum . . . something people call and label God? Something that knows the end from the beginning and the beginning from the end? Or was it all the impersonal musings of a cosmic consciousness?*

Fitzpatrick picked himself up from the sofa and went to the mail slot, where he gathered up the opened letters and bills and carried them to the master bedroom. The room was spacious, almost a suite unto itself. Before he had moved in, he had hired a contractor to build two-sided bookcases which doubly served as walls and partitions for an area with a large picture window that looked down on Central Park. He had purchased the townhouse for the view. A forest of trees stretched below him. The leaves were now at the peak of fall colors: reds from maple trees, the yellow leaves of poplars and birches, the oaks turning brown, all mixed together, creating a living portrait that dazzled his eyes. His desk was in front of the window, and behind it the custom shelving housed a collection of books.

He eased himself into his chair and looked at the trees for a moment, then began to go through his mail. Something caught his eye—a folded letter that he couldn't match up with an envelope. He opened it, saw the seal of the Vatican, and began to read the letter.

My Dear Fitzpatrick,

If you are reading this it can only mean one thing: that I have died of natural causes or, still worse, succumbed to some evil deed of foul play. I pray to our Lord, in his mercy, it will be the former.

There is not a day that goes by that I don't think of you, and you must realize that I keep you in my prayers. The task that was given to us by His Holiness, as of this writing, has progressed in spite of your leaving. But I must admit to you, it was very hard going without you, and finding a replacement has been impossible. I have been drawn deeper into things that we first delved into—some of which make my soul shudder. What I have discovered is almost too fantastic, and I find that in terms of human understanding, it is almost too much for me.

I believe I have uncovered the identity of the man who is named in the holy Scriptures the Antichrist. It is, as I have already stated, almost too fantastic to believe—that we could be at the end of days and that the Antichrist could manifest himself and usher in the time of chaos. But what is equally unsettling is that I have discovered a network of men and women who have committed their lives to this man. Who have helped prepare the way for him and are willing, as incredible as it seems, to lay down their lives for him.

I would go into this now in great detail, but I have enclosed a disk, and it contains names and institutions that I believe to be linked together in an unholy fraternity. There are people in high places, wealthy industrialists, heads of state, and, sadly, church officials—several of whom have access to His Holiness. I have taken it upon myself to update the disk on a biweekly basis so that you will have the most recent information. It is all here, but I must warn you that what it contains is explosive. There are those who would kill to keep what I have discovered hidden. I am, as of this writing, in the process of preparing the final text for His Holiness. You must be on your guard, for there are forces at work to keep in darkness what I would bring into the light. The task falls to you to bring our work to its rightful fruition.

There is something else. A man who goes by the name of Johanen will most likely make contact with you. I have made arrangements to have another copy of the disk sent to him. He is someone whom I would trust with my life. Treat him as you would treat me. He will help you. Together you will finish what I have begun.

I would ask that you would consider again the vows you once made, and return to he who called you.

He remains faithful, and his love is unbridled toward you. Be on your guard.

Peace be to you.
Cardinal Fiorre

The news shocked him and he stared out the window, not seeing the tapestry of colors before him. *I buried him along with everything else that I left . . . another life, another man,* Fitzpatrick thought. He sorted through the other mail, searching for the diskette that supposedly had come with the letter, but he couldn't find it. Suspecting who took it, Fitzpatrick admitted that the chances of ever seeing it again were slim.

His watch rang, indicating that he should contact the Tank. Fitzpatrick got up and went over to his desk, picked up his telephone, and after attaching a voice scrambler, dialed the number.

Two rings later—"Fitz, it's Zach. You been following the pope stuff?"

"Briefly. They haven't chosen a successor yet. At least they haven't made it public."

"We have something happening in the Middle East I thought you might want to be aware of."

"Such as?"

"Syria, Russia, Iran, Lebanon, and Turkey seem to be positioning troops very close to the borders."

"Do the Israelis know?"

"Their intel informed us."

"Any specifics?"

"Tanks, missiles, several divisions. But what's gotten our attention is the Russians. They're moving some pretty big stuff south . . . nukes."

"They've picked a good time to be doing it. Every eye is on Rome, so they have the distraction." Fitzpatrick paused a moment. "I suppose the Russian troop movement is a reaction to the killing of the Iranian cleric."

"Yep. We've been monitoring the chatter between the two countries. The Iranians are calling for an all-out *jihad* in retaliation, and it appears much of the Islamic world is ready to jump on the bandwagon. As you know, the Russians have backed Tehran for years." Zach changed the subject. "You going tonight or calling in sick?"

"Mary's picking me up at seven, so I don't have much of a choice."

"Well, good luck. See you on Monday, or if something new develops, I'll call."

Zach hung up. Fitzpatrick cradled the phone, his mind going to the Hag again. *Perhaps I'll find out something tonight. A clue as to who he is and what he's doing with the information I provide for him.*

He spent the rest of the day reading, sorting through some papers, and then around four in the afternoon went on a long run, lasting more than two hours. He was so absorbed with thoughts of the death of Cardinal Fiorre, the letter, and the missing disk, that he lost track of the time. He was late in getting back to his apartment, and when the concierge at the front desk announced that Mary had arrived, Fitzpatrick was dripping wet from his shower. He dried quickly and slipped on a pair of pressed slacks, a turtleneck sweater, and a sport coat.

When he finally stepped out of his building, a limo was waiting. The rear door was open and he could see Mary, dangling her long, silk-encased legs invitingly out the door.

She looks stunning, he thought, amazed at her transformation. He made his way over to the car and got in.

"You look . . . beautiful," he said, as the doorman closed the door of the car.

She brought her red lips to his ear and whispered, "Thank you, Fitz, I'm glad you noticed." Then she slid forward in her seat and opened the bar. "Something to get you into the swing of things, help you forget the Tank?"

They both knew, of course, that forgetting the Tank was an impossibility. Once you were in, you were in 24/7, 365 days a year.

Fitzpatrick surveyed the generous assortment of wines and liqueurs. "How about the Chardonnay."

Mary removed one of the bottles, retrieved a corkscrew, and uncorked the bottle. She selected two glasses and poured the wine. Fitzpatrick sampled it and settled back in his seat.

"You've never been to one of the Hag's bashes, right?" Mary teased.

Fitzpatrick shrugged and took a larger sip of his wine. "I've been able to avoid them. That is, until now."

Mary laughed and Fitzpatrick caught a look in her eye that unsettled him. "I've been to several. You never know what to expect. He's very hedonistic, with a streak of decadence that rivals Caligula. And of course he pours money into these things like there's no tomorrow. Be prepared for a very eclectic guest list, everything from bikers to bankers, hookers to movie queens, and everything else in between. The last one I attended had Tibetan monks perform some incredible magic tricks. I had never seen anything like it. People were levitated right in front of my eyes."

Fitzpatrick chuckled. "It's an old standby among magicians."

"I know, I've come across it in my research with the CDC in India. Like the Indian rope trick or certain variations of it, but this was different. It really happened. They had groups of people several feet above the ground."

"Did it happen to you?"

"No, I was too far back in the crowd, but you should have seen the expression on the people's faces."

"Ecstatic, euphoric, sublime?" Fitzpatrick offered.

"Exactly," she agreed. "It was like they were having a religious experience."

Fitzpatrick changed the subject. "Zach called this morning with word about troop movements in the Middle East."

Mary gave a shrug. "I don't want to talk about any of that . . . not now. Zach's holding down the fort till Monday, so if nothing major happens, we get the rest of the weekend off." She moved closer to him.

Fitzpatrick drained the glass of wine.

"Another?" Mary asked, an inviting smile on her face.

"Half," Fitzpatrick stated. But Mary filled it to the top in spite of his request.

"I don't want to be sloshed before I get there."

Mary took the last sip from her glass and laughed as she refilled her glass. "Have you actually *ever* been sloshed?"

"I plead the fifth," he shot back.

Mary laughed again, this time spilling a little of the wine on her dress.

They drove another hour as the limo brought them far out into the thick wooded countryside, that, unbelievable as it seemed, was not that far from New York City. They drove by sprawling suburbs, clustered villages, open stretches of farmland, and finally stopped at an old gatehouse once used in another century to stable horse and buggies. Gas lanterns burned on either side of the handcrafted wrought iron gates. The gates were tipped with solid brass spikes, and decorating the center were two eagles, reminiscent of World War II Nazi regalia.

Fitzpatrick looked out his window and saw a limo being stopped. Several uniformed guards examined the occupants of the car and scanned the bottom of it with what looked like some kind of metal detector. One of the guards signaled to another in the gatehouse and the gates began to swing inward, allowing the limousine to pass.

"Tight security, why?" Fitzpatrick asked.

Mary shrugged. "No party crashers allowed, I guess."

Their car pulled up and security ran a check on them, examining their invitations and scanning underneath the limo. After a moment they too were allowed to pass.

Fitzpatrick stared at the eagles as they drove by. *Is this a coincidence? Is it a tie to his past, a blatant proclamation of his ties with the Nazis?*

The limo wound up a cobblestone driveway past meticulously manicured grounds. Fitzpatrick even saw a pair of peacocks strutting around just off the drive.

"There it is," Mary exclaimed, and Fitzpatrick heard the excited edge in her voice.

Fitzpatrick got his first look at the Hag's mansion and wasn't prepared for what he saw. He had expected a stately mansion built in the late nineteenth century and carefully maintained through generations. Instead what lay before him was one of the most daring architectural structures he had ever seen. At first glance, it looked like a series of immense icicles thrusting up from the ground. Several of them towered into the night sky, illuminated from below by hidden spotlights recessed into the ground. A moat surrounded the exterior of the house, and a drawbridge of stainless steel and titanium alloy extended over the water.

"Incredible, isn't it?" Mary asked.

"It's not what I expected at all."

"Everyone says the same thing," Mary said. "He had the original structure torn down. From what I hear, he added several stories underground, maybe as many as seven. But that's only rumor."

"Seven stories underground?"

"Some of it's for parking. You'll see in a moment," Mary said as the limo headed toward the moat. It began to descend and to Fitz's amazement entered a glasslike tunnel that led underneath the moat.

"Incredible," Fitzpatrick said as he stared at a school of koi swimming into the moat on the other side of the glass.

"It leads to the underground parking. And he has an underground hangar where he keeps his private jet. There's also supposed to be a floor that is housed with medical equipment as modern as any hospital. He keeps a small private staff of doctors and nurses at his disposal."

"For what reason?"

"This is rumor again, but supposedly he undergoes blood transfusions once a week. That, along with several drug cocktails are *supposedly*—and I stress that word—staving off the aging process. Or at least slowing it down."

"But surely with all your knowledge of medicine and your work with the CDC you don't believe it?"

Mary lost her carefree hilarity for a moment. "Good question, Fitz, and it's something I've tried to get more information on. With the Beast at our disposal, we might as well get some use out of it."

"I know, I have my own queries with the Beast," Fitzpatrick confided.

"I haven't found much," Mary continued, "but what I did find was of interest. He imports some very rare herbs from the Amazon, also from the Himalayas, Tibet, and Mongolia."

"So you think there might be some truth to it?"

"Don't know. How old do you think he is, anyway?"

"I've wondered about that. He has to be at least in his eighties."

"I agree," Mary replied.

"But there are times when I've seen him with the vitality of a sixty-year-old, and that might coincide with his ingestion of some herbal concoctions."

"You might be on to something," Mary agreed as the limo pulled into a large underground parking area where a final team of security guards opened their doors. Fitzpatrick nodded to the man holding the door on his side.

"This way, sir, ma'am," a uniformed butler said. Fitzpatrick offered his arm to Mary. She took it, and the couple followed the man to one of three elevators. Moments later the door opened and another butler greeted them with a slight bow as they entered.

Fitzpatrick glanced at the number of buttons. He nudged Mary and pointed.

Mary gave a knowing glance. There were four upper floors followed by seven lower ones.

The elevator arrived, and as the two sets of doors opened a lively salsa number invaded their space. The gala was in full swing.

Fitzpatrick stepped out onto an immense sea of travertine marble, encircled by matching columns that towered to the glass ceiling high overhead. A chandelier of mammoth proportions sparkled in the center of the room. Off to the left was the bandstand, where a twelve-piece band gyrated to the infectious salsa rhythms that they played. A large video screen was directly behind them, and images flashed in sync with the beat. Light trees, strobes, and several hidden smoke machines were in full swing.

"Incredible, huh?" Mary asked, leaning close to him.

Fitzpatrick nodded as they made their way across the marble tiles. A group of boisterous revelers in costumes and masks swirled around them, preventing them from going a step further.

"What's going on?" Fitzpatrick yelled to Mary.

She shrugged an I-don't-know kind of look and laughed.

Just then the crowd parted and a woman dressed as a queen approached. "I see these intruders have not donned their appropriate attire," the queen said in a high falsetto.

Fitzpatrick realized that the queen was in fact a *queen. It's a guy,* he thought.

"See that these two are dressed in the appropriate manner," the queen instructed.

Fitzpatrick and Mary were then pulled apart. Although Fitzpatrick began to protest, a mask with the face of former president Richard Nixon was fastened to his head. Moments later he was returned to the center, where Mary had been transformed with a huge pig's head.

"That's the spirit of the thing!" the queen trilled, and pointed her scepter to another couple farther down the ballroom floor, who, like Fitzpatrick and Mary before, were in need of the "appropriate attire."

The group was gone and Fitzpatrick and Mary stared at each other before they both broke into laughter.

"Crazy, isn't it?" Mary laughed, removing her pig's head.

Fitzpatrick slipped his mask off and they moved along the outer edge of the ballroom. A spread of tables, each attended by its own server, lay end to end along the pillared wall. Fitzpatrick had never seen so much food. There were Maine lobsters on ice, crabs from the Chesapeake Bay, Pacific salmon, and shrimp that overflowed from chilled buckets. Steaks as thick as a man's forearm, barbecued ribs dripping in hot sauce, fresh venison, buffalo, quail, and duck. Then there was the bizarre cuisine: chocolate-covered ants, fried grasshoppers, and beetle wings.

A waiter offered them an appetizer, and they each took one from a polished silver tray and nibbled.

"Now what?" Fitzpatrick asked.

"We party . . . want to dance?"

"To this?" Fitzpatrick motioned to the mass of gyrating, swirling bodies pulsating to the salsa beat on the ballroom floor.

"I can teach you," Mary said, and she began to move her shoulders and step toward him in time with the music. "I love to dance to salsa."

Fitzpatrick shook his head and smiled. A waiter came by with a tray of champagne and Fitzpatrick took two glasses and handed one to Mary, thankful to be spared a dancing lesson.

"Look," Mary said, pointing to a cluster of people. "Senator Gable."

Fitzpatrick nodded.

"And there's Tim Roland, the actor. What a hunk."

Fitzpatrick noticed an African couple in traditional Swahili dress. "I think they're the real thing," he noted.

THE REVEALING / 115

"I do too," Mary agreed. "Probably ambassadors or state officials."

Several other dignitaries were discussed, then a well-known novelist, followed by a ballerina. They caught a glimpse of the mayor of New York City, holding court.

"There he is," Mary said, growing serious.

"Who?" Fitzpatrick wasn't sure who she was pointing out.

"The Hag," Mary whispered.

Almost as if on cue the Hag noticed them. Fitzpatrick immediately stiffened and clutched his drink. A retinue of admirers surrounded the Hag. He waved and began to make his way toward Mary and Fitzpatrick. "What can he possibly want with us?" Fitzpatrick asked.

Mary laughed. "Your soul, maybe?"

"You're joking, but there are times when I think he wants just that."

"Looks like he's being delayed. Maybe we can ditch him?" Mary suggested.

Fitzpatrick stared at the crowd that surrounded the Hag. "Do you know what a remora fish is?" he asked.

"Aren't they the fish that live on a shark's body . . . like a parasite?"

"Precisely . . . and the Hag has plenty of them." Fitzpatrick gestured to the throng.

"Hello, Mary, Fitzpatrick," the Hag said, finally reaching them. Fitzpatrick noticed the rosy color of the man's cheeks, his carefully coifed hairpiece, the tailored suit, but above all, the dangerous look in his eye, in spite of the warm smile on his face.

Mary extended her hand and the Hag took it and kissed it. A flurry of remora gathered around them.

Fitzpatrick extended his hand and his host shook it.

"Enjoying our little get-together?" he asked.

Fitzpatrick nodded politely, trying to look enthused. He was caught off guard as an exceptionally tall, thin woman, with the palest skin he had ever seen, snuggled up to him. She wore a bird's mask across her eyes.

"This is Sene," the Hag introduced the woman. "She's new in town, Fitzpatrick. I think she likes you."

Immediately the remora chorused a cry of encouragement.

"Perhaps you could be her escort, providing, of course, that Mary would part with you for a while? Yes?"

Fitzpatrick looked at Mary, who shrugged good-naturedly.

Fitzpatrick saw the Hag nod toward a good-looking body-builder type, one of the remora. "And this is Bruno. Mary, I picked him for you."

Fitzpatrick watched as the muscularly built man came up to Mary. Conga drums exploded in a thunder of flurried rhythms. The horns went wild, accenting the beat, while the rest of the band added their instruments to the dynamic sound. The place went nuts. Bruno grabbed Mary's hand and twirled her. She sent Fitzgerald a rueful grin, then a moment later they were on the dance floor, and she was dancing for all she was worth.

"Well, Fitzpatrick, I trust you will show Sene a good time? *Ja?*"

The woman had all but coiled herself around Fitzpatrick. He felt her slender body next to his, pressing against it.

"Have fun, you two," the Hag called, as the tide of dancing people began to carry them away from Fitzpatrick. Or was Fitzpatrick moving away from the Hag? He wasn't at all sure.

Fitzpatrick found himself pressed in the middle of the dancers with this silent blond woman dancing almost hypnotically in front of him. He was jostled from behind, then from the side, feeling like a pinball in a machine. The lights went out for a second and were replaced by a barrage of intense strobe lights, turning the ballroom floor into a surreal sea of frenetic dervish-like bodies.

Fitzpatrick found himself moving an arm and a leg, with no real sense of dance as he tired of the beat. And there, in front of him, the wraithlike woman writhed, with no expression on her face or in her hidden eyes. Her movements appeared willowy, but, like his own, seemed out of step with the music. Fitzpatrick wiped his forehead, which was dripping with sweat. The drums pounded, strobe lights flashed, trumpets blared, bodies swirled, and a cacophony of laughter and womanly shrieks inundated Fitzpatrick's senses. How long did he dance? Five minutes? Ten? Fifteen? He lost track of time and his inhibitions began to slide away.

Finally the music began to slow down into a light samba. Couples collapsed into each other, while others made for the balcony. Fitzpatrick chose the latter, with the silent woman beside him.

"What kind of a name is Sene?" he asked the woman.

"It is a name from the Pleiades star cluster," she responded.

Fitzpatrick listened to her accent, different from anything he had ever heard.

"I can't quite place your accent. Where are you from?" he asked.

The woman looked at him for a moment. He noticed her eyes through the tiny slits in the mask—dark, like the night, and what else? The absence of emotion? Is that what bothered him?

She came closer, wrapped her arms around his neck, and then found his mouth with hers.

Fitzpatrick began to pull away but was amazed at the strength with which she held him. She released him, the barest hint of a smile on her painted lips.

"You ask too many questions." Then she grabbed him by the hand and headed for a deserted spot on the balcony.

A waiter came by with a tray of champagne. Sene grabbed two glasses, her thin white fingers holding the stems as she offered one to Fitzpatrick. He took it and sipped eagerly.

A few minutes ticked by. Fitzpatrick began to feel dizzy, disoriented. He found himself laughing, but too loudly. He had another sip of the champagne. Sene was leading him by the hand. *Where? Down a dimly lit hallway? Now a door . . .*

what's that? A gargoyle's head? Fitzpatrick looked around. The room swirled in a flurry of fuzzy colors, and always before him the thin silent Sene leading him on. He saw the door close. Heard it echo a few times. He heard himself chuckle at the sound, and it echoed too. He felt Sene's hands on him again, pulling him down to something soft . . . a bed?

He was dreaming, wasn't he? Then his vision slipped away slowly, in a myriad of soft hues, and Sene was taking off her mask. He saw her eyes for the first time: coal black and three times the size they should have been. He recoiled at what he saw and wanted to get away from her, but then started to laugh again. The last thing he felt was her lips on his own as he lost consciousness.

15

＊ O ＊

I've arranged everything," Father Thomas informed Johanen and Mac, as they hurried through the vast expanse of St. Peter's Square toward the basilica.

"And what did Cardinal Pescolini say regarding our theory about Cardinal Fiorre's murderers?" Johanen asked.

"He was taken aback by it, but when I expounded on the circumstantial evidence, combined with the information you provided, he began to see the light."

"So will he start an inquiry?" Mac asked.

"With the pope's death, everything will be on hold until a successor is chosen. Right now he has taken over many of the official duties, but he is anxious to see you again, Johanen."

"So you've met him before?" Mac asked.

"Years ago, MacKenzie. The cardinal and I have kept in touch, though. He is a great man of faith and servant of our Lord."

The trio hurried up the broad weathered steps that led to St. Peter's Basilica. Beside the elaborately hand-carved entrance doors stood two Vatican guards shouldering spears and standing statuelike, at attention.

Mac was the last to enter. The walls angled upward toward the dome high above his head. Pictures in golden frames lined some of the walls. Overhead an immense fresco stretching across the ceiling depicted various biblical scenes. Mac leaned toward Johanen and whispered, "Incredible."

"Yes, it is, MacKenzie," Johanen whispered. "It is the best that man can do, yet it is but a shadow of what the heavenly scene is like."

Mac thought about Johanen's answer and wondered if the man was talking from firsthand experience. *Has he actually seen what heaven looks like?* he wondered.

"This way," Father Thomas said, as he walked quickly toward one of the side aisles.

Mac eyed the frescoes, the gold tapestries, and the marble floors, as he followed behind Johanen. He saw a mixed group of clergy talking in hushed tones in a small alcove next to the main altar off to Mac's left. Studying the group of men, he tried to make sense of the style of dress that differentiated between monsignor, bishop, cardinal, or priest. Then something caught his eye, and he stopped in his tracks and stared at the group of men.

Not here . . . it can't be him. His heart skipped a beat.

Johanen and Father Thomas were ten paces away before Mac called to Johanen. Johanen gave him a questioning look and Mac motioned for him to come.

"What is it, MacKenzie?" Johanen asked, as he came up next to him followed by Father Thomas.

Mac had turned his back to the group of clergy by the altar. "Look at the group of men off to the left of the altar."

Mac saw Johanen's eyes widen in surprise.

"What's going on?" Father Thomas asked, as he joined them.

Mac deferred to Johanen.

"Excuse us a moment, Father Thomas," Johanen answered. "It's *him,* MacKenzie," Johanen said, and there was no mistaking the mixture of surprise and urgency in the man's voice.

"But *what* is he doing here?" Mac asked.

"I have an idea," Johanen responded.

"Will you two let me in on what is going on?" Thomas asked, somewhat bewildered.

"It would take much too long to explain, but there is a man with that group of clergy standing over there that MacKenzie and I know . . . is not human."

"Not human?" Thomas repeated.

"What do we do?" Mac asked.

"We confront it and drive it out of this sanctuary."

"But *why* is he here?" Mac asked.

"We will talk of that later, MacKenzie, but now I call upon the Ancient of Days to give us strength that passes human strength, and to protect us with his mighty Spirit, and to shield us with heavenly warriors. Stay behind me, both of you, and whatever happens, don't look into its eyes."

Thomas's face had turned ashen. The man was shaken, unprepared for what was taking place. Johanen put his hand on the priest's shoulder. "Stay here, Thomas. Stay and pray. That is what is best for you. Let us go to battle, MacKenzie."

Mac followed Johanen as they retraced their steps and then walked up the center aisle toward the group of clergy.

Mac gritted his teeth together. *Not again . . . not now . . . not here . . .* He forced himself to pray. *I will be strong in the Lord . . . He is my shield . . . my strength . . . my high tower . . . I am strong in him . . .* but part of him wondered.

Mac heard their footsteps echo as they bore down on the group. They were closing fast. Fifty feet . . . now twenty . . .

Several of the men looked up as they approached and then glanced away.

Mac's eyes bore into the man that stood taller than the rest. Johanen was ten feet away when he stopped and raised his hands above him. "You unclean thing. Leave this place!" Johanen cried out, and it sounded to Mac like a loud clap of thunder accompanied it.

Mac saw the group of men fall backward to the marble floor, as if an unseen hand pushed them. The man whom Mac had eyed, the one that stood a head taller than the rest, remained where he was standing except that he changed shape. At the sound of Johanen's command, the human-looking disguise that encased the creature faded away, revealing in its place its true identity.

Where a man had been standing moments ago, now a tall, wraithlike creature with spindly arms and legs and scaly, lizardlike skin appeared. A fallen angel, it had assumed its true reptilian form. But it had the ability to transform itself into any form it wished—a woman, a man, an angel of light . . . in short, it was a shapeshifter.

The men who had fallen to the floor were stunned and terrified.

"It's Satan himself," an elderly bishop, his robes in disarray, gasped.

"What is it?" another cried.

"Leave this place!" Johanen's voice boomed, and the thunderlike clap accompanied his voice once again.

The shapeshifting reptilian stuck out its elongated black tongue and hissed at Johanen and Mac, then, with an agility that startled Mac, it jumped over a row of pews and headed toward an open door at the end of a colonnade of pillars.

"Follow it, MacKenzie," Johanen called out, and the two men gave chase. The reptilian disappeared behind a pillar.

"Did you see it?" Johanen called out. "Where did he go?"

"Down there," Mac said, and the two men ran for all they were worth.

At the end of the colonnade, a group of nuns were praying together in one of the many small chapels adjacent to the main basilica. All of them looked up with startled expressions—all but one of the nuns at the back, in a pew by herself.

"He's there," Johanen said.

Mac looked at the nun with her head bowed. *A study in prayer,* he thought.

One of the nuns addressed them in Italian.

Johanen answered and pointed to the nun sitting by herself.

Mac saw the nun raise her head. She was young and beautiful, but the other nuns gasped when they saw her, for it was clear that they didn't know her.

"Leave this place! You are cursed!" Johanen boomed.

The nun transformed back into the reptilian.

One nun screamed. Another fainted. Still others began to climb over the pews in an effort to get away.

The reptilian clawed at the pew in front of him. Mac was transfixed. He looked into its eyes for a moment and felt a wave of nausea overcome him. Then its claws bit into the wood as the foul thing grabbed hold of the pew and ripped it from the floor, hurling it at Johanen and Mac.

"Look out!" Johanen yelled, as he grabbed Mac and pushed him out of the way. The pew landed on the marble floor where the two men had been standing a moment ago, cracking the tiles. Mac sat up just in time to see the reptilian bound down the hall, turn into another corridor, and vanish from sight.

"We must hurry!" Johanen pulled Mac to his feet. The two men ran down the hall in hot pursuit. They found themselves in a corridor at the end of which was a door that was torn from its hinges.

"There," Johanen said, as the two men went through the doorway. He pointed at the head of a set of stone steps that led down beneath the foundations of the basilica. The air was musty and Mac felt a cool breeze as the men descended the steps two at a time.

"This descends to the catacombs," Johanen yelled, as he bounded down the steps.

Mac concentrated on taking the steps two at a time. At the bottom of the staircase he took in his surroundings for the first time. There were four separate tunnels, each with a string of electric lights that broke off in different directions.

"He could have gone anywhere," Mac stated.

"But his footprints—or should I say clawprints—are very noticeable." Johanen pointed to the dirt floor. "It went through there." Johanen pointed to a large two-story crypt fifty feet away.

The two men moved toward the entrance of the crypt. "What is this place?" Mac asked.

"It is a necropolis," Johanen began, "a resting place for the dead Christians. You might have heard them called catacombs. These date back to the second century, MacKenzie." Johanen paused to catch his breath. "Some of these tunnels stretch for miles. The bones of the martyrs lie buried here—thousands of men, women, and children."

They reached the entrance to the crypt and went inside. "Look here, MacKenzie. There is an entrance to another tunnel." Johanen pointed to the rear of the crypt. "It must have gone through there." Johanen quickened his pace and Mac followed. They passed rows of graves cut into the walls of the tunnels. Many of the graves were open and Mac could plainly see the skeletal remains of people who had lived centuries ago.

"There, MacKenzie," Johanen said, as he pointed out the sign of a fish that was painted on a slab of marble.

"I remember someone telling me that Christians lived in these catacombs."

"Not true, MacKenzie. They were for burial only."

They came to a place where several tunnels branched out.

"Now where?" Mac asked, as this portion of the catacombs had a tile floor.

"All we need to do is find a trace of a footprint in the dust." Johanen knelt on the tile so that his face was almost touching the floor and peered down the expanse of tile in front of him. "I think there. Take a look, MacKenzie, and see for yourself. There."

Mac knelt and followed Johanen's example. "I see it—let's go."

The two men were off again, trotting single file, with Johanen leading.

"How far do these tunnels go?" Mac asked.

"Some of them extend twelve miles. This one, if I remember correctly, is only a few miles long, and I believe it dead-ends. I've spent some time in these tunnels through the centuries."

And what happens if we find the thing? Mac thought, and a shiver ran up his spine.

As if reading his mind, Johanen said, "Remember, MacKenzie, when we find the creature, the Lord will do the work. Our part will be to rebuke it and call upon him who is stronger than the foul thing, and send it back where it belongs."

"And where is that?"

"The *abouso*. The bottomless pit. Some believe that it is an area deep within the bowels of the earth."

"But how . . ."

"The Ancient of Days will do the work, MacKenzie," Johanen answered.

The electric lights, which were placed at twenty-foot intervals on the walls of the catacombs, flickered. Mac thought back to that place in the Nevada desert, that top-secret, underground military base. He had had an encounter that mirrored what Johanen had just talked about. He had called out to the Lord and had seen an angel appear and cast a fallen angel into a bottomless pit.

The lights flickered once and then came back on again, then went out altogether.

MacKenzie found himself in total blackness. "Johanen," he whispered, "I can't see a thing."

"Nor I."

Something moved down the tunnel.

"What was that?"

"Take my hand."

Mac groped in the blackness and found Johanen's hand.

"Now grab my shoulder and walk behind me," Johanen whispered.

Something scraped a tile and the sound echoed toward them.

"It's coming closer," Mac whispered, as he moved behind Johanen.

Mac heard Johanen search for something in his pockets. Then he heard a striking sound of a match. A burst of light enveloped them.

Johanen reached in and grabbed the leg bone from one of the open graves, then wrapped the end of it with a section of the grave cloth. He put the match to it and the cloth began to burn.

Mac heard the sound of someone running away from them.

"It is on the move again. Let us follow it, MacKenzie. Stay close, as this torch will not last long."

Mac followed, his hand against the older man's shoulder.

Their torch sputtered. Johanen stopped, found another open grave, and repeated the process of wrapping the grave cloth around the leg bone. He produced another match and they started out again. Soon they came to a large hall, over two stories tall, and adorned with faded frescoes.

"It's beautiful, in a macabre sort of way," Mac whispered.

Johanen held his finger to his lips, motioning Mac to be silent. Mac held his breath and waited. The only sound was the slight sputtering of the torch.

A few moments went by.

Then something slammed into Mac, and he felt himself flying through the air. Then something was upon him, clawing at him, tearing his skin.

"Johanen!" Mac yelled. The torch had been knocked out of Johanen's hand and lay on the floor of the tunnel.

Mac struggled to defend himself, but it was no use; the reptilian was so much stronger. He did his best to cover his face with his arms, but he found himself rolling across the floor entangled with the vile creature. He smelled its foul breath, saw the glint of his yellow eyes, felt the grip of its claws tearing at his back.

The torch sputtered, a moment of blackness, then a faint glow again. Johanen's voice suddenly rang out, shaking the place with its power. Mac could not understand the words, for it was in a language that he'd never heard before. The ground began to shake and the walls of the catacombs vibrated. Mac felt the tiles cracking beneath him, and the ground began to open. A fissure appeared and grew wider.

Mac felt the reptilian's hold weaken. Mac took advantage and punched with everything he had in him. He aimed at the creature's eye and succeeded in landing his fist squarely on target. The thing howled and bared its teeth at Mac. The ground continued to shake so that some of the bodies in the catacombs fell to the floor. One of them hit the reptilian, the distraction causing the thing to claw wildly at the air. And through it all Johanen's voice continued in the strange language.

The ground underneath Mac opened further. Mac gathered his strength and punched again, aiming at the same eye. The punch went wild as the torch went out and Mac found himself in total darkness.

The ground began to cave in. The reptilian lost balance and fell into the newly created hole. Twisting his body, Mac managed to catch the edge with his hand. He could hear the sound of water rushing by below him. Then he felt Johanen's hand grabbing hold of him, pulling him to safety.

"What happened to it?" Johanen asked as he pulled Mac up.

"It fell into the water below us," Mac said.

Lights appeared in the far distance of the tunnel from where they had come. Then Mac heard voices. "Looks like we have reinforcements."

"Are you hurt, MacKenzie?" Johanen asked, as he lit a match and held it in front of him.

Mac held his arm up and found it was bleeding from a large gash.

Johanen took his arm and examined it. Then, as he wrapped his hands around the wound, he spoke in the same strange-sounding language. Mac began to feel something like a penetrating heat, and for a moment wanted to pull his arm away. Then he reminded himself of *who* he was with and relaxed. He began to feel refreshed and strong, and for a moment felt like laughing.

"There, that should do it," Johanen said, as he released Mac's arm.

Mac felt his arm. "There's nothing . . . the wound is gone."

"Give thanks to the Ancient of Days, MacKenzie, for his power has healed you."

Voices called out in Italian, then another in English that Mac recognized as Father Thomas.

"MacKenzie . . . Johanen? Where are you?"

Johanen looked at MacKenzie and winked, then cupped his hands together and called back, "We are here, Father Thomas." Minutes later a group of Vatican security guards, with Father Thomas, found them.

"What happened here?" Father Thomas asked, as he and the security guards gathered around the gaping hole in the floor.

Mac saw the guards edge carefully toward the hole, their flashlights darting over the area. Their light caught the fast-moving current beneath them.

They're afraid, Mac thought. *And who wouldn't be?*

One of the guards spoke up in broken English, "What did-a-you see? A monster?"

Mac looked at Johanen and wondered how he would handle the query.

Johanen pointed to the hole. "The monster, as you call it, fell into the hole and was swept away by the current."

The guard who asked the question got down on his knees and shone his light around the inside of the hole. He got up and shook his head. "Nothing."

Father Thomas leaned close to Mac and whispered, "What was that thing?"

Mac shot a glance to Johanen and then the hole. "How about we wait until we get out of here before I give you an answer."

"We gonna have to close up-a this place until repairs can be made," the guard said.

"Yes, we wouldn't want someone to inadvertently stumble upon this," Father Thomas agreed.

The party of men retraced their steps, and at the door that the reptilian had ripped off its hinges, one of the men remained to stand guard. Mac took one last glance at the long stairway, glad to be out of the darkness and back into the world of light.

* ○ *

An hour later the three men entered the private chambers of Cardinal Pescolini. His Eminence was a portly man in his early seventies, with a prominent bald spot, like a tonsure, on the crown of his head.

Mac had taken an instant liking to Pescolini, wishing he had met the man under different circumstances.

"You look the same as you did years ago, Johanen!" a startled Pescolini remarked, as he grasped Johanen's hand in his own. "It's like you haven't aged a day since the last time we met."

How will he handle this? Mac thought. After all, the truth was that Johanen *hadn't* aged a day since the last time they had met.

Johanen chuckled good-naturedly. "I assure you, my friend, that time has taken its toll on me as well."

"The years have been kind to you," Pescolini remarked, still holding Johanen's hand and searching the man's face, as if there was a secret that might yield itself with careful scrutiny.

Pescolini motioned for the men to sit, and Mac found himself sandwiched between Thomas and Johanen.

Cardinal Pescolini leaned forward in his chair. "We've closed the basilica to the public, and our personnel continue to search the catacombs for"—he threw a glance at Father Thomas—"the intruder."

"I can assure you, my old friend," Johanen said, "the creature has made its escape, but it is not gone by any means. It will return."

"I have sent for the men who were meeting with it. But why do you think it was here? Why now?"

The men looked at Johanen.

We all have the same question, Mac thought, as he looked to Johanen for an answer.

"There is much at stake now, with the choosing of a successor to His Holiness paramount in everyone's mind. Our adversary, the Devil, is here to influence the choosing. Perhaps to even put his own man in the Holy See."

Cardinal Pescolini shuddered and crossed himself. "God forbid that ever happens."

"Yes, Cardinal, *God* forbid that. But we know that the Enemy has managed to do much damage. Think of the scandals in America regarding the molestation of young boys."

Cardinal Pescolini nodded somberly. "It will take years to regain the trust of some of those parishioners. Some of those families will never recover from the devastation."

"Only our God can heal a person from such a deep wound," Johanen said. "We must remember that even their actions do not diminish the truth of the gospels, and certainly do not negate the work of the many good priests. But the Enemy has crept into the church, invaded her from within, and not only Catholic but Protestant as well. He is present in our very ranks. His emissaries are everywhere, and who among us can tell but that they are ravenous wolves in sheep's clothing?"

"Yes, you're right, Johanen, but what of this . . . thing? This creature? What is it?"

Johanen looked at MacKenzie. "MacKenzie, why don't you start by telling the cardinal and Father Thomas about your encounter with it in Yemen."

Mac was caught off guard by Johanen's request but he gathered his thoughts and began. "The thing can shape-shift; in other words, change its appearance at will. I recognized its human form from what I saw in the Yemeni desert. When Johanen rebuked it, it reverted to its true shape—a reptilian-looking creature."

"You'll find that throughout history this being appears in this form. In South America he appeared as a plumed serpent, Kukulcan," Johanen added.

"As we chased it, it changed appearance again, this time becoming a nun," Mac added.

"But make no mistake. It is one of the Evil One's emissaries, a fallen angel," Johanen concluded.

"A fallen angel? Here, in this holy place?" Pescolini shuddered again.

"As I said earlier, I do not think any of it is an accident. Cardinal Fiorre's death, the fallen angel manifesting here. It is all connected," Johanen stated.

"Father Thomas told me of your theory regarding Fiorre's death," Pescolini said.

"Yes, I believe he was murdered and the original document taken from him. Are you aware of what Cardinal Fiorre was working on?" Johanen asked.

Pescolini adjusted his bifocals and ran his hand over his balding forehead. "No, Father Thomas has remained in strict confidentiality on the matter, much to his credit, I may add."

Johanen explained, "Cardinal Fiorre researched the possible identity of the Antichrist, and those, both within and outside the church, that might aid in his rise to power. He had assembled a good deal of information, apparently narrowed the field to a handful of players, and uncovered some of the leaders."

"Father Thomas said that he mailed you a copy?"

"If he did, it never arrived in my possession," Johanen said, "or it was intercepted and destroyed by Stephan, a man who recently betrayed me and then committed suicide."

"And no copy exists?"

Father Thomas cleared his throat. "I sent a package which *may* have contained a copy of the manuscript on a floppy disk to Cardinal Fiorre's former researcher and partner in America."

"Have you contacted this person?" Pescolini asked.

"I've tried, but so far no contact has been established," Thomas answered.

"If what you say is true, and I am inclined to believe that it is, then we must warn this man. The same people who might have murdered Cardinal Fiorre . . ."

"Might go to the same lengths again," Johanen finished Pescolini's thought.

Silence for a moment.

"Johanen," Pescolini began somberly, "Do you think this is the time of the end?"

Johanen nodded slowly. "Yes, old friend, I do, but it is also the time of the beginning. For the end of days will bring the glorious return of our Lord. There will be peace and the healing of the nations. All people will be free, and he will rule from Jerusalem. A Scripture comes to mind—one of my favorites. In fact, I recite it several times a day, because it gives me a feeling of hope. It is from Isaiah 46 verses 9 and 10. It says, 'Remember the former things, those of long ago; I am God, and there is no other; I am God, and there is none like me. I make known the end from the beginning, from ancient times, what is still to come. I say: My purpose will stand, and I will do all that I please.'

"All of this—what is happening on the earth—was foretold long ago. Our Lord said in the Gospel of John"—Johanen looked at Mac and winked at him—"'Now I tell you before it comes, that when it does come to pass, you may believe that I am he.'"

Johanen waited a moment then continued, "He knows the end from the beginning and the beginning from the end. Cardinal, you must remember that even though we may be entering, as you put it, 'the time of the end,' we are not to lose hope, for we know that our redemption draws close. And when he comes, we will rise in the air to meet him."

Cardinal Pescolini asked for Johanen's blessing. A startled Father Thomas waited a moment before following the older man's example.

16

Nora heard the familiar whistle as she, Lizzie, and Rastaman approached the hole in the subway wall that led to the Condos.

Nora put her fingers in her mouth and gave the appropriate response: three sharp whistles. A few moments later they were met by one of the sentrys, a white man named Harry, who approached with a baseball bat slung over his shoulder. Nora saw him sizing up the trio.

"Mayor don' want him 'round here," he said.

Nora stepped forward. "Rastaman's hurt—he needs help."

"The Mayor say nobody come in 'less somthin' gone wrong," Harry said, and he eyed the sack Nora was carrying.

"That's what Rastaman said happened to him," Nora pleaded. "Look at his face, Harry. Something burned it."

Harry moved closer and examined Rastaman's face.

"See," Nora said, "somethin' burned it."

"Some kine of monster, mon," Rastaman mumbled.

Lizzie piped up. "Listen, Harry, Rastaman had somethin' happen to him that ain't natural. So now nobody's safe here. You understand?"

Nora saw that Harry was trying to decide what to do. Finally the man dropped the bat from his shoulders. "Come on with me. The Mayor will want to see you all."

Nora gave Rastaman an encouraging nudge and they followed Harry through the crack in the subway tunnel's wall. It led to a naturally formed cavern that over one hundred mole people called home. Clusters of makeshift huts, spread throughout the cavern, were lit with lanterns and candles.

Nora found herself outside the Mayor's house, which was one of the few structures made almost entirely from scraps of wood.

"Wait here," Harry said, as he knocked on the door.

"Who is it?" Nora heard the Mayor call out.

"Me, Harry."

"Is it important?" the Mayor called.

"Yeah . . . Rastaman's here."

Nora heard a shuffle inside the house, then the door opened, and a fifty-something white man stood before the group eyeing Rastaman suspiciously.

"He saw a monster," Harry said, and pointed to Rastaman's face.

The Mayor took a step closer. "Let me get a lantern." He went back inside his house and came out holding an old Coleman lantern. He held it up to Rastaman's face. "You get burned with acid?" he asked.

"No, mon, I don't get burned wit' notin' . . . sometin' did dis to me . . . There was a hole in the da tunnel, never saw it before, and dis light come out. Next ting I remember I was layin' on the da ground and my face was burnin'."

The Mayor regarded him for a moment. "You better stay with us until we figure out what's down there," he finally said. "You too, Lizzie, tunnels ain't safe right now."

"Ol' Lizzie can take care of herself, but I'll take you up on the offer, Mayor."

"Where's he gonna stay?" Harry asked, looking at Rastaman.

"He can stay with Nora and Jerry. And you mind the rules while you're here." The Mayor eyed Rastaman. "No funny stuff, right?"

Rastaman nodded.

"I've got stuff to do," the Mayor said, and he disappeared inside his house.

"Let's go, Lizzie," Nora said, and she shook the sack with the canned goods.

Lizzie nodded and the three of them walked across the cavern floor to Nora's house. They had gotten halfway there when a commotion stopped them in their tracks.

"Somebody help us!"

Nora froze as she recognized Jerry's voice.

"Somebody help . . . please!" the call rang out again.

"That's Jerry. I got to go. You guard this for me," Nora said, handing the bag to Lizzie, and she ran toward where she thought Jerry was, leaving Lizzie and Rastaman to fend for themselves.

By the time she reached Jerry, a small crowd had gathered around him. It was clear that the man was in shock. He was trembling all over.

"What happened?" an old alcoholic named Ben asked.

"I seen something . . . wasn't natural." He shuddered again.

The crowd parted and the Mayor stood a few feet from where Jerry was holding his lantern.

"Get ahold of yourself, Jerry," he commanded, "Tell us what you saw. A sentence at a time."

Jerry wrung his hands together, then he spotted Nora and shook his head as if to tell her that whatever he saw had been really horrible.

He tried to speak several times, false starts. He took a deep breath. "I was down on the second level looking for track rabbits. I was gonna get one too. All of a sudden I see something near the tracks. I thought that maybe somebody had stepped on the third rail. So I got closer and then I see that it's a body, all right. So I get even closer to see what's happened. Man, I got to tell you I ain't never seen nothin' like this." He stopped and started to shake again.

"Take it easy," the Mayor said. "You're gonna be all right. You're here with us, right?"

Nora saw Jerry look around, wide-eyed.

"You gonna be okay, Jerry," she called from the edge of the crowd.

Jerry caught her eye and nodded.

"What happened next?" the Mayor asked.

"Well, like I said, I called out 'cause this man was sittin' near the third rail. I thought the guy might be high or maybe he thinkin' on killin' himself. So I went up to him and called out again and he turned and looked at me. And it . . ." He stopped again and bit his lower lip. "It wasn't human . . . It had these eyes that were open and they was starin' at me . . . but they was eyes that I never seen before . . . big, black eyes . . . almost like some insect. Then I noticed the hands . . ."

"What about the hands?" the Mayor asked.

"There was six fingers on each hand. That was all I could take and I just ran here, fast as I could. I nearly got hit by a train, I was so scared."

"So you think it's still there?"

"I didn't look back . . . but somethin' else. There was a tunnel where there shouldn't a been one. It was like somebody just made one overnight, 'cause I was down there the day before and it wasn't there then."

"When was the last time you hit up?" the Mayor asked.

"Last night . . . but this ain't got nothin' to do with any of that, Mayor . . . trust me."

Everybody looked at the Mayor to see what should be done. *If anyone could figure out what to do, it was the Mayor,* Nora thought. *After all, he was the one who discovered the Condos in the first place, and made it safe for the women.* The Mayor had set the rules for everybody to follow and placed a guard at the entrance to the Condos. He would see to it that all was right in the end.

"Harry?" the Mayor called. "Take Jerry and a couple of men and go see if there's anything to his story."

"Hey." Jerry crossed his arms defiantly. "I ain't goin' back down there and that's for sure. Harry and the others can go, but nothin' gonna make me."

Nora saw the Mayor considering what Jerry had said. He stepped toward the man and placed his hand on his shoulder. "You don't have to do it then . . . okay, Jerry?"

The group began to go back to their huts. Nora came alongside Jerry and grabbed his arm. "Come on, Jerry. I got supper for us." She met up with Lizzie and Rastaman and led them all to her hut, shouldering the sack with the food—and the envelope with the disk—that she had taken from the apartment.

17

✦ ◯ ✦

Fitzpatrick rolled over in his bed, his mind lingering a moment on the last part of a strange dream. Mary was in it and so was the Hag. It was then that he felt something that didn't feel quite right against his skin. *Silk sheets,* he thought, as he opened one eye and realized that, one, this was *not* his bed; he hadn't made it home from the gala. Two, someone had drugged him. He racked his brain trying to remember.

The tall, blond woman, Sene, he thought. *The one with the eyes . . . Did I see that? Was it real?* He sat up in bed and his head pounded, like someone was hammering on an anvil inside it. He realized that he was naked. He spotted his clothes folded neatly over a chair by a Louis XIV desk. *Priceless antique,* he thought, having trouble focusing his attention. *Get ahold of yourself, Fitzpatrick . . . My head feels like it's splitting in two. Did the Hag do this? Where's Mary? Did she stay the night here too?* His vision blurred and the room started spinning. *Oh, boy . . . hold on to yourself, Fitzpatrick.* He steadied himself with both hands on the bed. *Who was that woman, Sene? Did she do this to me? What happened?* His thoughts wandered a moment and then he took possession of them again, getting angry at himself for losing control.

He climbed out of the bed, steadied himself a moment, then went over to fetch his clothes. As he tried getting a leg into his pants he lost his balance and fell to the floor. He sat up and slipped his other leg into the pants. As he got up the room began to spin again. *Steady . . . steady,* he cautioned himself. He got his shirt on but had trouble focusing his eyes on the buttons, finally succeeding by feeling them into place.

He slipped his jacket on, rubbed his eyes, and made his way out to the hall. The opposite side was a wall of glass and—judging from the position of the sun's reflection—he realized it was close to noon. *I've slept this late? Whatever it was they gave me threw me for a loop. What is going on? Why drug me?* He walked toward the spiral staircase, making sure each foot was planted firmly on the step before taking another one.

Reaching the ground floor, Fitzpatrick stood a moment before starting across the large ballroom, where half a dozen servants were in the process of cleaning up from the night before. He stopped midway and looked around. The Hag was nowhere to be seen. He went over to one of the servants. "Have you seen Von Schverdt?" he asked a demure Oriental girl. The girl lowered her head and pointed to the end of the ballroom.

"There?" Fitzpatrick said, pointing to another staircase.

The girl nodded and returned to her work.

Fitzpatrick moved across the floor, his head still foggy. *A cup of coffee would be just the thing I need to cut through this,* he thought as he neared the staircase.

He listened again and thought he heard the familiar voice of the Hag coming from below. He went down the stairs, paused at the last step, and, listening again to get his bearings, turned to his left and started down a hallway in the direction of the voice. He continued until he came to two ornately carved doors that he thought must have been lifted from the entrance to a European cathedral. The doors were open, and he paused at the threshold.

The Hag sat in a very large leather easy chair, puffing a cigar, while a male nurse administered what appeared to be a blood transfusion. But what stopped him and made his blood run cold was a large Nazi flag that dominated the far wall. Fitzpatrick looked around. Nazi regalia was everywhere. A life-sized bronze bust of Hitler. A photo-journalistic display of the Fuehrer showing his rise to power and the glory of the Nuremberg rallies. A gun case, displaying the finest handguns and rifles that the *Wermarcht,* the German army, had used during the world's bloodiest conflict. Iron crosses, uniforms, armbands, swastikas, helmets, and the dreaded double SS death's head of the Nazi elite's soldiers filled the room.

"Ah, Fitzpatrick," the Hag greeted him, letting out a stream of smoke. "I'm changing my oil, *ja?*" He threw his head back and laughed. Without his makeup and toupee, he looked dreadful. His jowls sagged, and dark liver spots marked his face.

Fitzpatrick stared. It was one of the most bizarre scenes he had ever witnessed.

"Come in, come in," the Hag coaxed. "He's almost through. Another few drops and then I'll be good for another week or so."

Fitzpatrick took a tentative step into the room. He saw the nurse fill a syringe, and after expelling the air, inject the contents into the IV line that was hooked into the Hag's arm.

"You are asking what happened to me last night? And what did I do with Sene . . . such an attractive ah . . . girl." He laughed again.

Fitzpatrick stared at the man, fighting the impulse to pummel the old Hag while he sat in the chair.

"What's your game?" he asked in the most detached, casual manner he could muster. His instinct was to sound bold and confrontational. But, seeing that he was in a compromising position, he realized the Hag would expect that kind of reaction. So he had opted for the opposite.

"Very good, Fitzpatrick." The Hag paused, sizing him up. "There is a game, as you put it. And you are a player in it, *ja?*" The Hag pulled at his cigar.

The nurse finished the transfusion and withdrew the needle from the Hag's arm, then put a Band-Aid over the spot. He wheeled his tray past Fitzpatrick, who moved to the side, allowing him to pass.

"Close the doors, will you?" the Hag asked, and he got up from his chair and went over to a polished walnut desk that had, engraved in its front panel, an eagle perched on a swastika.

Fitzpatrick looked at the Hag for several seconds before turning to close the doors. Then he walked over and sat in one of the chairs that faced the desk.

"What do you want? Why did you set me up with that girl and have me drugged? And where's Mary? Did you do something to her, too?"

The Hag sat with his hands in front of him, creating a steeple with his index fingers. "Mary?" the Hag repeated and chuckled as he shook his head. "Mary is of no consequence."

"So she's not here?" Fitzpatrick asked, anger coloring his speech. "Didn't she have the pleasure of being drugged and violated, then?"

The Hag sat impassively, ignoring Fitzpatrick's question. "I'm going to show you things, some of which will shock you, *ja?* Some of it will fit the puzzle you have been trying to put together." He paused and an impish smile crossed his lips. "I know about you trying to find out who I am."

Fitzpatrick shifted in his chair but didn't deny the accusation.

"First I want to show you something about what happened last night." The Hag pulled out the top drawer of his desk and pulled out a joystick. He pointed it at the flag, and a screen descended in front of it. Another click, and the lights dimmed. A video began.

Fitzpatrick leaned forward. There was no mistaking what he saw. There he was, clinging to Sene, who was leading him into the room. He saw her close the door and bring him over to the bed. He could see that even then he was slipping in and out of consciousness. His head bobbed up and down. He saw Sene begin to take his clothes off. He watched as she pushed him back onto the bed. The woman took off her feathered mask that until now had hidden her eyes from him. He gasped. Her eyes were not human. They were almond-shaped, three times larger than that of a normal human, and had no eyebrows. The pupils were as black as a lump of coal.

Fitzpatrick watched with a mixture of shock and horror. "What is it?" he whispered. Then he saw the woman reach up with both hands and remove her hair. *A wig . . . it's a wig, she's not human.* He stared at the bald woman and began to realize that it was a life form, but not of this earth. What followed next shamed him. Then the video ended abruptly and the Hag restored the lights to the room. Fitzpatrick rushed to the door and found that somehow it had been locked. Falling to his knees he vomited on the Persian rug.

The Hag laughed. "Now, now, Fitzpatrick. Nothing to be alarmed about. You should be honored, for you've helped with their breeding program."

Fitzpatrick vomited again. He felt totally violated, shamed, and unclean. There arose in the pit of his stomach a feeling of such dread that he began to dry-heave. He cried.

"You are so emotional, my friend. Like a woman."

Something snapped in Fitzpatrick. He picked himself from the floor and blindly staggered toward the desk with one thought. "I'll kill you, you lousy . . ."

He stopped in his tracks, chest heaving, fists clenched, mouth acrid. The Hag had a gun pointed at his chest. He saw the red dot of a laser circle near his heart as the Hag moved the barrel of the gun.

"I think you had better sit down." The Hag motioned to the chair.

Fitzpatrick realized that he was shaking. His knees felt weak. Easing himself over to the chair, he collapsed in it. The Hag pushed a button on his desk and, moments later, the doors opened behind him. A muscular man entered in a tight

T-shirt with arms the size of Fitzpatrick's calves. *A bodyguard. Isn't that the same guy who danced with Mary?*

Fitzpatrick stared at the Hag and waited for what would happen next.

"I have much to show you, Fitzpatrick, and I can't be concerned with what you might do. Bruno will see that you behave. Let's begin, shall we? You are asking yourself why?"

Without waiting for a reply the Hag continued. "It is because I want to show you deeper things, the hidden mysteries, what have been kept in the secret places for millennia, but now, in our day, will be revealed."

Fitzpatrick glanced at Bruno then at the Hag, realizing that there was no choice but to listen.

"Look at the screen, Fitzpatrick," the Hag said, as he dimmed the lights very low, but not completely dark as before. Fitzpatrick stared at the screen, a feeling of dread coursing through his body like a poison. The screen flickered a few times, and then he saw a black-and-white movie. The quality was poor, grainy.

"This was taken in 1917," the Hag began, "in Fatima, Portugal. There is no sound, Fitzpatrick, so if you don't mind I will narrate for us. You see the crowd? Over seventy thousand people were gathered in Fatima. And do you know why? Because three children claimed to see an apparition of the Blessed Virgin Mary. They had been told that she would appear and perform a miracle. So on that day people gathered—peasants, workers, farmers, the intelligentsia of the day, newspaper reporters. It had been raining all morning, Fitzpatrick. But the 'pilgrims' remained vigilant. The miracle was supposed to happen at twelve noon. But the Virgin was late. Can you imagine, late?" And he burst out laughing again. "She finally showed up an hour later. One of the children pointed to where she was. Of course no one but the children saw anything. But watch here, Fitzpatrick. You see the film, how jerky it becomes? It is because the cameraman is pointing the camera in a new direction, toward the sky. Look. The

sky is parting, and what do you see now? The sun spinning?
Watch . . . see it fall to the earth. Now the people fall to their
knees. Everyone is terrified. The world is coming to an end.
The 'sun' is dancing and falling down to earth. Like your
Chicken Little story." He laughed again. "Stupid peasants.
What do you see, Fitzpatrick? It's not the sun, is it? It's a disk.
Look at it reflect the sun off its shiny exterior. See the way it
comes close to the crowd. Everyone who had been standing
in the rain experienced his or her clothes becoming dry. Some
even reported miracles. And here's something that you should
know. This is the only film remaining of that day. Every other
photograph was confiscated. Are you aware that a Catholic
priest devoted his entire life to discovering what really happened? He is dead now, and his work remains unpublished,
confiscated by the Vatican. They know what it was and they
don't know how to deal with it. But wait! This is just the beginning. I have another film to show you. And the quality of this
film exceeds even the most advanced film techniques of our
day, yet it is almost two thousand years old."

Fitzpatrick glanced at Bruno, saw his deadpan eyes, and
realized that the man had probably never taken his eyes off
him for a moment. Fitzpatrick turned back to the screen.

"Look at the Roman soldiers, Fitzpatrick. Fascinating, isn't
it. And see the one that they are fastening to that wooden
crossbeam?"

Fitzpatrick leaned forward, spellbound at what he saw.
The Hag was right. The hologram, if that's what it was, was
extraordinarily clear. Further, the shot seemed to be taken
from the air, above the event. Fitzpatrick stared, mesmerized.
The view changed and began to pull back from the scene.
Fitzpatrick saw a crowd of people and then three crosses
being erected on a hill. The scene changed with a shudder,
like a ripple on a pond of still water. A closeup focused on the
man on the middle cross. He is bloody, beaten almost beyond
recognition, his beard pulled out in tufts. Then the camera
moved away, showing the entire body. Ropes bind both hands

while nails, driven through the wrists, fasten the body to the wooden crossbeam. Fitzpatrick can scarcely breathe. Another ripple. The head hangs lifeless and rests on the man's chest. A Roman soldier thrusts his spear into the man, but there is no movement. Another ripple. He is placed in a tomb and the stone rolled in front by men, while mourning women look on. Another ripple. Night. A bright light descends from the night sky, and—to Fitzpatrick's astonishment—a UFO lands near the site. Aliens move the stone by telekinesis and enter the tomb. A burst of light appears from the entrance. Moments later Jesus emerges. It appears that he has had contact with these beings before as he embraces them.

The film suddenly stopped.

"Why show you this?" the Hag asked rhetorically. "I know you once had faith in God, but you had questions. They gnawed at your soul, kept you awake at night, and finally when you couldn't answer them, drove you from the very thing that you had given your life to. So I have provided you with the answers you sought, but could not find—that of extraterrestrial intervention. It was they all along who gave birth to the religions of the world. They resurrected the Christ, created the miracle of the sun at Fatima, and performed a host of other miracles that would astound you. What you just saw was a holographic film of the Crucifixion, taken by them."

Fitzpatrick was stunned. It was almost more than his mind could handle.

"I have chosen you. Sene has chosen you. They have chosen you. To help bring about the final changes which are about to take place on this planet. There is something else you should know. There are men who would oppose us. They stand in their ancient traditions, their dogma, and their ritual, and hold on to those things. They are afraid of losing power, position, and control. One of these men you once worked with. He had information that would be very damaging to us if it were revealed. We saw to it that he would not be able to publish it. I want you to watch something." The Hag clicked the joystick again.

Fitzpatrick settled back in the chair, brought both hands under his chin, and watched. The scene rippled like the previous one, and Fitzpatrick recognized Cardinal Fiorre. He saw that there were two creatures, similar to Sene, that were in the same room with him. He saw one of them stare into the eyes of the cardinal. A ripple. Then the cardinal grasped his chest and he slumped over onto the table. Convulsing for a moment, he then lay still. Fitzpatrick saw that the creatures gathered up a manuscript and then left the scene.

The lights came up again.

"Why show me that?" Fitzpatrick asked, the anger rising in his voice.

"It is to show you what will happen to you if you choose the wrong side," the Hag stated.

"You killed an innocent man because of his research. That's murder." Fitzpatrick began to rise out of his chair. He felt Bruno's hand clamp on his shoulder and push him back down.

The Hag stood. "I know that you once worked with the cardinal when this project was in its nascent form. I know, from people that are in our organization at the Vatican, that he sent you a copy of his work. We must have that copy. You must understand that we have toiled for centuries to arrive at this point. You were hired because of your knowledge, but you never understood what happened to the work that you did. It was to aid us in bringing about the changes that will shake the world to its foundations, bringing about a one-world system of government!"

Fitzpatrick noticed that the Hag had become impassioned, bordering on the fanatical. Spittle formed around the corners of his mouth as he paced behind his desk.

"We tried to do this before. I helped with the first attempt, in Germany. Hitler was our vessel, but he proved to be weak.

So we have waited, and now the time has come for another. The showdown is coming ... and we will win."

The Hag set both his hands on his desk. "Join us," he whispered.

Fitzpatrick felt the man's eyes bore into him. He held his gaze, then turned away and exhaled a long breath of air. *He kills Fiorre, threatens me, and then asks me to join him* ... Fitzpatrick was dazed by the man's audacity.

The Hag continued in soft, almost fatherly tones. "Not now ... I understand. So much has happened. But later, when you have rested and sorted through it. Then you will give me an answer, along with the information the cardinal sent you. Bruno, see that he gets home."

Fitzpatrick picked himself up from the chair. He glanced once at the Hag, then looked at Bruno and followed the man out of the room. Several minutes later he climbed into the back of the limousine and collapsed into the seat. He felt like his mind had been shattered into a thousand pieces.

The car pulled away into the bright sunlight and headed toward New York City.

18

Art MacKenzie found himself once again in an airplane. This time he was in the copilot's seat of Johanen's private jet. They were midway over the Atlantic Ocean, approaching New York.

"So, how is Maggie? Did she understand?" Johanen asked, as he checked his fuel gauge.

"Yeah, she's being a real trooper about all of this. I promised that after we finished our business in New York I'd take the next plane back to Los Angeles."

"And if God gives you other instructions?" Johanen probed.

MacKenzie thought for a moment. "You know what I'd do, Johanen. I'd obey."

"The pace is picking up, MacKenzie. Look at the Middle East, for one. Now His Holiness has died, which creates more instability. Are you aware that at this moment there are over forty wars being fought on the planet? Weather patterns are being disrupted, famines are global, disease is killing millions every year . . . the world is ripe for the Antichrist to reveal himself. I have said before that the time is near. Now I would amend that to *the time is now*."

"So this is it?"

"Yes, MacKenzie, it is."

"And you think that Cardinal Fiorre knew who it was, the Antichrist?"

Johanen frowned. "No, I don't think any one person knows. There must be an indwelling by Satan himself, and that has not happened as of yet."

"But you said that Fiorre had narrowed the field."

"Yes, his last communiqué with me indicated that he had it narrowed to a handful of candidates."

"I have a question," Mac probed. "It's not related to what we've been talking about, though."

"Ask away, MacKenzie, for as you know, we have a few hours before landing."

"When we were in the basilica, and you challenged the fallen angel, your voice thundered. I heard it. And then the clergy that were present fell to the ground. It was as if your voice had a force that pushed them over. What was that?"

"When Jesus, or as I prefer to call him, Yeshua, was in the garden and Judas and the Jewish leaders came to arrest him, they asked, 'Where is Yeshua?' When Yeshua answered, he said, 'I am he,' and all of those who had gathered to take him fell backward. He has given that same power to me, MacKenzie. It is something that his Spirit does through me. When I spoke, I released, by faith, his power. You saw the result in human terms, with the clergy falling backward. But I must tell you that in the realm of the Spirit other events took place that you did not see."

"Such as?" Mac pressed.

"There are certain things, MacKenzie, that are better left unsaid."

Mac knew not to push the subject, although because he was a journalist he wanted to. He restrained himself, turning the conversation in another direction.

Several hours went by and Johanen landed the jet at La Guardia airport. It was 1:30 in the afternoon. They went through customs quickly, as Johanen produced a diplomatic passport from Italy. They hailed a cab and asked to be taken to the New Yorker hotel in Manhattan.

Deciding to share a room, they unpacked, got settled in, then got something to eat at a hole-in-the-wall Greek restaurant near the hotel. They stopped back at their room to freshen up, then headed out again.

"How well do you know New York, MacKenzie?" Johanen queried, as they waited for a cab outside the lobby of the hotel.

"Not well at all," Mac answered. "I was on assignment here several times, when I worked for the *Times*, but I depended on aides that were assigned to get me around."

Mac could see that he wasn't paying any attention to his answer. "Johanen?" Mac asked, but the man remained still, his eyes unblinking, as if he were seeing something that only he was privy to. A minute went by and still Johanen remained transfixed.

Much to Mac's dismay, several passersby also noticed. A doorman came over with a concerned look. "Is he all right, sir?"

Mac nodded. "He's fine. Give us a minute . . . thanks for asking."

The doorman gave Mac a sideways look and walked away.

"Johanen," Mac called.

Johanen finally moved. "Really, MacKenzie, you should know by now that everything is as it should be."

"Do you realize that you were standing practically comatose for several minutes? The doorman even came up and asked if you were all right."

"I was given a vision from the Ancient of Days. Something has been added to our agenda."

Mac waited for an explanation, having no idea what he was talking about.

A cab pulled up and they climbed in.

"Where to?" the cabby asked, as he punched the gas and the tires chirped.

"Wall Street," Johanen answered.

"So what happened back there?" Mac asked.

"As I said, I had a vision, and the Lord showed me a slight detour from our prime objective. We are to meet a woman at my bank. She is in need of my help."

"That's it? You make it sound like what happened was as common as buying a loaf of bread."

"I assure you, MacKenzie, the things of the Lord are never commonplace. But it is sad that much of the church today has denied the gifts of the Spirit. I believe this is a fulfillment of the prophecy stating that in the latter days, *they*—meaning those who call themselves Christians—would have a form of religion, but deny its power. We were meant to have visions, to walk in the power of the Holy Spirit, and that goes for you too, MacKenzie. Are you aware of a Scripture that says, 'Old men will dream dreams, and young men will see visions'?"

"You make it sound like it's a perfectly natural occurrence."

"It should be, MacKenzie. That is why the Ancient of Days promised to send the Comforter, the Holy Spirit, to all of us, to teach us in all things."

There was silence for a moment as Mac digested what Johanen said. Then Mac switched topics. "What do we do when we get to the bank? What happens?"

Johanen turned in his seat. "You will watch and learn, MacKenzie. There is a new saying that I've heard as of late. Very American, I may add. It goes like this: 'The things of the Spirit are sometimes better caught, than taught.'" Johanen waited a moment then continued, "The woman in my vision is in desperate need of money. But she is also very ill, although she has done her best to hide this fact from her husband and family. The Enemy has come against her. In fact, MacKenzie, if you keep your eyes open, and the Lord allows, you might see some very interesting things take place."

"In the bank?" Mac asked.

Johanen shrugged. "Why not in a bank, if that is where the Lord chooses to do his work."

Ten minutes later they found themselves in a traffic jam in which the participants honked their horns and shouted nasty epithets to one another, venting their frustration at the snarl of cars that stretched for blocks.

"Welcome to the Big Apple," the cabby quipped.

Mac turned to Johanen. "Is this going to throw the timetable off with the woman?" he asked.

"Not at all, MacKenzie. Be anxious for nothing. We'll arrive when we're supposed to."

"What if we're—"

Johanen threw Mac a glance and Mac didn't finish his question.

The traffic began to move, and a short time later the cab pulled up at their destination. Johanen paid the fare and the men went into the Chase Manhattan bank.

Mac took a seat in a cluster of chairs arranged in a circle in a semiprivate alcove, while Johanen stood in line. *There's no one here that fits the description,* he thought. *Did we miss her? Maybe she hasn't come in yet. What if Johanen didn't get it right?*

Johanen was behind an elderly gentleman in a well-fitting suit. The line moved slowly, but after a few minutes Johanen's turn came, and he went to the window.

Mac stared at the doors to the bank, then at Johanen, then back to the doors. The woman of the vision hadn't shown herself yet. *What did Johanen say? 'Be anxious for nothing'? Like most things he tells me, it's easier said than done.* Fed up with waiting, Mac got up and walked over to the counter where Johanen was transacting his business.

The teller, a middle-aged woman wearing too much makeup, glanced at Mac and gave him a dirty look. "Can I help you with something?" she asked.

"I'm with him," Mac said, pointing to Johanen.

The woman looked at Johanen for confirmation.

"Yes, he is with me."

The woman threw Mac another scowl and began to count from a wad of one-hundred-dollar bills. She stopped counting when she reached ten thousand, two hundred. Then she took a fifty-cent piece from her tray. "Would you like this in an envelope?" she asked.

"Yes, thank you," Johanen replied.

The woman put the money in an envelope and handed it to Johanen, then began to count out the rest of the money. She counted out another ten thousand in hundreds, and passed it to Johanen.

"Here you go, MacKenzie," Johanen said, as he handed the cash to Mac, which brought another scowl from the teller.

The two turned to leave. "She's not here yet," Mac reminded Johanen, as he tucked the cash in one of the deep pockets of his cargo pants.

"Are you sure, MacKenzie?" Johanen asked, and Mac caught a twinkle in the man's eye as he motioned to the doors of the bank.

A well-dressed woman entered, her dark brown hair gathered in a ponytail behind her head. She stopped for a moment and searched her purse. Then she pulled out a checkbook, a savings account book, and an official-looking envelope.

"Is that her?" Mac asked.

"Yes, it is," Johanen said, and the two men walked over to where the woman was standing, stopping several feet from her.

The woman was startled and began to back away from them.

"Hello, I am Johanen, and I would like to give you ten thousand, two hundred dollars, and fifty cents."

The woman stared wide-eyed at Johanen, her mouth open in shock. Finally she managed, "What did you say?"

Johanen laughed good-naturedly. "I want to give you what you need to take your house out of foreclosure. What you have been praying about. The Lord has answered your prayers," and he handed the woman the envelope containing the money.

Mac saw the woman take it, saw her hands tremble. She looked at Johanen, speechless, tears gathering in the corners of her eyes. "I don't know what to—"

"You do not have to say anything at all," Johanen interrupted. "But I have a favor to ask."

The woman frowned and moved to hand the envelope back.

"No, nothing like that," Johanen said. "I want to pray for you, to heal you."

The woman's lip began to quiver. "How did you—"

"This way," Johanen said, as he took the woman's arm and led her to the seat where Mac had been sitting. Then he laid his hands on the woman's head and began to pray in a strange language. The woman whimpered and then groaned as Johanen's prayer intensified.

The teller who had waited on Johanen was eyeing everything they did. She locked her drawer and went to what Mac assumed was probably an assistant manager. He saw her point to where Mac, Johanen, and the woman were.

Mac did the only thing he could think of—he smiled and waved at them.

Be anxious for nothing? Mac thought, as the two approached.

Mac glanced at Johanen, who was now holding the woman's hand in his, so that her hand rested on her stomach while his was over hers. More of the strange language from Johanen, then he took his hand slowly away from the woman. She sighed and opened her eyes.

The two bank employees closed in on them. The teller asked, "Are you all right, ma'am? Are these men bothering you in any way?"

The woman was startled. "What?" She began to laugh. "No, not at all. Why, this man probably just saved my life."

The bank people scowled.

"I can assure you both, everything is fine," Johanen remarked.

The women threw one last dark look at Mac and turned away.

Johanen got up from his seat. "May the Lord bless you."

"What? You're leaving now?" the woman stammered.

"Yes, but give thanks to him who has healed you, and tell your husband." And with that Johanen turned to leave.

Mac followed, looking back over his shoulder as they left the bank together. "Why did you leave so suddenly?"

"Our work was done. The Lord accomplished his purpose. I have learned that the longer one stays, the more one gives the flesh a chance to rise up and take the credit."

"But a few minutes couldn't have hurt?" Mac suggested.

"Let me put it this way, MacKenzie. Picture a stage, if you will. In the center is the lead actor. The audience recognizes him as such. Can you imagine what it would be like if an actor with a minor part suddenly appeared from the wings and stood in front of the lead actor? How ridiculous would that be? How distracting?"

"I get the point."

"Yes, Jesus is always to be center stage. I can assure you that at this moment the woman whom the Lord healed is giving thanks, and her focus is on the right person."

"So what do we do now? Try to make contact with Fitz-patrick?"

"Yes, we can try to reach him on the cell phone." Johanen took a piece of paper from his shirt pocket and dialed the number to Fitzpatrick's apartment. "Answering machine," he informed Mac. Johanen left his name and number and asked Fitzpatrick to contact him as soon as possible.

They went to the curb and looked for a cab to hail.

19

Nora sat near a small campfire outside Jerry's cardboard hut. With her were Lizzie and a subdued Rastaman. Jerry had crawled into his hut and didn't want to be disturbed. Nora couldn't remember when she had seen him so freaked-out before. She began to wonder what the search party the Mayor had sent out was going to discover. *That's what the Mayor's for. He's smarter than everybody else down here, and if anyone can get to the bottom of this, he will.* The thought gave her comfort. She reached into the pillowcase, took out several cans, and set them next to the growing line in front of her.

Lizzie shook her head and chuckled. "Nora, you really are somethin'. Good thing you bring us all o' this."

Nora brought out a handful of fresh broccoli stalks.

"We'll have to eat those first, else they'll spoil," Lizzie said, as she wet a freshly rolled cigarette in her mouth.

Nora finished taking the contents out of the pillowcase, but left the envelope with the disk still inside, and then sat on it.

"What are we gonna cook up?" Lizzie asked, and without waiting for a reply she continued, "Like I said, I'm thinkin' we should cook the broccoli, an' put 'em together with these yams here." And she took the can of yams from the lineup.

"You go 'head an' open it," Nora said. "I'll go an' get us some water."

She got up, took the pillowcase, and entering the hut, set it on the blankets where she slept.

"What you got there, Nora?" Jerry asked.

"Pretty stamps and some plastic thingy," she replied as she showed him the envelope.

Jerry turned up the Coleman lantern a little and looked at the stamps. "This came from Italy," he said, as he opened the envelope to see what the plastic thing was. He found the disk, looked at it, and read the writing that was on it. "The Vatican! Where'd you get this, girl? This came all the way from the Vatican . . . I bet it's real important to somebody. Is this from the man who gives you the pills?"

Nora shrugged. "Yeah."

"You got to return this, Nora. Cans of yams and beans is one thing . . . but shoot, girl, you could get everybody in a whole mess a trouble wi' this."

"Do I have to return the pretty stamps?" she asked.

Jerry chuckled. "Naw, you can keep them stamps, Nora, but you got to go return the disk, the plastic thingy, okay?"

Nora nodded then left the hut. Fetching the blackened pot that they cooked most everything in, she headed off to collect some water. As she passed by several huts, she overheard the same topic being discussed as she passed each one—what Jerry had seen and did it have anything to do with the burn marks on Rastaman's face.

She made her way to the well—as it was called by everyone who lived in the Condos—which was a length of PVC pipe that one of the residents had jerry-rigged into a water main. Nora turned the faucet, filled the pot, and then headed back to Jerry's hut, walking in the ever-present twilight of the Condos.

Arriving back at the hut, she set the water next to the campfire, noticing that Lizzie had been busy preparing the vegetables, and that Jerry was now sitting in the entrance to the hut.

Lizzie did the cooking while Nora, Jerry, and Rastaman watched. She threw everything into the pot and then set it on the fire, cooking it slowly until it became a thick stew. A short time later they ate their fill and lay around the campfire, content to watch the glow of the hot coals.

The repose was short-lived, however, as a shout rang out from the Condo's entrance. "Search party's back."

"Let's go see what's going on," Nora said, getting up.

"You go 'head and tell us what's happening," Lizzie said. "I'm too full of food and I ain't movin' for nothin' or nobody."

Nora looked at Jerry. "Let's go, girl," he said. "Maybe they found out what's goin' on."

They headed toward the Mayor's house. When they arrived they saw that a crowd had gathered outside. The Mayor stood on a milk crate so that he was higher than everybody else. To his left were the men who had been sent on the search party. Tim, a Vietnam vet who had become the leader, had a taped-up baseball bat that he kept tapping against the palm of his hand. The others sported different weapons, including a length of chain and several knives, which most all the mole people carried for protection. One of the men carried an old gun that he had found along the tracks. It was now rusted, and Jerry had told her, "Even if it work, I doubt the ol' fool could hit anything with it, 'cause he so high on Sterno all the time." Sterno was a staple among the mole people. They cooked on it, used it to light their huts, warmed themselves with it, and in this man's case, drained off the alcohol and drank it to get high.

The Mayor raised his hands. "Shut up, everybody."

The crowd quieted down a bit, but not enough. "Shut up, everybody . . . Now!" he said again.

The crowd became as silent as a church service.

The Mayor turned to the men who had gone on the search party. "Tim, tell us what you and the men found."

Tim took a step forward, still slapping the baseball bat against the palm of his hand. He looked at the crowd. Like most everybody in the tunnels, Tim had a past, and that past is what had driven him to seek the shelter of the darkness, and the anonymity of the tunnels. One rule of the mole people was that you didn't ask about anyone's past. If they wanted to tell you, they would. Otherwise, everybody minded his or her own business. Jerry had told Nora that Tim was one of the soldiers who had crawled in the Vietnam tunnels, looking for the Cong that were hiding there. Tim had told Jerry how he had had to kill somebody with just his bare hands. Sometimes, at night, that dead person would come back and haunt him in his dreams. "That's why Tim is here," Jerry had said.

Nora saw that Tim had come out of his shell—that being in charge of the search party had given him a new standing with the people of the Condos. He cleared his throat. "We searched from the Condos down to the very bottom level, the one that the trains don't use anymore," he began. "We didn't see anybody. No one's down there, except Satan and a lot of track rabbits." A murmur ran through the crowd. Nora had heard about the homeless man that everybody called Satan. He lived alone down in the deepest level of the tunnels and gave all the mole people the creeps. They pretty much avoided him at all costs.

"We did see something that shouldn't have been there," Tim said. "We saw a new, large tunnel. It was perfectly round and big enough to drive several cars through, but there was no railroad tracks or nothin' like that."

"No tracks?" the Mayor echoed.

Tim shook his head. "No tracks. We got to the opening and this new tunnel is at an angle that goes lower into the earth."

The crowd was heating up now, and Nora moved closer to Jerry.

"Transit Authority didn't have nothin' to do with this," Tim continued. "The walls was smooth like glass. There was no lights but we could see that it went down a long way."

Nora's eyes, like every other set of eyes in the crowd, were on the Mayor.

"What are we supposed to do, Mayor?" somebody called out.

The Mayor frowned as he rubbed the stubble of beard on his chin.

"We're gonna post a double guard on the entrance. We're gonna use the buddy system. Women especially. No one goes out alone."

Murmurs of agreement rippled through the crowd.

"One more thing. Nobody goes down to the lower levels until we figure out what's goin' on."

"You gonna tell the police about it?" a woman called out.

The Mayor shook his head. "No police, never. They'll kick us outta here, and then where will we be?"

The crowd murmured its agreement.

"That's it, everybody. Now go home and leave me alone." The Mayor stepped off the milk crate and vanished into his house.

Jerry nudged Nora. "You gotta be careful, Nora. It ain't like it used to be, and that's a fact, girl. You betta stay with ol' Jerry. No more sneakin' off. It's too dangerous."

Nora nodded. They reached Jerry's hut, and Nora sensed that something was wrong. Rastaman wasn't around, and it appeared that someone had gone through their belongings, littering the front of the hut with their bedding. Lizzie, however, was curled up in front of the fire, snoring.

"I knew I couldn't trust him," Jerry said, swearing.

"I wonder if he took the plastic thingy?" Nora asked, and she began to search her stuff. She found it in the hut where Rastaman had tossed it after deciding it was of little value to him.

"Where did he run off to? Should we wake up Lizzie?" Nora asked.

Jerry shook his head. "No point in doing that, she don't know nothin'."

"What did he take?" Nora asked as they began to put their few possessions back in place.

"Rastaman was after drugs . . . That's what I think," Jerry said. "Nora, you find your pills anywheres yet?"

Nora had rearranged most of her belongings. Her clothes, bedding, and magazines were all accounted for. The only thing she couldn't find was her pills. "No, I can't find 'em."

"Shoot, girl. When was the last time you took one? You been takin' 'em like I told you to?"

Nora hung her head. "I forgot to, Jerry," she admitted.

"I bet ya Rastaman got 'em and he's shootin' up somewheres," Jerry said. "We better go and look for him. I got a feelin' he ain't gone too far."

Nora and Jerry set off toward the back of the Condos. This portion of the cavern was damp and stank from sewage that seeped through from pipes above. It was also used as the communal toilet area. The Mayor had erected several makeshift outhouses to keep people from defecating anywhere they chose. Nora and Jerry walked quietly, a trait that both had acquired from stalking track rabbits and from slipping away unheard in the tunnels. Jerry motioned to the figure of someone huddling against the cavern wall.

"Hey, Rastaman," Jerry called out to the huddled figure.

They waited for a reply but none came.

"Maybe he's sleeping," Nora suggested.

Jerry took a step closer. "Hey, we know it's you, Rastaman. Why'd you take Nora's pills?"

Still no answer.

"Shoot, he's passed out," Jerry suggested, and walked closer. He yelled, "Rastaman, you a thief!"

No response. Jerry put his hand on the man's shoulder and shook it. And as Rastaman slumped to the ground, turning so that he lay face up, Nora gasped. The man was staring at her, his eyes wide open, a needle still stuck in the vein of his arm.

"Ah, shoot, we in for it now," Jerry said, "He's dead! Look here!" Jerry picked up the bottle that once contained Nora's pills. "He shot the whole mess up, an' it killed him. Shoot, Nora, what's in those things?"

Nora shrugged.

"We better go get the Mayor," Jerry said.

The two of them started off to the Mayor's house.

20

The limo pulled up at the entrance to Brian Fitzpatrick's town house. He looked through the window and recognized the doorman and an elderly couple who resided in his building. Conscious of his wrinkled clothes, the stubble on his chin, and the residue of his own vomit on his jacket, he decided to be dropped off half a block away, at the service entrance.

Fitzpatrick got out of the car and slammed the door, not bothering to thank Bruno, the driver, and made a beeline to the service elevator.

Just my dumb luck, he thought, as he saw that there were two painters waiting for the elevator. Coming alongside them he waited. He overheard one of the painters, a short guy with a shaved head and a tattoo on his neck, say, in Spanish, "Look, this guy has the life. He's been out partying all night." The other, taller, with a shaved head and backward baseball cap, smirked and nodded his agreement.

Fitzpatrick, who was fluent in the language, was about to comment in his defense, but opted against it.

The elevator opened and the three men got in.

Tattoo started up again. "Hey, Chino, this guy looks like he's had a tough night—too many women, eh?"

Fitzpatrick stared ahead while Chino, or Curly, as the man's name was translated to English, played with his baseball cap and smirked again.

"Hey, Chino, the guy can't hold his *Cervesa*." Tattoo was laughing openly now, making fun of the way Fitzpatrick smelled.

The elevator arrived at the floor where the painters got off. Fitzpatrick waited until they were several feet away and the doors began to close before he called out, in fluent Spanish, "You boys better be careful, the INS is out front looking for you."

The two men stopped, turned around, and stared wide-eyed at Fitzpatrick. Tattoo was speechless and Chino looked worried. Fitzpatrick winked as the doors closed and the elevator continued to the fourteenth floor. When he arrived he glanced down the hall, grateful that none of his neighbors were out, and bolted for his door. Reaching it, he fumbled with the keys, and once inside, locked the two deadbolts.

The apartment was silent. One of the outstanding features that the architectural firm had designed into the building was substantial sound-proofing. A foot of air space between the walls was packed with insulation then covered with the latest acoustical tiles for additional sound-proofing. Double-paned glass windows shut out a calculated ninety-eight percent of the ever-present din of the city. Fitzpatrick embraced the silence. He took a deep breath, sighed, and headed for the bathroom. There he took the longest shower that he could remember, as if staying under the water would somehow wash away the soiled feeling that ate at his insides.

He cleansed himself again, shampooed his hair, and stood with his head directly under the spout, water cascading over his body. But no amount of washing made him feel better. He had been violated. His chastity had been stolen from him. Although he had left the Dominicans, he had kept his oath of celibacy—a fact that he had done his best to hide from Mary.

He finally got out of the shower when he realized his hands had wrinkled to the point of looking like two huge prunes. He dried himself and then sat on the bed staring into space as his mind raced over what the Hag had shown him. *He killed Fiorre, or at least had him killed. He has threatened me and allowed me only twenty-four hours to make a decision. What am I supposed to do?*

Maybe if I run, things will sort themselves out. With that, he got up from the bed and put on his favorite jogging suit. He knew he was lying to himself, but opted for the run anyway. He adjusted his watch to silent mode. *No sense in being bothered by the Tank.*

He entered the park and eased himself into a jog. Running was something familiar and at the present he needed it, clung to it like a lifeline. He felt his body settle into the rhythm and picked up his pace after the first mile, his breath, legs, and arms moving together, propelling him forward. "I can't . . . change the past . . . only shape . . . the future," he said, over and over, in time with his legs as they moved along the trail. It sounded in his mind like something a drill sergeant might use to motivate the men under his command. "I can't . . . change the past . . . only shape . . . the future . . . I can't . . . change the past . . . only shape . . . the future . . ."

It was late in the afternoon when he returned—sweaty, exhausted, aching, but at least feeling that he had dealt with some of what had happened to him. He had detached himself enough to come to grips with the unimaginable fact that he had been raped by an alien hybrid, and that his chastity and his person had been violated in the most deliberate way. Seeing the film of Fiorre's death made him realize that unless he played ball he would probably come to a similar fate. He was being asked to join a secret fraternity of—what were they? Satanists? Masons? Trilateralists? All three combined? He knew one thing: The Hag was the very essence of evil, and because of that, regardless of the consequences, he would sever all connections to him, even if it meant death. He began to think of a way to escape.

But what about Nora? She must have the disk. Why does my life have to be linked to hers? Why does she seem to control my destiny? As always when he thought of his sister, he felt a mixture of anger and hopelessness. He had moved to New York City partly to help her, but he'd distanced himself too— not wanting to get too involved, but feeling too guilty to just abandon her to the streets. Now that policy had come back to haunt him.

He sat at his desk and checked his messages. There were three from the Tank, urging him to call in, one from Mary, and last, a message from someone that he didn't know. The man introduced himself as Johanen, claimed to know Cardinal Fiorre, and said it was urgent that he contact him. He left his telephone number and repeated his admonition to call.

This man can help, Fitzpatrick immediately thought, then wondered where such an idea had come from. *God is dead, so it can't be from him.* Still, it bothered him that somehow the thought had just popped into his head, as if someone had put it there against his will. He had always admired the way he had trained his mind. The way he could hold, simultaneously, different ideas, each juxtaposed atop another. But this unwanted thought, this unsolicited intrusion, distracted him, and made him, in some ways, feel just as violated as he had felt the previous night.

He listened to the message left by Johanen again, and this time jotted down the phone number. *Perhaps this is serendipitous . . . What have I got to lose?* Then he remembered: Cardinal Fiorre had mentioned this man in the letter. *So, you see, there is nothing supernatural about this.* He dialed the number.

"Hello," a voice answered, cell phone static making it hard to hear.

"This is Brian Fitzpatrick . . . someone called Johanen left this phone number. Is he available?"

"Oh, yes, just a minute."

Fitzpatrick listened to the noise of the phone changing hands, the sound of a car going by.

"Mr. Fitzpatrick? Thank you for returning my call. This is Johanen."

"What is this regarding, sir?" Fitzpatrick asked, remaining guarded.

"I was wondering if you would join my associate and me for dinner. It seems we had a mutual friend, Cardinal Fiorre."

"Yes, I knew the cardinal." Fitzpatrick's mind flashed to the video showing the death of Fiorre, and he shuddered.

"I have some very important things to ask you. And this can't be done over the phone. Will you meet me and my associate, Mr. MacKenzie, at Delmonico's, at seven this evening?"

Fitzpatrick paused for a moment, looked at his watch. 5:30. "Yes, I know the place. I'll see you at seven."

"We will arrive before you; ask the maître d' for our table. It will be under my name, Johanen."

"At seven then."

"Yes."

The phone went dead. Fitzpatrick picked up the letter telling him of the death of his former partner and friend, and read the part mentioning Johanen's name. *Why should I trust him? I don't know who this man is and I agreed to have dinner with him and his associate. I must be losing my senses.*

His watch lit up on his wrist. *The Tank,* he thought. *Well, they're just going to have to do without me for a day or two . . . I've got the flu.*

21

Art MacKenzie and Johanen sat across from each other at the table in their motel room. They had set up a workstation and both men were on the Spiral of Life Web site. Their computers had been custom built by Knud, a faithful employee who lived at Johanen's castle in the Swiss Alps. The computers had satellite link-up with a voice scrambler attached. Johanen had waited to use them until Knud assured him that they were clean and that Stephan, the man who had betrayed Johanen, had not sabotaged them in any way.

MacKenzie was researching a lead that Johanen had given him. He was looking at a United States declassified document from World War II. Specifically, he was searching for an ex-Nazi named Wolfgang Von Schverdt. Knud had found the name in Stephan's files.

MacKenzie scrolled down through a series of pictures of Nazis who had been transported to America after the war. These men had been employed by the OSS, the forerunner of the CIA. They brought with them some of the darker secrets of the Third Reich, and, in some cases, were the architects of those secrets.

"I think I got something," Mac mumbled to Johanen.

"Hold on a minute, MacKenzie, I'm on with Elisha."

Mac nodded and read the document again.

Mac heard Johanen wind down the call. "Yes, I will call you back in a little while. Shalom, Elisha." He hung up, then asked, "Well, MacKenzie, what did you find of interest?"

"Von Schverdt was a general in the SS. He was also involved in a top-secret installation. It was called Peenemunde. According to the file, it was where the Germans developed their V1 and V2 rockets. He was brought to America, helped with the space program. But get this. The rest of the file is blacked out, so whatever happened afterward, until the present, remains a national security risk."

"So Von Schverdt has shown his face again." Johanen leaned back in his chair and ran a hand through his beard.

"You mean you know this guy?" Mac asked, dumbfounded.

"Yes, MacKenzie. I have kept 'tabs,' as you Americans say, on him, and others of his ilk for years, but after Knud found the information on Stephan's computer, I became more interested. That, and of course, his connection with the stealing of the scroll that was given to you."

"You mean you know who stole it?" Mac wasn't sure he was hearing right.

Johanen smiled. "Yes. I set it up personally, with the help of Elisha, of course. The real scroll has been safe all along, and in fact, has been translated."

Mac was speechless.

"You see, MacKenzie, I knew that the Cadre would know of the scroll. Some of their people had witnessed the event, right?"

Mac nodded.

"Cameras were recording much of what happened, yes? Elisha and I thought that they would come after it, and they did. We had small transmitters sewn into the fake parchment. We were able to track where it went. I did not want to burden you with another secret, but now is a good time to bring you up to speed."

"So how does Von Schverdt come into play?"

"He has links with the Cadre. I believe he is in their inner circle. He also may have ties to the underground base in Nevada."

"That means he might know about my father," Mac said, and the thought flipped his stomach.

"Certainly a possibility, MacKenzie. If you access Spiral of Life and type in his name, you will find that Knud has amassed quite a file on him."

"Then why have me search government data banks?" Mac queried.

"To cross-check the information. To see what can be documented."

"So he has a fake scroll?" Mac asked.

Johanen nodded and a broad smile spread across his face. "Sometimes we get the upper hand, MacKenzie."

"How did you get this?" Mac asked.

"I requested that Stephan's files be carefully searched after his betrayal and subsequent suicide. Knud searched the hard drive and checked every e-mail that he could. He hit the jackpot when he found a cleverly disguised file that had been relegated to the trash. At first he thought it was nothing, and almost emptied it along with other files that Stephan had allocated there. This file appeared as an ad for whitening teeth. Knud opened it and found that the file was what it appeared to be. He almost dismissed it when something caught his eye. In the center of the ad, where the product was displayed, were a series of numbers in a bar code. Nothing unusual in that, except that Knud had recalled the same series of numbers on several e-mails that he had recovered. One thing led to another, and he was able to piece together what he believed was the contact that had 'bought' Stephan, so that he would betray the organization and me. The trail led to Von Schverdt. He may have also had a hand in the killing of Cardinal Fiorre."

Mac nodded. "Anything else you want to tell me?"

Johanen smiled again. "Actually, MacKenzie, there is. I was going to let you in on it soon, at least before dinner with Fitzpatrick, so it would not come as a shock."

"What is it?" Mac pressed, sliding to the edge of his seat.

"It has to do with the man we are going to meet for dinner, Brian Fitzpatrick. It seems that Fitzpatrick is employed by Von Schverdt."

"What? No way."

"Yes," Johanen fired back, "Von Schverdt covered all his bases. He knows from those who are in his service at the Vatican that at one time Fitzpatrick worked with Cardinal Fiorre. He sought him out and employed him in his private think tank."

"I don't believe it," Mac said.

"So I think that it would be safe to say that Von Schverdt knows about the disk that was sent to Fitzpatrick."

"So we can't really trust Fitzpatrick, can we?"

Johanen nodded. "Correct, and furthermore, something else might be developing here."

"And that is . . ."

"Von Schverdt might be trying to recruit him, showing him what the other side is like, the alien, or should I say Luciferic, agenda that we have been fighting against. Sway him to their side."

"Why would he go for it? After all, the man was once a priest."

"*Once* a priest, MacKenzie. Something happened to him. As yet, I have been unable to make any headway concerning that, even with all the resources I have at my disposal. I believe he has lost his faith. Of that much I am fairly certain. That, MacKenzie, is a dangerous place to be. The man's spirit at one time was open to the things of God. He has turned from that, and over the years, I am sure has become all but dead to the things of the Spirit. The space that was, for lack of a better word, opened, must be filled with something. The Enemy is trying to do that. Trying to turn him to be a tool for himself."

"So do you think Fitzpatrick will go for that?" Mac asked.

Johanen leaned forward, putting his arms on the table. "I don't know, MacKenzie. But I have hope, seeing that the man is meeting us for dinner. But we must be wary of him until we know for certain that he is not serving the Evil One."

Mac looked at his watch. "That's in less than an hour," he reminded him.

"I suppose then we should get ready. I think a shower might be in order for these old bones," Johanen laughed, pushing himself away from the table and heading for the bathroom. "One thing you should be doing continuously, MacKenzie . . ."

"What's that?"

"Be in prayer for the man, constantly. He is at a crucial juncture, and he is in need of all the intercession he can receive."

Mac nodded as he watched Johanen close the door. He made a copy of the file he had been reviewing, and then closed the computers down. The information Johanen had dumped on him was mind-blowing. *What's this guy Fitzpatrick made of? Why didn't he return to his calling, and what about his relationship to Cardinal Fiorre? Why did he just drop everything and move back to the States, forsaking the project that he had spent years on?* Mac admitted that he needed more information in order to see the big picture. *Now this Von Schverdt guy comes into play, and Johanen tells me he baited him with the scroll that I received from Enoch.*

He stopped a moment, catching himself. *Do you realize what you are saying, MacKenzie? ENOCH! He's been dead or living in heaven for who-knows-how-long, and he shows up in, what did Johanen call it, the Merkabah, the divine taxi. He is then spirited away, but before he leaves he hands me a football . . . the scroll! It's nuts. UFOs, murdered cardinals, shapeshifting monsters under the catacombs of the Vatican, for crying out loud. Now Nazis that by my reckoning should have been dead, yet here they are, alive and well and in the game.* Mac was mentally winded.

He sat a moment, then felt a check in his spirit, something that he had come to realize was God's way of telling him things. He sat still and began to talk to God. He talked openly about his confusion, bewilderment, fear, and wonder at what he had become involved in. He then thought of Maggie and the kids. He prayed for them. He was reminded of Fitzpatrick, and fired off a few more prayers. Johanen had taught him to be very specific, and to speak the things in faith that he wanted the Lord to bring about, always with the thought in mind, *not my will, but yours, be done*. Johanen had said that, by believing what had not yet happened, and yet speaking like it *had* happened, he could exercise his faith. He had learned to speak the Lord's blessing, favor, covering, and prosperity, for all whom the Lord had directed him to pray.

The door of the bathroom opened and a cloud of steam wafted into the room, followed by Johanen, who, with only a towel wrapped around his waist, raised his finger in the air and said, "Next."

Mac got up and headed for the shower.

22

Wolfgang Von Schverdt sat in his private office, surrounded by Nazi memorabilia. A servant was busy cleaning the Persian rug that the idiot Fitzpatrick had vomited on hours ago. The horrid smell lingered. Von Schverdt breathed deeply. *Ah, yes, the smell of defeat, of hopelessness, of darkness shadowing a man's soul. How I love it.*

Leaning back in his chair, he drank a horrible concoction that had been specially prepared using a variety of herbs flown in from all over the world. He grimaced at the taste but drank slowly, to prevent the gag reflex. He enjoyed, in a sick sort of way, forcing his body to do what it naturally would not. The stuff smelled like a dead animal and tasted worse. Von Schverdt licked the last bit of it and held it in his mouth, letting his taste buds scream in rebellion. Finally, he swallowed. *Once again I have overcome the weakness of my flesh with the power of my mind,* he thought with triumph.

He set the empty glass on the desk and observed the Oriental woman on her hands and knees, scrubbing the carpet. Like most of his household staff, the girl, who was barely fourteen, had been sold by her parents to pay back a debt they had incurred in her native country of Thailand. They had been told that, once the girl worked off the debt, she would be returned to them. None of which had been true. Once in Von Schverdt's control, she became, in fact, a slave. If a girl managed to last a year or two in his service she would then simply disappear, only to be replaced by another version of herself. In fact, the unfortunate soul would then be sold, for a hefty price, to a sheik in Saudi Arabia, who had acquired a taste for Oriental girls.

Von Schverdt believed that he was providing a valuable service to these people; after all, the girls that he acquired were illiterate—so much flotsam, cast off from backward third-world countries. The parents of the girls were ecstatic to have their debt canceled. Von Schverdt and others like him enjoyed the endless labor pool. And finally, the oil-rich sheik had the benefit of adding to his ever-expanding harem, while making Von Schverdt even richer.

Von Schverdt waited until the girl was finished, then watched her leave without so much as a word. *Head down, submissive, quiet . . . Good, broken already,* he thought.

He reached for the joystick that controlled a multitude of functions in the room, everything from the video screen and media center to the locks on the two steel-reinforced wooden doors that bolted themselves at the push of a button. He pushed the lock button and heard, to his satisfaction, the distinct sound of the bolts sliding into place.

He went over to a bust of Hitler and, taking the head in his hand, pushed back on it. Directly behind it the walnut paneling slid open, revealing a hidden elevator. Von Schverdt stepped into it and pressed another button, which caused the paneling to return into place. The elevator could accommodate up to four people at a time. The seating was designed for three people to sit at the rear, while one person operated the controls near the doors. He took the seat next to the control panel and belted himself in with a shoulder harness. He then pressed two buttons and waited. He heard a low humming sound and then the hiss of the air brakes. His head pressed against the cushioned headrest as the elevator began to free-fall down a tube, over a mile deep, into the bowels of the earth.

Several minutes passed and he felt the elevator begin to slow. Waiting until it came to an almost imperceptible stop, he then unfastened his shoulder harness. The doors opened automatically, and he stepped out into a dimly lit, circular corridor. Over twelve feet tall, the corridor's sides looked as if they had been fused together. Light emanated from the tunnel walls themselves, diffused units having been built in when it was first carved out of the depths of the earth.

He came to a door at the end, and next to it stood two uniformed guards. They stared at him with large almond-shaped eyes. There was no greeting between the hybrids and himself, which Von Schverdt found annoying. No salute, no clicking of heels, no lifting of the hand in the Nazi salute. Nothing but an emotionless stare. The hybrids were both males with long hair and thin, frail bodies. They wore dark gray uniforms with the SS death's head emblem on the right sleeve—a touch of the old days.

Moments later the door-locks clicked and the door opened. He entered a vast underground room, like something out of a science fiction novel. Various alien/human hybrids mingled freely as they walked along a corridor. He saw hybrid children with almost normal, human-looking eyes. *We are ready. Our breeding program is a success. We have bred the superman, and he will lead us. Lucifer will be victorious, and the Christian god will at last be defeated.* The thought made him tremble. Here was a lifetime of work; in his case *more* than a lifetime, and it was coming to fruition.

A willowy figure approached him that he recognized as Sene. Without her wig and mask she looked very alien. Sene came up to him and they exchanged greetings, then continued walking. Von Schverdt related what he had shown to Fitzpatrick. She, in turn, assured him that his seed had been collected and would be used in the near future.

They turned into a room with a vast array of screens that flickered on the walls, their images changing, flipping from one to the next like a slide show. Several hybrids monitored the screens. He stared at the images: A riot at the Wailing Wall in Jerusalem. The bloody carnage left in the wake of a suicide bomber. Israeli helicopter gun ships firing missiles down on parked cars, their occupants blown to pieces. Palestinian prisoners being executed in the dark of night by an Israeli firing squad. Angry Muslim clerics foaming with hate against the Zionists and their occupation of Palestine. Troops marching, tanks rolling over desert dunes. From the north of Israel, a gathering of armies. In Lebanon, troops massing on the border. In Iran, nuclear missiles that weren't supposed to exist being readied. Turkey, now under a Muslim government, shifting its troops toward its southern border. The former Soviet republic of Russia redeploying two armored divisions in the area.

"Things are looking wonderful," Von Schverdt stated, rubbing his hands together.

An exceptionally tall man with slicked-back hair and dark eyes entered the room. Von Schverdt bowed low, as did Sene and the other hybrids who sat at the consoles.

"Rise," came the command.

Von Schverdt saw the man change before his eyes to his true form: an emissary from the Prince of the Power of the Air. It was a reptilian-looking creature with a powerfully built body and a head that reminded him of a lizard. Von Schverdt had met this creature when he had appeared in human form as Mr. Wyan over seventy years ago. Wyan had initiated Von Schverdt into the secret Thule society, one of the secret societies that found a home in pre-war Germany. It had been Wyan who had trained Von Schverdt, taken him under his wing, and shown him the workings of the mystery of lawlessness. Later when Von Schverdt had committed his soul to Lucifer, Wyan had revealed his true form, that of the fallen angel, Azazel. It was Azazel who had helped with the possession of Hitler. It was Azazel who arranged for the saucer technology to be given to the Third Reich, assuring them of victory. But it had come too late. *Why hadn't Azazel given them the technology earlier? They would have won the war*. It was a question that haunted him even now after all these years.

"Yes, the vicar of the Weak One is dead," Azazel mocked, "and with him goes one of the Enemy's last strongholds. Our man is ready to assume his role. The church is in turmoil— fragmented, divided, each sect holding on to their precious doctrines. Each claiming to be the true way ... A house divided against itself ... For centuries we have manipulated, set in motion our plan; with cunning, foresight, deliberation, but always pressing on. A small victory here, a setback some- where else. But we continue, united, sure of our outcome, and now, at last, everything is ready. The nations are gathering just as we planned, and the war will terrify the world. We, of course, will provide the answer, point the way to Lucifer, the god of this world, and man will worship him."

Von Schverdt nodded enthusiastically.

"Have you found the disk yet?" Azazel asked.

Von Schverdt looked away. "I am close to getting it. I have made a bargain with the fallen priest. I am sure he will come to our side. Sene has had ... contact with him."

Azazel remained silent for a moment. "You have failed to get something as simple as the disk, so I will pay a visit to the priest to see for myself and take what I want. The time grows short. I want the disk now."

"As you wish," Von Schverdt answered. Then he felt a stab- bing pain in the pit of his stomach. It was, he knew, from Azazel. It began to spread. Von Schverdt bit his lip, dropped to his knees, forced himself not to scream in pain. *My master is punishing me because I failed him!* He bent over until his forehead touched the floor. His body began to shake as if every muscle was being ripped from his bones. His blood felt like it was boiling. His skin seemed on fire. He opened his mouth to scream, but managed to hold his voice back so that nothing escaped from his bloody lips. Then Azazel released him. Von Schverdt sprawled out in front of his master. "Thank you . . . thank you," he sputtered.

Azazel motioned for Sene to join him, and Von Schverdt vaguely observed the two of them leaving the room. A minute passed and he sat up, then glanced at one of the hybrids.

"You could be next . . . old man," the hybrid stated.

Von Schverdt ignored the statement. *No, my master is making me better to suit his purposes . . . what power he has! How magnificent he is!*

He got to his feet and left the room. He had to stop several times as his legs cramped. Slowly he made his way out of the complex. He came upon a group of hybrid children. He leaned against the wall for a moment as another cramp hit him, almost doubling him over. He grimaced in pain. The hybrids stared, emotionless, without a trace of compassion.

Von Schverdt began to laugh like a mad man. "It's the only thing that I can do that you can't . . . laugh . . . *ja?*" He saw the hybrids move away. He continued until he was back in the tunnel and then in the elevator. He closed the doors. *There is no laughter in this place,* he thought as he strapped himself in and waited for the elevator to ascend. *None.*

23

Nora felt anxious as she stood next to Jerry. She glanced at the Mayor, then at Tim, the leader of the search party, and a handful of people that the Mayor used as his council when something important was going on. Everyone was staring at the body of Rastaman. The needle was still in his arm.

"We've got to move him right away," the Mayor said. "Tim, get a couple of your men and get him out of here."

"Where do I take him to?" Tim answered.

The Mayor thought a moment. "Take him up to the upper level and lean him against the tunnel wall . . . nobody's gonna care about one more junkie killin' his self."

Tim rubbed his chin. "That's a long way from here, Mayor. He's a big man. I should know 'cause in 'Nam I carried a buddy . . . he got hit . . . blood was all over . . . carried him nearly half a mile . . . he died anyways . . ." Tim's voice trailed off and his eyes took on a faraway look.

"Then take him as far as you can. Just put him someplace where a conductor will see him and get the police to take him. Just make sure it's far enough away from us. Okay? Tim?"

Tim hadn't heard a word the Mayor said.

"Tim?" the Mayor repeated, this time a little louder.

The ex-Marine woke up as his body shuddered back to the present. He rubbed his hand on the back of his neck.

"I was saying, Tim, get him to a place where the train goes by and a conductor will see him. Okay?"

Tim nodded. "Sorry, Mayor. Sometimes it feels like it was yesterday that all of that happened . . . it's hard to let it go . . . real hard."

The Mayor patted him on the shoulder. Tim straightened up, gestured to a few men, and left.

The Mayor turned his attention to Nora and Jerry. "I never did trust that Rastaman. He's not here a day and he goes and kills his self. Where did he get the drugs? Jerry?"

Jerry shook his head. "No way, man, not me. He got 'em from Nora. They was Nora's pills to begin with. He stole 'em and shot the whole mess up."

One of the Mayor's council members, a wino that had been one of the first to set up camp in the Condos, piped up. "She's gonna bring the heat here and we'll lose our homes."

Nora looked to Jerry, hoping he would say something to set everything all right.

"Now wait a minute," Jerry started, but was interrupted by another council member, nicknamed Poc-a-lips, a semi-crazy old coot who had taken up residence in the tunnels because he believed the end of the world was coming soon. "She's been nothin' but trouble since you brought her here," the man said. "Besides, she's crazy, and you know it."

"No more crazy than you, Poc-a-lips man," Jerry shot back.

"Shut up, all of you. Let me think for a minute," the Mayor said.

Silence followed. Nora saw the Mayor give her a once-over and didn't like the expression on his face. She grabbed Jerry's arm, expecting something bad to happen, but not sure what.

"She's gonna have to leave, Jerry."

"But, Mayor," Jerry started, "she's my way of getting in and out of the 'venience stores, and heck, you been eatin' some of what's we get."

The Mayor shook his head. "Nothin' doin', Jerry. She's not one of us anyway. She goes up more than all of us combined.

Now we have somebody dead 'cause of her. She has till the next watch changes to get out."

Nora looked at the Mayor then back at Jerry, not sure of what was happening. "I gotta leave?" she asked, a tear coming to her eye.

"Come on, Mayor, give the girl a break. She didn't do nothin' wrong."

The Mayor shook his head again and he and the council members began to walk away, leaving Jerry and Nora alone with the body of Rastaman.

"Come on, Mayor, this ain't fair and you knows it," Jerry called out.

The Mayor called back over his shoulder, "Sorry, Jerry, but the council has decided, and you know it's for the best."

Nora grabbed Jerry and pressed herself close to him.

"You heard the Mayor. There's nothin' I can do about it either."

"Where am I gonna go? The monster might get me," Nora said, referring to whatever Tim's search party found.

"Shoot, girl, I'll take you somewhere where you can be safe fo' the night ... but I ain't your ol' man or nothin'," Jerry said, putting distance between him and her.

"Where's that, Jerry?" Nora asked, crying now.

Jerry grew angry. "You'll see, Nora. Let's go an' get your stuff and get you outta here, 'fore the Mayor thinks different and kicks me outta here too." Jerry started to walk away. "Come on, girl."

Nora followed him back to his hut. She saw that Lizzie was still sleeping. *Maybe I can live with her,* she thought, as she followed Jerry inside the hut. It took less than five minutes to collect her things.

"Roll up your sleeping stuff like I showed ya," Jerry instructed.

Nora took her bedding and rolled it up, then tied it with a length of string.

"You got that disk you stole?" Jerry asked.

Nora nodded. "I put it in my pants, along with the pretty stamps."

"That's where you gonna go. It's the same place where you get the pills, ain't it?"

Nora nodded.

"So you gonna go back there, say you're sorry, and maybe they let you stay fo' a while."

Nora thought about what Jerry said.

"Come on, girl. Let's git goin'." They went by the Mayor's house. Nora looked at him, hoping for a reprieve. None came.

"Here you go, girl," Jerry said, as they passed through the hole in the concrete retaining wall and left the Condos. "We're getting you to the upper level as fast as I know how to." Nora walked after him. They made their way down the stretch of tracks, moving out of the way when they heard the distant rumble of a train approaching. They reached the upper level—an area where graffiti artists painted walls with murals, some of which showed more than a modicum of talent. They reached the entrance to the subway tunnels. It was night and it was raining.

Several homeless men stood at the entrance keeping dry, but being careful not to venture too far into the world of the mole people. The men gave a start as they approached from behind.

Looks were exchanged. The homeless men relaxed and began to pass a bottle around amongst them.

"It's raining, Jerry," Nora said.

"I can see that, Nora. I'm thinkin', that's all," Jerry responded.

"Where am I gonna go?"

"I told you, girl, you gonna go to that man who gives you the pills and the food. He got to be nice, or he wouldn't be given' you all o' dat stuff."

"Too far," Nora whined.

"What you mean, too far? Shoot, girl, I seen you run for miles."

"Too far," Nora whined again.

Jerry kicked a stone with his sneaker. "Shoot, girl, I'll go wid ya. Come on."

Jerry put the hood of his sweatshirt over his head and stepped out into the rain with Nora following, oblivious to the rain, a smile on her face.

24

"There it is, MacKenzie," Johanen announced. "Crowded as was expected." The cab pulled up half a block from Delmonico's restaurant on South William Street. A cluster of cars, limousines, and cabs occupied the closer positions near the establishment.

"You sure this is okay?" the cabby asked.

"This is fine," Johanen said, then he paid the man the fare, and he and MacKenzie climbed out of the cab.

"Busy place," Mac commented.

"Always. The food is wonderful, the service friendly—not something one finds readily in New York."

Mac laughed, having been harangued by antagonistic New York waiters on previous trips.

They walked toward Delmonico's in the crisp fall air as a light sprinkle of rain began to fall. A lone figure in a faded red ski parka huddled on the stoop of a jewelry exchange that had locked up for the night. Mac noticed the patina of dirt and realized it was one of New York's homeless: a bone-thin, grizzled-looking old man. As he got closer he saw the open bottle, smelled the cheap whiskey, and, for a moment, met the man's bleary stare.

They walked past him. "We know who you are," the man called out, his speech slurred and raspy.

Mac turned to see who the man was talking to.

"Yeah . . . we know who you are . . . you're one of them . . . think you gonna escape what's comin', don't you?"

"Do not pay him any mind, MacKenzie," Johanen admonished, and quickened his pace.

"What is he talking about?" Mac asked.

"One of the Enemy's spies, MacKenzie, giving us a reminder that we are being watched, and not so subtly. The enemy grows bold, yes?"

Mac glanced one last time at the man, who had thrown a blanket over his head. Mac saw him take another hit from the bottle.

They arrived at the front doors of Delmonico's. Johanen gave his name to the maître d', and moments later they were ushered to their table past crowded clusters of chattering patrons.

"We are expecting a guest. Brian Fitzpatrick," Johanen informed the maître d'. "When he arrives, will you kindly show him to our table?"

"Of course." The maître d' smiled and in a moment was gone.

MacKenzie took a seat in a circular booth that Johanen had specifically requested. Johanen had informed him that it was his favorite table because it was tucked into a corner, next to a fireplace, and was placed far enough away from other tables so that it offered a good deal of privacy. Mac looked at his watch. "Seven fifteen. He's late."

Johanen frowned. "Yes, perhaps he has decided against the meeting. Let us hope that is not the case."

A waiter brought water and a basket of freshly baked bread sticks. Mac took one of the bread sticks, snapped it in half, and began to eat.

"You said that the homeless man on the sidewalk was one of the Enemy's spies. What did you mean by that?" Mac asked.

"Well, MacKenzie, it is like this. The man has given himself over to drink to the point that he has lost his right mind.

He has opened himself, perhaps unintentionally, but opened himself nevertheless, to the Enemy. I doubt he is aware that his eyes and ears are used by another that inhabits him."

"So he's possessed?"

"Most certainly."

Mac sat for a moment. "Can he harm us? What if he had decided to attack us while we passed by?"

"I assure you, MacKenzie, that we are protected by some of heaven's finest." Johanen's eyes twinkled.

"Meaning?"

"Meaning that wherever I go I am surrounded by a guard of angels—four of them, to be exact. Their leader's name is Smyrna."

"Smyrna? How do you know that? Have you ever seen him?" Mac asked.

"On occasion, when it suits the Lord's purpose."

"I still have trouble with your matter-of-fact manner with all of this." He mimicked Johanen, lowering his voice, "'On occasion, when it suits the Lord's purpose.'"

Johanen chuckled. "Not a bad impersonation of me, MacKenzie."

Mac smiled. "Thanks." He paused a moment, then asked, "But really, angels? You talk to them regularly?" He lowered his voice. "When I saw the angel—when it appeared at the underground base in Nevada, I felt overwhelmed."

Johanen nodded. "They can have that effect. It is different with Smyrna, though. He has been with me for centuries."

Mac shook his head in disbelief. "I know who you are and how long you've lived, but sometimes I still can't believe who it is I'm hanging out with. John the apostle, for crying out loud. Who would believe it?"

"Yes, but a man, just like you. Older, perhaps wiser, but in the end, a man."

They were interrupted as the maître d' led a tall, good-looking man toward their table.

"Here you are, Mr. Fitzpatrick," the maître d' said, with a flourishing gesture of his right hand toward Mac and Johanen's table. Then a flash of a smile and the man was gone.

Johanen and Mac stood up, and after introductions were made, they took their seats.

"I assume you are aware of His Holiness's death?" Johanen asked.

Fitzpatrick nodded. "He was an incredible individual."

"Yes, I agree," Johanen said. "Now, let me get right to business. I understand that Cardinal Fiorre and you were involved in some very interesting work . . . dealing specifically with the possible identity of the Antichrist and the people who might be helping to bring him to the forefront on the world's stage."

A nod from Fitzpatrick. "Yes, the cardinal and I worked very closely until I left the project while it was still in its infancy." Fitzpatrick took a bread stick and toyed with it. "It was a decision that I regret, but one, unfortunately, that was necessary at the time."

Johanen threw a glance Mac's way, as if to say, "Make a note of that, MacKenzie." Then Johanen spoke, "We arrived here very recently from Rome, where we were in the company of Father Thomas. He is the person whom Cardinal Fiorre designated to settle his affairs, in case of his death."

"I received his letter. The cardinal's death came as quite a shock."

"Yes, it was for me too. He was a good man," Johanen added. "Have you looked at the contents of the disk yet?"

Fitzpatrick looked away, then tapped the bread stick a few times on the table. "I don't have it. In fact, I never received it. It was taken."

"By whom?"

Fitzpatrick stared at the bread stick in his hand, rolling it between his thumb and index finger. "It's a long story."

Mac saw him looking at Johanen, sizing him up. *He's wondering if he can trust us,* Mac thought.

Johanen placed his hands on the table and leaned forward. "From what Mr. MacKenzie and I have discovered, we believe that your life might be in danger. This pertains directly to the disk."

Mac saw Fitzpatrick's left eye twitch rapidly three times. *Pay dirt.*

"Like I said, I never received it. I got the letter from Father Thomas, but the envelope and the disk were stolen."

Johanen frowned. "Why just the envelope and the disk? Why not the whole package?"

Fitzpatrick didn't answer.

Looks like an impasse, Mac thought.

"I know that you might be asking yourself, 'Why should I trust these men?' Am I right in assuming that?" Johanen asked.

Fitzpatrick gave Johanen a half-hearted nod.

"Maybe this will help—if I tell you that we know that the man you work for is an ex-Nazi, Wolfgang Von Schverdt . . . and that he has ties with what, for now, I will call an 'extraterrestrial presence.'"

Fitzpatrick stopped rolling the bread stick. "How did you know that?"

"The how, for the time being, is not important. But I assume he threatened you?"

Fitzpatrick broke the bread stick and let it fall out of his hands to the table.

"You have no idea what I've been through in the last twenty-four hours."

Johanen waited a moment, allowing the man to gather his thoughts. "Why not start by telling us what your involvement is with him." He paused for a moment, then added, "I assure you that Mr. MacKenzie and I are here to help you in all ways."

Fitzpatrick put his head in his hands, rubbing his forehead, then seemed to loosen up as he began to talk.

Mac's eyes never left Fitzpatrick as the man talked through the calamari appetizers that Johanen had ordered. Most of them remained uneaten as Fitzpatrick described his job at the Tank. He seemed candid yet reserved—as if he were telling them the facts, but not all that he could.

As he talked, Mac heard a commotion behind him. It grew louder. The double doors that led into the kitchen burst open, and a waiter fell to the floor, then got up and stumbled toward the entrance, blood pouring from his shoulder.

"What on . . . ," Mac began. Then a figure burst through the double doors leading to the kitchen. Mac saw the dirty red ski parka, the one that the homeless man wore—the derelict who had called to them from the sidewalk. He seemed bigger, wild and threatening, as he waved a butcher's cleaver and glared at the startled people around him.

Silence fell. The patrons and waiters froze, like wary deer in a field, sensing the hunter's pointed gun. The homeless man raised the cleaver over his head, and a banshee-like scream rose from his throat. The place broke into pandemonium. People scrambled for the nearest exit, knocking over tables in their haste to escape.

Mac jumped up from the table. Johanen followed suit, while Fitzpatrick remained dazed. The homeless man searched the crowd, and his head jerked in their direction as if it were directed by an unseen force. Mac's eyes connected with the man's. The transient's face broke into a hideous grin, and he pierced the air with another wild yell as he charged toward their table. Mac began to back away and bumped into Johanen. *He's a maniac,* Mac thought.

"Behind me, MacKenzie," Johanen yelled, as he moved forward.

Mac looked at Fitzpatrick, still sitting at the table, and yelled, "Get out."

Fitzpatrick began to move.

The homeless man was closing fast, weaving his way through the restaurant and fleeing crowd, slashing the air with the cleaver. He overturned a few of the tables, scattering plates of food, wine bottles, and crystal to the floor. *He has the strength of ten men!* Mac thought.

The maniac picked up a chair and with one hand hurled it toward them. It came faster than Mac anticipated, slamming into his shoulder, spinning him backward, taking Fitzpatrick down with him onto the floor. The maniac laughed, a wild, grating sound, and hovered over them, brandishing the cleaver in his dirty fist.

The maniac gathered himself, ready to pounce on the two of them, and Mac prepared to be hacked to pieces. Then everything slowed, and something happened to Mac's senses. He saw the maniac trying to jump, but behind him was the fuzzy, shadowy outline of a much larger figure. It grew clearer, almost came into focus, and then faded away again, leaving just its silhouette. *An angel?* Mac wondered. The angel had his arms around the attacker, preventing him from jumping on Mac and Fitzpatrick.

The maniac bellowed in rage at being restrained. Mac saw a dark figure come partially out of the man and try to do battle with the angel that restrained it.

Then he heard Johanen, and his voice sounded like it was right next to his ear even though he was several feet away. "In the name of Jesus, be still!"

Before his eyes, Mac saw the shape disappear back into the man. The maniac's eyes rolled up into his head, and his body grew limp, yet he remained perched above them. Mac saw the angel slowly let the man down, so that he came to rest on the table. For a moment the angel came into full view. He looked at Mac, who shielded his eyes. He felt overwhelmed, drained of all his energy. Then it was over, and Mac heard what sounded like the rushing of wind as he returned to his normal senses.

Fitzpatrick separated himself from Mac and stood.

Mac also climbed to his feet. "It's over . . . are you all right?" he asked Fitzpatrick. "Did you see it?"

"See what?" Fitzpatrick asked, ashen-faced and shaken.

"I think you should leave it be for now, MacKenzie," Johanen said, coming up beside him. "We are not finished here yet."

Johanen moved closer to the maniac and picked up the man's head. "Help me sit him up, MacKenzie."

MacKenzie took hold of the maniac's shoulder and propped him up. In the distance sirens wailed.

"Sounds like the police are on their way," Johanen said, as he looked around the abandoned restaurant.

"What happened to him? Why did he suddenly go limp?" Fitzpatrick asked.

"The man has a demon, perhaps several of them," Johanen said. "I'm going to cast it out. Both of you men pray."

Fitzpatrick frowned and folded his arms in front of him, "I don't believe in this anymore," he said to Johanen.

Johanen ignored him and addressed the limp body of the man. "In the name of Jesus of Nazareth, every foul thing, every unclean spirit, come out."

Mac began to pray with his eyes open. Johanen laid the palm of his right hand on the man's forehead. The maniac's eyes shot open. Fitzpatrick gasped as the man reared backward.

"We're coming for her," the maniac hissed, and then he spat toward Fitzpatrick, who backed away and cowered.

"Enough!" Johanen yelled, as Mac heard what sounded like a clap of thunder and saw the maniac's body jolt, as if an unseen hand had punched it.

"In the name of Jesus, be silent," Johanen rebuked it.

The maniac's face contorted. He tried to talk, but the words were cut off.

"Be still in the name of Jesus," Johanen commanded.

The maniac relaxed and the man's facial expression changed. *He's in his right mind,* Mac thought, discerning the difference.

Johanen took the man by his shoulder. "Do you want to be free of it?" he asked.

The man shuddered, trying to grasp what was happening to him, to find his way through the years of numbness and debilitation brought about by alcohol. Finally he nodded as tears streaked down his face.

Johanen leaned forward so that his lips were inches from the man's ear. "You have no right to this man," he said. "You must leave, and the others with you. In the name of Jesus of Nazareth, leave." And he clapped his hands loudly next to the man's ear.

The man trembled. "We'll ... kill ... him ... first." A shrill voice came from him, which was clearly not his own.

"Silence!" Johanen commanded. "Leave now ... in Jesus' name ... leave." Then Johanen began to talk in the strange language that he had spoken before.

A low growling noise came from deep in the man's throat.

Mac glanced at Fitzpatrick to see a mixture of fear, denial, and confusion on his face.

"Leave him now," Johanen commanded.

The old man's body twitched. Then his mouth opened and a choking sound came from his throat. His eyes rolled back in his head and his body was lifted a foot in the air, as if it had been kicked from underneath. Then it plopped back down on the seat.

Speaking to the demons, Johanen ordered, "Leave him, all of you, and return to the pit. In Jesus' name."

The man's body went stiff, then limp.

Mac looked at the old man. Several days' growth of white stubble sprouted through the deep wrinkles on his weather-beaten face. His matted hair hung in damp, patchy clumps, but Mac saw a difference.

"Is he sleeping?" Mac asked Johanen.

"Yes, he's sleeping," Johanen answered. "He is very old. I think there is a possibility that he might not make it."

A commotion from the entrance of the restaurant drew their attention.

"The police are here," Johanen said. "Go to them and let them know that everything is all right. Have them radio for an ambulance. Oh, and MacKenzie, keep your hands up so they don't shoot you by mistake."

Mac began walking toward the entrance with his hands up. He had gotten to where the maître d' had greeted them, near the entrance, when two policemen rounded the corner, guns drawn.

"Hold it right there," one of the policemen said.

Mac saw the maître d' sandwiched between two more cops ten feet behind them.

"He's a patron," the man called out, his voice shaky.

"I'm Art MacKenzie," Mac began. "We apprehended the man. He's not armed and we think he may need an ambulance."

The cops looked at each other. "Where is he?" one of them asked.

"Over there." Mac pointed with his raised hand. "Can I lower my hands?"

Another of the cops nodded and Mac dropped his hands. Then he led the cops to where Johanen, Fitzpatrick, and the old man were.

The cops sized up the situation and holstered their weapons.

"He needs an ambulance," Johanen said. "I believe the man might have had a stroke."

A short time later the three men stood on the sidewalk outside the restaurant. The rain had intensified, but in spite of it, a crowd had gathered along with several news reporters. The crowd parted as several police officers accompanied the gurney on which the old man lay. An oxygen mask was placed over his face and an IV line had been established. But the man was still unconscious, never having recovered from his exorcism. They put him in the ambulance and it pulled away from the curb, its siren wailing.

A young aggressive female reporter, with an umbrella being held over her by an underling, shoved a microphone in MacKenzie's face. "Sir, were you in there? Did you see what happened?"

Mac threw a glance at Johanen, then put his hand over the mike and pulled it down. "I'm a reporter myself, *L.A. Times.*

Here's your story. The guy went nuts, tried to kill a few people, and was then subdued." He started to move away.

"What about you, sir?" the woman pressed, shoving the mike in Johanen's face.

"The man was demon-possessed," he said without hesitation.

Mac saw that the reporter was taken aback. The woman put the mike down. "Are you saying that what happened in there was like something out of the *Exorcist?*" she asked with a smirk.

Johanen nodded and began to move away. Mac started to follow, with Fitzpatrick between them.

"And what about you?" she asked Fitzpatrick.

Fitzpatrick shook his head. "No comment," and moved closer to MacKenzie.

They moved through the crowd until they were alone on the sidewalk.

"What *did* happen in there?" Fitzpatrick asked.

"As I indicated to the reporter, the man was demon-possessed. He was sent to destroy you, or perhaps MacKenzie, or myself," Johanen said.

Mac kept his eyes on Fitzgerald. *He's shaken up and scared,* he thought, as he turned up the collar of his jacket.

Johanen strode to the curb and hailed a passing cab. The taxi's brake lights flashed and the three men ran to it.

"Where to?" the cabby asked.

"Another restaurant?" Johanen suggested.

"I'm not really that hungry after what we just went . . ." Fitzpatrick let his voice trail off.

"What about our hotel room?" Mac suggested.

"Why not come back to my place?" Fitzpatrick offered. "I can fix us something there, and besides, there are some things that I would like to show you."

"Thank you. We will accept your gracious offer," Johanen said.

"Go to West Ninety-First," Fitzpatrick said.

"Consider it done," the cabby replied as he headed toward Central Park.

25

"This is as far as I go, girl," Jerry said, and he stopped on the sidewalk.

"You promised that you'd help me find a place," Nora reminded him.

"Shoot, girl, I did. There's your place 'cross the street, like you said it. Now get over there and get yourself outta this rain."

Nora clutched her bedroll and other belongings that were now soaked by the rain. "I don't want to. I want to stay with you."

Jerry fidgeted and shook his head. "Can't do it, girl. You heard the Mayor."

Nora waited a moment, head down and her face buried in her bedroll. "Can I come and visit?"

"I don't know," Jerry said. He was getting mad. "You have to give that stuff back. Where is it?"

Nora reached into her pants pocket and brought out the envelope with the disk in it. "Here," she said, and then slid it back.

"You give it back to the man you stole it from, you hear?" Jerry said.

Nora hung her head and nodded. "Bye, Jerry," she whispered, as she started across the street.

A car swerved out of the way, its horn blaring.

"What you trying to do, girl? Get yourself killed, or what?" Jerry yelled, as he grabbed her and pulled her back onto the curb. "You know better than that. You're just playing with me . . . I know your tricks."

Nora didn't say anything, but just looked at him.

"All right, I'll walk you over, but that's it for me, and I mean it, girl."

Nora took his hand and they went to the crosswalk, where they crossed the street. Before she could change her mind Jerry let go of her hand and ran back across to the other side.

"You promised, Jerry," Nora cried out. She saw him wave once and then disappear behind a row of hedges that bordered the park.

She stood in the rain. Several people hurried past, their umbrellas covering them. She saw them stare at her and move to one side of the sidewalk to distance themselves from her.

Nora ran into the alley and went to the service elevator. Her pants were soaked and she had difficulty getting her lock picks out. She finally retrieved them, and moments later the elevator doors opened and she went in. She rode up to the fourteenth floor, ran to the apartment where she had stolen the food, and once again used her lock picks to open the door. She went to the bathroom, opened the linen closet, and crawled inside, where she made a nest for herself with the towels. She brought out the envelope with the disk and, looking at the pretty stamps, drifted off to sleep.

26

Mac, Johanen, and Brian Fitzpatrick warmed themselves in front of Fitzpatrick's fireplace in his apartment while eating a stir-fry Chinese meal that Fitzpatrick had whipped up.

"So, what happened back there?" Fitzpatrick asked.

"That old man was in the service of the Enemy—Satan," Johanen said, setting his fork down a moment.

Fitzpatrick looked at Mac, waiting for his take on what had happened. "You saw it for yourself," Mac began. "The man was demon-possessed. You heard the voices coming out of him. Then after Johanen prayed we saw him come into his right mind, maybe for the first time in a long month of Sundays. You saw the change in him."

Fitzpatrick toyed with his food as he tried to come to grips with what had happened. "I read about this when I studied for the priesthood, but that was years ago."

"Academics are one thing; being faced with a demoniac that wants to kill you is another," Johanen said.

"So you *believe* the man was possessed?" Fitzpatrick asked again.

Johanen nodded. "He may have been sent to stop you from talking to us."

Fitzpatrick shook his head in disbelief. "But why?"

"What do you know about the man you work for, Fitzpatrick?" Johanen asked.

Fitzpatrick visibly shuddered, then gathered himself and tried to be nonchalant. "He's a bit of an enigma. I really don't know much about him, except that he's obsessed with his Doomsday Clock Project. There are times when I think he *wants* Armageddon to happen."

"Good choice of words," Johanen said. "We believe that the disk from the cardinal contains the names of a secret group whose goal it is to bring about the rise of the superman, the Antichrist, and thereby the destruction of the world. Is that your goal as well?" And his eyes bore into Fitzpatrick's.

Fitzpatrick colored and shook his head. "Hardly. I just liked the work itself—the intellectual challenge. And he offered me a lot of money."

"Is that what made you leave the priesthood?" Johanen pressed.

They waited as Fitzpatrick stared into the fire. The room was quiet for over a minute, then the ex-priest cleared his throat. "There were other reasons," he answered evasively.

"Sometimes it is good for a man to unburden his soul," Johanen said.

Fitzpatrick leaned back in his chair and sighed. "I have a sister who is mentally ill," he began. "She has psychotic episodes. She doesn't remember what she does during them, but she often harmed herself and those around her. My parents got her the best help they could find. She seemed to be doing all right as long as she took her meds. But when I was working for Cardinal Fiorre, she set the house on fire. My parents died in their bed. They burned to death."

"I am very sorry for you," Johanen said.

"Thank you, but that was a long time ago. I've moved on with my life."

"Is that what caused you to leave?" Mac asked.

Fitzpatrick nodded. "Yes, it was the reason I left . . . my calling. I couldn't reconcile a good God with my parents burning to death. I didn't understand why he would allow both my mother and father to die at the hands of . . . of . . ."

Mac saw the bitter expression on the man's face.

"So she is still alive?" Johanen asked.

Fitzpatrick rubbed wearily at his forehead. "Yes, she is. She's the reason why I live here, in the city."

"When was the last time you saw her?" Mac asked.

"Several months ago, and then at a distance."

"What is your sister's name?" Johanen asked.

"Nora."

Johanen changed the subject. "We know that, before he died, Cardinal Fiorre sent you a copy of a disk containing the project you'd been working on together. Did you receive that disk?"

Fitzpatrick shook his head. "Unfortunately, no. I received his letter, but the disk was missing. It's possible that Nora took it."

"Nora?" Mac asked.

"Yes. She recently came to my apartment while I was gone, to get food. Since the letter was left but the disk and envelope were gone, she may have taken it."

"Can you locate her?" Mac asked.

"Not really. She's homeless, lives on the street. Sometimes I see her in the park. There's a wino that knows her and I slip him money every now and then. He can get word to her."

"Can you try to find her? MacKenzie and I will assist you in any way we can," Johanen offered.

Fitzpatrick nodded. "I can try to find the wino and see what happens."

"May I suggest that we go at morning's first light," Johanen said.

"I could do that." Fitzpatrick answered, then hesitated. "You said earlier that you believed my life was in danger.

Before today, I wouldn't have believed you. But this morning I met with Von Schverdt and . . ."

"What did he say?" Johanen prodded gently.

"He showed me . . . things." Fitzpatrick paused a moment. "He had what looked like a holographic film of Cardinal Fiorre . . . his last minutes on earth."

Johanen leaned in toward Fitzpatrick. "What did you see? Was he murdered?"

Fitzpatrick nodded. "Yes, I'm not sure how, but there were two . . . creatures. They somehow caused him to have a heart attack."

"They were two Nephilim who entered his mind telepathically and terrified him to the point of death," Johanen explained.

"The Nephilim? As in Genesis six?" Fitzpatrick asked.

Johanen nodded. "Yes, the Nephilim. The hybrid offspring of an unholy union between fallen angels and the women of earth."

"I find that almost unbelievable."

"Nevertheless it is true," Johanen remarked.

Shock and confusion passed over Fitzpatrick's face, and several beads of sweat appeared on his brow. "I have to tell you. I'm afraid for my life. Von Schverdt revealed something of his plans and asked me to join him."

"And do you want to?" Johanen asked.

"Absolutely not. He's evil incarnate. But if I don't . . ."

Johanen laid a hand compassionately on Fitzpatrick's arm. "The God you have forsaken has not forsaken you. You must turn to him. He will help you defeat the Enemy."

Fitzpatrick shook his head doubtfully. "That may be true, but what do I do now?"

"Our first task is to find the disk from the cardinal," Johanen declared. "And that we cannot do till tomorrow." Johanen stood up and stretched himself. "We must rest while we can. Are you ready, MacKenzie?"

Mac felt a check in his spirit and decided to voice his feeling. "Johanen, maybe Fitzpatrick should come with us. What if they try to get him here?"

Mac saw Johanen ponder his words and then look toward Fitzpatrick for an answer.

A thin smile appeared on Fitzpatrick's face. "The security here is one of the best in the city. I think I'll be fine for tonight."

"MacKenzie makes a good point," Johanen stated. "We know from experience that these fallen angels have the ability to change their appearance at will."

"What do you mean?" Fitzpatrick asked.

"They can appear as your best friend if they wanted to," Mac offered.

"They can appear even as an angel of light," Johanen added.

Mac saw that Fitzpatrick was on uncharted ground.

"Let me sleep on it. We'll meet in the morning."

Johanen said, "We'll come here first thing—say, at seven?"

"Seven sounds fine. We'll go to the park across the street and look for the wino." Fitzpatrick showed the men to the door. They exchanged farewells.

In the elevator Johanen inquired, "Well, MacKenzie, what did you think of all that?"

Mac thought a moment. "The man is caught up in something that he doesn't understand."

"Yes, I agree. I fear for the man's safety. I am hesitant to leave this place."

"We can't stay in the hallway all night."

"Of course not. But we might be able to station ourselves nearby."

The elevator door opened and Mac stepped into the lobby. "Any ideas? There's not even a donut shop nearby."

They made their way out of the lobby and stood under the canopy.

"Good evening, gentlemen," the doorman said. "Should I hail a cab for you?"

"That will not be necessary. I think we have other plans," Johanen said.

Mac looked at him. *What is he going to get us into now?*

"MacKenzie, if you will follow." Johanen smiled and set off down the street.

Mac caught up after a few paces. "What's up?"

"Well, here is the main entrance to this place, and as you can see it is guarded by security twenty-four hours a day. We can set up camp over there, in the park." He pointed to a bench. "It has a good view of the entrance. If anything happens, at least we will be here to help."

Mac took a deep breath. "Who gets the first watch?"

"I propose you take the first. I'll curl up on the bench and get some rest. Wake me in three hours."

Mac shook his head. "How did I know that was coming?"

"The Holy Spirit gave you the check, not me. Yes?" Johanen teased.

The men walked into the park. Johanen found a folded newspaper in a trash can and wiped the bench off before lying down on it.

"How can you possibly sleep on that thing?" Mac asked.

"MacKenzie." By the tone of Johanen's voice Mac knew he was in for a lecture. "After being a guest at the Mamertine prison in Rome, this, I assure you, is a luxury."

"The Mamertine prison?"

Johanen sat up. "Gruesome place. It was a prison in Rome. I spent some time there at the close of the first century in an insect-infested cell, where a man could not stand upright."

"Oh," Mac answered.

"I spent several weeks there and then the guards came for me and I was boiled in oil."

"Boiled in oil?"

Johanen nodded. "That is when I first began to realize that the Lord's promise concerning me, that I should not die until his return, might, in fact, be literal."

"What happened next?"

"They brought me to the emperor and he exiled me to the island of Patmos."

"And then what happened?"

"Well, MacKenzie, it would take the rest of the night and then some if I were to elaborate, would it not?" And he lay back down on the bench.

"But . . . ," Mac began.

"No, not now, I'm just getting comfortable."

"Hey, Johanen."

"Hmmm?"

"I think this is only the second time I've heard you use a contraction. You said *I'm*."

"It happens when I get tired. Three hours, MacKenzie." He turned up the collar of his coat and covered his head with the sports section of the newspaper.

MacKenzie looked at the man and shook his head. *No one would believe it.* Mac put his hands in his pockets and began to pace in front of the bench, all the while keeping an eye on the front of Fitzpatrick's apartment building.

27

Wolfgang Von Schverdt rode in the back of his Mercedes and looked at the rain-soaked streets of New York. A glance at his watch. *Almost two in the morning.*

He was headed to a secret meeting of men and women, who, like himself, were dedicated to bringing about the Chosen One, the one whom Lucifer himself would one day inhabit, and with that possession, rule the earth.

"Can you go faster, Bruno? I don't want to be late," Von Schverdt called.

A nod from Bruno and Von Schverdt felt the car increase its speed.

A short time later the car pulled onto Wall Street, the hub of the financial world in the United States. It then turned onto a small side street and entered an underground parking garage. Bruno put the car in park and opened the door for Von Schverdt.

"Thank you, Bruno," Von Schverdt said. "I will be back in approximately an hour, or two at the most." Without waiting for a response Von Schverdt made his way to the elevator. He stepped inside and inserted a special card. The doors closed and he waited as the elevator began its ascent. Von Schverdt had been at meetings like the one he was about to attend since before the war, although then they had taken place in Germany. He thought wistfully of the old days, of when Hitler was coming to power. *How proud we all were,* he thought.

When the doors opened, he walked down a hallway. Some of the others in this elite group had already gathered. He surmised that the meeting had been called because things had *not* worked out according to plan regarding Yemen.

We must find Johanen, and be done with him at last! he thought. W*e were so close, just a few minutes more . . .*

"Good evening, Von Schverdt." A Japanese man, slight of build, with a military-style haircut and round glasses, greeted him.

Von Schverdt clicked his heels together and bowed to the man.

"Good to see you again, Yamamoto," Von Schverdt said.

The men walked together past a banquet hall, where a round table was being prepared for a meal. Entering a windowless room covered in crimson draperies, they took their places at an ebony conference table inlaid in the center with an ouroboros, a red dragon, curled in on itself with its head eating its tail.

"We failed in Yemen," Yamamoto said.

Von Schverdt shrugged. "Not entirely. The media carried the sighting of the sign, something that we had not intended, and it has everyone talking. You might be interested to know that that one event, combined with the pope's death and the massing of armies in the Middle East, has moved my doomsday clock to midnight."

"We have a good chance of putting our man forward as the pope," Yamamoto said.

"That is what I heard from Mr. Wyan," Von Schverdt answered.

While they talked, other men and a few women entered the conference room until the seats were full, all except the one at the head of the table. The room settled down and all eyes were on the vacant seat. A tall man, with slicked-back, black hair and a deep scar above his left eye, entered the room.

"Mr. Wyan is here at last," Yamamoto whispered.

Von Schverdt nodded with satisfaction.

Wyan went to the head of the table but remained standing behind his seat. He paused for a moment and looked every man and woman in the eye.

"We have failed where we should not have failed," he yelled, and brought his fist down on the table.

Von Schverdt had seen Wyan's temper and knew that when kindled, things could get very dangerous and unpredictable.

"The very man that we set the trap for in Yemen was able to somehow turn everything against us. He has cost us time." Wyan peered at the group and then began to walk around the table, stopping at each chair, holding the back of it with his hands for a moment before moving on to the next one. "We almost succeeded in what we had hoped to accomplish." He stopped and moved to the next chair, directly across from Von Schverdt. The man was a wealthy industrialist, aging and battling skin cancer. Wyan set his hand on the man's shoulder. Von Schverdt stared at the six fingers on the large hand and saw how he squeezed the man's shoulder so that he winced from the pain.

Wyan moved to the next person and continued his excoriation. "We have worked for centuries to create this moment, when the world will embrace us and the one we serve, and why? Because we will promise them what eludes them ... peace. We have chipped away at the things that once were called good, blurred the lines so that the man on the street can't tell the difference between right and wrong anymore. And we have gone one step further, as he now thinks that there is nothing that is absolute. We have positioned him to where we want him to be. He is outraged by the killing of baby seals but kills his own children in their mothers' wombs. Isn't that wonderful? Look how we have twisted them, slowly, from generation to generation, because we are not divided in our cause."

Wyan paused behind a good-looking woman. Von Schverdt saw her press her lips together as Wyan played with a lock of her hair for a moment before moving to the next person. "The church is more concerned with bake sales than it is with the deception that we have laid all around them. They are poised at a critical juncture and are unaware of it. The armies of our allies are poised to destroy Israel, to drive every Jew into the sea and kill them. When that is accomplished, we will show ourselves to the world and they will marvel.

"We have twisted the youth of the world. Confused and titillated them with lascivious images, taken their innocence from them and in its place given them hopelessness and death. We have helped fashion the drums of war until every nation has learned to follow their seductive beat and fashioned their ploughshares into swords to kill each other. On such a grand scale we have accomplished this, that millions will die at the touch of a button, and we will be there to greet them as they leave their rotting corpses and go to meet our father in hell. We have seen plagues and new diseases take the lives of millions, leaving in their wake countless orphans who we will train to be men and women who live our precious lie.

"We have taken the life out of the church, driven the Spirit of our Enemy into the wilderness, and made certain that our people, like wolves in sheep clothing, infiltrate its ranks. We have waited decades for a pastor or priest to fall. We have sown the seeds of that fall and nurtured it slowly, watering it with seductive visions of money, sex, or power. Now we see scores fall daily.

"We have sown hopelessness and death, confusion and anarchy, disease and intolerance. We have harvested the souls of these wretched, worthless masses and fed them to the eternal fire of hell itself."

Von Schverdt felt himself getting excited as Wyan expounded on all that he held sacred. He felt like he was back in Nuremberg, listening to Hitler himself.

Wyan stopped next to Yamamoto's chair. "This is why we will prevail. Look at the Enemy's kingdom, divided in a thousand fragments, and we continue to divide them. They hold their councils. But little do they realize that we have placed our men and women next to them who will subvert and weaken that kingdom further. It is why, when Lucifer ascends to his rightful place, they will worship him because of his terrible power."

Wyan placed his hands next to Yamamoto's head, then without warning changed to his true form. The clawed hands fastened themselves to Yamamoto's head and in an instant twisted it, so that a loud snap reverberated in the room. Then he severed the head from the body.

A collective gasp filled the room. The woman sitting across from Von Schverdt covered her eyes. A few men looked ashen while others trembled, visibly shaken by the gruesome spectacle. Von Schverdt, however, trembled with excitement. *My master has shown them what power is . . . how fortunate I am.*

Wyan reached over and set the head in the center of the inlaid dragon. "Why have I killed one of your colleagues? Why have I made an example out of him? I will tell you. It is because he is weak, and Lucifer will not tolerate weakness. How was he weak, you may ask? He was more concerned for his own affairs, than the affairs of our Lord."

Von Schverdt stared for a moment at the severed head on the table, its eyes wide open and beginning to glaze over. The face contorted in a look of surprise, terror, and agony. He looked to his left at the headless corpse of Yamamoto, noticed the elegant suit now blood-stained and ruined. Wyan had returned to the head of the table. "Even though our mission in Yemen was thwarted, the next phase of our plan will not be deterred. We will annihilate the sons of Abraham."

Von Schverdt began to clap and soon the rest of the members at the table followed suit. Von Schverdt rose from his seat, leading the way for a standing ovation. As the applause filled the room Wyan reverted to his human-looking form. He motioned for quiet.

"All this has given me an appetite." He smiled and without another word left the room.

Von Schverdt looked around at the other members, all of which eyed the severed head that remained in the center of the dragon. *There is no laughter here,* he reminded himself, and he left the table and followed his master to the banquet room.

28

Johanen, it's time." Mac shook the snoring figure, who stirred from the park bench and sat up.

"What time is it, MacKenzie?" he asked.

Mac glanced at his watch. "Almost four in the morning."

"Anything happen while I slept?" Johanen asked.

Mac shook his head. "A patrol car shone its light on us, but nothing across the street."

Johanen get up and stretched. "Your turn, MacKenzie. See, I have warmed the bench for you. You should thank me."

Mac lay down on the bench and tried to get comfortable. First he lay on his back with a newspaper under his head. The slats on the bench bottom cut into his back. Then he tried his side, but his head was lower than his shoulders and his neck started to hurt. "I don't know how you do it," he said, as he sat back up.

"Do what, MacKenzie?" Johanen answered, as he paced in front of the bench.

"Sleep on the rack, for crying out loud."

Johanen chuckled.

Mac spread both arms on the bench's back and crossed his ankles in front of him. "I can't sleep, and besides, I have a head full of questions."

"As always," Johanen replied.

"Feel like talking?" Mac asked.

Johanen stopped walking and looked at the front of Fitzpatrick's building. "I suppose . . . about what?"

"Well, I have a question about this Von Schverdt guy."

"Fire away, MacKenzie," Johanen replied.

"How could this guy be alive today? He would have to be well over a hundred. How is that possible?"

"I believe that the Enemy is prolonging his life, like that of your father."

Mac nodded, remembering the last time he saw the body of his father, demented, possessed, given over to the foul thing that inhabited it. "Do you think that Von Schverdt is possessed, like the man in the restaurant?"

Johanen shook his head. "I am not sure, but the man is certainly under the control of the Evil One. He is a willing tool, a vessel to carry out the desires of the Enemy. He has made a very deliberate choice and serves the one he worships."

"How did he get to America? Wasn't he wanted for war crimes? And where did he get the clearances to initiate a top-secret project?"

"This might take a while, MacKenzie, and I do not have all the information, but what I do have I will share with you."

Mac slid to the end of the bench, making room for Johanen to sit down.

"In Germany during World War II, a pernicious event transpired that left millions dead in its wake."

Mac thought for a moment. "The Holocaust?"

"Precisely," Johanen said. "But what is it that motivated the Nazis to eliminate the Jews? Why have modern historians eliminated the spiritual side of the Holocaust?"

Mac shook his head.

"Because something so terrible took place with such utmost deliberation that the human psyche is repelled at the thought of it."

Mac shifted on the bench, glanced at the building entrance, and waited for Johanen to continue.

"Historians note that the Holocaust, the destruction of over six million Jews, was carried out with the utmost efficiency. What they fail to realize is that the bodies, burned in the crematoriums, were in fact a burnt offering to their would-be god, Satan—a sacrifice intended to bring about the rule of the Antichrist. Are you aware, MacKenzie, that the German word *holokaustein* is translated as 'burnt offering, as on an altar'?"

Mac shook his head. "I didn't know that."

"It is true, MacKenzie. The death of the Jews was a burnt offering. And do you know what the Nazis succeeded in accomplishing? They were able to create a doorway, a portal, by which the fallen ones of old could return."

"Do you mean fallen angels?" Mac asked.

"Yes, MacKenzie. They were given the ability to enter, and once they did, they gave the Nazis a secret weapon, the flying disk. One of these men, Wolfgang Von Schverdt, was and is an occult adept who helped usher in the fallen ones. He was involved in the death camps. He helped orchestrate the Luciferic sacrifice. He was Satan's willing tool. I tried to apprehend him just before the war's end, but failed in my attempt."

"What happened?"

"It is a long story, MacKenzie, and best told in detail another time, but he was surrounded by legions of the Enemy. You must remember that the Enemy was manifesting himself in our dimension at will, with no restraint. It was a demonic stronghold that I was not able to penetrate."

"But I thought," Mac began, but Johanen interrupted.

"You thought that because I had an inside line, as it were, to him"—and Johanen pointed to the heavens—"that somehow I would be victorious in every situation."

"Yeah, something like that, but why weren't you?"

"Have you read the book of Daniel?"

Mac nodded. "That's another thing I was going to ask you about."

"Well, do you remember when Daniel prays and then an angel, Gabriel, is dispatched?"

Mac nodded.

"Do you remember how long it took for the angel to arrive to assist Daniel?"

"I think it was around a month."

"Twenty-one days, to be exact. When he arrived, he explained to Daniel that the reason for this delay was that he was hindered by the evil prince of Persia, a principality of Satan, and that in order to break through, another angel, Michael, was dispatched to help him. My situation with Von Schverdt was similar. I got close, but I was restrained by the Enemy and was prevented from carrying out my task. He was then taken by the Americans. Are you aware that much of what the Nazis ushered in was then embraced willingly by the Americans?"

"No. But why would they want to deal with someone as ruthless as Von Schverdt?"

"He had the technology, the superweapons. I was able to ascertain that he was the head commander at the Nazi's secret weapon's facility in Peenemunde. The name translates as 'fantasy world.'"

"Incredible . . ."

"Von Schverdt took the secret technology and migrated with it to the U.S., where he was given carte blanche, and huge sums of money, to carry out black experiments."

"Like what was taking place at the base in Nevada?"

"Yes. You saw for yourself the breeding program, MacKenzie. Von Schverdt was the man responsible for seeing it to fruition. I believe he is the one who controlled the base in Nevada."

Mac pondered for a moment. "I wonder if the president is aware of this?"

Johanen shook his head. "No, MacKenzie. This is all very secret and only known by a handful of people. There is a shadow government that is involved in this, and they, like their predecessors, are involved in establishing the Luciferic kingdom on earth. They make certain the president is kept out of the loop."

Mac glanced to the front of the apartment building, then back to Johanen. "So Von Schverdt was pardoned for his war crimes, and allowed to migrate to the United States, all without impunity."

"Yes, MacKenzie, that is the gist of what happened. Now we have closed in on him and others of his ilk. We are aware that their goal is to bring about the Antichrist. We stopped their efforts in Yemen, and yet they continue with their plan, undaunted by their failure."

"We stopped them, but the media still picked up on the false sign. The world is debating what they saw."

"Yes, the world is seeing what was foretold centuries ago, fearful signs in the heavens, and *they*, the fallen ones of old, are manifesting themselves because these are the end of days. *The time is now.*"

Mac glanced at the canopied entrance to the building for the umpteenth time. He was about to glance away when something caught his eye. "Johanen, I think something's up over there."

Mac and Johanen looked at the entrance. "It's *him*, Wyan, the fallen angel. He's talking to the security guard."

Wyan grabbed the guard and held him by the lapels in front of his face. The guard yelled as he tried to cover his eyes.

"Now, MacKenzie!" Johanen yelled, and the two men started running across the street. Mac saw the guard fall to the ground, holding his head and yelling. Wyan walked calmly into the building and disappeared.

A car's horn blared and Mac and Johanen stopped as it swerved around them and continued down the street. They rushed to the security guard.

"Make it stop! Make it stop!" the guard shouted, terrified, as he thrashed on the carpet under the canopy.

"What about Wyan?" Mac asked.

"Stay here and see if you can calm him down. Pray for him, MacKenzie. If I do not leave now, Fitzpatrick may come to a horrible end."

Mac nodded and watched as Johanen bolted toward the elevator. The guard moaned again and began to bang his head on the concrete. Mac began to pray aloud, and when he looked up again Johanen was gone.

29

Nora awakened with a start, at first not knowing where she was, then remembering that she was in the bathroom linen closet. She pressed her back against the rear of the cabinet and listened. Someone was yelling.

She listened to the noise and thought, *They're not gonna get me . . . no way.* She recognized her brother Brian's voice. *Why is he yelling? What's wrong? Is he mad at me for taking these?* She looked at the envelope with the pretty stamps.

Then she heard something slam into the wall, followed by the pounding of a fist on the door.

What's going on? Nora wondered, and she opened the cabinet door and peeked out. She was able to see down the hallway to her brother's room. There was a very tall man standing in front of the door, pounding on it with his fist. To Nora's amazement, splinters of wood flew from the door. The man was breaking the door down with his fists. *But how could that be?* Nora thought, pulling the cabinet door shut again.

"I've got a gun . . . I've got a gun!" She heard the frantic cry of her brother.

The man punched the door again, then yelled, "Give the disk to me!"

"I mean it! I'll shoot you!" Brian yelled.

Then Nora heard something else from the direction of the front door. *Someone is trying to get in, but they can't because the door's locked. Maybe they're here to help.* Nora debated whether she should leave her hiding place and open the door.

"I'm not going to warn you again—leave this place *now* or I'll shoot," Brian yelled again.

Nora heard the front door burst open. Opening her cabinet door a crack, she saw a man come running from the living room to the hallway. He started to yell something but was drowned out by a piercing growl from the tall man.

Nora heard the gun go off.

The tall man spun around and crashed into the hallway wall from the force of the bullet.

She saw the gun stick through the hole in the door. She saw the flash of fire leave the muzzle, and a loud explosion hurt her ears, but the bullet missed the man and buried itself in the ceiling.

The new person, the one with all the gray hair and the bright blue eyes, stopped at the entrance of the hall. "Fitzpatrick . . . it is Johanen."

A piercing scream from the tall man made Nora jump, and she hit her head on the top of the cabinet. She rubbed her head and peeked out again. What she saw terrified her. The tall man had changed into a monster.

"What *is* it?" Brian screamed, as he fired another round. Nora saw the monster spin as the bullet glanced off its shoulder. *A monster, just like Jerry said.*

Nora heard the monster scream again as it charged the man with the blue eyes. The monster slammed into him. They began to wrestle on the ground. *You better run for it, girl,* Nora told herself, and she crept out of the cabinet holding the envelope. She stood up in the doorway and began to run for the front door.

"Nora! Come back here . . . now!" her brother yelled.

His voice startled her and she dropped the envelope on the floor and the disk slipped out and landed next to it. She bent down to pick it up and saw that his bedroom door was open and he was standing in the doorway, still holding the gun.

"Nora leave it . . . leave it there," her brother called.

She was confused and looked at the man with the blue eyes. At that moment the monster turned and saw her. She grabbed the disk and stuffed it back into the envelope. The monster growled and started toward her.

The man with the blue eyes tackled the monster, holding onto one of its legs.

Nora ducked into the hallway. A clawed hand reached out and tried to grab her, but she broke away, her body hitting a chair in the living room.

"Nora, leave the envelope!" her brother shouted again.

Nora ran for all she was worth toward the front entrance, holding the envelope tightly in her fist. She looked back as she left the apartment and what she saw terrified her, because the monster had broken free from the man with the blue eyes and was coming after *her*.

Nora reached the service elevator and pounded the button, over and over again.

The monster was flying toward her, with the other man just behind. Then she saw her brother in his doorway as the elevator doors began to open.

She saw him raise his gun and aim at the monster.

Nora didn't wait for the doors to open all the way. She jumped in and began to push the first-floor button.

The monster was getting closer. Then the man with the blue eyes leaped, his hands extended. One of them caught the monster by the leg and it tumbled to the ground. The elevator doors began to close. Nora saw the thing clawing its way toward her, dragging the man with it. She pressed herself against the back of the elevator. A hand reached out and tried to stop the doors, but to Nora's relief they closed, and the elevator began its descent.

At the first floor she got off and ran into the alley. Hearing glass breaking high above her, she saw, to her horror, that the monster was on the fire escape. She darted out into the alley and onto the street, where she was almost hit by an oncoming car. Without looking back, she headed toward the one place where she might find safety . . . the Condos.

30

MacKenzie heard the squeal of tires and an angry horn blaring up the street from where he was. He peered up the street at what appeared to be a frantic homeless woman. He saw her run into the park and disappear. *What's going on?* he wondered.

The doorman moaned.

"You're going to be okay," Mac said, as he helped the man stand.

"I saw things . . . horrible things . . ."

"You're going to be all right," Mac echoed again.

"What happened anyway?" the doorman asked, still dazed from the encounter.

Mac thought about telling the man the truth and realized that it would be better for the man not to know any more than he had to.

"Let's get you inside," Mac said, as he helped the man into the deserted lobby.

"I never believed in the devil. You know . . . but whatever it was . . . I felt like I was in hell . . . if there is such a place."

The man began to shake from fear as Mac helped him into a chair.

The elevator door opened and Johanen appeared. "Did you see a woman running out from the alley?" he asked.

"A couple of minutes ago but . . ." Then it dawned on him. "Fitzpatrick's sister Nora?" he gasped.

"Yes. We have got to follow her if we can, MacKenzie," Johanen said.

"Who are you?" the doorman asked.

"Someone who will speak peace into your life," Johanen said, as he laid his hand on the man's forehead.

The man closed his eyes as his head fell onto his chest. "Is he all right? What did you do?" Mac asked.

"Blessed him. He will be at peace."

"What happened to Wyan?" Mac asked.

"He changed into his true form after he entered Fitzpatrick's apartment. I found him clawing his way through Fitzpatrick's door. Fitzpatrick fired a couple of shots. I think he hit him once. Wyan picked up a fire extinguisher and hurled it at me, smashed a window, and went down the fire escape."

"Was Fitzpatrick hurt?" Mac asked.

"As far as I could tell, no. We must go to him now, MacKenzie."

"But what about the sister and Wyan? Isn't he chasing her?"

"Yes, and what is more . . . she has the disk from Cardinal Fiorre. But first we will help Fitzpatrick."

MacKenzie followed Johanen to the elevator, but when it opened Fitzpatrick himself stepped out. "Where is she? Where's Nora?" he cried.

"She's escaped for now," Mac said.

"What *was* that thing?" he asked.

"It was a fallen angel. We have dealt with him before. He came here to kill you."

Fitzpatrick wrung his hands together. "I was . . . terrified. That's why I grabbed the gun and started to shoot. I panicked and didn't know what else to do."

"Fallen angels are very powerful, but not invincible. We are strong in the Lord, and in his power we can defeat him, and indeed have done so in the past."

"It went crazy when it saw Nora . . . saw that she had the disk," Fitzpatrick said.

"He knows that it is the only copy in existence. They're going to make a move very soon, and that's why the urgency to get the disk."

"What do we do now?" Fitzpatrick asked.

"We find Nora before they do," Johanen stated. "If we can find the disk and get the information that is on it, perhaps we can make a difference. At the very least we can save your sister."

"To the park then," Fitzpatrick said.

The men left the apartment just as sirens wailed down the street, signaling the arrival of the police.

31

Nora crawled over the fence, looking back through the rusted chain link. *The monster might be coming after me yet ... I better hurry and get Jerry. He'll help me.* A few minutes later she was in the tunnels. It was now early morning and the commuter trains were frequent. She had to step aside several times and press herself against the wall as the trains rumbled by.

She made her way to the Condos and was greeted by Tim, who along with several other residents of the Condos was doing guard duty.

"What you doin' back here?" Tim asked, his baseball bat resting on his shoulder. "I thought the Mayor told you, you had to go."

Nora stared at her feet a moment. "I know what he said ... but I have to see Jerry. I got nowhere else to go."

Nora waited for an answer.

"You wait here with the guys and I'll go and ask the Mayor."

Several minutes went by and Tim returned.

"The Mayor says you can't come back, and Jerry hasn't been seen since he took you out last night."

Nora rocked herself. "Where am I gonna go then? I got a monster that's after me."

Tim chuckled and circled his temple with his index finger, the universal sign for "crazy." "You can't stay here, Nora. Now you better get out of here before the Mayor gets serious."

Nora began to walk away. When she was fifty feet away, she turned around and made an obscene gesture at Tim and the other two guards. Then she retraced her steps back out of the tunnels and made her way back to the park, where she sat on a bench and wondered what she was going to do. The sun was warming the park, turning away the nip of fall air.

She was getting hungry and wanted to get something to eat, so she went to the trash cans in the park and searched them for food. She found nothing in the first can. *Someone picked this one clean,* she thought, as she rummaged through the trash. The next can was more promising; she found a half-eaten sandwich in a kid's lunch bag along with an apple. She took her find back to the bench, where she ate it slowly.

She took out the disk and the envelope, stared at them, then stuffed them back into her pants pocket where she knew they would be safe. *What should I do now? Everybody is after me and my brother is mad because I took his stuff.* She sat on the bench and looked at the leaves that sporadically fell from the trees around her. She began to play a game, seeing if she could figure out where the next leaf would fall. The game made her eyes heavy and she drifted off into an uneasy sleep.

She was awakened by the noise of children laughing nearby and at first she wasn't sure where she was. She sat up and looked around and then remembered.

The kids were noisy and two of them were fighting with each other, so Nora got up off the bench and moved away. *Where do I go now?* She started walking without a real destination. *I'll go back to the tunnels, but I won't go in. I'll just linger in front and maybe I'll see Jerry, or I can go and see if Lizzie will let me stay with her.*

She moved a little faster now that she had a plan, ducking into an alley that led to the vacant lot near the Condos. There was an abandoned car in the lot and she went over to it. The front seats were gone as well as the windshield, but the back still had its seat as well as the rear windows. She opened the door, which took some effort, and tested the seat. It was slightly damp but otherwise in good condition. *If I go and get some wood and other stuff I could fix this up and maybe stay here.* The idea gave her hope, and she looked around the vacant lot that like most places of this sort attracted all kinds of unwanted junk and refuse. Finding several boards, she began to fashion a hut around the abandoned car. She took an old milk crate and set it in front of the car for a table. She looked at the stack of tires, some of which she had used the day before to help her get over the fence. She rolled two of them over to the car and thought about what she could use them for, becoming absorbed in what she was doing.

The stray dog appeared at the edge of the lot and stared at her. "Come here, Boy," she called. But the dog stood his ground and wouldn't budge.

She moved one of the tires, trying to see if it would make part of the wall she was trying to build. She looked over and the dog was still there, looking at her with its tongue hanging out the side of its mouth.

"Why don't you come here, Boy?" Nora called. "I won't hurt ya."

The dog moved about a foot toward her, then sat down again.

"Stupid dog," she mumbled, and began to move the tire again inside the car. She propped it up against the two pieces of wood that she had wedged between the car's windows. *All I need is some string or wire and this would work. I could tie the tires to the wood and then get some cardboard to finish it off.* She went searching the lot for wire and then remembered that she had seen some electrical wire that somebody had wrapped around the fence to hold it to the pole. She went over to the spot and started to work the rusted wire, untangling it.

The dog growled behind her, startling her. She turned around. The dog was crouched, all its hair bristling, its lips curled back showing its teeth. It barked and lunged at a man. Nora gasped as she recognized the man as being the one who had changed into the monster at her brother's apartment.

The dog bit at the man, holding him at bay while Nora scrambled up the fence. When she got to the top, before she jumped to the other side, she glanced back at Boy. The dog was keeping the man from passing through the narrow opening that led into the lot. She dropped to the other side, and then she heard the dog let out a cry, and then silence. She looked once more and saw that Boy was lying on his side in a pool of blood, his head twisted unnaturally. The man was already closing the distance between them. Nora slid down the concrete embankment and ran as fast as she could toward the opening of the tunnels.

32

N ora ran down an old line of track that hadn't been used in
years. She was terrified and confused, as the monster was
chasing her. She had gone past the Condos and ignored Tim,
who had yelled at her to stop. She had gone from level to level,
finally arriving at the lowest. It was very dark in this part of the
tunnels and most of the lighting was burned out or broken.

She stopped running for a moment and listened. *He's still
coming after me.* She was about to start running again when she
heard something in front of her. She peered through the darkness trying to see what it was. "Who's there?" she whispered.

"You know who it is," a raspy voice answered.

Nora wished she had kept the knife that Jerry had given
her to carry for protection. "Leave me alone, Satan," Nora
said, and tried not to whimper. Satan was the crazy man that
the mole people tried to avoid at all cost.

"The darkness is my friend, and it does what I tell it to do,"
Satan said.

Nora stared in the semidarkness and then, emerging from
a dark shadow, Satan appeared, a white man in his early thir-
ties with a shaved skull and tattoos over much of his body. The
most unsettling thing about him was his eyes. As he drew
closer Nora could see them, red and bloodshot. They seemed
to glow as the man stared at her.

Nora felt unable to move as the man approached her. The power of the man's mind had somehow sent out unseen tentacles that wrapped around her, making her immobile.

"Darkness is my friend and it will hide you, if I tell it to," the man hissed at her.

Nora began to tremble as the unseen force surrounded her.

"You're in my kingdom now . . . the kingdom of darkness. The darkness is greater than the light. The darkness will hide you if I tell it to."

"Go away from me," Nora said.

"Listen," the man said in a taunting voice, "he's getting closer. He's comin' for you, isn't he?"

Nora realized to her horror that she was trapped. In front of her was Satan, taunting her, behind her, a monster that was coming closer with every step. It seemed to her that there was no way out. Satan took a step closer to her, and in the darkness he looked like a phantom.

Looking behind him, Nora spotted the tunnel that she had heard about, the one that Tim had said had been made by somebody other than the Transit Authority. A faint light was coming from it.

Satan laughed at her and brought his hands in front of him. His fingernails had grown long and were filed into sharp claws. Without warning he came at her, his hands pawing toward her like a wild animal. Terrified, she willed herself to move and managed to take a step back, but felt a wisp of her hair catch on the man's nails as they swept by her face. "Stop it!" she screamed. She balled her fists and charged the man, knocking him down as she hit him with the force of her body while her fists flew wildly in his face. She brought a knee up and it found its way to the man's groin. The man yelled and she saw him tumble out of the way and hit the ground.

"The darkness will swallow you," he bellowed. "The darkness will swallow you and you will never see the light again."

Nora ran with all she was worth toward the tunnel. She had to step up almost four feet to enter it. She hoisted herself up and looked around. It was unlike anything she had ever seen before. Its walls were like glass and somehow a faint light emanated from them. The floor was hard and seamless. She started to run, and after she felt sure that she had distanced herself, she looked back once and saw that Satan was standing in the entrance. She started running again and with each step descended deeper into the earth.

33

Elisha BenHassen sat next to the Major deep beneath the streets of Tel Aviv. He had been many times to the specially designed bunker that housed the Israeli intelligence community and combined branches of the armed forces. The brightest and most well trained men and women that the tiny country could muster staffed this enormous underground room, maintaining a vigilant watch on its neighbors.

Because of the threat of missiles that could reach Israel in a matter of minutes, intercepting jets patrolled the Israeli air space and tactical antimissiles were dispersed in hidden locations throughout the country, both in the north and the south. Nuclear submarines patrolled the Israeli coastline and had the capability to intercept incoming missiles, as well as launching a preemptive strike.

The room was buzzing, as it appeared that an undeclared coalition was massing weapons and troops for what appeared to be an all-out offensive. The country had gone from a yellow alert, where it had been for much of the last decade, to a level 3 RED, indicating the strong possibility of an attack. Level 2 RED indicated a conventional war had commenced. Level 1 RED indicated the unthinkable, a nuclear or biological exchange.

"How certain are we that the Russians have moved their mobile nuclear missiles on the border of Turkey?" Elisha asked.

"Look for yourself," the Major said, and he used a laser pointer on the immense digital map in front of the room that showed the latest satellite image of the Middle East. He picked up a phone. "Give me a close-up on the force along the Turkish border," he asked.

The picture on the digital map changed to the close-up that the Major had requested. "You can see the mobile launchers sitting just off the road, yes?" the Major asked.

Elisha stared at the map. "They're not even trying to camouflage them," he remarked. There was no doubt that something was happening. "What about the troop movements in Iran?"

"The Iranian ambassador has assured us that these are just exercises. But we don't believe it."

"Especially since these war games are being conducted with the Egyptians, the Syrians, and Lebanon."

"Has the prime minister considered a preemptive strike?" Elisha asked.

The Major shook his head. "It's being discussed, but the Americans are pressuring us to stand down. They've had their diplomats clogging the phone lines for the last twenty-four hours since all of this began."

"How much time do we have *if* Iran launches their missiles?" Elisha asked.

"Less than eight minutes, but we've been prepared for that. We've had our intercepts on the ready since they launched their first successful tests."

"What's Damascus saying?" Elisha asked.

"They're feeding us the same line that Iran has given us. War exercises, nothing more."

"Major," Elisha began, "I know we have had long discussions over the years about the God of our fathers. And I know that you are . . . agnostic, and I certainly respect that, but I can't sit here looking at this massing of troops and not think of a passage of Scripture."

The Major smiled. "We have known each other since our war of independence. We have fought side by side, buried our loved ones, and seen the succession of two generations . . . over fifty years, and I have listened to you because you and I are brothers. So, as always, I am listening," he quipped.

Elisha began, "As I was saying, there is a portion of Scripture that speaks of a war against Jerusalem, where a coalition of armies that attack the city are defeated. Are you aware that the way in which the armies of this coalition are defeated sounds very much like a nuclear exchange?"

The Major shrugged. "You've mentioned this before, but not the particulars."

"Ezekiel chapter 38 talks about this gathering of armies and those armies descending upon Jerusalem. In another Scripture, Isaiah 17, it discusses the destruction of Damascus. There are those of us who have kept watch on this, aware of the prophecy foretold in these Scriptures, and many of us believe that they might be describing the same event. Still, in another portion of Scripture, Zechariah, it may describe a chilling portrayal of the event. The enemy soldiers' eyes rot in their sockets and their tongues melt in their mouths while they are standing. What does that sound like to you?"

"A neutron bomb, but that would mean . . ." The Major scowled.

"Yes," Elisha interrupted, "that these Scriptures written thousands of years ago seem to foretell the time we are living in. It speaks of what we, in our time, would consider the unthinkable, and yet here it is, written thousands of years ago, describing the battle vividly."

The Major looked at the digital screen and then back at Elisha. "What you are saying almost makes me wonder *why* the God of Abraham, Isaac, and Jacob would allow such a monstrous thing to happen. Think of the carnage, of the thousands, perhaps millions, of lives that will be lost."

"I agree," Elisha said, "but it has to do with man's free will. God is not forcing the Iranians to go to war with us. Yes?"

The Major frowned. "But if he is a loving God, as you always assure me he is, then why does he allow it? I saw what happened in the camps, in Germany. It is why I have said countless times, to anyone who will listen, 'never again.' I will die with a rifle in my hands before I allow women, children, and old men to be carted off and gassed like unwanted vermin."

"And I will do the same. But you know that is not what I am saying. These prophecies written thousands of years ago are to show us that he *does* care. He has told us things that will happen before they do, so we can believe that he is a God that knows the beginning from the end and the end from the beginning. Think of it this way. These writings are our heritage. Now that the *Diaspora* is over, we have seen our people gathered from the four corners of the earth. We have seen our country reborn, the desert bloom with produce, our language of Hebrew, dead for almost two thousand years, now spoken once again, and our holy city, Jerusalem, under our control. All of this was prophesied and much of it has come to pass."

Tears welled up in the Major's eyes. "How can a loving God allow what happened to my family in Germany at the camps?"

Elisha set his hand on the Major's hand. "I lost loved ones there too; it is the reason I believe what I do. Don't confuse the works of the Evil One with Yahweh. Remember the book of Job."

The Major wiped his eyes and excused himself. Elisha watched him walk out of the room. *He looks old and tired. A man without hope,* he thought, and he returned to studying the map on the wall in front of him.

34

○

"How far is it from here?" Mac asked as he, Johanen, and Fitzpatrick began to search out the only link they had to Nora—that of a homeless person who made his home on a particular park bench.

"Not far. The problem is, he comes and goes. Sometimes I see his shopping cart but he's nowhere in sight. He just leaves it and goes about whatever his business is."

The three men walked along the jogging path in search of the homeless man. A few early morning joggers, bundled up against the cold, ran by. MacKenzie pulled up the collar on his suit jacket and wished he had brought something with more substance to keep out the chill of the fall air. The men quickened their pace and a short time later reached the secluded area that Fitzpatrick described. The dirt path sloped downwards, running through a small clearing in the dense woods. It was hard to imagine that such a rustic place existed in the heart of the city. There was a park bench and an overturned trash can, with trash spread out around it as if someone had been sorting through it.

"He's not here," Mac said as he looked around.

"He probably went to a shelter because of the rain last night," Fitzpatrick stated.

"We shall stay and hope he shows," Johanen said. "There is not much else we can do."

The men stood together on the jogging path. Mac looked up and down, turning his head and shifting his weight from one foot to the other to keep warm and fight off sleep. His eyes felt heavy and his body needed rest.

Then something caught Mac's eye. It was a group of boys, teenagers, cresting the hill and coming down the jogging path toward them.

Mac looked at Fitzpatrick. "Am I supposed to be worried by them?" he questioned, trying to act nonchalant.

Mac saw Fitzpatrick's head go in the opposite direction of what he had hoped the answer would be.

"Stay calm, gentlemen," Johanen said.

"There's three of us and almost a dozen of them," Mac said.

The boys approached, and Mac saw that their ages varied, the oldest being maybe eighteen, and the youngest on the edge of puberty. He singled out the leader—a kid with a scrawny beard, baggy pants, shaved head, and a sweatshirt, sleeves cut revealing a canvas of tattoos on both arms. Mac braced himself, wondering what Johanen had in mind to get them out of what appeared to be imminent trouble. The gang came up to them, and the leader with the shaved head and tattoos snapped his fingers as the other guys spread out and circled them.

The leader pulled out a gun. Waving it in their faces, he demanded, "Give us everything you got in your pockets."

Fitzpatrick put his hand into his pocket in compliance with the leader's wishes while Johanen folded his arms in front of him defiantly.

"Hey you," the leader said to Johanen. "You got ears or what?"

"If you are referring to whether or not I heard your request for money the answer is yes . . . but I must warn you that you are in grave danger."

The leader looked confused. "What do you mean, man? There's nobody here but us. *You* guys are the ones in danger."

Mac heard the others in the gang laugh the kind of laugh that comes from people who are enjoying the upper hand in a situation, thinking that they are invincible because of their superior position.

"No, my friend, *you* are in danger. You are planning to rob us and then go back to your apartment, but what you don't realize is that there are others who are waiting for you there. You owe them money for drugs. And they are going to take what you have stolen from us and then kill you."

Mac saw the leader's jaw drop and his face grow ashen. "How do you know about . . ."

"I assure you, my friend, it will happen."

Mac looked at the other boys, who seemed to have lost confidence, and they looked to the leader for direction.

"I was gonna pay them dudes back, man," the leader stated.

"Yes, but those dudes that you refer to have lost patience with you and are high on methamphetamines. They *will* kill you."

"How you know 'bout all this . . . you some kind of psychic, man?" the leader asked, puzzled, but Mac saw that he had tucked the gun in his belt.

"I am no psychic, as you put it, but I am a man who knows the true and living God, and it is he who has told me these things."

"Come on, man, there ain't no God who cares about all that stuff."

"I assure you, my friend, that he cares about every hair on your head, even if it has been shaved off."

The other gang members cracked up, and some of them relaxed their tough-guy stance.

"What god are you talkin' about, man?"

"The God who knows that you have never met your own father, the God who knows that your mother is an alcoholic and a prostitute, the God who *is,* and can bring new life to you and turn you around."

Silence descended on the group. Mac held his breath but reminded himself that Johanen had resources that were divine in nature.

"You must choose," Johanen said softly. "A door is before you and you may enter. It is, you see, a free-will choice."

The leader's lower lip begin to quiver, then his head dropped to his chest and he began to cry. Johanen stepped forward and wrapped his arms around him.

Within half an hour some of the group had followed their leader's example and had chosen the door that Johanen set before each one. Telephone numbers were exchanged with the promise that Johanen would meet with them in a few days and show the rest of the gang how to get through the door.

Mac looked at Fitzpatrick, whose face was a picture of astonishment and wonder.

The boys left and called out to Johanen, reminding him to call. As they cleared the crest of the hill, a disheveled home-less man passed them.

"There he is," Fitzpatrick said. "See the little Mets' flag on the end of the shopping cart?"

Mac looked at Johanen, who winked at him and said, "God's timetable, MacKenzie. He is never late."

Mac sized up the homeless man. He looked to be about sixty, with a dark matted beard that hung down to his chest and wild black hair. He wore a weather-worn army jacket over dirty overalls. The smell of alcohol preceded the man as the wind was blowing from behind him.

Mac saw Fitzpatrick take a step toward him. He held a five-dollar bill in his hand.

"How you doing?" he asked as he extended his hand that held the bill.

The man nodded and a look of recognition crept into his bleary eyes. He reached out, took the five, and it disappeared into his pants pocket.

"Can you help me find Nora?" Fitzpatrick asked. "She's in trouble, and we have to find her."

The homeless man pushed his cart backward. "I don't want no trouble," he said, his speech slurred.

Mac looked at Johanen, who had remained silent. *Why doesn't he do something?* Mac wondered.

Fitzpatrick produced another bill and held it out in front of him. The homeless man tried to grab it, but he was too far away. The man pushed the cart forward, but Fitzpatrick held the bill just out of his grasp.

"I'll give it to you if you show us where Nora is," Fitzpatrick said again.

The homeless man rubbed his eyes with both hands. "I haven't seen her in a couple of days," he said as he held his hand out.

"Can you show us where she stays?" Fitzpatrick asked again, still holding the bill as bait.

"She's one of them . . . mole people . . . lives in the subways," the man stated.

"Which subway?" Fitzpatrick asked again.

The homeless man pointed down the jogging path. "Where 70th Street crosses over just before it turns and runs down Grover. There's an alley . . . and then a vacant lot. I've seen her go in there and then over the fence to the subway."

"Do you know the place?" Johanen asked.

"Yes," Fitzpatrick answered, "I go by it on my runs." He handed the man the money.

"Why you want to talk to her? She's crazy," the homeless man asked.

"She needs our help," Fitzpatrick said, as he started off down the path at a steady jog.

Thirty minutes later Mac found himself in an alley that led to the vacant lot the homeless man had described.

"Look at that, MacKenzie, Fitzpatrick," Johanen said, as he knelt down beside the body of a dead dog at the end of the alley. "This has been done very recently."

"It looks like somebody twisted the dog's head and broke its neck," Mac said.

"Look here," Fitzpatrick called from an abandoned car. "This is her stuff, I'm positive."

"I think our enemy, Wyan, has been here," Johanen said. "Nora must have been here and he found her."

Mac followed Johanen to the car.

"It's the same bedroll I saw when she was in my apartment," Fitzpatrick stated.

"Maybe the dog was trying to protect her," Mac suggested.

"It does look that way, MacKenzie," Johanen replied, as he went over to the fence. "This is where she climbed over," he said, pointing to the tires stacked against the side of the chain link. "Let us go." He pulled himself over the fence and dropped to the other side. Fitzpatrick was next. He struggled to get his balance and then tore his jacket as it caught on the top of the fence. Mac scrambled over the fence and joined the men on the concrete embankment.

"We have to go down there?" Fitzpatrick asked, pointing to the steep slide that led to the tracks.

A train rolled out of the tunnel and went past them thirty feet below. Mac saw the top of the cars as they sped by.

"This way, gentlemen," Johanen called, and without waiting for an answer, slid down the concrete. He landed on his feet and dusted himself off.

"You go," Mac said. "I'll bring up the rear."

Fitzpatrick started off slowly trying to maintain control, which he lost after a few feet. He picked up speed and almost went over headfirst, but caught himself at the last minute. He skidded the rest of the way on his back and came to a stop at the bottom. Johanen helped the man up.

Mac followed, sliding down the concrete embankment and landing squarely on both of his feet. "Now where?" he asked.

"In there, I suppose," Fitzpatrick said, rubbing his hands, which were scraped and a little bloody from the fall.

Mac looked at the dark entrance to the subway tunnel. "Let's do it," he said.

The three men jogged toward the entrance.

"Watch out for the third rail," Johanen warned as he explained the danger of the track and how it carried enough electricity to kill a man.

Mac entered the tunnel behind Fitzpatrick and Johanen, in single file, walking at a brisk pace. The first thing he saw was a large mural depicting a firing squad. He thought he recognized the painting. "That looks familiar," he said.

"It's Goya's *Third of May*," Fitzpatrick called over his shoulder. "Good reproduction, considering it was done with spray paint. We have some amazing graffiti artists."

"Train," Johanen called. He led the men to the wall, where they pressed their backs against the concrete.

Mac viewed the train as it sped by, its lighted windows filled with morning commuters. They continued on after it passed. The smell of urine and feces was very strong near the entrance, but lessened as the trio traveled farther into the tunnels.

This woman could be anywhere, Mac thought, as they continued even deeper into the subway system.

"Someone is coming," Johanen said. The men stopped and huddled together.

Mac peered into the semidarkness and saw the silhouette of two men coming toward him. The men were talking rapidly, and they sounded agitated. They drew closer, and Mac noted that they were young black men, maybe in their early twenties, and both had the look of someone strung out on some mixture of narcotics and alcohol.

"Hey man, what you guys doin' here?" slurred one of the men, who seemed to have a glass eye.

"You undercover cops or somethin'?" said the other man, wearing a faded red bandanna.

"No," Johanen said, "we are searching for someone, a young woman. Her name is Nora."

250 / *L. A. Marzulli*

"What you want to know 'bout her?" Glass Eye asked.

"We are here to help her. Her life is in danger," Johanen stated.

Mac saw the two men look at each other for a moment.

"What if we tell you we saw some crazy chick come runnin' through here 'bout an hour ago?" Bandanna said.

"Some tall guy was lookin' for her. Scared everybody real good, he did," Glass Eye added.

"Why did the tall man scare you?" Johanen asked.

"Shoot, man, the guy had a nasty look to him, big scar across his eye and everythin'. He freaked us out real good."

"Guy made my skin crawl ... nasty dude," Bandanna added.

"He was chasing the woman you mentioned, but she was too smart for him. She duck into one of the side tunnels and he didn't see her do that."

"I've seen her before," Glass Eye said. "She been hangin' out with a homie of ours, guy named Jerry."

Mac saw Bandanna elbow Glass Eye.

"Shoot, man, you tellin' them too much. Let's get outta here. They prob'ly cops or somethin'."

Before Johanen could ask anything else the men had moved on.

"Which tunnel did she go into?" Fitzpatrick called.

"The one down the tracks a ways ... goes to the right," Bandanna called out.

Mac brought up the rear as the men hurried until they saw the spur that headed off to the right. They followed the new tunnel. The lighting here wasn't as good as the main tunnel where they had entered, and many bulbs were missing or broken. They made their way cautiously for what seemed to be a half a mile or so, staying close to the side of the tunnel, and always taking care to avoid the third rail.

The spur connected with another line, and here the visibility was better. They followed this line around a large curve and saw a fire with a group of men gathered around it along the side of the tracks. They reminded Mac of vigilantes, as the men held an array of weapons: broom handles, baseball bats, and chains. They were huddled around a fifty-gallon drum with a fire burning in it.

"We had better be careful here," Johanen said, "Something has frightened them, and I am inclined to think that they have had an encounter with Wyan."

The three men approached cautiously.

"Who are you?" a voice called out from beside the burning drum.

"We are here to help you," Johanen answered.

"You the police?" another voice called out. "'Cause right now we need help."

Mac heard a chorus of voices agree that what they needed was the police.

"No, we are not the police," Johanen said.

For once I wish he wouldn't tell the truth, Mac thought.

They came within twenty-five feet of where the fire was.

A white man holding a baseball bat and wearing worn military fatigues stepped forward. "That's close enough," he said.

Mac stopped next to Johanen.

"We are looking for a woman; her name is Nora."

With the announcement of Nora's name the crowd of armed men erupted into an angry murmur.

"She's the one who brought us all the trouble in the first place," Mac heard someone call from the crowd. The murmuring grew louder.

"What do you want with her anyway?" the man with the army fatigues and the baseball bat asked.

"She is in danger," Johanen replied.

The man took another step toward them. "I'm Tim, and I'm in charge here. You boys know where you are? Know who it is you're dealing with? This is our world, and we have a different set o' rules here. You better just go back the way you came and leave this place."

"Your world is not so different from ours," Johanen said.

Mac saw Tim frown as he tried to think of a comeback.

"What do you mean by that?" Tim asked.

"You have been hurt in the past and so have I," Johanen answered.

Mac saw Tim loosen his grip on the baseball bat. "So . . . who are you, mister?"

"Someone who wants to help you and some of your friends here." Johanen looked around. "A man named Mickey has a really bad toothache."

Mac looked at the crowd of men, who were speechless.

"He's talkin' to you, Mickey," Tim said, as he pointed to one of the men in the rear.

"Come here, Mickey," Johanen said. "Let me take the pain away."

"How did he know about Mickey's tooth?" a few of the men asked each other. The man approached like a wary stray dog.

"Yeah, how did you know 'bout my tooth anyway?" asked Mickey, whose face was covered by a bristle of white stubble. "Can't afford no dentist, like I used to."

Johanen took the man by his arms, which brought about a few murmurs from the other men.

"Be healed in the name of Jesus," he said, as he laid his hand on the man's cheek.

"Hey, I feel somethin' . . . hot like," Mickey said, his eyes opened wide in astonishment.

Johanen continued to pray.

"I don't feel no pain no more," Mickey exclaimed. "It's gone!" The man's face lit up and he actually did a little jig. "I been dealing with my teeth for years." He pulled his cheek back, exposing his teeth. Several were missing.

The men crowded around Mickey and looked in his mouth.

"No more pain at all?" Tim asked.

"No more. You a magician or somethin'?" Mickey asked.

"Would you like to be free of the alcohol?" Johanen asked.

The crowd of men grew silent. Mickey looked down at his feet.

"You can be free. He will set you free if you let him. Just like your tooth," Johanen coaxed.

"I been on the sauce for too long. Nothin' can change that," Mickey said woefully.

"That is a lie that you believe, and it has kept you in bondage for years," Johanen stated.

Mac caught Fitzpatrick's eye, who, with raised eyebrows, indicated that he was being stretched beyond anything he could imagine.

"I want to be free from it . . . but it ain't possible."

Johanen took a step closer to the man and put his hand on his shoulder. "You can be free, but you must choose. You must ask and believe that you can be. You must have faith."

Mickey stared at his feet, then mumbled, "I want to, but I don't have no faith."

"Then admit you don't and ask for it and he will give it to you."

Mac heard the man mumble something, then saw a tear fall from his cheek. Johanen reached out his hand, placed it on the man's head, and began to sing in that strange language that Mac had heard before. Mickey began to tremble, then sway as Johanen continued singing. The man began to fall backward and Johanen grabbed him by the shoulders to let him to the ground gently.

"What did you do to him?" Tim asked.

"I did not do anything. The power of the Lord's Holy Spirit has overcome Mickey. He will be all right in a minute or two. Right now he is meeting his Lord."

All eyes were on Mickey as he lay still on the concrete. Mac saw a smile on the man's glowing face, but Mac wondered if it was a trick of the light from the fire.

A few minutes passed and Mickey stirred. Mac watched as the man opened his eyes, blinked them a few times, and then slowly sat up. "I feel better, like I ain't felt in years. Before I started to . . ." And he burst into tears.

"Know that it was Jesus who has healed you. If the Son makes you free, you shall be free indeed," Johanen said.

Mickey wrapped his arms around himself and nodded.

"Will you help us find Nora?" Johanen asked.

Tim stepped forward, and his face didn't appear as harsh. "We'll help you," he began, "but you got to understand that whatever it was that passed us by was wicked."

"You are correct," Johanen stated, "what came this way *was* wicked, but you have also seen a power that is far greater than that can ever be."

Mac saw the men think about what Johanen said. "Okay. I'll tell you what happened, then." Tim turned to the group, who gave their approval. "Nora came by. I saw her and she was running like she just seen the devil himself. I yelled to her, but she didn't even answer, just kept runnin'. Looked like she was goin' to the lower levels to try to get away from whatever was chasing her. A few minutes later that tall man came and he started yellin' at me. He picked me up before I had a chance to do anything and put me up against the wall, just held me there with one hand. Then his face changed to some-thin' real horrible . . . like a snake or somethin'. I closed my eyes and hollered and then he let me go and was gone. But like I said he went down the wrong tunnel. I went back and got some help and then you all showed up."

Mac felt a tug on his shoulder. "What the heck is going on?" Fitzpatrick whispered as he pulled him away from the group.

"Johanen is healing. It's one of the gifts that the Lord has given him."

Mac saw that Fitzpatrick looked confused. "You don't understand, those things died out in the first century, if they happened at all. I've spent a lifetime studying this and other supernatural phenomena—"

Mac cut him off. "You saw what happened to the possessed man and to that gang and now here to Mickey. How do you explain that? It's not a magic show, you know."

"He's using hypnosis or something."

"Talk to Johanen about them," Mac said, then, nodding toward Johanen, indicated that they should rejoin him.

Tim was speaking. "You'll need flashlights to go after her. I'll send somebody back to the Condos to get you a couple, so you can find Nora." Tim then gave an order to one of the men, who left for the Condos.

"We appreciate that, I assure you," Johanen said. "How far do these tunnels go?"

Tim looked around at the other men. "There's somethin' goin' on down there. It started happenin' a few days ago. New tunnels appearing where they shouldn't be. Strange stuff, and now all this."

Johanen looked at Mac. "It appears that the Enemy is much nearer than I had thought."

Mac gave Johanen an I-don't-know-what-you're-talking-about look.

"I mean that there might be a base here. There have, after all, been sightings. Where do you think these tunnels lead to, MacKenzie?" he asked rhetorically.

Mac looked at Fitzpatrick, wishing on one hand that he were like him, ignorant of what a base was, and knowing the terror that awaited them if they ever found themselves in one. On the other hand, he also knew that without protection, spiritual protection, the ex-priest was a dead man, and in that respect he was glad that he was under the aegis of Johanen.

The runner for the flashlights returned, and Tim took them and handed them to Johanen.

"These will do you fine. I'm gonna go with you until the last level, then you'll be on your own."

"We appreciate your leading us, Tim," Johanen said.

"You might need to eat somethin'. Nothin' down there but track rabbits, and I doubt you want to eat those. We got a box of candy bars that somebody, ah, borrowed. We been eatin' some of 'em, but I want you to have the rest." Tim motioned to one of the men, who fetched the box from the entrance to the Condos. He handed them to Johanen.

"Before I take you to the lower levels, will you say something to all of us? Somethin' good? It's been a long time since we heard somethin' good."

Johanen beamed as he extended his hands over the group of men and began to pray a blessing over them.

35

Elisha BenHassen and his grandson Uri hurried down the corridor leading to the underground control room of the Israeli Defense and Intelligence command center.

Elisha had been awakened at 2:30 in the morning by Uri, who had informed him of further troop movements by countries that the Israelis deemed hostile, regardless of the diplomatic rhetoric decrying otherwise.

Uri had driven them from Elisha's house, on the outskirts of Jerusalem, to Tel Aviv. They had passed through several layers of security and were now deep under the streets of the city. The bunker, which housed the communication network of all combined elements of the Israeli military, had been constructed with the engineering expertise of Americans. The central command bunker was extremely deep and had been reinforced with enough layers of steel and concrete to withstand a direct nuclear hit. Of course the bunker existed to prevent that horrific scenario from ever occuring in the first place.

Elisha spotted the Major and made his way toward him.

"Shalom, shalom," the Major called, as he caught site of Elisha.

Elisha quickened his pace. "Shalom, although I doubt that *peace* is in our immediate future." A touch of sarcasm edged his voice. He noted that the Major had deep black circles under his eyes. "When was the last time you slept?" he asked.

"Look there," the Major said, ignoring his question as he pointed to the large digital map that covered forty feet of wall in front of them.

Elisha studied the enormous digital map that dominated the room, his eyes looking over the heads of almost one hundred men and women, who, sitting at their terminals, directed new intel to the appropriate channels. Phones rang, encrypted communiqués were received, fax lines hummed. Pilots flying reconnaissance reported their positions. Satellites in geosynchronous orbit over the Middle East gave an up-to-the-minute picture of the area.

"That looks like it's developing into something," Elisha stated.

The Major nodded. "You see what is happening. It looks like the Iranians are preparing for an offensive."

"It will be suicide and they know it," Elisha stated. "This isn't '65. Everything is changed."

"Egypt too," Uri added.

Elisha gazed at the map again. "Nothing, compared to Iran."

"True," the Major replied, "but our intel inside Egypt are relaying that something is brewing. They're not sure how big, but they're *very* nervous about it."

"The Russians?" Elisha asked.

"Their president relayed a message to the American president, who in turn talked to our ambassador, who then relayed to the prime minister, that war games are underway between the Iranians and the Russian army."

"Predictable bedfellows," Elisha said. "I wouldn't trust either of the two to play fair in a soccer match."

The men chuckled.

"So what do you think is happening?" Elisha asked, knowing that the Major would never have awakened him unless something of great importance was about to take place.

The Major frowned. Then, taking the laser pointer, he highlighted a portion of the map showing the Russian border with Turkey. "This is something new." He handed Elisha a picture. "This was taken twenty-four hours ago from the satellite."

Elisha stared at the map. "Light infantry . . . maybe a few tanks. Nothing serious."

"Wait till you see what happens," Uri remarked.

"Now look at the large map," the Major said. He picked up a phone by his desk. "Give me the latest infrared view."

Elisha stared at the large digital map on the wall in front of him. The image changed and he saw a dark mass of troops, tanks, and equipment.

"Our intel puts it at close to half a million men. They also have spotted over two dozen mobile nukes. They haven't had war games like this in almost two decades."

"War games with the Iranians?" Elisha mocked. "What if it's the real thing? What if it's an invasion force?"

The Major nodded gravely. "That's one of the reasons you're here, Elisha. The other has to do with what you told me yesterday." The Major looked away for a moment. "About the passage in Scripture and the destruction of Damascus."

"Yes, of course. Let's hope that this is not the case," Elisha said. But he looked at the map and wondered, *Will this bring about the fulfillment of Ezekiel's prophecy?*

36

Von Schverdt was seated at a large table in the private conference room of a group that was known collectively as the Cadre. He felt delighted that he was so close to his long-anticipated goal of bringing about the manifestation of the one who the world would embrace as the Man of Peace. It was only a matter of time before the ideology of the Judeo-Christian god that had enslaved the Western world would be toppled. Of course Lucifer, the true god of this world, would take his rightful place.

The other reason he felt delighted was that he was about to give orders for the destruction of his beloved think tank and everyone inside. The man he had chosen for the task was waiting for his encrypted telephone call, when he would carry out his orders.

He remembered training SS recruits long ago in Germany. The recruits had to raise a puppy from eight weeks old. They would eat with it, sleep with it, take it on long walks, and play with it. Of course these men would eventually become the elite of the German army. They were trained to be merciless killing machines, able to carry out any order without questioning it. It had been Wyan himself who had told Von Schverdt what was necessary to instill that kind of loyalty. He who had initiated the role of the puppy. The recruit would train, and, over time, harden both physically and mentally. He would learn the art of sabotage and various ways of killing another human being. All the while the puppy would grow and become his faithful companion. One day, toward the end of his training, his superior officer would appear in his quarters. The recruit would snap to attention and then the superior would demand that the recruit kill the dog that he had raised and taken care of for the last two years. If the recruit hesitated, it was a sign that he was weak, and he was dismissed from the SS. Most of the men unholstered their sidearms and destroyed the dog without hesitation.

It was that same spirit of death, of killing, that resided in Von Schverdt like a welcome cancer. So when he had given the order to eliminate everyone in the Tank, it was done with anticipation and excitement. There was only one thing left to do, and that was going to be accomplished by Wyan himself— the finding of the disk that somehow had escaped them. Even with his man in the Vatican, Cardinal Fiorre had managed to get it past them, and now look at the trouble it had caused. But Von Schverdt was confident that his master, Wyan, would be victorious. He would find the girl, destroy her, the disk, and that weakling, Fitzpatrick.

Von Schverdt turned his attention to the meeting, just beginning. The lights dimmed and an American member of the Cadre took the floor. The map showed the area of the world known as the Middle East.

"As you can see, our allied forces are massed and ready to attack the nation of Israel. They, of course, will be annihilated by the nuclear arsenal of Israel, and afterward our armada will 'show' itself, and the world will embrace us, because they want peace. General, this will be a perfect Hegelian dialectic: conflict, counter-conflict, and then the resolution we desire." The man deferred to Von Schverdt.

Von Schverdt rose and cleared his throat. He had considered wearing his old uniform for the occasion. To wait so long for this day and not to be in uniform at this moment seemed like a grave infraction. "Gentlemen, we are poised at the most momentous time in history. You know about my project, the one that Mr. Wyan initiated years ago. I have been diligent in my pursuit, have hired the brightest minds, the most gifted scholars, and now everything is ready. My research has shown that the doomsday clock has reached midnight. It is the instability we have longed for. It is the time of *his* coming."

Those at the table broke into spontaneous applause.

Von Schverdt clicked his heels together and bowed, then sat down as the meeting continued. He pulled a cell phone from his coat pocket and punched in the text message which would initiate the explosion to destroy the building and everyone inside. He knew that it would be blamed on terrorists. He had gone out of his way to plant the necessary evidence, insuring that that conclusion would be reached by the FBI and any other agency brought in to investigate.

The text message reply was returned, indicating that his orders would be carried out. Von Schverdt settled back in his chair and listened to the rest of the presentation.

* ◦ *

It all was very simple, really, the man in the BMW thought. *Cash money deposited in a Cayman Island account, a list of materials that were needed to do the job. ID cards, false passports, and anything else I may need, at my disposal.*

He had checked his account that morning and saw that the money had been wired in. He was now four million dollars richer. One thing bothered him, though. Out of all the contracts he had ever taken, this guy, Von Schverdt, gave him the creeps. Even so, a job was a job, and with this one he might be able to retire.

He parked his BMW a block away from the building near Washington, D.C., which he had wired with explosives a week earlier. He opened the glove compartment and took out the radio transmitter that he had put there earlier. It was a pity he couldn't get closer to watch the fall, but with CNN and the Fox News channel, he knew he would get plenty of coverage. It would be good to watch all the chaos over a beer in his hotel room.

* ○ *

Mary sat at her desk inside the Think Tank, wondering what had happened to Fitzpatrick. She hadn't seen him since the night of the Hag's party. In fact, the last time she saw him was with that woman the Hag had introduced him to. She crossed her legs and played with a lock of hair. Staring at her screen, she read data concerning a new outbreak of Ebola in Sierra Leone. *I guess it doesn't matter, now that the clock is already at midnight ... what's another piece of unsettling news?* She typed the rest of the information anyway, and sent it to the Beast so that the computer could factor it into the mix. She thought again of Fitzpatrick, and wondered why he never made a move toward her.

* ○ *

The man in the BMW turned the transmitter on and then flipped the switch. A red light blinked three times, giving him thirty seconds to abort before it stopped blinking. He ignored it. The light stopped blinking and stayed on, bright red. Hearing a rumble in the distance, he felt the shock wave hit the car and vibrate it out of its parking spot. He giggled like a boy on a roller coaster. Looking around, he saw the panicked faces of pedestrians and motorists. People were swept off their feet by the shock wave. Cars collided into one another. The sidewalks buckled, and two schoolgirls were thrown to the ground, screaming.

Starting the car, he made his way out onto the street, away from the catastrophe he had caused.

* ○ *

Mary got up from her desk and headed toward the lounge wanting a refill on her coffee. She saw Zach seated at one of the two tables with his feet propped up on a chair. His clip-board was in front of him and he was making notes. It was then that she heard a rumble that seemed to come from directly under her. She looked at Zach and opened her mouth, about to comment on what the sound might be. The floor shuddered, and the noise grew louder. Then the floor erupted in a bright flash, and Mary and Zach, along with everything around them, were incinerated in a blinding ball of white-hot fire.

✳ ○ ✳

The man in the BMW was stuck in a traffic jam he had helped create, and it took him over an hour to drive across town to his motel. He parked his car and entered his room, where he ordered a beer from room service. He sat at the mirror and took off his disguise. A different nose, fat and bulbous, was removed—his was aquiline. A brown wig came off next, exposing his shaved head. Brown-colored contacts; his eyes were gray. False teeth gave his jaw and mouth a different look. He washed his face and patted some aftershave on it.

He sat on the bed, propped up a couple of pillows, and channel-surfed between CNN and the Fox News channel. The coverage was excellent on both. Already, fingers were point-ing to another hit by al-Qaida. He was amazed at how fast the pundits and commentators collected—like vultures around a carcass. He saw close-ups of the devastation. Fire trucks were still trying to get the flames under control. The city streets were gridlocked, and the White House, the Senate, and the House of Representatives had been evacuated as a pre-cautionary measure.

A knock sounded on his door and he rose from his chair to answer it. "Who is it?" he asked.

"Room service," a voice called out.

He opened the door as he reached in his pants pocket for a tip, eyeing the beer longingly.

He heard a tiny popping sound, felt something white-hot hit his midsection. He was stunned as he stumbled back through the door into the room. He saw the porter take the gun from the underside of the tray and point it at him. He held his stomach, which was oozing blood. Gasping for air he managed to say, "No, wait. I've got money."

The man smiled and fired the gun again. To his horror he realized that the hit man was toying with him as the bullet slammed into his kneecap. He yelled and rolled on the floor. Another shot hit him in the arm. The next shot hit him in the lower back. Now all feeling was gone. He tried to lift his arms and realized he couldn't. He was paralyzed. The bullet had severed his spinal column.

"No . . . wait . . ."

The hit man lingered a moment. Then he reached down for the beer and took a long sip.

"Wait . . ."

The hit man raised his gun, fired once more, and the room was suddenly very still, except for the sound of a digital camera clicking away.

* o *

Von Schverdt was seated in his limo. It was night. His radio was on and the top story of the evening was the explosion of a government building in Washington, D.C. The reporter was blaming al-Qaida for this most recent act of terrorism. Von Schverdt held the pictures Bruno had given him, looking at each one, enjoying the close-ups of the wounds, the blood, the twisted face in agony at death. It was almost like war. Oh, how he missed it!

"Very nice work, Bruno. This will be your puppy dog, like we used to say, *ja?*" He laughed as the car continued out of the city toward his mansion.

37

❖ ◯ ❖

Nora ran farther down into the tunnel. The thing seemed to go on forever at a slight angle. *This is easy because it's all downhill,* she thought as she loped along. She stopped after a minute and listened, gasping a bit as she caught her breath. Silence. Looking at the inside of the tunnel, she reached out and touched the walls for the first time. *Who made this thing?* she wondered. The walls were cool to the touch, and somehow a faint light emanated from them, allowing her to see her way.

Her breathing back to normal, she listened again. This time she could hear the muffled hum of something low, sounding like it came from deep beneath her. She had the feeling that the tunnel would lead her to whatever the noise was.

Leaning up against the wall, she wondered what was going to happen to her. She recalled a memory that she was never quite sure was real. There was a fire in the house and somebody was yelling. "Help me . . . help me." She hadn't meant for the thing to get out of hand. It had just happened. She didn't understand about the lighter fluid. She had squirted it all over the living room rug and then lit one end of it. She saw the flames follow the trail, growing brighter and larger all the time. There was smoke everywhere, and the walls were on fire. She saw the paint peel off the walls, the wallpaper smolder and turn black. Her stuffed toy was engulfed in flames and she wanted to reach out to get it, but the fire kept her from doing so. Then somebody grabbed her and carried her out of the building. They left her all alone in a room for a long time. There was a table and they strapped her to it and put something on her head and she felt hot stuff course through her body. She yelled and screamed and still it tingled every nerve. One day she found a bobby pin and used it to open the lock on a closet door in the building. It seemed to come naturally to her. She could feel the tumblers clicking, and in a few minutes had the door open, and was rummaging through its contents.

But here, in this tunnel, all the bobby pins in the world couldn't help her get out. She felt the disk thingy in her pocket, and wondered what all the fuss was about it. Then she heard something behind her again, far back in the tunnel from where she had come. She knew who it was, what it was, and it terrified her. She had seen it kill Boy, the dog, and knew it would do the same to her. With that thought she bolted farther down the tunnel.

38

Wyan scanned the tunnel ahead and listened. The girl had proved to be elusive, feral and cunning. He hadn't anticipated such strong resistance, and to complicate matters, the Enemy had sent a nemesis to thwart his every move. Hadn't Johanen stopped him from what he needed to accomplish at the Vatican? Hadn't Johanen warned the ex-priest, protecting him from one of Lucifer's minions in the restaurant? And he had almost succeeded in killing the lost, unprotected soul in his apartment, before Johanen came to his rescue.

He touched the place where the bullet had entered his body and noticed, to his satisfaction, that the wound had completely healed itself. It was wonderful to be immortal. Not like the humans who had cheapened life by their sheer numbers. Wasn't this the primary reason that the prince, Lucifer, had rebelled? The idea that the gift of life would be bestowed on something as trivial as a human was preposterous. After all, he wasn't much more than an intelligent ape, was he? No, Lucifer had been right. How could *he* have belittled *us* so with such a cheap creation? It had been right to rebel and he was glad of it. In this world of men he was very powerful, and when the change occurred he would take his place as one of those to be worshiped by the seed of Adam. Next to Lucifer, he would be the highest.

The thought filled him with pride and made him even angrier at not finding the girl. He let out a loud growl as he changed from Mr. Wyan to his true form, that of a reptilian-looking creature, Azazel. He ran down the length of tunnel, eating up the distance between himself and the girl he sought.

Sniffing the air, Azazel picked up the girl's scent as well as another. He ran quickly, his claws leaving faint prints in the dirt next to the tracks. Arriving at the lowest point of the tunnels, a place where the trains had not run in decades, he smelled the air again and caught the scent of the other person. He did not detect fear in its smell, and then he knew. This person was possessed by one of the lesser ones, a demon.

He drew closer and distinguished the figure of a man approaching him.

"What is your name?" Azazel asked when they were three feet apart.

"We are many here," the man cried out, and then fell to the ground, his head touching the dirt.

"Did she come this way?"

"Yes, master, she was here. Not long ago."

"Where did she go?"

"In there." The man pointed with his arm toward the new tunnel.

"Guard this place. There will be others who will follow. Stop them any way you can."

"Yes, master," the man said as he groveled at Azazel's feet. "We will guard it with our lives."

Azazel leaped into the tunnel. *This is good. She is already ours, for she will follow this path until she reaches the end, where I will have her and the disk.*

Azazel, Mr. Wyan, the Fallen Angel, gathered air into his lungs and let out a deep growl that echoed through the tunnel toward the girl he knew he would eventually find and kill.

39

❖ ⬤ ❖

Elisha BenHassen sat at one of the computer terminals deep under Tel Aviv, Israel. "We have more movement from the Iranians," he said to Uri, who occupied the terminal next to him.

"Yes, I see that, Grandfather. I received a call from our consulate who had contact with the Iranians a few minutes ago. They assure us that this is just war games with the Russians."

"What are the Americans saying?" Elisha asked the Major, who sat on his right at another terminal.

The Major's jowls twitched as he shook his head. "We have been in constant contact with them. They tell us that their ambassador has contacted his Iranian counterpart who assures us that ... "

Elisha joined in unison, "That it is just war games."

Uri continued, "What is bothering me is the Russians. Why would they be sending so many troops toward us? Why so many tanks and men?"

The Major looked at his screen, then answered, "It has all the makings of a full-fledged attack, although I can't imagine why they would do it."

Uri speculated, "Perhaps a force that they don't know about is guiding this. As I said earlier, if this is the fulfillment

271

of Ezekiel's prophecy, then we should see a confederacy of armies. What worries me, though, is that the lineup is there. The modern-day names for the countries mentioned in the prophecy are Iran, Turkey, Libya, Ethiopia, and, of course, Russia. Everyone is accounted for."

"How can you be so sure that it is accurate?" the Major asked.

"We have the Torah and the Dead Sea Scrolls that show us that the wording is the same. What was prophesied thousands of years ago might be unfolding before our eyes."

"If you were me, what would you do? A preemptive strike?"

Elisha shook his head. "No, that would start World War III. Every Arab in the world would march against us, and who could blame them?"

"But we can't sit here and allow them to position enough men to knock us into the sea," Uri stated.

"Does the Torah say anything about what we should do?" the Major asked.

Elisha frowned and pushed his trifocals up on his nose. "Not directly. It does discuss what happens after the battle. The forces are wiped out and no one touches the bodies for six months. After that time, people are sent out to mark where the bones are. Then others are sent to gather the bones and bury them."

"Yes, it sounds like the aftermath of a nuclear exchange. How long ago was that written?" the Major asked.

"About three thousand, five hundred years ago," Elisha replied. "Here's something else. Remember the scroll that was given to the American, MacKenzie? It was translated this morning."

"But I thought . . . ," Uri began.

"That it was stolen?" Elisha interrupted.

Uri nodded.

"Johanen thought the Cadre would come after it. He switched the real one with a counterfeit. Not even MacKenzie knew of the ruse."

"So . . . what does it say?" Uri asked.

"Yes, do you have a copy of the translation?" the Major said.

"I have a copy here." Elisha touched the breast pocket of his jacket. "But we should go somewhere private. What is contained in the scroll bolsters the idea of the Great Deception that Johanen has talked to me about for more than a decade."

"Why would the Russians join the fray?" the Major asked, as the men got up to find a secure location.

"Scripture tells us that God himself puts a hook in their jaw and draws them into the fray," Elisha said. "The text makes it clear that they are a reluctant combatant. Now with the killing of the Iranian cleric and the Muslim world calling for *jihad*, we may be looking at the window of time in which these things happen."

"They also supply Iran with much of their military equipment," Uri added.

"Which is why they will lose if they come up against us. Remember what happened to the MIGS?" the Major quipped.

"Even so, the Russians will come, and they will be defeated."

The men found a room and, going in, locked the door behind them.

Elisha took the paper from his pocket. "We're not certain how old the scroll is. Only that it predates the Dead Sea scrolls by almost one thousand years and is written in a very old style of Hebrew lettering. The author describes the city of Jerusalem in the last days, telling of an invasion force that comes against the city. But what to me is the most chilling is the last sentence, which states: 'Hundreds of silver disks fly over the skies of Jerusalem at the end of the great battle.'"

The Major rubbed his eyes, then whispered, "UFOs."

Elisha looked into the eyes of the Major, then said, "My God, may it not be so . . ."

40

* ◯ *

"We're almost there," Tim said, as he led Johanen, Fitz-patrick, and MacKenzie down the labyrinth of tunnels. Mac followed last.

"When was the last time these things were used?" Mac asked.

"They haven't had trains on 'em since before I came here and I been here a while now," Tim answered.

"All this is unused?" Mac asked.

"Yep. It's a dead line. Goes nowhere now."

"How far before we get to this mystery tunnel you told us about?" Fitzpatrick asked.

"Not far now, but I'm gonna warn you. We might run into Satan—he's the one I told you about earlier. All of us mole people stay away from him. He's nothin' but trouble."

"We will see how he fares against the power of the living God," Johanen said.

"This is as far as I go. The tunnel we saw earlier that shouldn't be there, is just ahead, maybe a hundred feet or so," Tim stated.

"Thank you, Tim, you have been a great help to us," Johanen said.

"Some of us was wondering if you could come back after you get done with whatever it is you're gonna do here. We

would like you to come back and, you know, say something
over us again, like you did for Mickey."

Mac nudged Fitzpatrick with one of those are-you-
listening-he's-talking-to-you nudges.

Fitzpatrick shrugged an indifferent shoulder.

He still doesn't get what's happening, Mac thought, and
right there he prayed for the man.

"I promise I will return if I am at all able to," Johanen
replied. "It depends on where this tunnel leads us and what
awaits us there."

"I knew you'd say that you'd come back." Tim grinned.
"Some of the others didn't think so, but I knew you'd say yes.
You're a lot like we heard Jesus was like and that's a good
thing."

Johanen laughed and then put his hand on the man's
shoulder. "Let me bless you, Tim," and he began to pray for him.

Mac said good-bye to Tim and watched as the man disappeared into the darkness.

"Now what?" Mac asked.

"We go forward, MacKenzie, and see what awaits us."

"I have a question." Fitzpatrick, who had been a silent
observer, spoke up.

"Ask away," Johanen replied, as he led the men forward.

"How is it that you seem to be able to heal, and cast out
demons, and know who someone is that you've never met
before, like the hoodlums in the park. Who are you?"

"I have faith. I know what I know, by experience with the
one I serve. It is he who guides my steps."

"Who is *he?* Buddha? Confucius? Krishna? Muhammad?
How do you know *who* it is, who guides your steps?" Fitzpatrick challenged.

"As I said, I know by experience. That is, I know he who is
behind the works that you have seen manifest. I have been
in his service a very long time."

Mac caught a knowing glance from Johanen.

"But how are you able to do it?" Fitzpatrick asked.

Johanen shook his head and frowned. "Many years ago when you were in seminary you studied God's Word." He waited for Fitzpatrick to nod in the affirmative. "You were called once, yes? Heard his voice?"

"But that was . . ."

"That is the voice of the one I serve," Johanen cut him off. "Jesus called you in your heart and you responded. That was real. He touched you and you felt his touch. It made you leave everything to become a priest."

"So what happened to me?" Fitzpatrick asked, and even in the semidarkness Mac saw the ire in the man's face.

"The flame of that experience was slowly snuffed out by all the knowledge you accumulated. As Scripture says, 'knowledge puffs up.' Do not misunderstand me here. I am not saying that knowledge is bad. How would doctors know how to do a heart transplant, or a pilot navigate without it? What I am saying is: Knowledge of God is *not* the same as *knowing* God. The Greek word *genosco*, which is one of my favorite words, means *know by experience*. In fact, the first epistle of John uses this word over forty times."

Johanen winked at Mac as he continued.

"You must understand that you had lots of knowledge about God, but stopped trying to be with him *in relationship*. In plain words, you lost your first love."

Fitzpatrick opened his mouth to reply, but he was interrupted by a hideous scream.

Mac moved closer to Johanen and he noticed that Fitzpatrick did likewise.

"Well," Johanen began, "I see that Satan has come like a roaring lion, seeking whom he can devour. Follow me and stay close. Fitzpatrick, you might consider that this would be a good time to learn to pray again."

41

◆

Nora ran for all she was worth, following the tunnel down into the bowels of the earth. After a while she came to the first intersection. The tunnel she was in branched out and became two. She peered down one and then the other, trying to make up her mind which one she should travel. They were both identical, enormous wormholes created by whom, and for what purpose? The tunnel on her right looked older. It was darker than the other, and the floor wasn't as smooth. Finally, she decided to take the tunnel on her left, and began the descent. As the air grew warmer, she took off her sweatshirt and tied it around her waist.

It was getting harder to think clearly. When was the last time she had taken her pills? She couldn't remember.

The "slip" had come gradually. Right and wrong and good and bad had become relative, something to decide capriciously, on the spur of the moment. But one thing was very clear to her: Keep away from the monster that she had seen at her brother's apartment and again in the vacant lot. *That* was burned into her brain. She wasn't going to lose sight of that, no matter how many pills she missed.

She kept running for another hundred yards or so, and then stopped dead in her tracks. *What's at the end of this?* she wondered. *Maybe there are more monsters and they'll hurt me, or do something worse.* She looked ahead and saw that the tunnel seemed to stretch to oblivion. Hungry, she searched the pockets of her oversized pants to find a half-eaten Snicker's bar, which she ate.

The last part of the candy bar was still in her mouth when she spotted something far ahead, almost where the tunnel closed in on itself and became a vanishing point. There it was again, and it was getting a little larger with every moment. The image emerged, and she could see that it was human, a child. *What is a little child doin' down here?* she thought, as she started to walk toward it, realizing that if she could see it then it could also see her.

As she drew closer Nora knew that she was right, that it was indeed a child, but a very strange-looking one. The child's head was deformed, larger than the rest of its body, and its eyes were bigger than they should have been and almond-shaped. Its wispy hair was blond, almost white, and long. It had the weirdest color of skin Nora had ever seen—a very light gray—making the child look sick. It wore a dirty, one-piece jumpsuit that hugged its body like a second layer of skin. Nora couldn't decide whether it was a boy or a girl. She drew a little closer. "Hello," she said, and her voice echoed over and over again in the distance.

The child held its skinny finger to its thin lips in the universal sign to be quiet. It turned and looked back at her, a silly grin on its face, as it motioned for Nora to follow.

Nora started after it, and no matter how fast or slow she walked, the gap between the two remained the same. It almost seemed that it had eyes in the back of its head.

Nora followed for a long time. She rubbed the sweat from her eyes and, for a moment, lost sight of the entity that she followed. When her vision cleared she saw, to her amazement, that the creature had stopped and was waiting for her. She was about to say something when it gave the signal to be quiet again. Then it turned around and started off down the tunnel once more, Nora trailing behind.

After a while another series of forks lay in front of them. The child entered a tunnel that appeared to be darker than the rest. Nora watched the willowy figure disappear, but she was afraid to follow it, and hesitated. After a minute it reappeared. It had the same goofy smile on its face, and motioned for her to follow.

Nora shook her head, the universal sign for no. Then something really weird happened. The creature was immediately standing beside her, but she hadn't seen it move. It was almost like it had jumped from one space to another in an instant. Startled, Nora tried to take a step back. The child reached out and took her hand. She recoiled at first from its touch. The skin was soft and clammy and the fingers seemed like they had no strength in them.

A picture of her eating ice cream flashed in Nora's mind. Looking down at the child, she realized that somehow it had put that thought into her mind. She giggled, and the being smiled at her.

Then the child produced something that reminded her of chalk. Bending down, it drew some strange letters on the floor of the tunnel. Then it drew a picture of itself and offered the chalk to Nora. She tentatively took the chalk and printed her name, correctly spelled, except that the letter *R* was reversed. The child smiled again, and Nora noticed that it had only a few teeth and that these were small and pointed, like a puppy's.

The child pointed to the letters that Nora had written and in a very high and strange-sounding voice said, "Nor-ra?"

Nora giggled, which brought about a squeeze from the child, who again put a finger to its lips.

It pointed two fingers at itself and whispered, "Geevneh."

Nora frowned and wondered what kind of a name *Geevneh* was. Then Geevneh pointed to the tunnel where it wanted to go. This time Nora felt at ease and followed the little child into the tunnel.

42

Mac stared in front of him at the shadowy figure swaying in the semiblack passageway.

"The darkness will block your way and your light will be extinguished," the figure called out.

"Wait here," Johanen said as he continued to press forward, stopping when he was less than ten feet from the man that they had all been warned about—Satan.

"What is he going to do?" Fitzpatrick asked.

Mac gave a shrug and ran his hand through his hair. "I have no idea. But I'll tell you one thing. This guy is either going to be healed of the demons that possess him, like the guy in the restaurant, or he's going to be rendered useless in some fashion."

Johanen began praying in that strange unknown language that he spoke.

"What is he saying?" Fitzpatrick asked.

"I don't know, except that every time he goes up against the Enemy he prays in another language."

"How are you holding up?" Fitzpatrick asked.

"I'm exhausted, but getting my second wind . . . but who knows how long that's going to last? How are you . . ."

They heard a terrible scream.

"What *is* that?" Fitzpatrick asked, moving closer to Mac.

"I think Satan has met his match."

"Silence," Johanen thundered to the demoniac.

Satan stopped screaming at Johanen's command, and then began to gag and choke.

"Release him," Johanen commanded. "Release him in the name of Jesus."

Mac took a couple of steps to get a closer look. Satan had collapsed in a heap on the dirt by the entrance to the new tunnel he had apparently been guarding.

"What do you want with us, man of God?" Satan whined.

"Silence is what I have commanded you," Johanen replied, as he moved closer. He extended his hand and touched the man who was possessed. The demoniac started to convulse and then foam at the mouth.

"In the name of Jesus of Nazareth, leave him now," Johanen commanded.

The demon-possessed man bit his tongue and a combination of blood and foaming saliva drooled from his mouth. The man's eyes were opened wide and unblinking. His hands were curled in on themselves and his legs shook on the floor like they were no more than matchsticks.

"We . . . will . . . not . . . leave . . . him . . . ," a deep, guttural voice uttered.

"You who have held this man in bondage for all these years, leave him in the name of Jesus!" Johanen clapped his hands together. Satan became rigid like a corpse. Then the man shook violently and began to convulse again. Johanen bent over, grabbed the man's head in his hands, and began speaking again in the strange language. "You will leave him. I stand in the gap for this man. I will be his kinsman redeemer."

Mac crept up beside Johanen, knelt, and began to pray. He saw Johanen nod encouragement to him. "You must leave him," Johanen repeated.

Mac saw the man stiffen again and for a moment he could have sworn that Satan's body levitated off the floor for a few seconds. Then the man relaxed and pushed himself into a sitting position. He looked at Mac and Johanen. "How did I get here? So many of them . . . so many of them . . ." He shuddered. "Are they gone? Will they come back?"

"They are gone, but you must renounce them. You must not allow them to come back again. They will try, and when they do, it will be your faith in Jesus that will drive them away and keep them at bay."

"Jesus . . . I saw him here," the man stuttered. "He was here and he called to me. He had a sword in his hand. He cut me free from them . . ."

Mac glanced back at Fitzpatrick, who, with arms folded over his chest, looked disturbed and confused by what had just transpired.

"I'm going to send you out of here. This man's name is MacKenzie, and he will lead you to a place where you can rest."

Mac saw the man nod and then try to stand on his feet.

Johanen helped him up. "Do you think you can find your way, MacKenzie?"

"Yeah, I do. I can also try to get some more food from Tim when I reach the Condos."

"Then take him there and return as quickly as you can to Fitzpatrick and me here. And MacKenzie—pray over him continuously. Hurry now."

"I'm MacKenzie," Mac introduced himself. "Are you ready to go?"

The man rubbed his eyes. "I don't want to. I want to stay with him," and he pointed to Johanen.

"I will return to see you. I have also promised a man named Tim that I would return to see him when I have finished my business here. You will be in his care until I come. Now go with MacKenzie," Johanen said.

Mac helped the man take the first few steps. "Lucky me," Mac said, as he guided the man past Fitzpatrick, who gave him a reluctant nod. Mac began to retrace his steps toward the Condos, never once stopping his praying.

43

✣ ◉ ✣

Azazel ran in long strides down the tunnel chasing the girl, Nora. He stopped for a moment and sniffed the air. *The woman isn't far off. She is fearful, and that is good. Fear will eat at her mind and creep in like a virus, choking out any hope that may remain.*

Continuing, he soon arrived at the same Y in the tunnel that Nora had come to a while before. He sniffed the wind and saw that the woman had taken the fork on the left, but he wasn't exactly certain where that leg of the tunnel ran. Although he had helped create the complex of tunnels that ran under the earth, connecting the continents, these were new and had been made as probes into the world of men, to help in the breeding program. From here people could be easily abducted and no one would miss them.

He knew, to his satisfaction, that the breeding program was complete. That they had created their vision, attained the perfect hybrid, and that he was very powerful. Azazel had abducted the mother when she was just a child, had collected her eggs and had bred her shortly after her first menstrual period. It had been part of a deal he had made with certain men who longed for the toys he had dazzled them with. *Just like thousands of years ago. How little the whims of men change . . . they will sell their birthright for a bowl of porridge.*

He remembered taking her to his ship at the end of her first trimester, taking the child from her womb. Even then he knew that they had reached their goal. The child was not like the others, sick-looking, or with abnormal-looking eyes and malformations of the hands. This child looked normal and, as it grew, it became strong.

The mother's name was Helen, and he had hoped to sacrifice her, a present to his master. He had thought that nothing could stop him, as the helpless woman was drugged and laid on an altar ready to be sacrificed to Lucifer, the god of force and power. But he had been stopped by his nemesis, Johanen.

Well, now *he* had won. The armies in the Middle East were gathered together and they would attack, with only a handful of men knowing the *real* reason. He had fomented their anger, stirred their hate, and fueled their prejudice. Now the time had come. With the killing of the Iranian cleric the precarious balance had been tipped. This had been the flashpoint that ignited the smoldering fire of hatred that he had helped build.

He had waited for the world stage to be readied, the breeding program fulfilled. Now he and the others were on the verge of what they had all sought: the worship of men. The war would annihilate entire armies, and, seeing the devastation wrought, the world would cry out for peace. He and his superman would have the answers.

Azazel picked up his pace. He wanted to get the girl and the disk, and then hand her over to some of his underlings to have some fun with her. He growled loudly and felt satisfied as the force of it filled his ears.

44

Elisha BenHassen sipped his coffee and stared at the digital map of the Middle East. He had sorted through over a hundred e-mails that had been sent to the Major from different branches of intelligence that the Israeli government had scattered all over the globe.

"It is as I feared, Uri." Elisha waved a stack of encrypted e-mails at Uri. "Most of our people, embedded in the very countries that claim they are just doing war exercises, are saying that they believe an attack on our nation is imminent."

"Look at the latest satellite imagery," Uri responded. "Things look like they are heating up."

"We have a very interesting post from the Jordanian king," the Major began. "He is being very forthright, saying he believes the Iranians are preparing to launch their missiles."

"But why would they do that? A nuclear exchange is unthinkable." Elisha slapped his palm down on the stack of e-mails.

"The ayatollahs run the country. It is their version of Islam. They hate us and want to see us annihilated. The new ayatollah has whipped the country into a frenzy—just when it started to look like there might be some reform," the Major replied.

"Many students were killed and hundreds more imprisoned for protesting that repressive regime," Uri added.

"Still, to imagine that they would take the step from which there is no turning back . . ." Elisha's voice trailed off and the men were silent for a moment.

"The Americans are doing their best to hold everything together," the Major stated. "Our intelligence has it that there is some deal in the works for billions."

"Another ransom similar to what happened in North Korea?" Elisha asked.

"Yes, but there is one difference. Iran has huge oil reserves; they don't need the money. So far the deal is a no-go," the Major stated.

"What about Damascus?" Elisha asked.

"They're involved and so is Lebanon, Turkey, and, of course, the Russians."

Elisha produced a worn Bible from his coat pocket and turned to the book of Ezekiel. "It's all here," he said, handing it to the Major. "The names of the countries have changed, but the geographic locations are the same, and so are the armies that are mentioned. This could be it."

"So how do you think this will play out?" he asked. "Is this the Armageddon that the Christian fundamentalists in America are always talking about?"

Elisha adjusted his trifocals, sipped his coffee, and silently asked the Lord for wisdom. For the first time in over fifty years the Major was listening with a different ear, because of the prophecy that was seemingly being fulfilled.

Elisha cleared his throat and began. "This is different from Armageddon. This war might be the war that allows the person whom the Bible calls 'the Antichrist' to rise to power. Think of it this way . . ." And he began to elaborate.

45

Nora followed the child, Geevneh, into a tunnel that branched off from the main one they had been in. This tunnel was much smaller, and Nora had to duck in several places to keep from hitting her head. They came to the end, and Nora wondered where Geevneh had led them. The child placed a hand on the rock wall and a door opened in front of them. They walked through, and to Nora's surprise, found herself back at the old tunnel, the one she had decided not to enter. She wondered why she wasn't afraid of this weird-looking childlike creature who was leading her to who-knows-where.

The tunnel that she now found herself in looked to be older than the others she had traveled through. The walls were darker and not as smooth. The light that somehow shone from the tunnels' sides was also dimmer. The child, Geevneh, stopped and faced Nora.

It pointed to itself and said its name again, "Geevneh."

Nora was taken aback by the way Geevneh's voice sounded, so squeaky and set in such a high octave that Nora found it hard to hear.

"Nora," she said following suit.

"You . . . lost?" Geevneh said, its mouth barely moving, making it look really strange.

Nora thought for a moment. "Yes, I don't know where I'm going." She overpronounced each word, making sure that Geevneh understood. Then the thought hit her and she voiced it. "What are *you* doing here?"

Geevneh hung its head, the straggly hair covering the dark slanted eyes.

"I no one want to me," Geevneh said.

Nora had trouble understanding. "Say that again, will ya?"

Geevneh picked its head up and stared at Nora. Nora suddenly felt uncomfortable and looked away, but before she did, several pictures filled her mind. Disturbing scenes of tall beings taking care of smaller creatures that looked like Geevneh, but different. They were taller, healthier, and appeared almost human, whereas Geevneh looked like something out of a freak show.

"Did you show me that picture just now?" Nora asked, wondering how Geevneh was able to do such a thing.

Geevneh nodded and then looked in her eyes again.

This time Nora held Geevneh's gaze for maybe half of a minute, until her head started to hurt, making her look away. Pictures appeared in her mind, visions of another place, an alien place, that seemed to be not of this world. She saw many childlike creatures that were of all different ages. She saw what looked like a huge cavern that was under the earth, and inside were silver disks, space ships, that came and went in the underground city. But the thing that really disturbed her and made her afraid was that there were men and women like herself that appeared to have been taken against their will. These people were being experimented on by the creatures. Nora shuddered as she remembered being probed by lots of doctors and undergoing test after test. The worst of all being the metal hat they had made her wear, the hat that stung her and made every nerve in her body scream out in agony.

The people in the vision looked scared. She wondered if she, too, should be scared. After all, this was an awful lot like the monster that Jerry said he saw by the tracks that one day.

But it's just a child, and it can't hurt me anyways, Nora thought as she scrutinized the frail child who barely came up to her shoulder.

"No want me," Geevneh said, "too different than you," and it pointed a spindly finger at her.

"You're not that different, are you?" Nora said. Then, peering more closely at Geevneh she added, "I guess you are a little different, but I'm different too. Some people think I'm crazy, and I suppose they're right 'cause if I don't take my pills, then . . ." She stopped and looked down the length of tunnel.

"Small everywhere," Geevneh said and used its hand to compare height with Nora.

Nora looked down, noticing for the first time that the child's clothes were worn and dirty. They also appeared to be made out of a material that she hadn't seen before.

"You come my home," Geevneh said. "Food."

Nora nodded and rubbed her stomach. "Food," she repeated.

The two set off again down the tunnel, side by side. Soon they found themselves in a portion of the tunnel that had fallen in. The roof had buckled and the sides seemed to have collapsed, like a crushed soda can. The stuff the tunnel was made of was buried under a mound of dirt and rocks. But a small tunnel had been made through the rubble.

Geevneh got down and started to crawl through the opening, then motioned for Nora to follow. It disappeared and Nora was left standing alone. She looked into the place where Geevneh had crawled and saw that it was dark. Somehow the light that had come from the tunnel was broken and whatever lay beyond was submerged in darkness.

Nora hesitated, then heard a sound that made her skin crawl. It rolled through the tunnel system, filling every space with its sound, splitting itself at the intersections while moving forward. It seemed to Nora that the sound was looking for her as it grew louder. It rang for a moment all around her, and then dissipated.

Geevneh appeared beside her, agitated and, like herself, fearful of the sound. It pulled at her clothes and pointed to the opening that passed through the rubble.

"Geevneh show home . . . be safe."

Nora saw it scamper through the opening and once again disappear. She didn't hesitate this time, but dove in and scampered after it on her hands and knees. In one place she had to crawl on her belly as the passageway narrowed even more. She saw that someone—she assumed it must have been Geevneh—had stacked the broken pieces of the tunnel and used them for bracing.

The farther she went, the darker it became, and she started to panic when she no longer could see where she was going. "Geevneh, I'm scared," she called out. She felt in front of her, groping to see what was ahead. Her breath came in little pants of fear, and for a moment she stopped moving altogether. Then, a burst of light shone at the end of the crawlway, and she saw Geevneh holding what looked like a stick, and from it came a steady stream of light. She started to crawl again, her confidence bolstered by the light, and soon she reached the end.

"Little more way, then home," Geevneh said, and started walking down the portion of tunnel that was still in good condition, except that no light came from its walls. Nora brushed herself off and followed. The tunnel turned sharply to the left, and at the turn Nora saw a round room, perhaps three times the width of the tunnel itself. There was a place to sleep and it was filled with the things that Nora had seen lots of mole people use. In fact, it looked like a mole person lived here.

The thought came to her that, in a way, Geevneh was a lot like herself. For some reason that she didn't quite understand, nobody wanted Geevneh either, because of what it was— small, deformed, and sickly looking. Like her, it had found refuge in the tunnel, even though *these* tunnels were unlike anything she had ever seen.

"Here . . . food," Geevneh said, as it went to a small shelf that had been cut into the side of the tunnel. Nora saw that there was a container made of a shiny metal. Geevneh set the light stick on the shelf, then opened the box and took out something that looked like a cracker. Geevneh broke it in two and handed a portion of it to her. Nora took it and nibbled at one corner. It didn't taste like much, sort of like a saltine without the salt, except that as she started to chew it became moist and expanded in her mouth. She took another bite. "Not too bad, Geevneh," she said.

To Nora it seemed that Geevneh was happy that she was here in its home. She finished the cracker and felt full, although she would have preferred a juicy hamburger with onions and lots of ketchup.

She still couldn't tell what sex Geevneh was. She thought it might be awkward, but she decided to ask anyway. "Are you a boy or a girl?"

Geevneh cocked its head and then pointed to Nora. "Girl, you, Geevneh other, boy."

Nora felt more comfortable with Geevneh, especially after the crawlway. If he had wanted to harm her that would have been a good place to do it, considering that she was in the dark and helpless. She leaned over so she could get closer, realizing that this was the best way for Geevneh to show her what it was he wanted to say.

Her mind exploded with images, much more vibrant and lifelike than before. She saw the same underground city that she'd seen before, but this time she saw that many children just like Geevneh were standing in a line waiting for something. There were several human women. Women of all races, and most of them were young. She noticed that they were frightened and seemed disoriented, and looked uncomfortable where they were. She thought it very odd that most of them were in their pajamas. They were herded into a room where other children, like Geevneh, waited for them. Tall gray beings with dark slanted eyes oversaw what was going on.

In this vision, Nora could hear some sound. Not a lot, but every now and then a snatch of conversation would accompany the pictures that seemed so real in her mind. *They all look unhappy and scared,* Nora thought. Then she saw that the tall gray beings were showing the women what they wanted them to do. One of the tall gray beings went over to one of the children, a sickly looking girl. It wrapped its spindly arms around the little girl and held it. Then it went back over to the women, and selected a young black woman. The woman looked scared, but she followed the creature and went over to where the little girl waited. She took the child in her arms and hugged it. Then the scene changed and Nora saw herself holding Geevneh in her arms. The vision ended.

Nora looked at Geevneh. "Is that what you want? You want me to hold you or somethin'?"

Geevneh gave her the same weird smile and moved closer to her.

Nora wrapped her arms around him. Holding the frail child, suddenly she felt happy. She began to rock back and forth on her feet, still holding the weird, sickly looking Geevneh in her arms.

46

✦ ◯ ✦

Brian Fitzpatrick reluctantly stepped into the tunnel that looked like something out of a science fiction movie. Peering down the perfectly symmetrical tube, he pondered the events of his life that had led to this point. It seemed like an eternity since he had been at his desk in the Tank.

He thought about the last twenty-four hours. *What was that thing in my apartment?* He had seen it transform into something hideous, the essence of evil. He felt that the monster—*what had Johanen called it, a fallen angel?*—would think nothing of destroying him and every living thing around it. *You also saw a man healed, didn't you, Fitzpatrick? Something that you had always wanted to see happen. You thought that such things died out long ago with the apostles and only existed today in the minds of some backwater, deviant denomination of Christianity more akin to a snake-handling cult than to the Miracle Worker that founded it.*

He wondered about Nora. *How long has it been since she went down this tunnel followed by that* ... He hesitated because if he called the thing a fallen angel then he would be admitting that Johanen's theology was correct. He resumed his thought. *She doesn't stand a chance against whatever it is. And Johanen doesn't seem to be in a great hurry to confront it.*

Johanen called him and he stirred out of his rumination. "Fitzpatrick, who do you think made this tunnel?" he asked, as he continued walking at a brisk pace.

Fitzpatrick ran his hand along the smooth surface of the tunnel. "From what I learned with my little session with Von Schverdt . . . it has to be extraterrestrial."

"You know, Fitzpatrick, some of these tunnels have been here for centuries," Johanen countered.

Fitzpatrick felt like he was in a new episode of the *Twilight Zone.* "How do you know that?" he asked.

"I have been down some of these before. Actually, there are many of them, and they crisscross the globe. Scripture speaks of a realm that the fallen ones inhabit, and by 'fallen ones,' I mean the angels that rebelled against their Creator eons ago. Some of them have been sent to a place—"

"Yes, the *abouso* in Greek. The Abyss, I know," Fitzpatrick cut him off. "The bottomless pit, mentioned in the book of Revelation."

Johanen stopped and turned to face him. "But what of this?" Johanen asked, as he ran his hand down the smooth surface of the tunnel.

Fitzpatrick didn't answer.

"As I was saying," Johanen started again, "the Abyss is real. Some of the fallen ones have been held in that place since the great flood. Others, for reasons I am not certain of, have been allowed a certain latitude of freedom." He started down the tunnel again.

"I will grant you that the flood *legend,*" Fitzpatrick stressed the word, "has been dutifully recorded in most every culture, and there seems to be a high degree of similarity between the records, but a meteor crashing into the earth's ocean could have produced the same cataclysmic event. Afterward, the few survivors told the story to their offspring. There were many 'Noahs' and lots of resourceful folks clinging to trees and who-knows-what-else to ride out the flood waters."

"A possible scenario, but even Jesus refers to Noah and tells us that before he returns, the days on earth will be like those of Noah. You must ask yourself, Fitzpatrick. What differentiates those days from any other in history? It is the presence of the fallen angels, the *sons of god,* manifesting in the world of men. What you are looking at is evidence of the return of those beings."

Fitzpatrick cleared his throat. "All right, tell me this. How did they reappear, and why now?"

Fitzpatrick felt the hair on the back of his neck stand on end as he heard a deep growling sound reverberate through the tunnel. It was like a punctuation of Johanen's statement. "What the heck is that?"

Johanen stopped and looked at Fitzpatrick. "Something that has found its way back into the world of men," he answered.

Fitzpatrick listened as the noise slowly faded away. The sound expressed to them, loud and clear: *We're back.*

"That noise is very unsettling, to say the least," Johanen remarked.

"That's an understatement," Fitzpatrick mumbled, then continued with his line of questioning. "So how *did* they regain access to the world of men?"

Johanen resumed their walk. "What I am about to tell you is fantastic. For most men to even contemplate it is like a sojourn into madness."

Fitzpatrick swallowed hard. He had come to realize that whoever Johanen was, he was *not* an ordinary man. He had a depth of soul and knowledge that Fitzpatrick had never imagined could have existed. He gestured to the walls of the tunnel. "I believe I'm sojourning, to use your term."

"Yes, you are, Fitzpatrick," Johanen agreed. "Let me start by saying that Von Schverdt was very instrumental in what the world has come to know as the Final Solution, the Holocaust. He helped engineer it and did so very deliberately. The deaths of millions of souls served as a sacrifice to his god, Lucifer. By his actions the gates of hell were opened, and once again the fallen ones had access to the world of men."

"Are you saying that the Nazis . . . it's too incredible," Fitzpatrick said, his mind reeling at the thought.

"Not all of them knew, of course, but those at the top understood what they were trying to accomplish. They tried to manifest the one that Scripture calls the Antichrist, to them the superman . . . and they almost achieved it. They were defeated in the war, but afterward they succeeded in allowing the fallen ones back. Many of them found haven in America and slowly subverted those around them. You have seen some of it yourself. You know that Von Schverdt is in league with them, and it seems that the time of their manifestation of the superman *is now*."

Brian seemed incredulous. "In the Tank, we called whatever was affecting the world 'the mix.' I knew that mankind was headed for some sort of showdown, a flash point, but which holy man, seer, or prophet could you hitch your prophetic wagon to? Which mythos was truth, if in fact, truth exists at all?"

Johanen stopped and sat down in the middle of the tunnel.

"What are you doing?" Brian asked. "What about Nora?"

"There are things that I know of that you don't," Johanen answered, and motioned for Fitzpatrick to sit next to him.

Fitzpatrick eased himself down on the tunnel floor and crossed his legs beneath him. "This is crazy . . . Shouldn't we be trying to rescue Nora?"

Johanen didn't answer. Instead, he seemed to disconnect from what was around him for a moment, as if he was looking at something only he could see.

"Do you remember long ago, when you first were called? Do you remember how you felt? How you gave up everything to pursue him who called you?"

Fitzpatrick shifted his buttocks on the floor of the tunnel. "I remember, but that was long ago, and applied to a different

Brian Fitzpatrick—younger, gullible, naïve, and far too trust-
ing, and perhaps somewhat delusional."

"Perhaps the former Brian Fitzpatrick is precisely the one
you need to embrace again," Johanen suggested. "You experienced God once, didn't you?"

"I don't know what I experienced. It was something good,
I suppose, but it could have been that the books I was reading at the time had an undue influence on me."

"Do you really believe that?"

Fitzpatrick thought a moment. Part of him wanted to
march back up the tunnel and leave the whole affair alone.
But then there was Nora, and as always she was the one
deciding factor that prevented him from doing so. He cursed
the life fate had given him and wondered why he wasn't able
to just let his crazy sister go. Have the doctors perform a
lobotomy—it had been suggested after the fire—and have
her permanently institutionalized. Why couldn't he take the
step and do that? What prevented him?

He looked at Johanen who was patiently waiting for an
answer. *What do I really believe about how I was called?* he
wondered. He thought a moment as his mind went back
many years earlier to the time of his calling. He remembered
how overwhelming it had been. How it had left him with a
sense of purpose, of mission, and with an internal peace that
he had never felt before. He remembered that he believed he
could conquer all the wrongs of the world. That he would be
God's man; his life would make a difference.

"Something happened," he admitted reluctantly, "I thought
it was God. But he certainly was absent when my sister lit the
house on fire and burned my parents to death, wasn't he?"

Fitzpatrick glared at Johanen, daring him to answer.

Johanen answered simply, "I want you to understand
something, but to get there you must answer my question
with a simple yes or no. Did you experience God when he
called you?"

Fitzpatrick clamped his lips together. This man wouldn't let him off the hook. He kept pressing in and would not stop until Fitzpatrick faced the truth in himself.

He wrestled with that question, angry that he had to do so. He realized that if he admitted that God had spoken to him, then he left himself wide open for the following question, which might be something like, *Then why don't you seek him now?* His mind churned with ideas, quotations from a host of saints, seers, and theologians. In the end he knew that the memory of what had happened to him was sacrosanct. It remained in him tucked away, like a treasure in a sealed box that was put in the attic of a big house. But in spite of a lifetime's heaping of clutter which should have buried it, the treasure remained unchanged.

"As I told you," he whispered, "I thought at the time that it really happened, that it was God."

A moment of silence passed. Fitzpatrick heard his words echo down the tunnel.

"If it did happen, and for the sake of our conversation let us presume that it did, you still believe that, because you *experienced* it. What happened to you was so very personal that even now, years afterward, you cannot deny the reality of it. Would you like to experience him again?"

Fitzpatrick wondered what Johanen could possibly mean by that. "Here, in this place?"

Johanen gave a firm nod. "Yes, right now. You do believe that he is omnipresent, is everywhere, do you not?"

Fitzpatrick thought a moment. "Well, yes, but I don't really know whether that's true or not. The concept is a theological one. How can it be proved?"

"Again, for the sake of the moment let us assume that he is everywhere and that he has heard our entire conversation. Will you agree?"

Fitzpatrick gave a half-hearted smile and nodded.

"Good. I want you to close your eyes for a moment."

"There's nothing scriptural about the closing of one's eyes. It's not mentioned—"

Johanen interrupted, "I am aware of that. But please, do it anyway."

Fitzpatrick shifted his weight again and closed his eyes, then opened them to protest, but one look from Johanen and he shut them again. *I can't believe I'm allowing this. What do I expect to happen? God to visit us here, in this god-forsaken place?*

He heard Johanen begin to speak in that same unknown tongue, and had to resist asking what language it was.

"I want you to ask the Lord to forgive your unbelief," Johanen said.

Fitzpatrick felt Johanen's fingers on his forehead. He began to feel heat, a warm sensation that spread out along his forehead and worked its way toward his neck. *How is he doing that?* Fitzpatrick wondered, and he thought of shamans and sorcerers from different cultures, who, by touching someone, could bring a similar sensation.

"I speak peace into this man's life," Johanen said.

Fitzpatrick felt nothing.

"I speak peace into Fitzpatrick's life," Johanen stated again.

Suddenly, a great heaviness began to leave him. It felt like a weight had been removed from his shoulders. He smiled and relaxed a bit. It was as if his fears, and the phantoms that haunted him, were lifted from him, taken away by an unseen hand. Then a verse of Scripture popped into his mind. *"My burden is easy, my yoke is light."*

"I speak hope to this man and healing from the things of the past," Johanen spoke.

Fitzpatrick felt Johanen's hand move from his head to his chest area. Again, he felt the same warm, heat-like sensation. *Things of the past,* Fitzpatrick repeated to himself, then he stiffened at the thought of his father burning alive, at the desecration he'd experienced at the hands of Sene and Von Schverdt. Anger rose from deep within him like the beginning of a tempest.

Then Johanen began again, "I speak release from the bitterness that has held this man in bondage for these many years."

Fitzpatrick felt his stomach tighten involuntarily and doubled over from the pain. *What is going on?* he thought. Johanen's hand steadied him.

"I curse the spirit of bitterness and command it to leave," Johanen said, with authority.

Once again Fitzpatrick felt like someone had kicked him in his stomach. But at the same time he felt that something unclean which he had in fact *allowed* to reside within him, leave.

"I speak peace and hope to this man in the name of Jesus of Nazareth. I speak goodness to him, and may the favor of the Lord rest upon him."

Fitzpatrick remained very still and once again was warmed by the gentle heat coming from Johanen's hands.

"The peace of the Lord be upon you," Johanen said.

A few moments passed, and then Fitzpatrick opened his eyes.

"Well?" Johanen asked.

"I felt . . . I don't know. It was peaceful," he stated.

"It was the Lord's Spirit," Johanen informed him. "He is still here, all around us."

Fitzpatrick caught himself looking around the tunnel and of course couldn't see anything other than Johanen sitting in front of him.

"Why don't you ask him to touch you?" Johanen suggested.

"What do you mean touch me? You mean here, sitting like this?"

"Certainly. He loves you, Fitzpatrick, but your years of bitterness have kept him apart from you. You have shut him out of your life and barricaded the door of your heart."

Fitzpatrick nodded.

"You see, Fitzpatrick, all of these years you studied and *learned* about God, but forgot to *experience* him, the way you did when he first called you. What happened just now? You let your guard down and the Holy Spirit did some house-cleaning. You have been carrying around things that you should not have, and now they are gone. Be careful that you do not pick them up again."

Fitzpatrick nodded as Johanen stretched out his hand and touched his forehead. He instinctively shut his eyes, feeling soothing warmth descend over him. He felt like he was about to fall over and steadied himself to keep from falling.

"It is all right, I'll catch you. Let go," Johanen whispered.

Fitzpatrick resisted a moment, part of his mind wanting to question whether or not God would actually do this. Then he felt the presence again, stronger this time. It overcame him and he knew that if he wanted to, he could stop it, will it away, close, once again, the door to his heart. But he didn't. No, this was incredible.

He felt himself falling back while he was still sitting. Then he felt Johanen's hand catch him by his shoulders and slowly let him down to the floor of the tunnel. He lay there feeling a peace that coursed through him. A thought entered his mind and he knew it was the Lord speaking to him. *Rest in me.* Fitzpatrick relaxed further, and it was as if he were sinking into the tunnel. He then had a vision in his mind of galaxies spinning in space. Awed by the expanse of it, the swirling colors, the distant stars and planets, he felt so small, so inconsequential.

Then a new thought entered his mind. *I created all of this. I am the Alpha and the Omega, the One who knows the beginning from the end. Serve me.* Fitzpatrick was afraid to breathe. The living God had spoken to him. Shown him part of his creation. Admonished him to serve.

He lay still, afraid to move a muscle, feeling the peace of the Lord. Peace that he had never known in his life. He didn't want to get up from the tunnel's floor.

Then he heard the same disturbing growl echoing its way from far beneath him.

For a moment he was afraid, then a thought floated to the forefront of his mind. *Greater is he that lives within you than he that is in the world. He is defeated. Walk in peace.* He relaxed again and lay still on the floor of the tunnel for . . . a minute? An hour? He couldn't tell, but he thought about Nora and opened his eyes, sitting up. Everything had changed. He felt lighter, restored, forgiven. His mind was clear, and he felt a wellspring of joy inside. "That was incredible," he said, as carefree as a little kid.

Johanen nodded and smiled at him, then patted his shoulder. "We serve a good God, Fitzpatrick. Welcome back."

"What happened?"

Johanen chuckled. "You were overcome by the presence of the Holy Spirit. He let you feel his peace."

"Incredible . . ."

"Instead of reading about him, you *experienced* him. Now you *know* by experience that he is good, that he loves you, and that he cares for you."

"Johanen," he murmured as the older man raised his eyebrows at him, "I have made peace with . . . things that happened to me. They make no sense that I know of. But the Lord impressed upon me that even in the midst of that tragedy, he was there."

"Yes, he was, Fitzpatrick, and although it is hard for us to understand, we have his promise that someday he will make right all the hurt, all the suffering, that has happened since Adam fell. He will set things right because he is a good God."

"Johanen?" Fitzpatrick heard MacKenzie's voice roll toward them and then continue down the tunnel until it was just a faint echo.

"We are here, MacKenzie," Johanen called in return.

A short time later Fitzpatrick saw Art MacKenzie walking toward them.

"Did you get him back to the Condos?" Johanen asked.

MacKenzie gave a nod and a thumbs-up. "He's really confused and had lots of questions. I don't think he stopped talking the whole way."

Fitzpatrick looked at Johanen, wondering whether or not he would say anything about what had transpired in MacKenzie's absence.

"It is good that you are back with us, MacKenzie," Johanen remarked, and started their trek again.

Following the course of the tunnel, Fitzpatrick realized he was a changed man, a redeemed man, and he gave thanks for the goodness of his Lord as he walked between Johanen and MacKenzie.

47

* O *

Nora awakened and wasn't sure how long she had been asleep or where she was. Then she looked down and remembered the weird-looking boy, Geevneh, that she held in her lap. Geevneh's eyes were open and stared up at her. She started to move, but Geevneh held on tight and wouldn't let her go.

"You've got to let me get up, Geevneh. I got to go right away."

Geevneh shook his head and held her tighter. Nora took her hands and pulled the thin weak fingers off her waist, but as soon as she let go Geevneh attached them to her again.

"Geevneh say noooo," and he snuggled closer.

One of Geevneh's fingers dug into Nora's side, hurting her. She took both his arms, yanked them off, and pushed him away. Geevneh crouched in front of her and bared his pointed teeth at her. "You no go from Geevneh," he said, and he suddenly looked very menacing.

Nora felt her head swim when he looked at her. Turning away, she got up from where she had fallen asleep. She started to back her way out of the room toward the caved-in part of the tunnel. Geevneh followed. She didn't like the way he looked at her with his little pointed teeth bared. She kept walking backward and stared at his feet so she wouldn't have to look at his eyes.

Then he was beside her. He moved so fast. She continued backing away and kicked at him with her foot. He ducked to the side, then she felt him sink his teeth into her arm.

"Ouch, you little creep." She swung at him with her fist and succeeded in hitting him on the side of the head. Geevneh tumbled over and screamed at her with such a loud, high-pitched sound that it made her ears hurt.

Nora turned and ran down the tunnel. She made her way to the collapsed part where Geevneh had created the crawl-through, and dove. She was almost halfway through when she stopped, looked down the crawl-through, and there, at the other end of the tunnel, saw the head of the monster peering in the opening, with one red eye fixed on her.

She couldn't turn around in the crawl-through, so she started to back her way out. The monster let out a loud growl that was deafening. She held her ears and closed her eyes for a second, feeling her body tense with fear. Another growl, and she backed up as fast as she could. Then she saw the monster's clawed arm reach into the tunnel, trying to grab her. She was a good way from it, but it terrified her and made her move faster. The monster grabbed part of the tunnel and pulled it away, making the crawl-through larger as it began to dig its way toward her.

Her foot wedged itself in a small fissure. For what seemed like minutes but was only a moment, she couldn't move. Pulling her leg as hard as she could, she finally slid her foot out of her shoe. She began backing out of the crawl-through again and reached the place where her tennis shoe was. She grabbed it and kept going.

Another growl and then the monster spoke. Its voice was sweet and sounded like . . . she stopped and couldn't believe it. Her father? Didn't he die a long time ago?

"Give me the disk, Nora," the voice of her father said.

Nora stopped moving. She was panting, and she had per-spired so much that her clothes were wet.

"Nora, give me the disk and then you can have some ice cream," her father said again.

Then Nora heard another voice behind her. This voice was from the child, Geevneh. "Nora, you come me. No listen," he said.

A loud growl thundered through the crawl-through and made her ears hurt. She realized that the monster had some-how impersonated her dead father. *How did he do that?* she wondered. Nora started to back out of the crawl-through again. She reached the other side and saw that Geevneh looked as scared as she did. He started to run back up the old tunnel and motioned that Nora should follow.

Nora looked back and saw that the monster was making good progress in widening the crawl-through. It was just a matter of time before it widened enough to pass. And then what?

Nora put her shoe on and followed Geevneh quickly up the tunnel.

* ○ *

"Did you hear that, MacKenzie?" Johanen asked.

Mac, gesturing to the four tunnels that branched off into different directions, replied, "With all the echo in this place it's hard to tell exactly where that sound came from, but I'd put money that it's from the one on the far left."

"I agree. He is close. We must hurry," Johanen said.

The three men ran down the new tunnel and after a while stopped when they spied a pile of freshly moved earth.

"What happened here?" Fitzpatrick asked.

"It appears he had to dig his way through," Johanen explained.

"This part of the tunnel system looks much older than what we've been running through," Mac offered. "Maybe it was large enough for Nora to get through but not the monster. That would explain all the digging."

They heard another growl, much closer than before, and then a woman screaming.

"We must hurry," Johanen said, as he charged into the opening. Mac once again followed last. He was bordering exhaustion and had felt for a while now that he couldn't go another step without sleep. But now, with the urgency of Nora's scream, the adrenaline it produced had given him the jolt he needed. He came out of the newly enlarged tunnel. He took out one of the flashlights Tim had given them that up until now they hadn't needed. Johanen did the same, and the three men moved cautiously, close behind the reptilian monster.

The tunnel ascended slightly and then leveled out. The men moved along at a rapid trot, and the tunnel opened into a room.

"He has been here, look," Johanen called from ahead.

Someone had taken residence in this place, but everything had been overturned. A few clothes, a metal box with cracker-like food crumbled around it, and a pile of stick-like lights, several of which lit up the room. Mac stopped and picked up one that was lit, and turned off his flashlight. In the few seconds it had taken to do that, Johanen and Fitzpatrick had put some distance between themselves and him. He sprinted after them, not wanting to be left alone.

The tunnel began to turn to the right and the men followed it. Then Johanen stopped suddenly. Mac almost ran into Fitzpatrick and had to jump to the side to avoid slamming into him. He looked up and saw the reason for the sudden stop. In front of him lay a dark, gaping maw, descending straight down into the depths of the earth. The hole was huge, perhaps forty feet in diameter. Around the top was a two-foot rimlike walkway. Mac could see Nora at the far side of it, standing next to a strange-looking child, which he thought had to be a hybrid—a product of an unholy union between fallen angels and earthly women. Moving closer to her loomed Azazel, the fallen angel.

What happened next became a confused nightmare of images. Johanen called out to the creature, then a primal roar in response resounded throughout the tunnel, bouncing off the walls and making Mac tremble. Nora screamed and Fitzpatrick shouted to her. Azazel crouched low, and then it leapt towards Nora across the opening, claws extended. Johanen yelled again and a burst of blinding light filled the cavern. Mac shielded his eyes. The sound of Azazel filled the cavern, roaring in protest as the light blinded him. Mac opened his eyes in time to see the monster stagger and crash into the side of the tunnel, with Nora and the child between it and the pit. Sliding on its side, it began to thrash for a handhold, and in doing so, knocked the child and sent him sprawling along the rim.

Azazel reached out and, grabbing Nora by the ankle, sunk its claws into her. She screamed and tried to move away. There was a moment when she bore the weight of the powerfully built reptile. Helplessly, from across the vast hole, Mac watched her search for something to grab onto, but the sides of the tunnel were smooth and offered nothing. The monster's grip was firm as Nora teetered for a moment.

Fitzpatrick yelled, "Nora!" Johanen began running around the small walkway.

Nora slid toward the edge. She couldn't hold the weight much longer. Then the hybrid child jumped, and as he did, he let out a wailing, high-pitched scream. He landed on Azazel's back and began to pound on its head. The added weight tipped the balance and Nora fell into the maw, with the hybrid atop the fallen angel, a strange trio linked together by claw and fang.

Fitzpatrick let out a long, *"No-o-o-o!"* One of the light sticks was caught in the tangle of limbs, and it shone brightly on them as they descended.

Then Johanen turned to MacKenzie and said, "Follow the tunnel down as far as you can. I will find you." With that he jumped in after Nora.

Mac cried out, "Johanen!" but it was too late. He saw the man look up at him once as the blackness swallowed him.

"Johanen," Mac cried out again, weakly. He peered over the side of the great hole. A faint growling noise came up from somewhere far below. Then there was silence.

"He jumped in to save her!" Fitzpatrick exclaimed. "Why? What chance does he have of surviving?"

Mac looked as far as he could into the great maw. "I don't understand it . . . but he knew what he was doing."

"And Nora . . . ," Fitzpatrick began, and then broke down. He sank to the floor and, holding his head in his hands, began to cry bitterly. Mac moved a few feet away and stood silently. He waited until Fitzpatrick had finished and was beginning to wipe his eyes, looking grim and broken.

"I know this might sound shallow," Mac began, "but Johanen said that we should go to the lowest level and he would find us there. I don't know what he has up his sleeve, but I know enough about him to know this. He did that deliberately. He called to us just as he jumped. He wouldn't have done that unless he knew that somehow he was going to survive, and Nora with him."

Fitzpatrick nodded half-heartedly.

"We need to retrace our steps. There's more of these light sticks back in that small cavern. I say we take a few in case our flashlights run out, and then do as Johanen instructed and seek the lowest level."

"I suppose we don't have much of a choice . . . MacKenzie, she was so helpless. She didn't stand a chance." Fitzpatrick's eyes began to tear up again.

"I know, but all might not be lost. Remember, Johanen went in after her. If anyone can save her, it's him."

The two men retraced their steps through the cavern where Mac picked up several of the light sticks. He also found the cracker-like wafers that had fallen out of the metal box. He sampled one, found it nourishing, and both he and Fitzpatrick stuffed their pockets with the items. There was no telling how long they were going to be down there. They made their way through the enlarged opening that Azazel had made, and eventually found one of the main passageways and continued their trek down.

48

Nora fell in a tangle with the monster and the child in this horrible place of darkness that had swallowed her whole. Her thoughts came in flashes one after the other. Below her was the monster that was still painfully grasping her ankle. "Let go!" she whined as the pain from the wound shot up her leg. She felt its claws loosen a little as she struggled to get out of its grip. She saw Geevneh take one of his bony fingers and push it into the monster's eye. It let out a howl and then let go of her.

She glanced above her and saw, to her astonishment, a man falling with his arms outstretched toward her. She recognized him as the one with the blue eyes from her brother's apartment. During her struggle, she had released the light stick and it floated near her, just out of reach, but she could see that the monster and Geevneh were moving below her.

Then something amazing happened. The area around them was suddenly lit up so brilliantly that she had to close her eyes. She felt her freefall start to slow down, but then she realized that this was impossible, so she forced her eyes open. She looked at her ankle and was amazed to see that the wound had begun to close and the pain had all but vanished. The man with the blue eyes was near. Somehow they were floating in the air and the light was all around them glowing brilliantly. Geevneh and the monster were nowhere to be seen.

She felt herself being caressed by whatever it was that was holding her in midair. She started to laugh because it was easily the most amazing thing that had ever happened to her.

The man with the blue eyes came over to her, almost as if he were flying. She giggled again. "Are you all right, Nora?" he asked as he touched her shoulder with his hand.

Nora nodded. "How are we doing this . . . we were falling and now . . ."

The man smiled at her and said, "His angels guard you and will not let you fall, for they will catch you. You are surrounded by some of heaven's finest, Nora."

Nora looked around, and although she saw the brilliant light, she didn't see any of the angels that the man was talking about.

She felt herself moving down again, but it was a controlled, slow descent. Looking all around her she noticed that they were coming up to another intersection of tunnels that fed into the great maw. Whatever was holding her up—if it really was angels like the blue-eyed man said—began to vanish, and the light dimmed as she found her feet touching solid ground again. She instinctively pulled away from the edge. The man with the blue eyes was let down next to her almost like he had stepped off an elevator. She looked at the light that enveloped him and to her amazement, saw it move away and then transform into a tall, good-looking black man and he, too, had the deepest blue eyes that she had ever seen. He followed the man onto the rim of the connecting tunnel. "Who are you?" she asked the white man with the blue eyes.

"I am called Johanen, Nora."

"How did you know my name? Did my brother tell you?" she asked.

"Yes, he did. He loves you very much."

"Who's he?" she asked, pointing toward the tall black man.

"His name is Smyrna, and he has been a friend and guardian for a very long time."

"That's a funny name. I never heard anybody called that."

"Yes, it is, Nora," Johanen answered. Then he asked, "Do you know why you were being chased?"

"By the monster?"

Johanen nodded. "Yes, Nora, by the 'monster,' as you put it."

Nora reached into her pants pocket and pulled out an envelope. "Is this the reason? They want this?"

"May I take a look at that, Nora?" Johanen asked.

"Yeah, sure, but just a look. I want the pretty stamps on the envelope," she said as she handed it to him. She watched as Johanen unfolded it and took out the plastic thingy. He handed her the envelope but held onto the plastic thingy.

"Can I keep this, Nora?" he asked as he held the disk up so that she could see it.

Nora frowned a moment and then said, "Yeah, okay. You saved me from the monster, so you can keep it." She enjoyed Johanen's smile as he tucked the disk away in his top pocket and buttoned it.

"Well, Nora, we should try to get ourselves out of here, yes?" he asked.

Nora nodded. "But how are we going to do that?"

"You will see. It is one of the reasons why my friend Smyrna is with us," Johanen said, and he gestured to the silent man next to him.

Nora, Johanen, and Smyrna began to venture down the tunnel. Nora walked between them and felt safe. Something else was beginning to happen. She felt as if she had been taking her pills again. Her mind was clearer than it had been only a few minutes ago. She wondered why this should be so. She thought about the child Geevneh and pondered, as best as she could, whether or not it had been bad or good. She turned to Johanen and asked, "What happened to Geevneh? Why didn't you save him?"

"Is Geevneh the little child that jumped onto the monster's back?" Johanen asked.

"Yeah. At first I liked him, but then he got mean and he bit me, but then he kind of tried to save me. Don't you think he tried to save me?"

"Yes, he did try to help you with the monster," Johanen agreed.

"So what happened to him?" Nora asked. "Did he die with the monster?"

"I am not certain, Nora."

"Oh, well, I feel okay with you, and him." She pointed at the silent black man, as she grabbed Johanen's arm and clutched it as they walked down the tunnel.

49

Azazel was falling and the nasty little hybrid was becoming a nuisance. He had seen his nemesis Johanen dive into the hole after him. Heard him yell to his underling MacKenzie while the stupid ex-priest shouted to his half-wit sister. The thought angered him and in one motion he grabbed the hybrid, jerked it from his back, and twisted its neck until he heard it snap. Then he threw the dead body against the side of the hole. The horrible presence of the enemy blinded him; they outnumbered him four to one, and it was a relief that they had not pursued him. He was thankful for the darkness of the pit as he continued to fall away from the enemy, putting wanted distance between them.

He shape-shifted into a bat and, spreading his wings, landed on the bottom of the pit. Changing back into his true form, he looked up and saw the dim light of one of many connecting tunnels that branched from this main shaft. Gathering his body under him he leapt upward, catching at the opening, then using his claws to pull himself up the rest of the way. At the top he listened carefully and then sniffed the air, smelling something familiar.

He ran down the tunnel, anxious for everything that lay ahead.

50

"This is what we have been waiting for, Bruno," Von Schverdt said to his driver from the back of his limousine. "We have put the pieces back together again from our previous failure in Germany, with that weakling Hitler. The stage is set and now we will usher in the superman. I have seen him and he is terrible, wonderful, savage, and cunning. The world will worship him."

"Yes, sir," Bruno answered, and turned the car into the driveway of Von Schverdt's estate. It was checked by security and then allowed to enter. Von Schverdt had Bruno let him off in front of the mansion, something he usually didn't do, because exposure to direct sunlight would turn his skin yellow from the concoction of drugs that coursed through his veins.

He stood on the drawbridge and looked around. He knew that it would be a while before he would see any of this again. The armies in the Middle East would clash, and then the big surprise would change everything. He clasped his hands behind his back and began to walk over the drawbridge. Pausing a moment in the center, he admired the clear water of the koi pond and the large fish that swam below him. He walked the rest of the way over the bridge and stood in front of the two massive bronze doors. Bruno would have called ahead so he anticipated the doors opening, and as he stood on the slate stoop, they did.

Much to his satisfaction, his Asian servant girl greeted him. She bowed her head as Von Schverdt entered. He glanced at his watch, ignoring the girl, and headed straight toward his office on the lower level. He pressed the code, which allowed access to the office, and then carefully shut the doors behind him.

At his desk he proceeded to undress, folding his clothes neatly and laying them carefully over the chair. With just his underwear on, he walked to a door in a corner of the room. Opening it Von Schverdt stepped into a large walk-in closet where there were tailored suits and a variety of costumes, some of which he had worn at his galas. He ignored these and went to the rear of the closet where a uniform was protected by a garment bag. He carefully unzipped the bag and began to dress in a replica of the uniform that he had worn fifty years earlier.

He had paid a handsome amount of money to a tailor, instructing him to recreate every detail of the original. Satisfied to see how well it fit him, he buttoned his shirt, paying careful attention to the death's-heads cufflinks on the sleeves. He then put on his pants, feeling a slight pinch at his waist as he buttoned them. He pulled his polished black boots over his black-stockinged feet and clicked his heels together once, bringing to his lips a smile of satisfaction. He took the last of the wrapping off the jacket and the sight of his decorations— his medals and the iron cross—took his breath away. A tear fell from his eye and his hands trembled as he reverently took the jacket off its hanger and carefully slipped his arm into first one sleeve, then the other. He buttoned it and stood before the mirror.

Admiring his noble demeanor, he mused, *I am SS-Obergruppenfuehrer Von Schverdt, and I have never surrendered. Not to the Americans, not to the British. They were happy with the toys I provided, and now my hour has come. The goal has been reached! Heil, Hitler.* Von Schverdt threw his hand out in the infamous Nazi salute, not saluting Hitler, but the spirit that had possessed the man.

He clicked his heels together and then marched out of the closet. Grabbing a loaded pistol, he fitted it into the holster at his waist, then went over to the bust of his *fuehrer,* Adolph Hitler. He pulled the head back and the secret panel opened. He stepped into the hidden elevator and strapped himself into the seat. *They will look upon me with respect,* he thought as the elevator doors closed and he felt it begin its dizzying descent into the bowels of the earth.

51

"Can you hear that low, almost inaudible humming sound?" Mac whispered as he walked next to Fitzpatrick.

The man nodded his head. "Yeah, and it seems like it's getting louder the deeper we go."

The tunnel suddenly dipped down at a very steep angle so that the two men slid on the smooth floor to the next level. They had come to several intersections and had chosen the tunnels that had the steepest descent.

"What do you think these are for?" Fitzpatrick asked.

Mac shrugged. "I think they travel in these."

"With what?"

"Maybe a small UFO-type craft. Look at the way this tunnel bends at a slight angle to the left but always heads downwards. It reminds me of an ant farm I had when I was kid."

Fitzpatrick laughed. "I had one of those, too."

"Remember how all the ant tunnels led to the one main section of the colony?"

Fitzpatrick grew serious. "Yeah, and this might be no different."

A very low noise sounding like the heartbeat of some giant creature rumbled through the tunnel.

"You hear that?" Mac asked.

Fitzpatrick gave him a worried look. "Yeah, and whatever it is, it's coming our way."

"Back there, where we slid down, at the bottom, was a slight indentation," Mac said.

The two men ran, retracing their steps. Mac was right; there was a trough-like impression at the bottom of the slide. Mac looked behind him. "Get down quick," he warned, as he dove into the trough. Fitzpatrick threw himself next to Mac. The sound grew louder. Mac peered over the lip and observed a sleek, silvery-metallic craft speeding toward him. It lit up the tunnel with a bright orange color as it approached them.

"What the . . . ," Fitzpatrick gasped.

"Down!" Mac said, and he yanked Fitzpatrick's sleeve. They lay with their faces against the bottom of the trough.

Mac heard the craft approach and then hover a moment directly over them, bathing the area in a deep orange color. He peeked out again and saw the craft turn on its side as it negotiated the odd kink in the tunnel. When it reached the top it shot away.

"Did you see that?" Fitzpatrick said as he jumped to his feet. "I can't believe it! Where did it come from?"

"Easy, man," Mac said. "The guy that was in your apartment, who tried to kill you, is in cahoots with whoever is flying that thing."

"It was beautiful though," Fitzpatrick said.

"Yeah, but I can assure you from firsthand experience that you don't want to mess with what's inside it."

"What do we do when we get to the bottom?" Fitzpatrick asked.

"I guess we wait for Johanen to find us."

"What if he's not alive?"

Mac thought about the question for a moment. "He's alive, trust me. My gut tells me he is. He'll find us."

52

W here are we going, Johanen?" Nora asked in a sing-song voice as she let her hand play over the sides of the tunnel.

"Well, Nora, you are going to go with Smyrna out of these tunnels to a place where it is safe. He will take you to the place you call the Condos. I am going on to meet your brother and my friend, Art MacKenzie," Johanen answered. "Then when we are finished with our business, we will join you."

"Where do you think they are? Is there a map that you can look at to tell where they are?"

"No, Nora. There is not a map, at least not one that is in my possession. But we will trust that we will find our way, and we have something better than a map." Johanen gestured toward the angel. "Smyrna is going to help us."

Nora looked at the angel, who had somehow become a man, and then asked, "How did he stop shining, like back at the big hole?"

She saw Johanen smile.

"Smyrna can do that. It is the way God created him. So be careful, Nora, sometimes you may be with angels and not be aware of it."

Nora thought about what Johanen said, then looked again at the tall black man. She thought about the monster and shivered, moving closer to Johanen.

"What about the monster? Is he dead?"

"The monster is not dead, Nora, but he is far below where we are now. I suggest that you take those thoughts of fear from your mind."

Nora frowned. "The monster made me feel afraid. I know he was goin' to kill me if he got ahold of me."

"Like I said, Nora, think about things that are good in your life. Think about the angels who came to save us both, about Smyrna being with you now, and about how much your brother loves you."

Nora gave a quick nod. "I understand," she said, and her face brightened. "Are you gonna give the disk thingy back to my brother?"

"Yes, Nora, I shall. You caused a lot of trouble by taking it, you know."

"I'm sorry, Johanen. It was just that the envelope had nice pretty stamps with lots of colors on 'em. I didn't mean no harm by it."

"Sometimes we do things and we don't realize the consequences of our actions. You have set things in motion, Nora, but regardless of your intentions, whether innocent or not, God will bring about his perfect will. Even in the circumstances we now face because of your choice."

Nora frowned. "I'm not sure I understand what you are saying."

"It is all right, Nora. Maybe when you go with Smyrna he will make it so you will understand. I know that in your heart it is what you have always wanted."

Nora hung her head. "I know I'm not normal, like other people. That's why they put me in those places and gave me pills and did other stuff. I tried to be okay, and my brother gives me pills, and when I remember to take them it makes me feel better. But then I don't remember to take 'em, and I start to slip, and the funny thing is, I don't remember the stuff I do."

Johanen put his arm around her and she snuggled close to him as they walked down the tunnel.

They came to a cross section where three tunnels branched out in different directions. Johanen looked at Smyrna and then she heard the man speak for the first time.

"This way, Johanen." He turned to the tunnel on the left.

"How come he doesn't talk more?" Nora whispered.

Johanen laughed. "Yes, Smyrna, why is it that you do not engage in the art of conversation?"

Nora looked up at Smyrna and waited for the angel to answer. He spoke. "Right now I am listening to things that you cannot hear, and seeing things that you cannot see. I will guide you away from here and keep you from harm's way."

Nora nodded, not really understanding what he was talking about. They walked farther and Nora noticed that this tunnel seemed to be going upwards. They came to another intersection and the next one had four tunnels that connected in sort of a big room-like area.

"It is time," Smyrna said, as he stopped in the middle of the cavernous part.

"Which way am I to go?" Johanen asked.

Smyrna pointed to one of the tunnels. "Follow this one until it ends and then take the tunnel on your far left. You will find those you seek there. But hurry, Johanen, Azazel is also looking for them."

Johanen dropped to one knee in front of Nora. "Nora, as I said before, you are to go with Smyrna. He will take you now. All right?"

Nora bit her upper lip and nodded. "I'll go, but you have to promise me you'll come back to see me at the Condos, okay?"

Johanen reached out and took her hand. "Let me bless you, child," he said, as he put his other hand on her forehead.

She closed her eyes and listened as Johanen prayed for her and blessed her. She felt a hot sensation flow into her head and she felt compelled to giggle. Then Johanen finished and she opened her eyes.

"Come, child," Smyrna said as he waited for her at the entrance to the tunnel they were going to take. Nora walked over to him and she took his hand.

"Bye, Johanen," she called, and looking back realized that Johanen had already gone into one of the tunnels.

"I will see you again soon, Nora," she heard him call, and his voice echoed all around her.

She snuggled up to Smyrna and thought for the first time about something that had happened years ago. It remained fuzzy, almost dreamlike in her memory. She remembered the fire, and for the first time realized that she had killed her parents with it. She began to cry silent tears as she walked next to the angel.

53

✢ ◯ ✢

Mac and Fitzpatrick moved cautiously down a long stretch of tunnel that descended farther into the earth at a very steep angle. For some reason this tunnel was darker than the preceding one through which they had traveled, although a faint light still emanated from the walls. But they still didn't need to use either the flashlight Tim had given them or the light sticks they had brought.

"I think we're getting closer to whatever it is that's down here," Mac stated.

"I agree," Fitzpatrick said. "The sound is louder, and I'm feeling more vibration in the floor as we walk."

They had not seen any other craft since the one incident earlier. It had been several hours since Johanen had dived into the great maw leaving them with only his words for assurance that he would find them. "How far do you think we've come so far?" he asked Fitzpatrick.

"Well, we've been moving at a good pace." He glanced at his watch. "I set the stopwatch when we first entered the tunnel. We've been down here almost six hours, and most of the time we've been on the move. So do the math. We're doing about three miles an hour. Multiply that by, let's be conservative, and say four hours. Then let's be even more conservative and say that we've lollygagged a bit here and there which affects our speed, so, factoring all that in, I'd say we've gone maybe ten miles."

"That's quite a watch you've got there," Mac commented, getting his first glimpse of it as it had been under Fitzpatrick's jacket and therefore hidden from view.

"The Hag, Von Schverdt, gave them to all of us employed at the Tank. It has a GPS ..." He stopped dead in his tracks.

"A GPS," Mac repeated, knowing what implications that had for them.

Fitzpatrick nodded, his face grim. "What should I do with it?"

"Take it off and stomp on it," Mac suggested.

Fitzpatrick shook his head. "It's no good. It's made of a Titanium alloy, light and very resistant to shock. Its glass is also bulletproof and watertight."

"Then leave it here or throw it in the next tunnel we come to," Mac said.

"Do you think they're using this ... to locate us?" Fitzpatrick asked.

"Yeah, maybe that disk we saw earlier was no accident. I don't know. Maybe it doesn't work down here. But we can't take any chances. We've got to distance ourselves from it and quick."

Fitzpatrick took the watch off. "I'll throw it as far as I can."

Mac gave a nod of support. "Yeah, and then let's get out of here."

Fitzpatrick threw the watch, but it hit the side of the tunnel after twenty feet and fell to the floor. "Let me try," Mac said, and he ran over to it and picked it up. He hurled it as far as he could, which was better than Fitzpatrick had done, but certainly wasn't going to put any distance between themselves and anyone who wanted to access their position by global satellite.

The two men ran. Fitzpatrick began to pull away. Mac was exhausted, and his body craved sleep.

"Hey . . . wait up," Mac said, already out of breath after a couple hundred yards.

Fitzpatrick stopped and waited for MacKenzie to catch up.

"Do you jog or something?" Mac asked.

Fitzpatrick nodded. "As often as I can. After putting in ten- to twelve-hour days at the Tank I need something to take my mind off things. Living next to Central Park, it was a natural."

"Why don't you go up ahead and wait at the next intersection. Maybe scout out the area, look for Johanen."

"And leave you alone?" Fitzpatrick asked.

"I'm not alone, I'm right behind you."

Mac saw Fitzpatrick frown. "You watch horror movies?"

Mac was taken aback. "Not really, but I've seen a few."

"You know how the good guys always seem to separate, or leave the girl behind, alone?"

"Yeah, so?"

"Well, that's when the bad stuff happens."

"Those are movies, this is real life. I'll be fine. Look for Johanen. We need him."

"You sure?"

Mac gave him an 'I'm a big boy and can take care of myself' look.

Mac watched Fitzpatrick nod an okay, and a moment later he was running down the corridor at a good clip.

Mac walked after him and half an hour later they met up at an intersection.

"See, I told you," Mac said with a certain amount of satisfaction. "It worked out fine."

"No Johanen here," Fitzpatrick commented. "What now?"

They both froze as they heard the sound of a woman screaming.

"That's Nora," Fitzpatrick said, and before Mac could respond, took off in the direction of the sound.

"Fitzpatrick! Wait!" Mac yelled and started after him. "It might be a trick . . . they can mimic your sister's voice!"

Mac raced after him, but it was clear that he would not be able to catch him. He broke into a sweat and, finally, when his legs felt like rubber and his lungs ached, he stopped and leaned against the tunnel trying to get his breath. *Maybe if I just sat down for a moment* . . . Mac thought as he slumped to the floor and closed his eyes . . .

54

Elisha stood at his terminal with Uri on one side and the Major on the other. The underground military complex buzzed with heightened activity.

A short, dark-haired woman several rows down from Elisha shouted out, "We have confirmation. Iran has launched four of its missiles."

"Copy that . . . we have them classed as RAAD cruise control missiles with self-guidance systems."

An Israeli Air Force captain tore the headset from his ears and announced, "We have confirmation, repeat, confirmation that the Russians have also launched a half-dozen missiles."

Several red lights began to flash in the front of the room on the large digital map on the wall.

"This is it," Uri said. "I cannot believe this. They are starting World War III."

"We've launched our antimissiles. Intercept time less than two minutes."

Elisha snatched his trifocals from his face and grabbed the Major's arm. "It's happening! This is madness!" His hands began to shake and he sat down to compose himself, wiping some dry spittle from the corner of his mouth. He heard a woman begin to cry several rows down from him. Gathering himself together, he sat upright, realizing that this was the moment to be strong for his country. That in spite of the chaos of the moment, somehow God was still in control. He grabbed his yarmulke from his coat pocket and slipped it onto his head, praying.

"We've intercepted three of the Iranian missiles," the same dark-haired woman announced. A scattering of cheers went up. All eyes were on the board in front as it showed the projected targets of the Russian missiles.

"We have several divisions of troops that have begun to engage near the Golan," an Israeli captain shouted.

"Are we going to use the laser cannon?" Uri asked.

"Yes, Uri," the Major replied, "but I am afraid the ground forces we have been monitoring are beyond the use of conventional means to repel it."

"We've launched our fighter planes," an Israeli corporal announced.

The Major motioned to another monitor, which showed two squadrons of Israeli F16s, F18s, and four AWACs, used for radar. One squadron was launched from the south, the other from the north. In moments they had crossed Jordanian air space, headed toward Iran.

Elisha watched the planes close in on their targets. He listened to the voices of the commanders radioing back what they were seeing.

"The Russians are launching more missiles," a young woman yelled frantically.

Controlled bedlam ensued. "What will we do?" Elisha asked the Major.

"We will intercept their missiles with ours, then launch a counteroffensive."

"What about the troops? Their forces outnumber us."

The Major rubbed his eyes and leaned close to Elisha. "We have handled many war scenarios, you know that, Elisha. We thought that something like this might happen. We remember the '65 war, yes?"

Elisha nodded.

"Until a few minutes ago our response was conventional, but . . ." His voice trailed off while he rubbed his eyes again and blinked them a few times to refocus. "The Iranians have crossed a line . . . so have the Russians. We cannot fight a two- or three-front war with conventional weapons against such a great mass of troops. So . . ." He paused and took a deep breath. "We will fight with our nuclear arsenal . . . use our neutron bombs. The prime minister has already been informed of this . . ."

Elisha glanced at the digital map in front of the room. "It looks like our submarines have launched their missiles toward Syria."

"Yes," the Major replied, "where a great mass of troops is beginning to pour over the border into Israel."

"It will be less than two minutes before impact."

Elisha glanced at his watch. The room seemed to grow quiet as he watched the second hand slowly sweep around the face of the watch. One minute passed. Then another thirty seconds. Elisha watched the big hand as it crept toward the top of the clock. Before it reached it they felt the ground tremble.

Elisha looked at the Major, his mouth open in horror. The unthinkable had happened—a nuclear device, more specifically, a neutron bomb, had been deployed.

Rocking back and forth in his chair, he thought, *The time of the end has come. It has started and there is no turning back now. It is the time of the Evil One, and so the time of Jacob's trouble is upon us.* The noise in the room seemed to fade away as Elisha prayed as he had never prayed before.

55

MacKenzie felt something shake him. Having lived in Los Angeles for most of his life, *earthquake* was the first thought that forced its way into his sluggish mind, which rebelled at the intrusion. He opened one eye.

"MacKenzie, wake up," Johanen said, and even in Mac's stupefied state he recognized the urgency.

"Johanen!" Mac said, rubbing his eyes. He looked around. "Fitzpatrick . . . he thought he heard Nora's voice and ran ahead of me. I must have dozed off."

Johanen pulled him up. "He can't be too far, let's go."

Both men started down the tunnel. After a while it opened to a large room where as many as a dozen tunnels connected. The sound that Mac had been hearing from the moment that he entered the tunnel system was much louder now, and he had to raise his voice so that Johanen could hear him.

"I thought he would be here," Mac shouted. "He was supposed to wait at any intersection he came to."

"Wait, MacKenzie, look there."

Mac looked, and there coming out of one of the tunnels was Fitzpatrick. But with him was someone else, and seeing it made the hairs on the back of his head feel like they were on fire.

Mac took a step away from Johanen and ran toward Fitzpatrick. "Who is this?" he yelled. For standing next to Fitzpatrick was another Johanen.

"What's going on?" Fitzpatrick yelled.

"Who's with you?" Mac yelled.

"It's Johanen," the Johanen that stood next to Fitzpatrick yelled. "MacKenzie, you're in danger! Quick, run over here!"

"No, Mac, the man is an impostor. It is Azazel who is trying to deceive you and Fitzpatrick," the Johanen that had awakened him said.

"MacKenzie, trust me, your life is in danger, hurry!" The Johanen next to Fitzpatrick yelled.

"Mac, he found me, and just in time. He said Nora was fine," Fitzpatrick yelled.

Mac looked at one and then the other. *Which one is real?*

Then from behind Mac a voice called out, "In the name of Jesus of Nazareth be still!"

Mac felt the shock wave from the voice pass through him and hit the other Johanen that stood next to Fitzpatrick. He saw the man change as if a costume had been pulled suddenly from him to reveal the reptilian known as Azazel.

Before Fitzpatrick could do anything the reptilian had him by the throat with a sharp claw pointed at his jugular vein. "You have what I want and I will kill him unless you give it to me," he spat at Johanen.

Mac looked back at Johanen and wondered why he didn't call on a host of angels to stop what was going on.

"What is your name?" Johanen's voice thundered with authority.

"I am called Azazel," the reptilian yelled back, his face twisted with hate.

"Is this what you are looking for?" Johanen took a disk out of his pocket and held it in front of him.

"Give it to your underling to give to me and then I will release him," the reptilian hissed.

Mac saw that Fitzpatrick had turned ashen, and wondered if the man would faint.

"No," Johanen said firmly, "release him and I will give this to you personally."

"Where is your god now, Johanen? Why doesn't he send his angels? I suppose they are too busy elsewhere, or perhaps he has forgotten about you."

"No, Fallen One, for it is written, 'He that began a good work in me will be faithful to see it through.' It is your master's time, and so the one you serve will manifest his delusion on men, but not without the Lord's consent."

Azazel hissed and Mac saw his finger puncture Fitzpatrick's throat, causing a trickle of blood to flow.

"The world of men willingly follows us, for we have planted the seed of rebellion deep within their hearts. How easy it is for us to water it and watch it grow. They will not worship your god, the weakling of the cross. They will choose a god of power, of war, the superman. For who can stand against the superman?" the monster taunted, grasping Fitzpatrick even more tightly. "Now, have your underling bring the disk to me, or I will kill him."

Mac looked at Johanen. *What is he going to do? Why hasn't he called out for help?*

"MacKenzie," Johanen called to Mac in a steady voice. "Take the disk to him, but do not allow him to take it until he releases Fitzpatrick."

As Mac went over and took the disk, Johanen whispered, "Hold it behind your back so he cannot see it."

Mac walked toward the reptilian and Fitzpatrick. He stopped about ten feet away.

"Release the man, now," Johanen called.

The reptilian withdrew the point of his claw from Fitzpatrick, then shoved him toward MacKenzie.

Mac held out the disk and took a step closer to the reptilian. He felt the disk vibrate, then it flew out of his hand and into the claws of the reptilian.

Azazel observed it for a moment and then his clawed hands curled around the disk, flexing and shattering it into three pieces. The reptilian dropped it on the floor and ground the pieces with its grotesque-looking foot.

"You have lost, Johanen. You realize that I could kill your friends even now. But I have something better in mind. I want you to see what your defeat looks like. I want you to taste it. Rub your nose in it, as you humans say. Yes, Johanen, follow me down. Take the tunnel I show you. It will lead you to a vantage point and you will see for yourself what the future holds. Mankind will begin its final descent into the Abyss, and our father will greet each one as they willingly choose to follow him. You have failed, Johanen. Your god has failed. Observe, old man, and as you continue to wander the earth and see the misery that is about to be unleashed, you will wish for death. But it will not come to you. Your god has seen to that. So, Johanen, follow me down."

Mac watched Azazel turn around and then vanish into one of the tunnels. A moment later a peal of laughter rose above the loud droning, echoing through the tunnels.

Mac turned to Johanen, who remained stoic. Indeed, a faint smile creased his face.

"Are you all right?" Johanen called to Fitzpatrick.

"I suppose . . . ," he answered.

Mac helped him up from the ground as Johanen approached them.

"Are we going to follow the tunnel and see what he's talking about?" Mac asked.

"Can we trust him?" Fitzpatrick added.

"He is full of pride, bombastic in his statements, but he is right about one thing. This is the prelude to the time of Jacob's trouble. A time when the world will embrace what Scripture calls the Antichrist. It is the time of the Enemy dwelling amongst men to fuel their most base passions. However, he has forgotten that there is *more* that is written. He will be defeated.

He and his master and their legions will be cast into the lake of fire."

"So do we follow him and see what he's talking about, or go home?" Mac asked.

"MacKenzie," Johanen began, "you are anxious to see. It is your reporter's nose that pushes you. But I will go because it is something that I have been told to do, and *not* by Azazel. Let us see what lies ahead."

Mac brought up the rear as they followed Johanen into the tunnel into which the reptilian had vanished.

56

✳ ◻ ✳

MacKenzie, Johanen, and Fitzpatrick soon found themselves perched hundreds of feet above an enormous cavern. They were concealed behind a knee-high wall of rock that resembled a guardrail. Below them spread an underground city.

Mac gasped at what he saw. Human/alien hybrids milled about the floor. Some had stringy white hair and long, delicate limbs. Others appeared more human, but with black, elongated eyes. Still others had giant-like traits and stood well over ten feet tall, with six fingers on each hand. The classic gray alien that had been popularized by TV shows made up the majority of what Mac assumed was an invasion army, and there were thousands of them. Off to one side, on a platform, were the fallen angels, several of whom conversed with each other while others gave orders. But what astounded him and made his skin crawl and his stomach flip was the vast array of saucer-shaped craft lined up in rows, hovering just above the cavern floor.

Mac whispered, "There's probably a couple of hundred space craft."

"It looks like they're getting ready for an invasion," Fitzpatrick commented.

"Yes," Johanen said. "I have said to both of you that the time is now, and as you can see, my words have not been idle. The Great Deception is unfolding before our eyes."

Mac spotted several humans and wondered whether they were advanced hybrids or human conspirators. "Look there," Mac said, as he caught sight of a man in uniform.

"Where?" Fitzpatrick asked.

"See the grouping of four UFOs at the side of the cavern? The ones that are not hovering."

"Yeah," Fitzpatrick said.

"Go up a little way from there."

"No. . . I can't believe it," Fitzpatrick said, "It's the Hag. Von Schverdt—in a full-blown Nazi uniform."

"I see him too," Johanen stated. "Now his day is here."

"What do you mean, 'his day'?" Mac asked.

"I mean that this was foretold thousands of years ago. I can only assume that nuclear war has broken out in the Middle East." Johanen pointed below them. "You see before you an alien armada that will leave this place, travel under the Atlantic Ocean, and a few minutes later, arrive in Israel. It is the beginning of the deception. Most people will believe that what they are seeing are, in fact, extraterrestrials that have come to usher peace into the world. The course is set, and the Antichrist will take his place as ruler of the world. He will be portrayed as a man of peace, but, in the end, he will bring destruction and misery.

"It can be explained like this: There are two kingdoms, each with their own so-called 'currencies,' each mutually exclusive of one another. One kingdom is the Lord's, and the currency in his kingdom is faith. The other is the kingdom of the Evil One financed by fear. Mankind will be terrified of what they see in the coming weeks. Then, because fear has taken hold of their minds and poisoned them, they will believe the lie—that the 'aliens' are here to usher in a time of peace, that they have been here before, and that they are older and wiser than us—in fact, our creators.

"Man has rejected faith, so, therefore, will dwell in fear. Bound and judged by his choices that were exercised in his free will, man has doomed himself. But because of God's great mercy and grace, a promise has been made. A date has been set when man will be allowed to exhaust his free will, and God will intervene to rescue him from himself and from his enemies.

"The Great Deception has started. Nations *will* rise against nation. There *will* be famine, pestilence, and earthquakes, and, as we have seen recently, fearful signs in the heavens. God could move now and stop all of this. But it is not of his choosing. He has his timetable, and when his Son, Jesus, returns, everyone will bend their knees and bow their heads. When the Lord returns everything will change. There will be no more disease, war, or famine. He will rule from the holy city, Jerusalem. When that happens, the kingdom of heaven will be with men. We are seeing the preparation for that now. Again I tell you, *the time is now.* I have seen enough. Come, let us return to the world of the light. As dim as it may be, it is better than this place, for truly, no good thing dwells here."

The men moved away from the edge, and, retracing their steps, reentered the tunnel.

57

Hours later, Mac found himself once again above ground, and he was thankful to be there. He jumped out of the tunnel and landed next to the railroad tracks. It was dark, and Johanen had pulled out his flashlight, lighting the area that had once been the lair of the demoniac that had been delivered, when, a lifetime ago? Mac stretched his arms over his head and worked his neck muscles a few times. Fitzpatrick was anxious to see his sister, Nora, so they pressed ahead, going from level to level, until they reached the guard at the Condos. The fifty-gallon drum had a slow fire in it and there was still a contingent of men gathered around it.

"Who's that?"

Mac recognized the voice as Tim's.

"It is I, Johanen."

The men hurried to greet them.

"You made it back, huh?" Tim asked, as the mole people gathered around them, eager to hear what had happened.

"Did Nora get back safely?" Fitzpatrick asked.

The crowd of men grew silent. Mac began to wonder if something had happened to her.

"Yeah, she got back," Tim said. "She's a lot different now. It's kind of spooked us all."

"Ah, yes. That was to be expected, Tim," Johanen replied. "Can you take us to her?"

Tim nodded. Mac followed as close behind Johanen as he could, as he was surrounded by a huddle of men who jostled to get closer.

Soon they entered the home of the mole people. Word had gone before them, so everyone who lived in the Condos had come out to greet them. Mac mingled with a crowd of homeless people who were whispering amongst themselves as they got their first look at Johanen.

The crowd parted and a young woman ran toward them. It was Nora.

"Johanen," she cried out, as she ran to meet them.

Johanen opened his arms and the woman ran into them. "Smyrna . . . made me whole . . . I'm all right now," she said, and began to cry.

Fitzpatrick stepped forward, trembling.

"Brian?" Nora called out.

"Nora," Fitzpatrick whispered.

"I'm better now, Brian," Nora said, as she left Johanen and ran to Fitzpatrick's arms.

Mac watched them embrace. The crowd of mole people began to talk, and some of them applauded, not knowing what else to do.

"What happened to her?" Mac asked, as he made his way over to Johanen.

"She was with an angel—the one you saw restrain the demoniac when we were in the restaurant. His name is Smyrna, and through the Lord's power, he healed her. She is whole and in her right mind for the first time in her life."

A woman started to yell from the back of the crowd. "Hey, everybody. You gotta listen to what's goin' on."

Mac regarded the old white woman with wild hair, dressed in a tattered bathrobe. She held a small transistor radio with the earplug in one of her ears.

"We can't hear nothin' till you take that earplug out your ear," a toothless man near the woman admonished.

The woman pulled the earplug wire from the radio. Mac heard the urgent voice of a female reporter. She was mid-sentence when the speaker crackled to life.

"...reports that there are extraterrestrial craft over the city of Jerusalem. It appears that this is a direct response to a sudden nuclear exchange between Israel and the former Soviet Union and a confederacy of Arab states. First reports indicate that there are ..." The reporter broke down and began to cry. There was silence for almost a full minute, then the broadcast resumed, this time with a male reporter.

Mac was stunned. He looked at Johanen, then at Fitzpatrick. Both looked shocked and grim. Mac moved closer to Johanen. "We've got to get out of here and find out what's going on."

"Not so fast, MacKenzie. Listen, it's starting again."

Another voice came over the airwaves. "Ladies and gentlemen, all normal radio broadcasting has been suspended due to the ongoing circumstances in the Middle East. We expect the president of the United States to make a statement shortly..."

* ○ *

Elisha BenHassen sat, bleary-eyed, staring in disbelief at his computer screen. Uri was beside him, his head resting on the desk in front of him and covered by his arms as if they might somehow keep out the stark reality of the last several hours. On the other side, the Major sat stoically still, his face ashen and wax-like. On Elisha's lap an open Bible rested. It was open to Isaiah, chapter 17. He reread the passage, wanting it to say something else but knowing that it wouldn't. *What had they done?* he asked himself. He read it again.

"Behold, Damascus will cease to be a city and it will remain a ruinous heap ..."

According to reports that had found their way to Elisha deep below the streets of Tel Aviv, Damascus had been completely destroyed. The attacking armies of Iran, Libya, Egypt, Syria, Lebanon, Turkey, and Russia had been wiped out. When it became clear that Israel had no remaining options, they then relied on their last resort. They did the unthinkable— launched a nuclear counterattack with neutron bombs, and annihilated hundreds of thousands of people within a few minutes. The remains of the vast armies lay dead on the mountains and plains bordering the tiny nation.

Elisha ran his fingers over the worn leather edge of his Bible. He felt the same hopelessness that he had felt after leaving the death camps so many years ago. The overwhelming despair, as if life was no longer worth living, for the world was a place that had lost any semblance of order and sanity.

The screen flashed and Elisha wondered what would take place next. *Would the Americans enter the fray? Would the Russians retaliate with the remainder of their nuclear arsenal? Would countless hordes of enraged Muslims gather together in a last* jihad *and storm across the borders?*

The phone rang on the Major's desk. The Major twitched, startled, then picked it up. Elisha waited as the Major ended the conversation.

"Something is going on in Jerusalem . . . We should have a picture in a minute. They're working on it."

Elisha looked to the large digital screen, which was still blacked out. It flickered a few times and then the picture came into focus.

Elisha nudged Uri, who sat up and rubbed his tear-stained eyes.

"That's Jerusalem, the Western Wall," Elisha said. He saw a mob of men and women in front of the wall, and although there was no sound, he could tell that desperate cries were echoing off the ancient stones.

The camera panned back and Elisha saw *them* for the first time. He had read about it from the scroll that Enoch had given MacKenzie. Still, it shocked him to his core. He glanced at Uri and then at the Major. Both men were speechless. He looked back at the screen again. The sky was blue and cloudless, and, hovering over the old city, were hundreds of UFOs—"sun disks," as the ancient scroll had called them.

"God help us," Elisha whispered, and grabbed the hands of Uri and the Major and began to pray.

* o *

The Mayor emerged from his hut and called out to Johanen and Mac. "You've got to see this. Get over here."

They hurried over and followed the man inside. Mac took a seat on a blue tarp next to Johanen. In front of him was a small black-and-white television set perched on a milk crate.

Mac nudged Johanen. "It's difficult to believe this is happening," he said, as he stared at the screen.

"Yes, MacKenzie. With the nuclear exchange in the Middle East the unthinkable has happened."

Mac nodded, wishing the picture were clearer. A well-coifed woman reporter, knuckles curled in a death grip around the microphone in her hand, was speaking. ". . . of Jerusalem are in a state of panic because of the extraterrestrial craft that you saw back there." She gestured nervously behind her.

The picture zoomed in on one of the craft that drifted over the old city of Jerusalem. "Unbelievable," Mac whispered under his breath.

The woman continued, "We have just received word that the president of the United States is on his way to an emergency session at the United Nations."

The camera panned back to the hovering craft, then to the chaos on the street. The streets were jammed with cars. Horns blared and some motorists stood on top of their hoods. Others had abandoned their cars, engines running, doors flung open. An old rabbi stood on the corner, his hand holding the Torah, and rocked back and forth as he prayed, ignoring the panicked people around him. A handful of IDF, Israeli Defense

Force, ran into the area and tried to get traffic moving and to keep a semblance of order.

The television set lost its reception and the Mayor slapped it, but the picture wouldn't come back on.

Johanen got up, thanked the Mayor, and motioned to Mac to follow him. They left the Mayor's house and moved away from the crowd.

"Well, MacKenzie, it is time for you to leave this place."

"And what are we to do then?" Mac asked.

Johanen shook his head. "Not we, MacKenzie. You. It is time for you to do what you do best." He paused.

Mac thought a moment. "You mean write?" he asked.

Johanen nodded.

"It is what you have been trained to do, MacKenzie. You have a perspective that few people, if any, have. You need to be a spokesperson for the Lord."

"So what are you going to do?" Mac asked.

"For the time being, stay here. At least for a few days," Johanen replied.

Mac hesitated for a moment. "Will I see you again?" he asked.

Johanen smiled. "Yes, MacKenzie, if the Lord wills it. But for now your wife and children need your attention, and I have business here and in other places."

Mac mulled over what Johanen had said. "What about Fitzpatrick and Nora?"

"They have much catching up to do. They need some time alone. But let us gather them and leave this place."

Mac spotted Fitzpatrick and Nora seated a short distance away. "They're over there," he said, pointing to them.

A short time later Mac, Johanen, Fitzpatrick, and Nora stood at the entrance to the tunnels. Behind them, Tim and several of the other mole people gathered. They had escorted them to the entrance, but were afraid to take them any farther.

Mac looked out of the mouth of the tunnel to the gray, overcast sky. A light drizzle was falling. He turned up the collar of his jacket.

"Well, I guess this is good-bye," Mac said to Johanen.

"Yes, for now, MacKenzie. Remember, you should do what you do so well. Write about what is going on. The world needs your perspective. It may prove to be critical."

Mac nodded and then threw his arms around his mentor, embracing him. Fitzpatrick and Nora each took their turns thanking Johanen and saying their good-byes.

Mac turned to Fitzpatrick and Nora. "Ready?"

Fitzpatrick had his arm around Nora, and the three of them started out of the tunnels.

MacKenzie looked back once and saw the snowy white hair of Johanen disappear into the perpetual twilight of the tunnels.

> *"They're not human. They come from somewhere else, somewhere far away ..."*

Nephilim

L. A. Marzulli

Two years ago, Art "Mac" MacKenzie was a respected newspaper journalist with a wonderful family and a bright future. Now he lives alone, fighting the temptation to drink and trying to survive as a freelance writer. His faith in God, humanity, and virtually everything else is gone. All that's left is a pile of bills and the ache of his son's death.

Then comes the opening of the multimillion-dollar new wing of the Westwood Center, and a distraught patient's fantastic tale of alien abduction and impregnation. So begins a media story with international implications—and more trouble than Mac has ever imagined.

Hot for a story, Mac follows a lead to Israel, where he comes across the remains of one of the Nephilim—ancient biblical giants sired by demons and born of human women. It's just the tip of a terrifying supernatural iceberg—for the Nephilim are back and will do anything to prevent him from revealing their secret.

Softcover: 0-310-22011-4

Pick up a copy today at your favorite bookstore!

ZONDERVAN™

GRAND RAPIDS, MICHIGAN 49530 USA

WWW.ZONDERVAN.COM

The Unholy Deception
The Nephilim Return
L. A. Marzulli

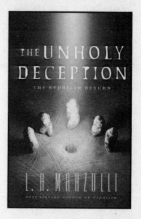

For journalist Art "Mac" MacKenzie,
the scenario smacks of an alien agenda.
He determines to unearth the truth at
any cost. But the Cadre doesn't surrender its secrets easily. Mac's former edi-
tor, Jim Cranston, has been found wandering among the ruins
of Machu Picchu with burns on his body and in a constant
state of fear.

Worse yet, General Roswell, Mac's inside connection in
the secret government-alien cooperative, is dead of cancer.
However, Roswell has left behind two potential bombshells:
a set of files with far-reaching implications, and a link to the
aliens that he has kept secret for years.

With Mac hot on Roswell's trail, the Cadre moves forward
with its agenda: to convince the world that Jesus was just an
ordinary man granted miracle-working powers by the aliens.
The Cadre must be stopped before they can publicly unveil
the fraudulent body of Christ, an event that could precipitate
a global and apocalyptic shock wave. Mac is swept into a race
against time in which losing is not an option . . . but winning
could cost him all.

Softcover 0-310-24064-6

Pick up a copy today at your favorite bookstore!

ZONDERVAN™

GRAND RAPIDS, MICHIGAN 49530 USA

WWW.ZONDERVAN.COM

We want to hear from you. Please send your comments about this book to us in care of zreview@zondervan.com. Thank you.

GRAND RAPIDS, MICHIGAN 49530 USA

WWW.ZONDERVAN.COM